Praise for

Heidi Swain

'Sweet and lovely. I guarantee you will fall in love with Heidi's wonderful world' **Milly Johnson**

'Wise, warm and wonderful – a real summer treat!' *Heat*

'Sparkling and romantic' *My Weekly*

'The most delicious slice of festive fiction: a true comfort read and the perfect treat to alleviate all the stress!' **Veronica Henry**

'A fabulous feel good read – a ray of reading sunshine!' **Laura Kemp**

'Sprinkled with Christmas sparkle' **Trisha Ashley**

'A story that captures your heart' **Chrissie Barlow**

'Fans of Carole Matthews will enjoy this heartfelt novel' **Katie Oliver**

Heidi Swain lives in Norfolk with her family and a mischievous black cat called Storm. She is passionate about gardening, the countryside and collects vintage paraphernalia. *The Christmas Wish List* is her ninth novel. You can follow Heidi on Twitter @Heidi_Swain or visit her website: heidiswain.co.uk

Also by Heidi Swain

The Cherry Tree Café

Summer at Skylark Farm

Mince Pies and Mistletoe at the Christmas Market

Coming Home to Cuckoo Cottage

Sleigh Rides and Silver Bells at the Christmas Fair

Sunshine and Sweet Peas in Nightingale Square

Snowflakes and Cinnamon Swirls
at the Winter Wonderland

Poppy's Recipe for Life

Heidi Swain

The Christmas Wish List

**SIMON &
SCHUSTER**

London · New York · Sydney · Toronto · New Delhi

A CBS COMPANY

First published in Great Britain by Simon & Schuster UK Ltd, 2019
A CBS COMPANY

Copyright © Heidi-Jo Swain, 2019

The right of Heidi-Jo Swain to be identified as author
of this work has been asserted in accordance with the
Copyright, Designs and Patents Act, 1988.

1 3 5 7 9 10 8 6 4 2

Simon & Schuster UK Ltd
1st Floor
222 Gray's Inn Road
London WC1X 8HB

Simon & Schuster Australia, Sydney
Simon & Schuster India, New Delhi

www.simonandschuster.co.uk
www.simonandschuster.com.au
www.simonandschuster.co.in

A CIP catalogue record for this book is
available from the British Library

Paperback ISBN: 978-1-4711-8568-7
eBook ISBN: 978-1-4711-8569-4
Audio ISBN: 978-1-4711-8687-5

Typeset by M Rules
Printed and bound by CPI Group (UK) Ltd, Croydon, CR0 4YY

MIX
Paper from
responsible sources
FSC® C020471

To Paul,
this one was always going to be for you

Chapter 1

As my fingers itched to click open the calendar on the computer for what would have been the fiftieth time in the last five minutes, I began to question my resolve about not taking superstitions seriously.

That morning, before I started my double shift on the hotel reception and merrily checked my weekend to-do list, I hadn't given the date a second thought. So excited by the prospect of a whole weekend away from work and with the flat I shared with my partner, Jonathan, to myself that I hadn't even noticed, but now I knew without any shadow of a doubt that Friday the thirteenth of September was going to be etched on my brain for ever.

What with lost key cards, a malfunctioning lift and two sacked sous-chefs, the morning had been bad enough, but events of the afternoon had sent the day soaring from tough to a total disaster.

'I seem to have done it again,' beamed Mr Lost Key Card Number Two from earlier. 'I'm sure I had it with me when I left,' he continued, patting down his jacket and trouser pockets as he approached the desk, 'but now . . .'

Now the computer was telling me my long and gruelling shift was over and he wasn't my problem. Ordinarily I wouldn't have left until everything on my watch was on track and running like a well-oiled machine, but right then, quite frankly, I didn't care.

'If you take a seat,' I told him, 'my colleague will be over in a minute to help you.'

'Oh right,' he murmured, clearly affronted that I hadn't jumped into action. 'I'll just wait then.'

He sauntered off and I resisted the urge to stick my tongue out behind his retreating back.

'Bloody hell, Hattie,' hissed Stuart, my deputy who, as always, was right on time but never early for a shift handover. 'I've just heard. I'm so sorry.'

I nodded, but didn't comment and signed myself out of the check-in system.

'Mr Oakley over there has lost his key card for the second time today,' I swallowed, 'and the catering agency are sending over a couple of temps. They should go straight round to the kitchen, but if they turn up here—'

'I'll send them over,' Stuart interrupted, fixing me with a searching stare. 'You really didn't know, did you?'

'I told you I didn't,' I said, reaching under the desk for

2

my bag. 'I've been telling you all for weeks that I didn't. I thought it was just a rumour, the same as you lot.'

It was a balmy September evening, far too warm for a bubble-filled bath, but that was what I was looking forward to. On the bus home I imagined myself slipping into the muscle-relaxing tub where I could have a good cry in peace and telephone my dear friend, Dolly. At almost fifty years my senior we were unusual BFFs but I knew she was the one person in the world who would be able to offer the comfort and soothing counsel my bruised ego craved. I would talk to Jonathan, who would most likely see the situation as an opportunity rather than a disaster, once I had the benefit of Dolly's wise words ringing in my ears and had cried myself out.

Dolly and I had actually met through the hotel. She had been a regular guest for years before I secured what was supposed to be a temporary housekeeping position the summer I left school almost fourteen years ago. The hotel had been run by the Lucca family then and the whole set-up had been family friendly; warm and welcoming, abuzz with laughter and nothing like the sleek operation it had been turned into when they sold up four years ago and moved back to Italy. Now it was all corporate clients and fine dining.

Dolly and I had properly bonded the year I turned eighteen. My personal life had taken a battering and my relationship with my parents was hanging by the thinnest of threads, but professionally things were better.

I had just moved into a room at the hotel and been promoted to front of house when Dolly broke her wrist during an excursion into town. Too uncomfortable to travel back to her home town of Wynbridge alone and unwilling to ask anyone to collect her, she decided to stay on. The Luccas, knowing certain tasks would be difficult for her, and that I could do with the distraction, asked if I would mind taking special care of their much-valued guest. Initially, Dolly hadn't been keen on the idea.

'I'm sure the last thing Hattie wants is to be traipsing about picking up after me,' she had told Mr Lucca. 'The poor girl will be bored witless by the time I'm well enough to go home.'

Thankfully the Luccas knew best and had stuck to their guns and Dolly's concerns were completely unfounded. I discovered in her a sympathetic confidante and we ended up spending a very companionable two weeks together. I had never had the opportunity to spend so much time with someone her age before – my grandparents had gone long before I was old enough to form memories of them – and having no children of her own meant I filled the role of granddaughter for her.

She hadn't been able to heal my recently broken heart – nothing was capable of that – but she had stopped me from severing all ties with my parents, imploring me to give things time to settle. We chatted together for hours and she told me all about her life in Wynbridge and her job as a teaching assistant, scattering her monologues with hilarious classroom anecdotes, and when I escorted her back home, I fell in love with both her beautiful cottage and the town as well as her working life.

As a result, during the years that followed I became a regular visitor, even occasionally volunteering alongside her in the school and eventually falling to wonder if I should consider a career in education myself. I loved working with the children and was certainly capable of doing the job, but I never took the plunge. Swiftly promoted when the Luccas left, and with a pay rise to match, I stayed working at the hotel and my plans soon became nothing more than an eventually forgotten daydream played out on the train to and from Wynbridge.

Glossy, groomed, efficient and the consummate professional, I was now knocking on the door of thirty and matched the transformed hotel and the manager's expectations to a T. Or at least I thought I did. Dolly hadn't stayed since the hotel's overhaul – she hadn't been impressed by the plasma TVs and sleek electric curtains – but she was proud of my achievements and we still kept in touch. Not quite as regularly as before, and increasingly by telephone rather than me visiting her in person since I had started dating Jonathan a couple of years ago, but she was always there when I needed her and boy, did I need her now.

Jonathan had never been able to understand why I was best friends with someone five decades older and, having no grandparents of his own and no other older influence in his life, couldn't grasp it when I tried to explain, but Dolly was my best friend and after such a disastrous day she was always going to be my first port of call.

'Hattie?'

I crossed the lobby, my heels slipping slightly on the polished floor as I rushed towards the lift which would take me up to the flat.

'Hattie,' came the voice again, more insistent this time.

I told myself that the events of the afternoon must have sent me into shock. I was so looking forward to hearing Dolly's voice I had conjured it in my head.

'Hattie, it's me, dear, Dolly.'

I spun around and there she was. Tiny in stature, but large of heart and surrounded by bags. She always reminded me of Miss Marple as interpreted by Geraldine McEwan. Only perhaps slightly more eccentric, if that were possible.

'Oh Dolly!' I gasped. 'What are you doing here? I was going to call . . .'

My voice trailed off as the lump in my throat threatened to betray me.

'And so was I,' she smiled, her green eyes twinkling, 'but then I just got the feeling that it would be better to visit in person.'

She eyed me astutely and I nodded and stood up a little straighter.

'You look tired,' I observed, returning her scrutiny and feeling surprised by what I found, 'and pale.'

It was unlike her not to be sporting a rosy glow, especially after a summer spent tending her beloved garden.

'Just what every woman of advancing years wants to be told,' she chuckled, raising her eyebrows.

'Sorry,' I said, shaking my head. 'It really is wonderful to see you. Was your journey horrid?'

'Not at all,' she replied. 'Travelling on the train was quite pleasant, but it's the start of term and, as you know, all the excitement takes it out of me a bit these days.'

'Of course,' I nodded. 'I was forgetting you were back in the thick of it again now.'

I knew this was to be her last academic year and given her pallor I couldn't help thinking that next summer couldn't come soon enough. She had added fifteen years of volunteering to her working life since her retirement, so it was little wonder she looked worn out.

'Anyway,' she said, reaching out for my hand. 'That's enough about me. I was rather hoping you were going to tell me what you've been up to, and a hug wouldn't go amiss.'

I managed not to cry all over her and once we were all hugged out, we went up to the flat. Dolly perched herself at the kitchen island, watching me closely while I boiled the kettle, kicked off my heels and released my hair from the pins which held it in a tight bun.

'It's so lovely to see you, Dolly,' I said, running my hands through the tangle and thinking what a relief it was to finally relax. 'But I can't help wondering what exactly it was that made you decide to call in person rather than pick up the phone?'

'Well, you hadn't rung for a couple of weeks,' she said

shrewdly, 'and the last time we spoke I could tell there was something bothering you. I figured it was either man trouble again or something at the hotel so I thought I'd come and see if I could winkle it out of you. I am right, aren't I?'

'Yes,' I said, clearing my throat as I splashed water into the pot. 'Yes, I'm afraid you are, but it's not man trouble, as you put it. That little bit of bother I had with Jonathan was literally months ago.' Not that I was keeping count. 'It's long forgotten, Dolly. Everything's been fine since I moved into the flat.'

'I'm delighted to hear it,' she nodded, 'although I'm not all that sure about your description of it.'

Given the fallout at the time, I was surprised I could so easily downsize the disaster myself, but given what I was now faced with it felt like a tiny splash in life's ocean.

'Oh Dolly,' I sobbed, 'I've been made redundant.'

'Oh, my dear girl, no,' she gasped, her mouth falling open as I banged down the kettle and began to cry all the harder.

She slipped off her stool and rushed to pull me into another hug.

'I've only just found out,' I sniffled, resting my chin on her shoulder, 'by the end of November, I'm going to be out of a job.'

I still couldn't really believe it. Following the takeover I had worked tirelessly to meet the needs of some increasingly demanding guests and I always went above and beyond when it came to customer service and yes, I know, some would say that was all part of my job, but I prided myself on going the extra mile in the misguided assumption that it would make me indispensable. But at the end of the day, it turned out that my impeccable work ethic and unpaid hours had counted for nothing. I might as well have spent the last few years being as slapdash as Stuart for all the good my commitment had done me.

'Have you been told why they're letting you go?' Dolly eventually asked, as she released me and carried on making the tea herself.

'Staff streamlining or something,' I said, noisily blowing my nose on a sheet of kitchen roll. 'From what I can work out the highest paid in each department has been given the chop and they're giving us plenty of notice so we have a chance to look elsewhere.'

'So, it's about saving money,' Dolly said kindly, 'not about you personally.'

'I suppose,' I shrugged. 'But what am I going to do?'

'You'll find another position easily enough,' Dolly rallied. 'You have years of experience and no one can fault your dedication. You've worked every Christmas for as long as I can remember. There aren't many employees willing to sign up to do that, Hattie.'

Dolly didn't approve of my willingness to forgo the joys of Christmas year on year. She was a huge fan of the season herself.

'I didn't work last Christmas,' I reminded her.

Jonathan had surprised me with a trip to Abu Dhabi. It was lovely to leave the grey skies of England behind but I hadn't much enjoyed the seasonal celebrations under the sun. It was true that Christmas had come to mean less and less to me, especially now I had no contact with my parents at all, but it turned out that not even the spectacular Winter Wonderland on Al Maryah Island could reignite my festive spark. Like me, Jonathan didn't care much for Christmas either, but he loved the city and had been backwards and forwards to work on various projects there throughout the year.

'Yes, well,' Dolly sniffed. 'You might not have been working, but Jonathan was and I hardly think a week or two in the searing sun is very festive!'

'It was only twenty-six degrees,' I hiccupped. 'In the summer it's nearer forty.'

'Never mind that,' she tutted, handing me a mug of sweetened tea. 'What you need is a good old-fashioned Christmas to remind you what you're missing out on and you might want to think about that before you sign up for another job and commit to working every December the twenty-fifth. You should view this as an opportunity to make some changes in your life, Hattie. Redress the old work–life balance a bit. You've hardly taken a proper break since the Luccas sold up.'

'Well, I don't know about that,' I told her. It was far too early in the year to be thinking about Christmas and whether or not I wanted to carry on working through it. 'But I could do with some company this weekend.' I didn't much want to be on my own now. 'You will stay, won't you?'

'Of course,' she agreed. 'I wouldn't dream of leaving you

alone after a shock like this. I take it Jonathan is away again at the moment?'

I opened my mouth to answer, but stopped as the flat door opened and then banged shut.

'Hattie!'

'Not away then?' Dolly questioned.

'I don't know,' I told her, abandoning my tea. I pulled off another sheet of kitchen roll and peered at my reflection in the oven door. 'I'm not sure, I mean, I wasn't expecting to see him until next Tuesday. I was planning to talk to you on the phone and get everything straight in my head before I shared my news with him.'

My mascara, in spite of the promises about being completely waterproof written on the expensive packaging, had proved to be anything but and my face was smeared with the telltale signs of an emotional offload. I quickly began to try and scrub it away, making my eyes look even sorer in the process.

'Given the circumstances,' said Dolly pointedly, 'I hardly think you need to worry about a bit of smudged make-up, my dear, do you?'

'I have news!' Jonathan shouted along the hall. 'Get your best gear on, Harriet, because I'm taking you out to dinner!'

He burst into the room, simultaneously popping the cork on a bottle of champagne and grinning from ear to ear. His smile faltered a little as he spotted Dolly perched back at the island and I knew she would have noticed.

'Dolly,' he said, quickly collecting himself, 'how absolutely lovely to see you.'

11

'Hello, Jonathan,' she smiled back.

'I hope you will be able to join us?' he asked. 'As always, you're more than welcome.'

'I wouldn't dream of it,' she said, 'but it's very kind of you to ask.'

'Oh well,' he said, turning to me, his dark blue eyes registering surprise as he took in my tear-stained face and unkempt hair. 'What on earth . . .'

'And as you can see,' Dolly continued, 'Hattie here isn't much in the mood for a celebration at the moment either.'

Jonathan dumped the bottle on the counter and rushed round, wrapping his strong arms tightly around me. I forgot all about my dishevelled state and clung to his warm body, the smell of his aftershave simultaneously comforting me and making me want to cry all over again. It might have been Dolly I turned to first, but it did feel good to have Jonathan home too, not that I had been expecting him.

'What on earth's happened?' he asked, planting a kiss on the top of my head. 'What's going on?'

Fresh tears started to flow and Dolly handed me the last of the kitchen roll before Jonathan steered me towards a chair under the window. He took the one next to me, still holding my hand which made mopping up my tears awkward.

'It's the hotel,' I told him, dabbing ineffectively at my nose which needed another good blow. 'I've been made redundant.'

I let out another sob, still unable to really take it in.

'If I can't find another job, I'm going to be unemployed by the end of November.'

Jonathan was silent for a second, then let out a cheer and jumped up to retrieve the champagne and a trio of glasses. I frowned up at him as he began to fill the flutes, handing one to Dolly before sitting back down.

'But that's just perfect, Hattie!' He laughed, merrily clinking his glass against mine. 'Couldn't be better actually.'

'I don't think Hattie feels that way,' interrupted Dolly, putting her glass down and pushing it away untouched.

'But she will in a minute,' Jonathan carried on, beaming.

'I think you'd better tell me why,' I said, feeling nettled that he looked so thrilled about my bad news.

Whatever he had to say was going to have to be nothing short of miraculous if it was going to lift my spirits high enough to match his.

'So, do I,' Dolly snapped, 'because at the moment you're coming across as pretty heartless, Jonathan.'

Jonathan shook his head and laughed.

'I've been offered a new job,' he grinned. 'A permanent one in Abu Dhabi. I had the interview on Wednesday and they offered it to me there and then.'

'Oh,' I said, as another layer of shock melded itself on top of the one I'd been subjected to earlier. I had no idea he'd even been looking for another position. 'I see.'

'I didn't want to say anything before, in case I didn't get it,' he carried on. 'It's another corporate finance role, but the top spot this time, overall manager.'

'My goodness,' I swallowed, 'that's quite a step up the ladder.'

'I know,' he agreed. 'It's with a private healthcare group.'

'Congratulations.'

'I'll be starting at the end of January but relocating in the new year.'

'So soon?'

'It's not that soon,' he said, running a hand through his thick blond hair, 'especially as I have notice to work and the flat to sell.'

'Of course.'

I could understand that he was excited about his good fortune, but why he thought that finding out I was losing my job *and* my home *and* my boyfriend in the same day was thrilling for me I couldn't fathom. I had given up my room at the hotel when I moved in with him and given that I'd just been made redundant I couldn't very well ask for it back again.

'Excuse me for interrupting,' Dolly cut in, clearly riding on the same train of thought as I was, 'but how exactly is this new job of yours good news for Hattie?'

'Because I want her to come with me of course!' Jonathan shouted, laughing again as he drained his glass. 'I want you to move with me to Abu Dhabi, Hattie!'

His words settled in the silence around us.

'You want me to go with you?' I eventually asked, the question coming out as little more than a squeak. 'You actually want me to move to Abu Dhabi with you?'

'Yes,' he said, 'that's exactly what I want. That's why I said that you being made redundant couldn't be better timed. You're always on about fate and how it steps in to lend a hand when you most need it. Well, on this occasion, I think you might be right. We've been a couple for over two years now. It's time we moved our relationship along and by December there'll be absolutely nothing stopping you from coming with me and doing exactly that!'

I had to admit, I was always banging on about destiny and how things happened for a reason, but surely this was too fortuitous for words?

'I've been wracking my brain on the plane home trying to work out how to convince you to give up your job,' Jonathan carried on, 'but I needn't have bothered. This is meant to be, Hattie.'

'Perhaps . . .' I said, biting my lip.

'You see,' said Jonathan, turning his attention back to Dolly. 'I'm not quite so selfish and self-centred as you might think.'

Dolly sniffed, but didn't comment.

Jonathan's mobile began to buzz and he rushed out of the kitchen to answer it, closing the door behind him.

'Oh, my goodness, Dolly,' I croaked. 'I can't believe it!'

I shook my head and took a swig from my glass, the bubbles tickling my nose and making me want to sneeze. Was it really possible that in less than two minutes Jonathan had waltzed in and magically solved all of my problems?

'Abu Dhabi . . .' I sighed dreamily.

'I thought you didn't like it?'

'It was the strangeness of seeing Christmas in the sun I didn't like,' I told her. 'Not that I'm all that bothered about it, as you know.'

That might not have been strictly true, it wasn't just the sight of a scorching Santa which had jarred, the city had felt different too, but then it would, wouldn't it, because it was. Perhaps fate was suggesting I should give the place a second chance? Maybe it was time to try something completely new and, as Jonathan had suggested, move our relationship along.

'You aren't really thinking of saying yes, are you?' Dolly frowned. 'At least not straightaway?'

'I don't know,' I said, shaking my head. 'It's all such a shock.'

'A culture shock,' Dolly said cautiously. 'Taking a holiday is one thing but settling in another country would be a completely different kettle of fish. You need to think this through very carefully. I mean, until Jonathan just made his announcement, you've never mentioned any desire to live abroad.'

'I'm beginning to think you don't want me to go,' I pouted. 'Not ten minutes ago you were telling me to take this redundancy as an opportunity to make some changes to my life.'

'But I want you to be able to take your time and make those changes on your own terms,' she said sagely, 'not get railroaded into something when you're still reeling from shock.'

'But what if it is fate?' I laughed. 'What if the universe has lined this all up for me with perfect timing?'

Dolly looked doubtful.

'Even if it has, that doesn't mean you just have to accept it,' she told me. 'Don't forget how you *really* felt about the city when you spent Christmas there.'

Clearly, she wasn't about to gloss over my memories and first impressions, even if I was.

'Can you honestly imagine building a whole life for yourself there, Hattie?'

She was right of course. It wasn't something I had even considered since we arrived home, not like when we came back from a weekend in Paris and I'd secretly fantasised about living in one of the chic apartments for months afterwards. However, I had given plenty of thought to the plethora of stunning hotels which graced the streets of Abu Dhabi. I wondered now if I would be able to find a position in one of those. Perhaps my years of hard work at the hotel would pay off after all.

'And there's your family to consider,' Dolly reminded me.

'I don't see why,' I shot back. 'What difference would it make where in the world I was living when we don't have anything to do with each other anymore?'

She couldn't argue with that.

'Well, what about your marital status then?' she carried on.

'My marital status?'

'Yes,' she said. 'If you do decide to go, you'd have to marry first, wouldn't you?'

'Well, yes,' I stammered, only just realising. 'I suppose so.'

'Is Jonathan really the man for you, Hattie? Is he

someone you can imagine spending the rest of your life with? Have you ever considered a long-term future with him, because marriage isn't something to enter into lightly, you know and don't forget . . .'

'Please don't bring up what happened before again,' I cut in. 'Everything's fine now.'

But was Jonathan the everlasting man for me? I suppose, given the length of time we'd been together, we were travelling down the serious relationship road, but like moving to Abu Dhabi, it wasn't something I'd consciously thought about. Not all that long ago our relationship had encountered more ups and downs than a rollercoaster and, in spite of what I had told Dolly, I was only now beginning to believe that the track had properly levelled out again. I certainly hadn't had time to consider committing to the long haul.

But Jonathan obviously had because he wouldn't have asked me to go with him otherwise, would he? We'd spent our Christmas holiday in separate rooms but if we were actually going to move there then that wouldn't be an option, and he would have been well aware of that before he asked me to go with him.

'I don't think I'd better drink any more,' I said, putting down my glass. 'I'll never be able to think straight with a head full of bubbles.'

Dolly moved her glass next to mine.

'This was not how I was expecting my day to end.' I sighed.

'I'm sure it's not what either of us were expecting when we got up this morning,' she said squeezing my arm.

Jonathan came back in then, still grinning like the Cheshire Cat as he loosened his tie and undid the top button of his shirt.

'So,' he said, topping up our glasses and looking at me, 'have you made up your mind?'

'Oh, for goodness sake, Jonathan,' said Dolly, gathering up her bags. 'You mustn't rush her.'

He winked at me and I shook my head. I wished he didn't take quite so much pleasure in winding Dolly up.

'You aren't leaving, are you?' I asked her. If she went, I wouldn't be able to think any of it through in my own time because Jonathan wouldn't give me the chance. 'You've only just arrived and I need you to help me decide.'

'No, you don't,' she said firmly. 'This has to be your decision, my dear and yours alone. I'm going back to Wynbridge, where you know you are always welcome. You need to take some time to yourself, Hattie, and have a long hard think about things.'

I knew she was referring to much more than the move to a sunnier clime.

Chapter 2

I had been right to think that Jonathan wouldn't give me a moment's peace to think his offer through. The second I returned to the flat after helping Dolly into a taxi he had whisked me off to bed just as he always did after a trip away. Evidently, I was still as incapable of resisting his seductive charms as I had been when he switched from hotel guest to local resident.

I had just about managed to keep him at a professional arm's length whilst he was a guest, but four months later, the moment his work relocation was complete and he had moved into the flat, I had succumbed and we had gone on our first date. We had been together ever since and had recently celebrated our two-year anniversary. And, aside from the 'little bit of bother' I had mentioned to Dolly earlier, everything was wonderful.

'In Abu Dhabi,' he whispered, as he set about slowly liberating me from my hotel uniform, 'we won't have to worry about all these layers.'

I breathlessly reminded him that it was the end of summer

and a thin blouse and silk camisole hardly constituted layers, but he silenced me with a lingering kiss and had been smoothly answering any questions I had come up with about the move ever since. I couldn't deny he had a knack for making it all sound straightforward and the beautiful images he showed me of the city were all picture perfect.

There could be no doubting his determination to make me fall in love with the place and his plans, but during the first couple of weeks after his surprise suggestion I did my best to follow Dolly's advice. I even had a notebook listing the pros and cons and initially they were pretty evenly matched, but Jonathan's excitement combined with the unusually wet autumn which morphed into a bitterly cold one, meant that by the time I'd worked my notice I was feeling every bit as keen to settle in a warmer clime as the swallows who had already taken flight. My mind was made up; I was going and Jonathan was thrilled.

'Do you really have to go to this leaving thing tonight?' he asked as he kindly filled my insulated cup with coffee on the morning of my last shift. 'Only I was hoping you could cut and run. I thought we might crack open some champagne and have a little celebration of our own.'

'It's not a leaving thing,' I reminded him. 'Those of us getting the chop didn't want one, remember? I'm just going for a meal with the rest of the Surplus to Requirements Gang. I won't be late. We can have the champagne and celebrate when I get back.'

'All right,' he said, handing me the cup and pulling me in

for a kiss, 'and while we drink it, we can look through the photos again.'

We had been looking online at the places we'd most like to live; scrutinising the practical and fantasising about the completely out of our league super-rich options.

'And tomorrow,' I added, kissing him back, 'I'm going to look at some jobs.'

Jonathan pulled away a little and I knew I'd taken the shine off his celebratory mood. This was a conversation we'd had before and even though it had the potential to turn into an argument I was determined not to back down.

'I know you keep saying I should wait until we're there,' I quickly carried on, closing the gap between us again, 'but I really need to have a proper idea of what's going to be on offer for someone with my experience.'

'Even though I've told you there's the small matter of visas and permits to work through,' Jonathan reeled off, 'and that you won't have to worry about money because I can easily support both of us?'

'Yes, even though you've told me all of those things many, many times,' I answered, with another kiss. 'I know it's a bit complicated but I'm only going to be *looking* at jobs, not applying for one.'

Jonathan sighed.

'I need to know I'm going to have a professional future there,' I told him. 'I don't want to be just a girlfriend hanging on to her other half's coat-tails. If this move is going to be a success, then it needs to work for both of us. It has to offer me something professionally as well as personally.'

'Personally,' he said, now changing tack and kissing me lightly along my collar-bone, 'I can't see what's so wrong with being "just a girlfriend", as you put it.'

We still hadn't talked about getting married which, given how quickly the time was rushing by, was something of a surprise but knowing Jonathan as well as I did, I felt certain that he would have some grand proposal in the pipeline.

'Well, try seeing the situation from my point of view,' I told him, stepping out of his seductive reach, 'I don't want to have to be financially dependent on you, Jonathan.'

'And I get that,' he said, following me across the kitchen and helping me into my coat, 'I really do, but it wouldn't be for long, just a few months.'

It was an extremely generous offer, but I was struggling to accept it.

'I just want you to have the chance to settle in properly,' he shrugged, sounding glum, 'have the opportunity to get to know the place as well as I do.'

I wrapped my arms around him again. I knew it was unfair to keep spurning his kind offer, but I had never been out of work and hated the thought of having to go to him, cap in hand, every time I wanted to hit the shops. Even if it was as he had suggested, just for a few months. I knew that all he wanted was to be my knight in shining armour but the independent streak in me was determined to keep kicking his trusty stead out from under him.

'You know what,' I said, planting a kiss on his cheek and

trying to lighten his mood, 'I reckon this is all some sort of trick you've planned to turn me into one of those *Real Housewives* types. You're actually just taking me with you to starch your shirts, aren't you?'

'Of course not,' he said, a hint of a smile reappearing. 'I don't think the Real Housewives do that sort of thing and anyway, there's the laundry service for that. Unless of course, you'd prefer to do it.'

'Like your mother, you mean.'

Jonathan properly laughed then.

'You know as well as I do that she wouldn't know one end of an iron from another!'

I laughed along with him. The thought of Jonathan's mum, the flawless corporate wife, in an apron at the ironing board was an amusing one.

'All I'm saying is,' Jonathan reiterated again, but this time with a smile, 'don't be in such a rush, Hattie. Surely it would make more sense to get there and work through a few of the formalities before you sought out a new job?'

I supposed there was plenty of sense in what he was saying and he did know a whole lot more about how things worked out there than I did.

'Well, all right,' I said, but nonetheless determined not to give in completely. 'I might still have a quick look but I promise I won't set my heart on anything.'

'So,' said Dolly, when I called her the next morning, 'that's you finished at the hotel then.'

'Yep,' I sighed, 'that's me done.'

My final shift had ended quietly with no fanfare or fuss. Not that I wanted either, but it had been a far cry from what the Luccas would have laid on, not that they would have willingly let me go, I was sure.

'One chapter of your life has ended, my dear, and another even more exciting one, is about to open.'

'Yes,' I sighed. 'I know.'

'You don't sound all that sure.'

'I'm sorry, Dolly,' I said, trying to inject some enthusiasm into my voice. 'I am more excited than I sound, I promise. I just drank a little too much champagne last night and this morning I'm feeling a bit overwhelmed by it all.'

I really needed to perk up a bit. My dear friend had listened to me go back and forth at least a hundred times while deciding whether or not I should move and she certainly didn't need to hear me sounding so flat about the conclusion I had finally reached, even if I was a little hungover.

I still didn't think Dolly was certain that my decision to go was the right one. Not that she'd said as much. But I knew her well enough to pick up on the words she didn't say as well as the ones that she did.

'There's just so much to think about,' I told her, trying to sound breezier than I felt and detonate the ammunition my doubtful tone was supplying her with. 'But I'm sure it will all get sorted.'

'And have you thought any more about contacting your parents before you go?' she asked.

These were words she had definitely had no qualms about saying before.

'I have,' I told her.

'And?'

'Well, I talked it through with Jonathan and he agrees with me. As we're no longer in contact with them, where in the world I'm living won't make any difference to the situation.'

I heard Dolly sigh.

'Look,' I said, beginning to feel ruffled, 'you know as well as I do what Mum said that last time Jonathan saw her, and I can't forgive either her or Dad for that on top of everything else, I just can't—'

'And yet you forgave Jonathan last year,' she interrupted, 'and his behaviour was—'

'Can we just change the subject, please?' I cut in. 'How are your plans for Christmas shaping up?'

Another sigh.

'I'm not going to talk about my parents, Dolly.'

'In that case,' she said, finally letting it go, 'and as you've asked, I do want to talk to you about Christmas.'

'Oh?'

'Yes, I was wondering if there might be a chance that you would come to stay with me in the run-up to it. You said yourself that Jonathan is going to be away a lot and that you had no festive plans of your own.'

I had said that.

'So, I was thinking,' she carried on, 'that it would be nice, for me especially I suppose, if you could come and help me with mine. You know how much I love it all and it would mean so much if we could have this very last Christmas together.'

'What do you mean by very last Christmas?' I frowned, even though she couldn't see me.

The way she had said it made it sound so final.

'Your last Christmas here, in the UK, of course,' she went on. 'I can't imagine you will be rushing back here next December to celebrate something you aren't all that bothered about. I'll be lucky to get so much as a phone call before you head off to the beach for your barbecue, or whatever it is you'll be having.'

'I think that's an Australian thing,' I told her.

'Well, whatever,' she said. 'What do you think?'

'Can I let you know?'

'Of course, but I hope you'll say yes. I've decided I'm giving up work at Christmas now, instead of in the summer and it would be lovely to have you here with me when the time comes.'

That was almost more of a surprise than Jonathan asking me to move to Abu Dhabi.

'Oh, my goodness,' I gasped. 'Why the change of plan?'

Dolly took a moment before answering.

'Because, loath as I am to say it,' she said, sounding annoyed to have to admit it, 'I'm not much enjoying getting up and out so early on these chilly mornings. I think I've done as much as I can with my working life. It's time I had a rest.'

That didn't sound like Dolly at all. She didn't even rest

at weekends. There was always something going on in Wynbridge that she was a part of.

'But surely the school would be happy to have you start a little later in the day.' I suggested.

'That's no good,' she said, sounding impatient. 'You need to be there the moment the children arrive. You can tell a lot about how a little one is feeling when they walk through the door and that can impact on their whole day, and besides, this is always the best term. There's so much excitement surrounding Christmas, what with the nativity play, concerts, activities and fairs. It's always been my favourite time of the school year so it's an ideal time to bow out really.'

I couldn't imagine Dolly would ever really bow out of school life and I was sure the teaching staff couldn't imagine the place without her either, but I could understand where she was coming from about Christmas at school. In the past, before my festive spirit had been knocked on the head and I had fantasised about properly working in a school, I had always pictured myself helping out with the play, adjusting angel wings and making special cards, squelchy with glitter and glue, to take home to parents.

'Have the school got a special assembly planned for you?' I asked.

'I hope not,' said Dolly with what I imagined was a shudder. 'We had all that palaver when I officially retired at sixty-five.'

'They're bound to want to mark the occasion in some way though, aren't they?'

'All the more reason to have you here to help me through it then,' she said quickly. 'You know how I hate a fuss.'

'I bet she's going to try and make you change your mind about moving,' was the first thing Jonathan said when I relayed Dolly's request. 'I could tell she hated the idea right from the moment I asked you, and what about Christmas?'

'What about Christmas?' I snapped, ladling steaming risotto into bowls and feeling shocked by his reaction. 'We don't bother with it, do we? We aren't even having decorations this year so I can't see how my not being here in the weeks leading up to it will impact on you. Besides, you aren't even going to be here half the time.'

I snatched up the bowls and walked over to the island, roughly shoving one into his hands before I poured us both a glass of wine. It had been a while since he'd sounded so narky and I didn't much like this sudden reappearance of the version of himself that he'd promised to leave behind the day he gave me a key to the flat.

That said, I was certain the thought of me going to Wynbridge again reminded him of the circumstances of my last visit, and he was no doubt feeling flustered as a result, but that still didn't justify him being impolite about my friend.

'I don't know what it is that you've got against, Dolly,' I began.

'I haven't got anything against her,' he interrupted but I cut him off.

'I know you think our friendship is an unusual one and so what if it is? You seem to have forgotten that I have no family to turn to. Dolly is the only person I've got.'

'Thanks to your parents,' he interrupted again.

I wished Mum and Dad wouldn't keep winkling their way into practically every conversation.

'We'll be moving in January,' I carried on, 'and this may very well be the last opportunity I have to spend the run-up to Christmas with my friend.'

'I don't suppose she is getting any younger, is she?' Jonathan mused.

'I meant because we're going to be so far away,' I shot back, 'and I want to be with her when she finishes at the school. That place has been her life, and even though she says she's ready to give it up, she's bound to find it hard. I want to be there to support her, just like she's always been there for me.'

Jonathan took a moment to take my words in.

'Of course,' he said, shaking his head. 'I'm so sorry, Hattie. It's just even talking about that place . . . it reminds me of the reason why you were last there . . .'

The way his voice caught in his throat was proof enough that he was feeling upset by the memories the mention of Wynbridge had dredged up.

'I know,' I sighed. 'I do understand.'

'Of course, you should go,' he said. 'It's important and I shouldn't have reacted like that. When will you leave?'

'I'm booking the train for Friday,' I told him.

There was no need to say that I'd already downloaded the tickets to my phone.

'So, you won't be around next weekend?'

'No.'

'Damn,' he tutted. 'That's a shame. I was planning something rather special.'

'Sorry,' I swallowed, my heart hammering as I realised there was only one 'something rather special' he could be talking about. 'I didn't know. I assumed you'd be gone again by then.'

'Not to worry,' he smiled. 'I probably will fly out early as you won't be here.'

'OK,' I nodded.

'I really do understand that this visit to see Dolly is important, Hattie,' he said, reaching for my hand, 'and what I've got in mind will keep. Though not for much longer.'

I felt my face turn a shade brighter as he squeezed my fingers and grinned.

'In that case,' I conceded, 'if you let me know when you've got your schedule sorted, perhaps I'll see if I can come back a little earlier than planned.'

Chapter 3

I assumed that Jonathan had made his peace with the thought of me heading back to Wynbridge again, but he still had one last-ditch attempt to try and make me change my plans. However, given what he was suggesting, I couldn't help thinking that his motivation was well meant rather than meddlesome.

'You could fly out with me,' he said just as I was about to leave. 'The weather's glorious right now and you know I'm going to be viewing the apartments. I can easily book another room and you could fly home in a week or so and go straight to Wynbridge then. You'd still be with Dolly in plenty of time for the end of term.'

'I'm not going to do that, Jonathan.' I told him, even though it really would have been lovely to see the apartments for myself.

'Don't you want to help me choose where we're going to be living?' he asked, sounding a little peeved.

'Of course, I do,' I told him, looking out of the flat window as the taxi I'd booked pulled onto the forecourt. 'And I can choose with you from the extra photos you send. We've already narrowed it down to three places.'

'But it won't be the same. You won't be able to get the feel of them from a photo.'

'Look,' I said, hoping I wasn't making a mistake in turning him down. 'I know the layout of all of them now and if I can't decide, I'm certain you'll pick the right one for us. I trust you, Jonathan.'

Truth be told, I was surprised he hadn't jumped at the chance to be in charge. The old Jonathan wouldn't have given my preference a second thought if he didn't agree with it, but then we'd banished him, hadn't we? Really I should have been feeling grateful that he valued my opinion rather than annoyed that he was so keen for me to express it.

'Well, all right,' he sighed, 'as long as you're absolutely sure.'

'I am,' I said, 'and now I really do have to go otherwise I'll miss my train.'

He did nothing to help me along and I began to wonder if his behaviour was a little reminiscent of the clingy conduct which had preceded my last trip to Wynbridge. Perhaps the old Jonathan wasn't completely exiled after all.

'And you're sure you're going to be all right travelling alone?' he asked. 'It's been a while.'

'Of course, I'll be all right,' I laughed. 'What are you talking about? It's only a train and a taxi journey.'

'Sorry,' he shrugged, 'I know I'm making a fuss but I worry about you and it's quite a trek. You should have agreed to let me drive you then you wouldn't have to struggle with all these bags.'

I felt a little ashamed then, to have mistaken his current concern and kind consideration for his former suffocating clinginess. His offer to drive me to Wynbridge couldn't have been easily made given his memories of the place.

'I'll be fine on the train,' I told him, 'but thank you for offering to drive.'

'All right,' he shrugged. 'I'll walk you down.'

'No,' I smiled, planting a swift kiss on his cheek. 'It's all right. I can manage.'

He stepped closer and kissed me softly on the lips. I pulled away before it really was too late.

'I have to go,' I whispered.

I left quickly, thinking how strange it felt to be the one going. Jonathan popped in and out of the flat regularly, but the only place I ever ventured off to on my own was to work. Or should I say, had been to work? The journey to Wynbridge was, as he had pointed out, the first trip I'd taken on my own in what felt like a very long time. It was hardly a global adventure, and I didn't for one second think he'd intended to, but his concern had made me feel a bit jittery about it.

Unfortunately, my sudden attack of nerves were completely justified because the journey was far from straightforward. The taxi had barely set off when Jonathan rang to say I'd left the paper copy of my ticket behind. It didn't really matter because I had it on the app on my phone, but then I started worrying something would go wrong with that. The traffic through the city was crawling and when I did eventually arrive at the station, I pushed through the crowds to discover the timetable was completely off-kilter thanks to a series of signal failures.

Consequently, the few trains that were running were heaving and there was no hope of securing the seat I had reserved or finding a spot for my bags. I ended up wedged by the steamy window with them piled on my lap and around my feet and next to a mum with a screaming toddler with a toy xylophone and opposite the ultimate manspreader who stared at me from the second the train set off to the moment I fought my way off at Peterborough.

Conditions there were little better. Rain was pouring from a slate-grey sky and the wind was roaring along the platform. It was all I could do to hang on to my luggage and stay upright as I made my way towards the taxi rank. I kept my head bent and pushed on, hoping the lift was working and I wouldn't have to tackle the flights of steps to get out of the station. I could hear someone shouting ahead of me, but I didn't look up.

'Hey!' bellowed the voice again. 'Hattie!'

I risked a brief upward glance; my face was soaked in an instant and I found myself blinking at what appeared to be a human wall. The bitter wind stung my eyes and I just knew that my newest mascara had let me down every bit as spectacularly as the old one.

'Sorry,' shouted the man-wall. 'Did I make you jump? I didn't mean to. You are Hattie, aren't you?'

'That depends,' I shouted back, the wind carrying my voice off and away as the rain ran down my face. 'Who are you?'

'I'm Beamish,' the guy, who I guessed was about the same age as me, beamed.

Did he really say his name was Beamish?

From under the hood of his waxed coat, I could see his large brown eyes smiling into mine. His lashes were thick, long and dark and his jaw was covered in stubble. How he could even bring himself to think about smiling given the conditions was beyond me, but it was a great smile. In fact, given the bad mood my rotten journey had put me in coupled with the atrocious weather conditions, it must have been a spectacular smile for me to even notice it.

'Dolly asked me to give you this,' he said, pulling an envelope out of his coat pocket. 'She's asked me to come and pick you up.'

'I wasn't expecting a taxi to come out from Wynbridge,' I sniffed, feeling a little wrong-footed and not only because of his unexpected presence.

I swapped one of my bags with him for the envelope and turned out of the wind before pulling off a glove so I could open it. My fingers were numb within seconds. The note confirmed what the block of masculine masonry, had said. His name was in fact Beamish and he was here to collect me.

'Let's go then,' I said, turning back and stuffing the note deep into my pocket, 'before we freeze to death.'

36

Beamish didn't seem to notice the cold, the rain or the weight of my luggage, which he carried out of the station without so much as a grimace. I had to practically trot to keep pace with him but didn't feel much warmer for the effort.

'What's happened to your face?' I asked, catching a longer look at him as the wind blew back the saturated hood of his coat and he stowed my soaked bags into the boot and behind the driving seat of his mud-splattered Toyota truck. It was an unusual choice of vehicle for a taxi, but then Wynbridge was rather rural. Perhaps it was what was needed to ferry passengers around the country lanes at this time of year.

'I came off worst in the scrum last weekend,' he told me, as he pushed his soaked hair away from his face.

I had no idea what he was talking about.

'Rugby,' he elaborated. 'I play rugby for the town.'

Given his bulk I shouldn't have been surprised. He really was extraordinarily well built. Almost as broad as he was tall.

'Oh,' I said, still taking him in. 'Right.'

It was a shame to subject a face like his to what was probably a weekly battering. Had it not been for the bumps and bruises he could have been quite handsome, in a rough and ready sort of way.

'Do you want to hop in,' he said, 'and we'll get off. Dolly can't wait to see you.'

'Yes,' I blushed, embarrassed to have been caught staring. 'Thanks.'

He looked somewhat taken aback as I climbed into the space behind the passenger seat but didn't say anything.

There was no way I was getting in the front. The foot-well looked filthy and besides, travelling alone I didn't feel it was appropriate to sit next to the driver even if Dolly had sent him.

'Are you comfortable back there?' he asked, his smile making the corners of his eyes crinkle. 'With any luck,' he carried on, firing up the engine, turning up the heat and quickly cutting the volume of the radio which blared out, 'we'll be in town before it gets dark and you can get a look at the place, even if it is from the back seat. We're really gearing up for Christmas now.'

He sounded every bit as excited by the mention of the 'C' word as Dolly.

'Oh right,' I said, rummaging in my bag for some tissues to wipe my face and my phone so I could text Jonathan and let him know I'd almost arrived. 'Great.'

From the number of notifications, I could see my other half had been messaging throughout the duration of my journey and I couldn't help but wish that I had taken up his offer to drive me to Dolly's. A part of me, a very soggy part, was even wondering if I should have relented about flying out to spend a few days in the sun. I settled back in the seat and began to type a reply as Beamish cranked the radio up again and pulled out of the station.

The wind had died down a bit by the time we crossed the bridge into town and we weren't getting quite so buf-feted as we had been on the A47. The flat, Fenland horizon had stretched for miles there with little other than the odd farm and occasional tree to ineffectively halt the gusts in their tracks.

'Here we are then,' said Beamish, cutting the music and slowing down to take a lap of the market square.

He sounded proud to present me with the view but as I peered out of the window, I couldn't see what all the fuss was about. It didn't look all that different to the last time I'd visited.

'Lovely,' I nodded, not wanting to quash his enthusiasm. 'Is that a new shop? I don't think I've been in there.'

'It's quite new,' he explained, 'the latest Cherry Tree venture. It's a gallery and studio for local artists and crafts people. You might want to take a look if you still have Christmas shopping to do.'

I didn't tell him that I didn't have anyone, other than Dolly and Jonathan to shop for and that their presents would be ordered online and delivered direct already gift-wrapped.

'It's not looking very festive, is it?' I commented, taking in the rest of the shops. 'I thought you said Wynbridge was gearing up for Christmas?'

'It is,' he said, sounding unimpressed by my lack of seasonal spirit, 'everything's up but it won't be lit until tomorrow, will it?'

'Why, what's happening tomorrow?'

'The town switch-on of course. That's when it will all kick off properly. Dolly's absolutely over the moon that you're here in time to enjoy it with her.'

'Is she now?' I frowned.

For a taxi driver, he seemed to know an awful lot about my friend.

'Oh, yes,' he said. 'She's told me she has great plans for the time that you're going to be staying with her.'

'Do you think we should be getting on?' I primly suggested.

I had no desire to hear what Dolly had planned from anyone other than the lady herself. I hoped she hadn't gone overboard though. She knew I hated a fuss about things as much as she did and that I certainly didn't share her passion for Christmas these days.

'All right,' said Beamish, sounding deflated. 'I'll take you to the cottage.'

Located just a short walk from the town, but tucked away enough to feel a part of the nearby countryside, Dolly's little cottage was not all that dissimilar from the one Kate Winslet owned in *The Holiday*. I hadn't seen the festive film myself, but Dolly had shown me a picture and apart from being built and tiled from different local materials it did bear a striking resemblance with the classic covered front door in the centre, a window either side and two above. There were even roses around the wooden arched porch, or there were when the temperature was higher and the weather kinder. The little place always put me in mind of the sort of houses I drew as a child.

'Here we are then,' said Beamish, jumping out almost before he had pulled on the handbrake. 'Home sweet home, for the next few weeks at least.'

He rushed round to open my door and I stepped out.

'Here we are indeed,' I sighed, suddenly remembering the head bumps I was going to be subjected to until I remembered to duck coming down the stairs and through a couple of the doorways. 'I'd forgotten how cramped this place is.'

I wished I didn't sound so tired and grumpy. This wasn't the mood I had wanted to arrive in at all, but the journey from hell and the subsequent soaking, added to my recent lack of sleep, had rather taken the edge off my arrival and usually upbeat attitude.

'It's not cramped,' said Beamish, justifiably correcting my disparaging tone. 'It's cosy.'

I didn't have time to say that his was a far kinder and better suited description.

'Here you are!' Dolly shouted, flinging open the front door but not venturing down the path. 'Here you are at last. What were you doing sitting in the back? For a minute I thought you hadn't come!'

Beamish started to laugh and I left him to deal with my bags.

'Dolly,' I called, rushing to meet her and feeling my bad mood and some of my tiredness ebb away.

She opened her arms and I hugged her tight, but not too tight. She felt even smaller than the last time I held her, if that were possible, and she was stick thin.

'How are you, Dolly?' I asked, noticing her hair was definitely whiter than before.

'I'm fine,' she said releasing me, 'but I won't be if we let

41

the cat out. Let's get inside before she makes a dash for it. Hurry up will you, Beamish!'

Rather than drop my luggage at the door, he followed us inside, remembering to duck, and deposited my bags at the bottom of the stairs.

'What cat?' I questioned as Beamish quickly closed the front door. 'You haven't got a cat, Dolly.'

'I have now,' she said, indicating a small basket next to the stoked open fire. 'Come and meet Tiddles. And don't look so worried, she doesn't live up to her name.'

The little tortoiseshell cat was sound asleep. A most unlikely looking scrap to make a bid for freedom.

'Now, I know you aren't a huge cat fan.' Dolly said, squeezing my arm.

That was putting it mildly.

'But I don't think you really are allergic, are you?'

'Well, I guess we'll find out soon enough, won't we?' I said tentatively. 'But she's not really yours, is she?'

'She belonged to my old neighbour, Bob,' Dolly explained. 'He died a month or so ago and his family refused to give a home to either of his cats so I took on Tiddles.'

'And I took on Tiny, her sister.' Beamish added.

He didn't look like the cat-loving kind to me and there was a certain irony about the name of the puss he had taken on, but I forbore to comment.

'Don't they mind being apart?' I asked instead. 'Tiddles looks pretty ancient to me, doesn't she mind being away from her sibling?'

'Not at all,' said Beamish, 'they used to fight all the time. They're both far happier in separate homes.'

'But it's such a big commitment,' I said, turning back to Dolly. 'What if you want to go on holiday once you've properly retired. What's going to happen to her if you want to leave Wynbridge for a few days?'

Dolly had been practically tied to the town her entire life and now, just as she had the opportunity to explore fresh horizons and find a new hotel to visit, she'd taken on something else to tether her down.

'Why would anyone ever want to leave Wynbridge?' Beamish belted out, his booming laugh making Tiddles' ears twitch.

He might have been supersized in nature, but he was obviously a local lad with a small-town attitude.

'And who am I going to go and see?' Dolly asked. 'You certainly aren't going to be just a train ride away now, are you, Hattie dear?'

'No,' I said, 'I suppose not.'

'Anyway,' she carried on, 'now the introductions are over, let's have some tea, shall we? I've baked some scones especially for the occasion.'

'Not for me, thank you, Dolly,' said Beamish, somehow assuming he'd been included in the party. 'I still have another job to do this afternoon.'

It was on the tip of my tongue to suggest that he should give his truck a bit of a clean before he picked up his next fare, but I bit it back. Given our rural location, his next passengers might have been a gaggle of geese for all I knew.

'In that case, let me wrap a couple up for you,' Dolly insisted, bustling through to her little kitchen. 'One of each, in case you don't have time to stop for dinner.'

He gratefully accepted the greaseproof package of a sweet and savoury scone and ducked back through the front door as a van pulled up outside.

'Welcome back to Wynbridge, Hattie,' he called to me before he disappeared. 'I'll see you tomorrow, Dolly.'

The van turned out to be delivering a parcel for Dolly, and a large one at that.

'What on earth could this be?' She frowned, looking at it suspiciously. 'I haven't ordered anything.'

It turned out to be a beautiful hamper from Fortnum & Mason packed full of delicious treats including tea, coffee, biscuits, chocolates and wine. It was all exquisitely packaged and stylishly presented, as you would expect.

'There's a note,' I said to Dolly, handing her the card.

'To dearest Dolly,' she read aloud, 'a little something for you and Hattie to enjoy after dinner. With much love, Jonathan.'

I looked from the hamper to her and back again.

'Well now,' she smiled, her cheeks finally gaining a little colour. 'What a lovely thought.'

After poring over the hamper contents and devouring Dolly's delicious but carb-packed afternoon tea, she showed me up to my room which somehow felt smaller than I remembered even though it wasn't all that long ago that I'd stayed in it. The cream metal-framed bed took up much of the space but there was just enough room for a small wardrobe with drawers beneath, a dressing table and stool, a tiny bookcase and a pair of lamp-topped nightstands.

'I know you love this room,' said Dolly as she smoothed out the floral-patterned eiderdown and turned on the lamps, which cast a warm and welcoming glow. 'And I hope you enjoy being back in it.'

'I'm enjoying it already,' I told her, with a warm smile.

I still felt bad for labelling the cottage as cramped, even though I had been grumpy, but then I supposed I had gotten used to having so much extra space at the flat I was bound to notice the difference. The wardrobes there were practically of walk-in proportions and the dining table could easily seat eight, not that we ever held dinner parties. Jonathan had always preferred to keep our time together for just the two of us.

'Good,' Dolly nodded. 'I'm delighted to hear it and I'm delighted you've come. It's a big day for Wynbridge tomorrow and it will be wonderful to have you with me to enjoy it.'

'Ah yes,' I said, 'the switch-on, Beamish did mention it.'

'I know you don't hold much truck with Christmas, my dear, but I'm still hoping you will enjoy some of our little customs and events. It will be a comfort to know that you carry some of the Wynbridge winter in your heart when you head off on that plane.'

All of a sudden, I thought I was going to cry. I must have been feeling even more tired and emotional than I realised.

'I'm sure I will,' I said huskily, before reaching for one of the fluffy towels Dolly had piled on to the end of the bed. 'Would it be all right if I just have a quick shower to freshen up? I feel a bit grubby after my journey and I still haven't properly thawed out.'

'Of course,' she smiled, 'but it will have to be a bath. I still don't have a shower. They've always struck me as being in too much of a rush.'

Later that evening I pulled my coat over my dressing gown – a fluffy affair borrowed from my host who was appalled to discover I didn't have one of my own – and headed down the garden to message Jonathan again. I had barely reached the shelter of the apple trees at the end of the lawn when my phone began to ring.

'Hattie?' Jonathan called out the second I answered.

'Yes.'

'Oh, thank goodness. Are you all right? I've been trying to get hold of you for hours.'

'I told you there's no signal at the cottage,' I reminded him. 'I've had to come down the garden and I can't be long because it's absolutely freezing.'

'You said you'd let me know when you were in a taxi,' he said, sounding stressed.

'I did,' I told him. 'I did send a text in response to the ones you'd sent me, but it mustn't have sent for some reason.'

'Oh well,' he said, letting out a long breath, 'as long as you're all right.'

'I am,' I said, 'and I'm ever so sorry,' I added, even though it wasn't my fault.

'I kept checking the trains and I could see you were most likely caught in some hold-ups.'

That was putting it mildly, but given that he hadn't wanted me to use the train in the first place, I didn't say as much. If I hadn't been so stubborn, I could have arrived far sooner and far drier.

'It wasn't too bad,' I said playing it down, 'and I'm settled now.'

'That's all right then,' Jonathan replied, sounding calmer. 'So, how's Dolly? I've sent her a present. Has it arrived?'

'It has,' I told him, 'and she's absolutely thrilled with it. It was a really lovely thing to do, Jonathan.'

'I wanted to make amends for questioning her motive for inviting you,' he said. 'I know she doesn't know what I said, but I've been feeling bad about it.'

'Well,' I said, 'whatever the reason for sending it, she loved it.'

'Good,' he said. 'So how are things in Wynbridge? What are your plans for tonight?'

I didn't tell him that I had been taken aback by Dolly's appearance or that she'd arranged to have a taxi pick me up. I didn't think Jonathan would much appreciate knowing she'd lined up the Fenland equivalent of Dwayne Johnson to rescue me from the typhoon. Not that Beamish looked like

The Rock, but he was certainly built like him.

'Much the same as usual,' I sniffed, jiggling about to stop the blood freezing in my veins. 'And Dolly's planned a wild night in for us. She's warming cups of cocoa as we speak.'

Jonathan chuckled.

'And she's lent me one of her fluffy dressing gowns to keep me warm,' I added, to further boost his mood.

'I'm sorry I got so stressed,' he apologised. 'I was just worried about you, that's all.'

'I know,' I said, 'I know you were.'

I was grateful to have someone in my life who cared for me so much, but I was still planning to quickly end the call and get back indoors before my toes dropped off.

'I'll feel better once we've moved,' he said brightly. 'Then I'll know where you are all the time.'

I stopped moving, a frown knitting my brows as I let out a long breath and watched it stream away.

'Not all the time, Jonathan,' I said. 'You can't know where I am all the time.'

'You know what I mean.'

I wasn't sure I did, but I was too cold to ask him to explain.

'Look,' I said, 'I have to go. It really is freezing out here.'

'All right,' he said. 'I'll message you when I land and we can talk about how to cut your time there short and maybe even skype for a bit later in the week?' he added hopefully.

'That will depend on the signal,' I reminded him, glossing over the part about leaving Dolly earlier than planned. Now I'd had eyes on her, I wasn't sure I wanted to. I should never have suggested it. 'Have a safe flight and we'll definitely talk again soon.'

'Definitely,' he said, 'I love you.'

'I love you too,' I said back, racing up the path towards the warmth of the kitchen. 'And thank you for sending that hamper, Jonathan. Dolly really loved it.'

Chapter 4

When I went to bed that evening, I had absolutely no expectations that I would fall asleep. I'd been struggling to get any real rest since the day I discovered I was surplus to requirements at the hotel and when I did manage to nod off, my downtime was filled with odd dreams of deserts and being abandoned on unfamiliar shores.

However, the soft, deep mattress on Dolly's spare bed and the sound of the crackling fire in the sitting room below must have worked some magic and I was surprised to see a little daylight peeping around the curtains the next time I opened my eyes.

In fact, I think I would have carried on sleeping were it not for a persistent tapping sound outside the bedroom window and the old familiar weight on my chest, which had also been present since Friday the thirteenth of September.

'What on earth,' I gasped, as I struggled to sit up in the bed.

The weight was even heavier than usual and as I began to move it started to purr.

'Tiddles,' I groaned. 'What are you doing up here?'

The little cat was heavier than you would think at a dead weight and she was incredibly reluctant to move. I managed to carefully push her to one side without eliciting a hiss, actually, she didn't even open her eyes so I couldn't be sure she was even conscious, and then swung my legs out of the bed as the tapping grew louder.

Annoyed to have my first peaceful sleep in weeks ruined, I rattled the curtains along their pole and flung open the window to seek out the source of the noise.

'Oh, fuck me!' Were the first words I heard as I launched myself forward and with one hand caught hold of the top of the ladder I had just sent flying, with a very startled looking Beamish balanced near the top of it.

I clung to his wrist and between us we pulled the ladder back so it was resting just underneath the ledge of my window.

'Bloody hell,' he gasped, breathing heavily and shaking his head as he peered down at the frost-encrusted ground below. 'I thought I was a goner there for a minute.'

I didn't answer. I couldn't. It was all I could do to stop my heart from hammering out of my chest.

'Good morning, Hattie,' he said, turning his attention back to me. 'Did I wake you?'

We both looked down at his wrist which I still had hold of.

'You can let go now,' he winked.

I dropped him like a hot stone and took a step back. He had regained his composure far faster than I had.

'What the hell are you doing?' I demanded. 'It's ...' I looked around for my phone to check the time but couldn't see it. 'Well, it's too early to be banging and crashing about outside someone's bedroom window on a Saturday morning.'

'It's half eight,' he informed me. 'And I was only banging, you would have been the one responsible for the crashing, had you pitched me off completely.'

I put my hand over my mouth to stifle an unexpected giggle.

'It's not funny,' he said, raising his eyebrows.

His comment made me laugh all the more. I had no idea what had come over me.

'I know,' I said, clearing my throat. 'I'm so sorry. I think it's the shock.'

'Anyway,' he went on, now wearing a smile which matched my own. 'I would have had you down as an early riser. One of those running before work types with a neon vest and a Fitbit strapped to your wrist.'

I bit my lip to stop myself from telling him I'd forgotten to pack my Fitbit and realised I wasn't the only one capable of making assumptions. The truth was, I did used to run before my shift at the hotel, but I wasn't about to give him the satisfaction of telling him that, was I? The next thing I knew, he'd be quashing my small-town lad theory.

'Well,' I said instead. 'I'm not at work, am I? I'm on holiday and as such, fancied a lie-in for a change.'

'Fair enough,' he said, looking back up at whatever it

was he was up the ladder doing. 'I'll be finished here soon. Perhaps you'll be able to nod off again.'

I didn't actually want to, given that I'd just had my first full night sleep in months.

'I doubt it,' I said, 'anyway, you still haven't told me what it is that you're doing.'

'Getting an eyeful of your figure by the looks of it,' snapped a cross voice behind me. 'Put some clothes on for pity's sake, Hattie, before you catch your death.'

I hastily snatched Dolly's borrowed dressing gown off the bed and thrust my arms into it as Beamish chortled. I had quite forgotten that I was still in my scanty nightwear and it was so cold. If Beamish had noticed he hadn't let on, but that didn't stop my cheeks glowing as I fumbled to tie the belt.

'And you've let the cat up here,' Dolly tutted disapprovingly. 'I hadn't made up my mind about whether or not to let her on the beds yet.'

I opened my mouth to protest but didn't get the chance.

'Oh honestly, Hattie,' said Beamish.

'Still,' said Dolly, handing me a mug of tea from the tray she'd carried up before passing one out of the window to Beamish, 'at least we know you aren't really allergic. If she's been up here with you all night you would be sneezing and itching all over the place by now.'

'I didn't notice any scratch marks.' Beamish unhelpfully put in, earning himself a stern look from my friend and a head shake from me.

'Have you nearly finished up here?' Dolly asked him.

'Almost,' he answered. 'By the time you've made me that bacon butty you promised I'll be ready to set up the Santa and reindeer.'

'You still haven't told me what you're doing,' I reminded him yet again.

I was beginning to feel as if I was the star turn in some silly bedroom farce.

'He's putting up my Christmas lights,' said Dolly. 'It's the Wynbridge switch-on tonight, surely you haven't forgotten?'

'No,' I said, thinking how very resourceful Beamish was for a taxi driver, 'of course not. I just didn't realise that your cottage was part of the attractions, Dolly.'

'Oh, we've all signed up to do it now,' she said, taking back the mug Beamish had already emptied. 'Well, lots of us have anyway. This is our second year. It's all part of the festive fun.'

Beamish went back to his tapping.

'I'll come and give you a hand with the breakfast,' I said to Dolly. 'I'll just get dressed first.'

'Well make sure you close the curtains,' she said pointedly. 'It was quite a shock coming in here and finding the pair of you in such a compromising position.'

She disappeared back through the door and Beamish began to laugh again.

'Excuse me,' I said, carefully closing the window and drawing the curtains again.

I could still hear him chuckling so decided to get dressed in the bathroom.

After a hearty breakfast which included eggs, tomatoes

and mushrooms as well as bacon and doorsteps of thickly buttered bread, Beamish went back to dealing with Dolly's exterior illuminations and I helped clear up. He was obviously much more than just a rugby-playing taxi driver, but I didn't want to ask about his other skills. I was too embarrassed about where I had chosen to sit during the journey from Peterborough to Wynbridge and had no intention of drawing attention to my faux pas. Perhaps I shouldn't make assumptions or jump to any more conclusions while staying under Dolly's cosy roof?

'Just exactly how many lights are you planning to have out there, Dolly?' I asked as I spotted Beamish unloading yet more boxes from his truck. 'I think you might need to rein your friend's enthusiasm in a bit.'

'Plenty,' she said, joining me at the window as he began to set out a sleigh and eight reindeer on the front lawn. 'And don't worry, these are all mine. They're a brand-new addition to the display. Beamish has been storing them at his place as he has the room.'

'Aren't you worried that they'll make the cottage look tacky?'

Dolly looked up at me, her eyes wide.

'What I mean is,' I faltered, 'wouldn't a simple wreath on the door and some warm white lights around the windows be a little more in keeping?'

'With what?'

Clearly, I wasn't explaining what I meant particularly well and I had upset her, but that hadn't been my intention.

'I just meant with the style of the cottage,' I rushed on, trying to make amends.

'If you're suggesting my decorations are Christmas tat, Hattie—'

'No,' I interrupted, 'no, of course not.'

'Then you're probably right,' she laughed, 'but the children love them and for that matter, so do I. The town produces a little map of the most illuminated streets now and my cottage is one of the furthest. Lots of families come to enjoy them, so where's the harm?'

'There is none,' I said, shaking my head and feeling suitably chastened.

'I can remember you once telling me that your father went in for something similar.'

That was true, or it had been. Obviously, I didn't know how he and Mum decided to decorate now, but Dad had always favoured a slightly over the top attitude when it came to Christmas. It had driven Jonathan to distraction the one and only December we had visited together before I snipped that thread. Come to think of it, lots of things my parents liked hadn't met with my partner's approval.

'And when the Luccas owned the hotel you were always first in the loft to bring the boxes of decorations down, weren't you?'

'Yes,' I said, smiling as I remembered. 'I suppose I was.'

'You used to work through your days off to help put them up. What happened to that girl, Hattie? Where's she disappeared to?'

'I don't know,' I said, my smile faltering as Beamish gave us a thumbs up and Dolly waved back. 'I haven't seen her for a while.'

The hotel still had Christmas decorations, but they came and went with a professional designer and were stylishly coordinated and confined to a corner of the reception and dining room. It was all very chic, not unlike my festive holiday in the sun with Jonathan. There was certainly no room or allowance for the so-called 'tacky Christmas tat' that Dolly favoured.

'Well,' she said, rubbing my arm, 'I'm sure we're going to find her in the next few weeks, whether she wants to stay hidden or not.'

The little town of Wynbridge was heaving that evening and Beamish was lucky to find a parking space. He had insisted on driving Dolly and me in and had made a great show of opening the back door of the truck, telling Dolly that I preferred not to sit in the front. I smiled sweetly and climbed in knowing that if I tried to explain then I'd never hear the last of it, from either of them.

'Don't feel obliged to stick with me, Hattie dear,' Dolly said as we made our way amongst the crowd towards the market which had stayed open and looked to have a few extra festive stalls. 'I've promised to help on the WI stand, so you can go off and explore if you like.'

'I might in a while,' I told her. I felt a bit out of place among the throng who all seemed to know one another and met with hugs and smiles. 'I'll see how I feel if that's all right.'

'Of course,' said Dolly, waving to a woman who I guessed was calling her name. It was a job to hear anything above the rousing chorus of the Salvation Army band. 'Whatever you like.'

'Here you are, Dolly!' said the woman, handing her an apron the second we reached her. 'We were hoping you would make it. How are you feeling?'

'I'm fine,' said Dolly dismissively. 'It was just a cold and I'm over it now. Hattie, this is Catherine Connelly. She owns the country pile, Wynthorpe Hall and I suppose she's the closest to gentry the town has got.'

'Oh Dolly,' tutted Catherine, 'you are naughty. I'm pleased to meet you, Hattie. Dolly tells me you're going to be spending the run-up to Christmas with her before you move abroad.'

I flushed as I remembered my promise to Jonathan that I would try and cut my visit short and how I had glossed over his mention of it during our telephone conversation the evening before. I knew I wouldn't be able to get away with doing that for much longer and felt my face redden to what must have been a deep shade of crimson.

'Hopefully,' I said, meaning my visit rather than my move. The move was definitely happening.

Dolly looked at me quizzically but didn't comment.

'Well, we have plenty going on at the hall during the next few weeks,' said Catherine. 'It would be lovely if you could come along. We're expanding our Winter Wonderland this year and of course there are the sleigh rides around the grounds.'

'Perhaps,' I said, cutting her off before she got carried away. 'I don't much go in for Christmas, I'm afraid.'

'Don't go in for Christmas!' cried a voice behind me. 'Whatever next!'

'Here you are, Hattie,' said Dolly, 'here's a familiar face.'

I turned around and found myself in the midst of a hug from a woman with thick dark curls and the prettiest green eyes.

'Rose,' I said, hugging her back. 'How lovely to see you. How are you?'

Rose Gardner, was one of the teachers at the school where Dolly worked and I myself had worked with her too when I had volunteered. She was always brimming with bubbly charm, very much a glass half-full kind of woman.

'I'm very well,' she said, looking me up and down, 'but not as well as you it seems. How fantastic do you look? But then with your height and slender frame, you always did put us little country dumplings to shame.'

'I don't think so,' I said, feeling another blush blooming.

I had hated my height when I was growing up and sometimes still felt that it wore me rather than the other way around.

'Dolly tells me you're here for the holidays,' said Rose, linking arms, which wasn't easy given our height difference, before moving us away from the stall. 'I'll bring her back in a bit, Dolly!' she called over her shoulder.

59

'Take your time!' Dolly called back.

I glanced over and saw she was already in the thick of things, handing out mince pies and gingerbread biscuits as if they were going out of fashion.

'So,' said Rose, once she had treated us both to a cup of fragrant mulled wine. 'What are your plans? I know Dolly said you're moving abroad in the new year, but what are you going to be doing while you're here?'

'Nothing in particular,' I told her, blowing into my cup.

I wondered if Dolly had said that I was moving with Jonathan when she'd been telling everyone about my imminent move. They all knew my last visit to the town had been prompted by man trouble but I still didn't know how Dolly had explained my swifter than planned departure. I would have to ask her about that.

'I'm here for Dolly really,' I went on. 'I want to spend as much time with her as I can before I go.'

'In that case,' Rose rushed on, her eyes twinkling, 'you should definitely sign up to volunteer at the school again.'

'Oh . . .' I said, shaking my head, all thoughts of Jonathan suddenly forgotten. 'I don't think . . .'

'No, I mean it,' she interrupted. 'That way you could spend far more time with Dolly and I can guarantee that by the time you go, you'll be feeling completely different about Christmas.'

She said that as if it was a good thing.

'I couldn't believe it back there when you said you didn't go in for it. What on earth were you thinking? I don't know where your festive spirit has slunk off to Hattie, but just one week working with our excited lot and you'd be as mad keen on Christmas again as the rest of us!'

She was almost bouncing up and down at the thought.

'Well,' I said feebly, 'I really don't know.'

'We have so much coming up,' she went dreamily on, 'what with the fair and the carol concert and the play. We're really swamped. An extra pair of hands would be a godsend right now.'

'But what about health and safety and all the checks?' I gabbled, giving voice to the first excuse I could come up with. 'By the time all the relevant paperwork comes back it would be the end of term. Wouldn't it?' I hopefully added.

I wasn't sure why I was so set against the idea, but my head was telling me it was something I should avoid doing at all costs.

'Not at all,' said Rose, shaking her head. 'There's a check we can apply for which comes back almost straight away and besides, you renewed your DBS the last time you were going to volunteer with us, didn't you? I know your boss at the hotel was desperately under-staffed and you had to cut your visit short, but the paperwork had been sent off by then and it came back almost as soon as you'd gone back to work.'

So that was the line Dolly had taken – I had arrived because of man trouble, but rather than tell everyone I had gone again because Jonathan and I had worked things out, she'd said I'd left to go back to the hotel. I didn't want to think too deeply about why she had done that and I certainly wouldn't be asking her. Clearly, Jonathan's flat key, honeyed words and heartfelt promises at the time had soothed me, but not my friend.

'Oh yes,' I swallowed, 'of course. I seem to remember Dolly did mention it.'

'Well there you are then! I'm sure we'll still have it all on file,' Rose rushed on, 'so there's really nothing stopping you, is there?'

Our conversation was interrupted by a sudden fanfare at the far end of the square in front of the towering tree. It was time for the lights to go on.

'Promise me you'll at least think about it,' said Rose as the first of the celebratory fireworks rocketed into the air and the crowd began to cheer.

I looked around at the happy faces, flushed with excitement and caught sight of Beamish laughing with a group of friends right next to the platform where the magic switch-on was going to happen. He waved when he spotted me, a look of pure joy lighting up his bruised features. I couldn't help but smile and wave back.

'I'll think about it,' I told Rose, 'but I'm not making any promises.'

Chapter 5

When I woke the next morning, with Tiddles thankfully settled further down the bed, I could feel the air was cooler than the morning before and there was no light peeping around the curtains. I could hear Dolly moving around in the kitchen and I gratefully wrapped myself in her warm dressing gown before heading down.

I had laid awake the night before, mulling over what Rose had said about Dolly's explanation of why I had left Wynbridge as hurriedly as I'd arrived the last time I had been in town and was still convinced that it would be best not to ask her about it. It was well over a year ago now, and everything had turned out fine, so why go fishing for a catch I didn't want? I was certain Dolly had had her reasons for not telling the truth; I just wasn't sure I would benefit from knowing what they were.

'Good morning,' said Dolly, quickly taking something off the table when she heard me on the stairs. 'Tea? I thought we might try this blend from the hamper.'

'Yes, please.' I said, with a little shiver. 'It'll warm me up.'

'There's a hard frost this morning,' she said. 'The path was quite slippery when I went out to dress the bird table.'

It was on the tip of my tongue to remind her to be careful when she went out, in case she fell, but I didn't.

'Is Tiddles up there by any chance?' she asked, with a nod to the stairs.

'Yes,' I said. 'She is. Do you want me to turf her off the bed?'

'No, there's no point now she's got the taste for it. I always knew it was only a matter of time before she negotiated the stairs and as they're open plan she'd only go straight back up again if we carried her down.'

'She isn't doing any harm and she doesn't take up much room.'

Dolly looked at me and raised an eyebrow.

'In that case,' she said, 'we'll definitely leave her. Now, come and sit down. I have a present for you.'

'A present,' I laughed. 'It's a bit early in the month, isn't it? Even for you.'

I did as I was told, relieved that I hadn't come down all guns blazing and demanding an explanation, but not because I was being given a gift. Dolly handed me an A4 envelope.

'Open it then,' she encouraged.

Inside was an advent calendar.

Oh, Dolly!' I gasped. 'It's lovely.'

'You can't start December without a calendar,' she said. 'And I thought the picture on that one was rather pretty.'

The intricately painted houses had a dusting of snow on

their roofs and glitter-covered trees in the windows. Santa, resplendent in his shiny red sleigh, was flying across the star-studded sky behind his eight purposeful reindeer, a packed sack of toys at his side.

'Where on earth did you find it?' I asked, examining the old-fashioned details.

It was years since I'd had an advent calendar and I hadn't even realised they made ones like this anymore. Some of the girls I had worked with at the hotel had gone in for the expensive beauty variety last year and when I was growing up, I had always had a Cadbury chocolate one, but this vintage-looking treasure was a first of its kind for me.

'In town,' said Dolly. 'A couple of the shops still stock this sort so I picked up one for you and one for Beamish.'

I was sure he would be every bit as thrilled as I was, more so probably, given his apparent love of the season. His face as the lights came on in the market square the night before had been a picture. That was something else I had thought about before I went to sleep but I had no idea why.

'Well thank you,' I said, leaning over and giving Dolly a kiss on the cheek. 'I know my Christmas spirit has done a bunk, but I still love it. Have you got one?'

'Of course,' she said, pointing to the shelf above the sink. 'It's a bit battered, but then it would be. I've been opening and closing it for the last twenty odd years.'

Dolly's calendar was the same sort as mine only hers featured a nativity scene, complete with manger, lowing cattle and one very bright star.

'Let's open them together,' I said, jumping up and handing Dolly hers.

'I know what I've got,' she laughed. 'I know them all off by heart now.'

'Don't spoil it,' I told her, as I carefully lifted the corner of the little window marked one. Once I'd peeled a bit back, I slid a teaspoon underneath to help with the rest.

'You could just tear it off,' Dolly remarked as she revealed an angel behind her door. 'I think mine needs a little more Sellotape,' she added, getting up.

'But then I wouldn't be able to use it again next year,' I said, thinking it might be nice if I could keep my calendar for as long as Dolly had had hers.

'I suppose you could take it with you.'

For a moment I'd forgotten that this time next year, I'd be spending December in the sun, and every month before and after it, come to that.

'What have you got?' she asked. 'Haven't you got in yet?'

'Yes,' I swallowed, 'yes, here we go. It's a teddy bear. A lovely big bear with a bright red bow.'

'Now,' smiled Dolly, coming back with the tape. 'How lovely is that?'

It was very lovely indeed.

Dolly was a fairly regular churchgoer and she was determined that I should join her that afternoon for the first advent service of the year.

'But I don't do church,' I told her. 'I'm not a church person.'

Beamish, playing the part of chauffeur once again and with his calendar carefully grasped in his bear-sized mitts, shook his head.

'You call that an excuse,' he tutted, his trademark grin in place.

'You be quiet,' I told him.

My rebuke made him smile all the more. He might have been the size of the Hulk but he had Puck's mischievous spirit.

'But I would really like you to come,' Dolly wheedled. 'The first candle on the advent wreath will be lit today and it's quite unusual for the first day of December to actually fall on a Sunday, you know.'

I wasn't even sure what an advent wreath was, but I could see it meant a lot to my friend.

'I'll get my coat,' I said resignedly.

'And I'll get the truck warmed up,' said Beamish, bounding out the door and banging it shut behind him.

I was surprised to see the church so packed and the service, which was all about hope, stirred up memories of Christmas past, many of which I hadn't thought about in years. The first purple candle in the evergreen wreath was lit and 'O Come, O Come, Emmanuel' was sung with such enthusiasm I thought I was going to cry. Beamish handed me a tissue as the hymn drew to a close and I felt a little foolish to have been found out. I turned to say something to him, but he was staring straight ahead and I was certain his own eyes were a little wetter than usual.

'Now that wasn't too bad, was it?' asked Dolly as the three of us made our way to the back where tea and mince pies were being administered.

'It was lovely, Dolly,' said Beamish. 'But if you'll excuse me for a moment, I'm just nipping out to catch a word with someone, but you take your time. I'm in no rush.'

More than one pair of eyes were trained on his retreating back and I guessed that Dolly's driver and handyman was highly regarded among her churchgoing friends.

'Hello, Harriet,' said a man's voice behind me as we stood in the queue for tea. 'Rose tells me you're going to ask about joining us until the end of term.'

'Mr Matthews,' said Dolly, 'I thought I heard your baritone somewhere near the back. What's this you're saying about Hattie?'

Rose waved at me from where she was handing out colouring sheets and crayons to keep the youngsters occupied, and I shook my head in response.

'I think I'm right,' Mr Matthews, the headteacher, continued with a frown, 'aren't I?'

'I did talk to Rose last night about the possibility of volunteering for a few days,' I began to explain.

'Well that's wonderful,' interrupted Dolly, her cheeks positively glowing. 'Why ever didn't you tell me?'

'Because I still haven't made up my mind,' I rushed on. 'I know Rose said that all my checks and things would still be up to date, but ...'

'We really could do with an extra pair of hands, couldn't

we, Dolly?' Mr Matthews quickly cut in. 'We've had a new boy join us recently and he's diabetic so Mr Patterson's teaching assistant spends quite a bit of her time out of the classroom now. Some extra help, especially in the run-up to Christmas, would be very much appreciated. I still haven't worked out how we're going to cope without Dolly next term.'

The poor man really did look genuinely worried and I knew from some of what Dolly had told me that school budgets were being squeezed and cut all the time. That said, I still wasn't prepared to say yes until I'd given offering my services – or should I say Rose offering my services – some more serious thought.

'Are you waiting for tea, dear?'

I hadn't realised I was holding up the queue.

'Yes,' I said, 'sorry. Can I have two cups, please?'

'I'll see you both tomorrow then,' said Mr Matthews, moving off to speak to the vicar before I had a chance to correct him.

'Now,' said Dolly. 'That really will be a treat.'

Rose somehow managed to slip away every time I got close enough to tell her that I still hadn't made up my mind and with Dolly looking happier and healthier than I'd seen her since my arrival, I didn't have the heart to make a fuss.

'I think it's about time we were heading back, don't you?' she said, after finishing her third cup of church tea. 'It's going to be a busy week, what with the school fair happening on Friday afternoon. I daresay we could both do with an early night.'

Beamish had set up a timer for the lights at Dolly's cottage and I could see it had worked the second he swung the truck back into her road. I had thought Dolly would want them on the evening before but that night, she told me, was reserved solely for the town. Now however, her little place positively glowed like a festive beacon. Other houses were also decorated but none as brightly as Dolly's. The old-fashioned red, blue, yellow and green bulbs, which Beamish had hammered in place under the eaves and around the windows looked very jolly indeed and, on the lawn just inside the gate, Santa appeared poised to launch, his reindeer straining to take flight.

'There now,' Dolly exclaimed as she leant forward in her seat to get a better look. 'What a welcome sight to come home to.'

'It looks great,' agreed Beamish as he unashamedly admired his handiwork. 'I hope Mum's looks this good.'

'I'm sure it will,' said Dolly, patting his arm. 'Do you still think it looks tacky, Hattie?'

'Tacky!' gasped Beamish. 'Is that really what you think?'

I could hardly deny the accusation given the conversation Dolly and I had had just the day before.

'I admit that yesterday I did think it was going to look a little . . . naff,' I said, wishing there was a word which would describe my former feelings a little less harshly, 'but now it's all lit I think it's great.'

'She wanted warm white lights,' said Dolly, unclipping her seatbelt, 'and a holly wreath on the door.'

'You've been reading too many glossy magazines featuring country cottage Christmas styling,' said Beamish.

'No, she hasn't,' said Dolly, 'she doesn't go in for Christmas, remember? So, she won't have seen any of those.'

'Oh yes, that's right.' He went on, 'You're not a fan are you, Hattie?'

I really didn't think it was fair that they should both tease me like that.

'I used to be.' I said, jumping out to help Dolly. 'Perhaps I've just forgotten what it's all about.'

'In that case,' she said, taking hold of my hand as she carefully lowered herself on to the road, 'it's just as well that I've come up with the perfect plan to help you remember.'

Later that evening as we sat either side of the fire, Dolly with Tiddles on her lap and me rocking gently in Dolly's grandmother's chair, I fell to thinking over my first weekend in Wynbridge and all the feelings and memories the place had already stirred up.

Before I arrived, I had thought I had most things in my life in order, what with the fresh start in a new country poised to happen and a proposal of marriage from the man I loved waiting in the wings, but now it felt as if someone had come along with a big stick and stirred everything up, muddying the previously clear waters and stopping me from seeing the bottom.

It seemed inevitable now that I would be heading into school with Dolly the next day but I still couldn't decide why

I was so reluctant to go. It wasn't as if I had a hundred and one other things to be getting on with while Dolly was at work and I had always enjoyed my time there, but then perhaps that itself was the problem. Perhaps, on some subconscious level, I was worried that I would love it all over again and regret that I hadn't done more to turn the fantasy I used to play out on the train into reality.

Or maybe it was the thought of being surrounded by all those excited under-eights. Jonathan and I may have never discussed get married but he had made his feelings about starting a family very clear. He didn't want to. As far as he was concerned, we, as a couple, were perfect as we were, just the two of us.

'I don't want to share you with anyone,' he had told me very early on in our relationship, 'and I never will.'

And given everything I was coming to terms with from my past, that had been OK for a while. It was even OK now, but would it be OK for ever? I wasn't sure. I still didn't know if I would want a baby one day but I supposed my silence on the subject had led him to believe that I had accepted his pronouncement. After all, I wouldn't have been banging on about finding a job in Abu Dhabi if I was harbouring a secret desire to start a family, would I? Truth be told, I probably wouldn't have agreed to go at all if I had baby fever.

I began to wish that I had taken Dolly's advice and gone off somewhere to make up my mind about moving instead of letting Jonathan's smooth talking and the deteriorating weather influence my decision. I loved the man, of course I did, but I suddenly realised the enormity of what I was going to be giving up for good when I accepted his impending proposal and our global relocation.

'Penny for them.'

'Sorry?'

'For your thoughts,' said Dolly. 'You've been staring into the flames for the last half an hour and looking as though you've got the weight of the world on your shoulders. What are you thinking about?'

'Actually,' I fibbed, 'I was trying to work out what it was that you've come up with to try and help me remember what Christmas is all about.'

'I knew you wouldn't be able to resist asking,' Dolly smiled, accepting what I had said as she transferred Tiddles from her lap to mine. 'I'll get my notepad and pencil and then I'll explain.'

'I hope it isn't anything to do with making a list,' I told her, 'because that's cheating. You know how I love a good list. I won't be able to resist if there are bullet points involved.'

'It has *everything* to do with making a list,' said Dolly, settling herself back into her seat, now with her squishy beanbag lap tray, reading glasses and notepad in place. 'A Christmas Wish List.'

'A Christmas, what?' I frowned.

'Wish List,' she said again, licking the end of her pencil and deftly flicking the notebook open on to the next clean page.

'What's one of those?' I asked.

I couldn't imagine she was going to ask me to start writing

a list of longed-for presents. Dolly was the least materialistic person I knew.

'Well, it can be all sorts of things,' she said seriously and I suddenly got the feeling she was going to aim straight for my heart, 'to all sorts of people, but this one is unique to you, Hattie. I saw your face light up this morning when you opened that advent calendar and I'm certain there are plenty of other things about Christmas that you've missed every bit as much, it's just that you've forgotten about them.'

I wasn't sure she was right, but I did love the calendar.

'So, the point of the list is . . .'

'To experience them again,' she said, scribbling something I couldn't make out at the top of the page. 'I want you to create a list of all the things you either haven't done for ages or won't be able to do when you move, or even both. Like I told you before, I want you to make some memories to take with you, my dear.'

'I see.'

'You keep insisting that Christmas isn't all it's cracked up to be, but I'm not sure if you're simply accepting Jonathan's opinion about it as your own, or if you've worked through the holidays for so long you've hardened your heart against it, or if you're in denial about the joy it can bring because you don't talk to your parents . . .'

'Dolly—'

'I know,' she carried on, flapping her hand, 'I know, you don't need me to point all this out to you and you probably think I'm a little cruel to do it—'

'A little cruel—'

'But I'm only saying it because I know that somewhere deep inside, you've still got the capacity to have some festive fun. Your reaction when you opened that envelope this morning was proof enough of that.'

She was silent then, sitting with her pencil poised and wearing a neutral expression. I knew exactly the game she was playing. She was waiting for me to make a suggestion and if I didn't, we'd end up sitting there all night.

'Well I suppose I could think of something,' I caved after about a minute and a half.

'Marvellous.'

'But only if we do it together.'

'Together?'

'Yes,' I insisted, 'we'll both add things to the list.'

If I was going to have to go along with the idea, then she was going to have to join in too.

'But I've always done everything I've ever wanted at Christmas,' Dolly frowned. 'You know that.'

'Those are my terms,' I told her. 'A joint list, or no list at all.'

Dolly chewed the end of her pencil and rubbed her forehead.

'Oh, oh,' she gasped a few seconds later. 'Actually, there is something I would love to see.'

'Right then,' I said feeling pleased to have drawn her in and caught her in the web she had spun for me, 'you'd better write it down.'

We spent the rest of the evening compiling a list of all the things I had missed out on in recent years. Dolly came up with far more than I did and lots of them were silly things like wearing a Christmas jumper, but she said they were every bit as important as the bigger things because they all formed part of the spirit of the season.

'I think that's going to be my highlight,' Dolly sighed, as she re-read her wish to take a trip to the Norfolk coast. She was hoping to spot some of the pink-footed geese which visited there every winter. 'If we can find a way to get there, that is.'

'I'm sure we'll manage it,' I told her.

Truth be told I was more interested in ticking off the things Dolly had added for herself than working through what she had included for me. As lovely as her idea was, I knew it was going to take a whole lot more than wearing a spangly sweater to get me in a merry mood.

'Is that it then?' I yawned. 'Surely, that has to be enough to be going on with for now?'

'There is just one more thing,' said Dolly.

'What?'

She looked up from her notes and fixed me with a serious stare.

'I know this isn't the first time I've said it recently, but more than anything,' she said, 'I want you to get back in touch with your parents, Hattie.'

I shook my head. She couldn't add that, it had nothing to do with Christmas.

'You know that's impossible,' I said quietly. 'You know what they said.'

'I know that you'll regret it if you don't,' she carried on. 'I'm not suggesting you turn up on their doorstep, or even telephone. Just send a simple card with the return address for here, or your email written inside.'

The sneaky thing. She was going to use a Christmas card to make her request fit the list.

'That way,' she carried on, 'should they need to, or want to, they'll be able to get in touch.'

I shook my head.

'You wanted me to write the Wish List with you, Hattie,' she said firmly, 'and this is the one thing I want to add to it more than anything else. I know you've told me that you can never forgive them and, given everything you've been through, I do understand, but if you move to the other side of the world without telling them I really think it'll be game over for you and them, for ever.'

I sat back in my chair and let out a long slow breath. I thought I had been so clever making Dolly join in with her own additions, but now it seemed she had pulled me into the web along with her. What a clever woman she was.

Chapter 6

The sky above Wynbridge the next morning was slate-grey to match my mood as Dolly and I set off for school, after a fortifying breakfast of honey-sweetened porridge, carrying a thermos apiece. Apparently, I was the newest Wynbridge Infants recruit whether I wanted to be or not.

We hadn't walked far before my phone pinged and a message from Jonathan showed up. I read it quickly and fired one back to tell him all was well, but that I was still struggling to get a signal. I made no mention of my temporary new job. My head was still whirring with everything my brief time in the town had stirred up and, as I didn't know exactly what to say, I thought it best not to say anything at all.

'If I could just ask you to sign in?' asked Alison Anderson, the school's receptionist. 'And wear this lanyard, then Dolly can take you through to the staffroom. It's lovely to see you again, Hattie.'

Alison was the epitome of efficiency, running not only the school office with extraordinary proficiency but the staff as well. Nothing ever fazed her and she always had a solution to every problem. Mr Matthews often joked that the school would descend into chaos if she ever phoned in sick but we all knew he actually meant it.

'And don't worry, all your checks are up to date,' she added before turning her attention to the queue of parents waiting to try her patience even before the morning bell had rung. 'I've put all the paperwork on Mr Matthews' desk.'

'Thank you, Mrs Anderson,' I said, trying to smile.

That was my 'Get Out of Jail Free' card scuppered then.

'Right,' said Dolly, 'I'm going to have to leave you to it, I'm afraid. Andrew knows you're here and will be along in a minute. Is that all right?'

My stomach was churning as if I was a new pupil rather than a grown-up trying to do the school a favour. I couldn't remember ever feeling like that before.

'Yes,' I squeaked. 'I'll be fine.'

The staffroom was already deserted and I could hear the photocopier in the next room churning out A4 as people called to one another along the corridor. My eyes were drawn to a huge sheet of cartridge paper which had been stuck on the whiteboard and almost completely covered one of the walls.

It announced 'the countdown to Christmas' and listed all the things which were going to be happening during the last few weeks of term. Dolly had been right. There were a fair few things on our Wish List which could be ticked off just by turning up on the right days. My stomach churned again as I looked at the busy calendar. What with the school schedule and Dolly's list, there really was going to be no escaping Christmas this year.

'Hattie,' said Mr Matthews as he rushed in looking harassed. 'Sorry to keep you hanging about.'

'It's fine,' I told him. 'I've only just arrived and I was looking through the Christmas plan.'

'Yes,' he said, a deeper frown forming, 'as you can see there's plenty to do so your timely arrival couldn't be more appreciated. I was hoping to give you the lowdown on what we were thinking you could help with as well as a quick tour as a few of the rooms have been repurposed, but I have to see a parent.'

'That's all right,' I said. 'I can come back later if it will be more convenient. I know we have to go through safe-guarding before I'm assigned a class.'

Someone began whistling 'We Wish You a Merry Christmas' in the corridor and at the sound of it, Mr Matthews' frown was instantaneously smoothed.

'Coming in for that later might not be a bad idea,' he said as he rushed back to the door, 'but don't worry about the tour. You stay there, I know just the person who can help with that.'

I waited as instructed, straightening my lanyard and wondering if I'd packed the best outfits for dealing with the onslaught of glitter and glue which no doubt awaited me.

'That would be such a help,' I heard Mr Matthews say as he walked back to the staffroom, 'it's not even nine and I'm already swamped.'

'You know me,' a voice answered. 'I'm always happy to help if I can.'

'That you are,' answered Mr Matthews as he came back in. This time he was smiling rather than looking harassed. 'I take it you already know our school caretaker and grounds-man, Hattie?'

'Do I?' I asked doubtfully.

I thought I recognised the other man's voice, but surely it couldn't be?

'You're more familiar with me in my taxi driving and head of festive illumination roles really, aren't you, Hattie?'

'Beamish,' I said, taken aback.

He was the last person I had been expecting to see in school and I wondered if there was any area of Wynbridge where he didn't play a crucial role. He'd got looking out for the elderly sorted, as well as town sports and chauffeuring, and now it appeared that even the youngest academics were covered by his all-encompassing skillset.

'Yes,' said Mr Matthews, 'Beamish. He's hardly been with us any time at all really, but he's already our male equivalent of Mrs Anderson.'

'I'm not sure what you mean by that,' Beamish laughed.

'You mean that Beamish here is an expert in his field of expertise, don't you, Mr Matthews? Just like Mrs Anderson in the office.'

'Exactly,' Mr Matthews confirmed. 'And Mrs Cook in the kitchen. Although,' he added thoughtfully, 'Beamish has so many fields of expertise that, by rights, he should be one of the largest landowners in the county.'

Mr Matthews laughed at his own joke, but was pulled up short when Mrs Anderson's head appeared around the doorframe, a stern expression on her face.

'Andrew,' she hissed, 'Mrs Jones is waiting.'

'Sorry,' he said, banishing the laughter, 'I'll be right there. Hattie, I do apologise for not being able to give you a better welcome back to the school, but . . .'

'It's fine,' I told him. 'I understand. As I said before, I can easily pop back at the end of the day and we can talk about everything then.'

'Bless you,' he said, rushing off, 'and bless you too, Beamish.'

'Right,' said Beamish, clapping his hands together once he had heard Mr Matthews' office door close, 'as that's us well and truly blessed, I suppose we'd better get on. Shall we start with the tour?'

Not all that much had changed since my last visit but some of the rooms were now being used for different things and there was a new kitchen area where the children had cooking and science lessons. I knew that Dolly ran a cooking club, as well as a knitting group, and that with the exception of the summer term, when the weather was generally more favourable, she was always over-subscribed.

Whichever room we poked our heads into Beamish was greeted with smiles from both the staff and the children, who had now been led inside and were getting ready to begin their day of learning.

'We've recently made a wildlife area,' Beamish explained as we reached the kitchens which were set behind the large school hall. 'There's a pond with a dipping platform and lots of bug homes and bird boxes. I would show you that too, but it's a bit muddy and I'm not sure your smart boots would appreciate it.'

'You could give her a fireman's lift!' someone hollered from the depths of the kitchen.

Beamish pushed open the door and leaned inside.

'I'm not sure *she'd* appreciate that,' said Beamish. 'We hardly know each other.'

'You can practise on me, if you like,' said a plump girl wearing a blue hairnet and matching tabard apron.

'You leave him alone,' said Mrs Cook, the matriarch in charge.

She'd worked at the school for, well not quite as long as Dolly, but not far off. Every September, with the new intake, she had to put up with the hilarity her name caused but she bore it all with good grace.

'How are you, Harriet?' she asked, appearing with a ladle in one hand and a spatula in the other. 'I heard you were coming back. You really are a glutton for punishment, aren't you? And at Christmas of all times! You'll be exhausted come the big day.'

'My goodness,' I laughed, 'good news travels fast around here, doesn't it?'

'This is Wynbridge, love,' she said with a wink, 'nothing stays secret for long.'

When we found ourselves at the car park, I told Beamish I would walk back to the cottage and come back, as I'd promised Mr Matthews, at the end of the day.

'I'm heading into town for some materials,' he explained. 'I'll give you a lift if you like or, if you're feeling strong, you could give me a hand first and then I'll drop you back at Dolly's after.'

'What are you collecting?'

'Some timber. The stage needs a couple of repairs and the teachers need to be using it for rehearsals to get the kids used to the space as soon as possible. We don't want anyone diving off the front like last year.'

I thought it best not to ask. I knew that by the end of term I'd have enough educational anecdotes to dine out on for months. Not that I could imagine Jonathan would find them particularly amusing, should I ever decide to tell him about my time in school.

'All right,' I agreed, 'I'll help you first, although I'm sure you could get it all delivered.'

'We would as a rule,' he said, pointing out where he'd parked the truck, 'but the van the store uses is off the road today.'

'Couldn't you order from somewhere else, or try online?' I suggested. 'It would probably be cheaper.'

'No,' he said, 'we shop local around here. Now,' he smirked, 'you go and sign yourself out with Mrs Anderson and when you return you can tell me if you would prefer to sit in the front or the back.'

I gave his comment the full eye roll it deserved and sauntered back to the reception.

I mulled over what Beamish had said on the journey to the timber yard, the 'shop local' part that is, and I realised that the ethos most likely extended far beyond buying big stuff like we were collecting. I had noticed there had been a few individual stalls selling homemade and hand-crafted gifts at the switch-on, including one run by the Cherry Tree Café team, and folk couldn't seem to get enough of everything.

Perhaps I should add local shopping to the Wish List? Or maybe even try my hand at making something myself? But then who would I give it to? I could just imagine the expression on Jonathan's face if I presented him with a bag of homemade festive fudge or a handmade card. Like me, he might not have gone in for the fun and frolics which made Christmas for most people, but he was always happy to accept an expensive designer gift.

His idea of something special was the latest bit of tech or an aftershave blended to his own specifications. I couldn't imagine that anything crafted by my own fair hands would cut the mustard with him. Jonathan appreciated the finer things in life, as did I now too. I quickly banished the homespun idea, knowing it would be a waste of time and effort and feeling a little annoyed that I had been sucked into thinking about the list again.

'How do you fancy a coffee at the Cherry Tree Café?' Beamish asked, once the truck was loaded with timber. 'I know it's still a bit early, but it's criminal that you've been here for practically half a week and not been in.'

I was beginning to feel a little peckish now my first day at school nerves had settled, but couldn't resist the opportunity to question Beamish's work ethic.

'Shame on you,' I tutted, 'and during the working day. What would Mr Matthews say?'

'Thank you for turning up at five this morning to sort out the dodgy boiler again, probably.'

'Oh,' I said. I should have known better.

'I haven't had any breakfast yet.'

'Sorry,' I blushed.

'It's all right,' he grinned. 'I'm only winding you up. Although, I was there at five sorting out the boiler.'

He really was worth his weight in gold. I didn't think I'd ever met anyone as indispensable in so many areas. From what I had discovered so far, he was always on hand to help anyone and everyone at the drop of a hat and I wondered if there was a reason why he always kept himself so busy. It made me feel a little guilty when I considered my own life. I hadn't been doling out many acts of kindness lately and, as uncharitable as it might have been to think it, Jonathan was no better. We were both pretty self-centred, placed firmly at the top of our own lists, whereas Beamish, I was sure would add himself at the very bottom of his.

'What would everyone do without you, Beamish?' I laughed.

He ducked his head and shrugged, but didn't answer.

It was a struggle to stop my jaw hitting the floor when we crossed the café threshold. I almost got a sugar rush just from walking in. The scent of cinnamon and orange filled the air and I made a bee-line for the jars of iced gingerbread characters which were lined up along the counter. The café was always pretty, but even I had to admit, dressed for Christmas it was exquisite.

'If you take a seat,' said a lady wearing a candy cane patterned apron, 'One of us will be over to take your order. Good morning, Beamish,' she added with a smile.

Ladies' favourite, as well as worth his weight in gold it seemed. Although that wasn't really fair because, from what I'd deduced so far, he was every bit as popular with the men too.

'Good morning, Angela.' He smiled back.

We found a table in what had originally been the area set aside for Lizzie Dixon's crafting classes. Lizzie, Beamish explained, now ran her classes and courses in the gallery.

'And of course, they have the vintage caravan tea room and seasonal market stall too.'

'Wow,' I said, 'it's quite a business they've built up, isn't it?'

I had always known that the perfect pairing of Jemma,

the café owner and Lizzie, her clever crafting pal, were hard-working and a force to be reckoned with, but now their business was turning into an empire. I admired them very much.

'It certainly is,' Beamish agreed. 'From what I've heard since I moved back, the town's recent turnaround has been largely down to the dynamic duo.'

After Angela had taken our order – a latte and a gingerbread man for me and an Americano and bacon and avocado bagel for Beamish – my interest in him was somewhat piqued.

'So,' I began, 'you haven't always lived in the town then?'

My assumption about him being a local who'd lived his whole life here was obviously wrong and I should have realised that as soon as I'd made it; he was such a good friend of Dolly's that had he lived here for ever we most likely would have met before.

'No,' he said, 'but I did grow up here. I left when I went to university and only moved back for good a couple of years ago. Not that I realised that I was moving back for good at the time.'

I surmised that he would have quite possibly been around when I last visited. He was probably even working at the school when I went in to renew my paperwork, but I was certain I would have remembered him if I'd seen him. He had the sort of face and physique you wouldn't forget in a hurry.

'Why did you come back?' I asked.

'My dad died,' he said, one eye on the kitchen, 'so I came back to support Mum.'

'Oh, Beamish,' I swallowed. 'I'm sorry.'

I was sorry about his dad *and* my nosiness. I shouldn't have asked.

'I knew straightaway that there was something more than grieving wrong with my mum the second I saw her,' he carried on, rearranging the napkins as Angela appeared with our tray.

He stopped talking while she unloaded the delicious-looking food and drinks.

'And I was right,' he continued, after she had returned to the kitchen, 'Mum had cancer. She died six months to the day after Dad.'

'I'm so sorry,' I said again, feeling even worse than before.

He looked and sounded absolutely wretched and without thinking, I reached across the table and laid my hand on top of his. He turned his over and grasped mine. I felt a buzz, an unexpected tingle as his warm fingers closed around mine.

'Thank you, Hattie,' he said. 'I'm waiting for it to get easier, even took on the job at the school because I thought it would help, but so far . . .'

'It hasn't,' I finished for him, squeezing his hand tighter and ignoring the fluttering sensation in my chest.

Perhaps this was the reason why he kept himself so busy. Perhaps working so hard and helping everyone else was his way of coping with his grief.

'Aren't you going to answer that?' he asked, letting go of my hand.

It was only then that I realised my phone was ringing. I pulled it out of my pocket and then put it straight back.

'It'll keep.' I told him.

I didn't think that having just held hands with another man, and still feeling the palpitations the moment had elicited, made it quite the right moment to answer a call from my beau, even if nothing more than compassion had prompted my spontaneous gesture.

'Well this looks good,' said Beamish, picking up his knife and fork. 'Just what I need.'

I drew my spoon through the love heart decorating the top of my latte and waited until my own heart had stopped skittering quite so much. If Beamish had felt anything when we touched, he certainly wasn't letting on. I decided not to dwell on it and moved the conversation on.

'Do you think you'll ever leave Wynbridge?' I asked. 'I mean, you don't need a degree to be a school caretaker and Christmas illuminations expert so I'm guessing you once had a very different life to the one you're living now.'

'Oh, I did,' he said. 'I was an architect working in a busy London firm so it was, as you say, completely different, but I don't miss it in the least and no, I'll never leave. Not for more than a couple of weeks anyway. I only wish . . .'

His words trailed off.

'What? What do you wish?'

'I wish I'd spent more time here before I lost my parents,'

he said sadly, 'but there was always something to stop me coming back. I kept telling myself I'd wait until the next big project was finished, but then there'd be another one, more impressive and with a tighter deadline than the last. In the end, my time ran out. We always think we have enough of the stuff but we don't and what we do have we often take for granted and end up wasting.'

'You're probably right,' I said, snapping a leg off my gingerbread man.

'I know I'm right,' he said, looking straight at me, 'and I know this is none of my business, but Dolly mentioned that you don't talk to your parents.'

I sat back in my seat. Ever since he'd told me what had happened to bring him back to his hometown, I'd been thinking about Dolly's addition to the Wish List; that she wanted me to get in touch with Mum and Dad.

'She's right,' I said, 'I don't.'

'Then you should,' he said. His voice was firm but tender. 'Don't be too proud to be the one to make the first move, Hattie. Make the most of the little time you have left to see them before you board that plane.'

'You make it sound so simple,' I said huskily, 'but it's anything but. They broke my heart, you see. They interfered in my life and I ended up losing something very precious as a result.'

I don't know why I told him that, but I was grateful that he didn't ask what it was.

'Were you very young?'

91

Heidi Swain

I wasn't sure if he was guessing or if Dolly had told him more than she should.

'Does that matter?'

'It might well have had a bearing on their actions,' he said softly. 'If they thought you were heading for trouble then surely it would have been remiss of them not to step in.'

'I suppose,' I conceded.

I could appreciate that Beamish was trying to make a reunion sound like the easiest thing in the world, but he didn't know the full story. If he knew everything, he wouldn't even be suggesting it.

After the crisis I had moved out of home and into the hotel and miraculously, thanks to Dolly and her gentle advice and words of wisdom, our relationship had just about survived. Had it not been for my friend's subtle coaxing I was certain I would have snipped that fragile thread which attached me to my parents the day I moved out.

However, for a while and with Dolly's help, things were bearable. With the benefit of time, I could almost understand why they had done what they did, even if I couldn't come to terms with the outcome. There had even been a time when I believed that a proper reconciliation might be possible, but then I started seeing Jonathan and things went downhill almost from the moment I told him what had happened to make me leave home.

In the end, I had to accept that my parents and I would be better apart and made Jonathan go and tell them what I couldn't bring myself to say. He returned with a response so shocking that it blew my world apart. I had begged Dolly never to mention them again and she had kept her word until the move to Abu Dhabi was thrown into the mix.

Beamish looked poised to say something else, but I cut him off.

'It really is all much more complicated than you can possibly know,' I said quickly, thinking of how Jonathan had struggled to tell me what my parents had said. 'Do you mind if we change the subject?'

'I'm sorry, Hattie,' Beamish frowned. 'I didn't mean to upset you.'

'I know.'

'But please,' he said urgently, this time his hand reaching out for mine, 'please don't let past grievances mess up your future happiness.'

I squeezed his hand and nodded as I realised that I had found it surprisingly easy to talk to the man I barely knew sitting opposite me. It felt like he was fast becoming a firm new friend.

Chapter 7

That afternoon, sitting in Dolly's cottage waiting for three o'clock, with Tiddles in her basket next to the fire, I shut out all thoughts of how touching Beamish had made my skin tingle and focused instead on my parents. Not the grievances and rows of my tempestuous teenage years, but the time before that, the special moments; birthdays, holidays and bedtime stories. All the time my life had been busy, filled with either shifts at the hotel or with Jonathan, it had been easier to brush those memories to one side, but it wasn't like that in Wynbridge.

I had hardly been back in the town any time at all before I had realised just how different the priorities here were. Family, friendship and a strong sense of community were more important than anything else to the folk I had met and I wondered if Dolly and Beamish were right – should I let Mum and Dad know where my life was taking me?

Given what they had told Jonathan a part of me believed

they didn't deserve to know but, the thought of ending up like Beamish, unable to resolve anything because it had been left too late, made my eyes sting with tears. In spite of knowing what Mum and Dad had said, would I be able to comfortably carry the guilt of not even trying to make things, if not completely better, then bearable, when I had the chance?

I jumped up as my heart began to race. This dramatic realisation was a shock, I had always been adamant that I would never talk to them again, but the anguish in Beamish's eyes and hearing him talk about his own dreadful experiences had given me a jolt and I knew I had to try. I would send the Christmas card of reconciliation that Dolly had suggested and see what happened.

I glanced up at the clock. It was almost time to head back to school to find out what festive fate awaited me. I grabbed my coat and was just reaching for the door when my phone struck up again. I stayed rooted to the spot for fear of losing the signal.

'Hattie?'

'Jonathan.'

'Oh my god,' he laughed. 'I've been trying to get hold of you for ages! The signal in that place really is rubbish, isn't it?'

'I know,' I said, feeling guilty that I had ignored his earlier call. 'I'm sorry. Did you get my last text?'

'Possibly,' he said. 'I think so. They've been arriving out of sync, but never mind.'

'Have you seen the apartments yet?'

'No, not yet, but I'm going to later.' I could tell he was

smiling. 'I wish you were here to view them with me, but I'll send lots more photos.'

'That will be great,' I told him, but I wasn't filled with the same excitement about it all as I had been before.

I guessed that was because of the distance between us and I couldn't help wishing that I could be in two places at once. It would have been lovely to see our future home together for the first time, but further photos would have to do.

'Are you all right?' Jonathan asked. 'You sound a little preoccupied.'

'No, I'm fine,' I said, trying to sound brighter. 'I've just got a lot on my mind, that's all.'

'Like what? You're supposed to be on holiday, Hattie! Although how you can call a visit to Wynbridge a holiday is beyond me. I still think you should have flown out with me, if only to see the apartment—'

'I've been contemplating a few things I want to sort out before the move,' I interrupted, thinking now was as good a time as any to broach the issue.

'Such as?'

'All sorts really,' I swallowed as my heart began to skitter again, 'family stuff.'

'What family stuff?' Jonathan asked sharply.

I could sense his smile had slipped and hear the frown in his tone. With just those two words I'd managed to knock his excitement about the apartment straight out of him.

'Well,' I swallowed again. 'Things with Mum and Dad. I've been thinking it perhaps wouldn't be a bad idea . . .'

'Is this Dolly's doing?' he snapped, the line crackling. 'Has she been putting ideas in your head?'

'No,' I lied, 'of course not.'

'Really?'

'It wasn't Dolly.' I told him, which was almost true. It had been a combination of her and Beamish.

'Who then?' Jonathan demanded. 'I know you wouldn't even be thinking about this if someone hadn't suggested it. It's private, Hattie. Nothing to do with anyone else.'

Given that I hadn't felt able mention that Beamish had picked me up from the train station when I arrived, I certainly couldn't now say that I had been sitting in a café chatting with him over a coffee and a festive biscuit, could I? Jonathan didn't always have the best reaction to my interactions with other men, even though they were completely platonic, and that was most likely why I'd kept quiet, only now my silence about Dolly's right-hand man had landed me in hot water.

'Was it that Rose?' Jonathan barked. 'That teacher from Dolly's school?'

'Yes,' I said, clinging to her name and feeling amazed that Jonathan had remembered it. 'It was Rose and I'm sorry.' I added. 'Forget I said anything. I just got a bit carried away what with it being almost Christmas and everything.'

He didn't say anything.

'Are you still there?' I asked quietly.

'Yes,' he said, 'I'm still here, but I have to go. I have to meet the agent. I wish more than ever that you were here with me now.'

'Me too,' I admitted. 'And I'm sorry we've spent our time arguing over this.'

'So am I,' he agreed. 'I do appreciate that you have a lot to think about ahead of this move, Hattie, but please try to stick to the important stuff.'

Now they were back in my head, my parents were the important stuff, but I didn't want to fire him up again.

'I will,' I promised. 'Sorry,' I said again.

'And I'm sorry too,'

'What are you sorry for?'

'Accusing Dolly of interfering in things,' he tutted. 'I shouldn't have jumped to conclusions.'

That made me feel even worse.

'But I do love you, Hattie,' he went on. 'I love you more than anything and I just want our lives here to be perfect. I'm trying to make this transition as smooth as possible but it's hard bloody work.'

'I know,' I said. 'I know. And I hate the fact that there's nothing I can do. I feel so helpless.'

'There'll be plenty for you to do when you get here,' he told me. 'Don't worry about that. I'll be expecting you to keep me in ironed shirts, remember?'

'Yes,' I laughed, thinking back to our conversation about his own mother. 'I remember.'

'Now,' he said, 'I really must go. I'll send you the photos when I can and I'll call again soon, OK?'

'OK.'

'Love you.'

'I love you too.'

As I walked back to the school, I tried to banish the unexpected excitement which had started to build around the prospect of getting back in touch with my parents. Talking to Jonathan had been a timely reminder that he had been the poor soul charged with delivering their poisonous message. Perhaps sending the card wasn't such an inspired idea after all?

While the staff were finishing up for the day, I familiarised myself with the relevant updated school policies and then, after further deliberation, it was decided that I would be best placed in the year two class where the teaching assistant, Mrs Newton, now spent quite a lot of her time looking after the new child Mr Matthews had mentioned who had diabetes.

The class teacher, who I hadn't met before, was called Mr Patterson and he was thrilled to have an extra person to help out, especially as there was a lot left to do in preparation for the school fair which was happening at the end of the week. In fact, I soon discovered, there was everything left to do.

'I can turn my hand to most things,' Mr Patterson told me, 'but baking isn't my strong point and I still haven't got a clue about the craft project. Each child has to make something unique to them so the parents will be keen to buy it, but I seem to have run out of ideas and Mrs Newton has been so busy she hasn't had a chance to give it much thought.'

The poor man looked frazzled and I quickly scanned the sheet on the staffroom wall to get an idea of what each of the other classes were doing.

'No one's put down stained glass biscuits.' I noticed. They had been a firm favourite when I was at school. 'They're ever so easy to make. Each child could make three or four and we could bag them up and name them so the parents would get roped in to buying those as well as the craft item.'

Mr Patterson grabbed a pen and quickly scribbled the suggestion in the gap next to Dragonfly class.

'You better call me Paul,' he smiled, looking happier already.

'All right, Paul,' I smiled back. 'How about, before I go home with Dolly, I have a quick look at some simple Christmas tree decorations online? I can't do it at the cottage because Dolly doesn't have Wi-Fi and I still haven't found a reliable phone signal hotspot.'

Given the look of relief on his face you could have been forgiven for thinking that his Christmas had come early.

'That would be wonderful,' he sighed. 'I'm also the music teacher,' he added, no doubt feeling the need to justify the fact that things had been left a little late, 'so as well as organising my own class, I'm responsible for the carol concert at the church and some of the music for the school performance.'

I wasn't at all surprised it was all a bit much and I was already feeling pleased that Rose and Dolly had coerced me into helping out.

'Well,' I told him, 'don't worry about things for the fair. I'm sure I can pick up what we need in town before I come in tomorrow and then we could make a start first thing in the morning.'

'Brilliant,' he said, pushing his glasses back into place, 'absolutely brilliant.'

Dolly was delighted that I had been officially teamed with Paul Patterson and loved the tree decorations I had come up with.

'What a clever idea, including each child's photo,' she nodded, when I showed her the sheets of instructions I had printed off. 'The parents won't be able to resist these.'

'I hope not.'

'You're a clever girl, Hattie.' She told me. 'A natural at this sort of thing.'

I had to admit, it had been fun trying to decide what would work best. In the end I had opted for, with Paul's approval of course, a simple tree bauble made out of card. The round shape was plain at the back so the children could decorate it however they chose, but the front had a circle cut out so a photograph could be inserted. I planned to give the children paper hats to wear and while they were designing and decorating, I would photograph them all individually. I would then add sticky back plastic to protect the photo and assemble them once the glitter and sequin creations had dried. A hole punched in the top with some ribbon threaded through would make them easy to hang.

'You know,' said Dolly thoughtfully. 'I have a spare

Christmas tree in the loft. It's a bit sparse in places, but you could set that up in the hall and hang the baubles for the parents to find.'

'That's a great idea,' I agreed, imagining how lovely it would look. 'I could even hang the bags of biscuits on there too, couldn't I?'

'I don't see why not,' said Dolly. 'I rather wish I'd thought of that myself now.'

The crafts and bakes I had come up with might have been the simplest I could find, but eighteen excited six- and seven-year-olds soon added their own brand of creativity, tantrums and styling into the mix and by the end of Thursday I was absolutely exhausted.

The crafting had happened in class en masse, and took up most of Tuesday, but the biscuits were baked in batches on the Wednesday and Thursday, with Mr Patterson selecting groups of four or five, depending on ability, attitude and whether they were needed in the hall for play rehearsals, to come down to the kitchen with me and Mrs Newton.

'I have to say,' she said as I helped one little lad pick out which sweets to add to his biscuits, 'you seem to have a bit of a knack for this, Hattie.'

'Do you think so?'

Dolly had already told me as much, but it was flattering to hear it from someone else.

'Definitely,' she said. 'During my first week, I went home in tears most days, but you've taken to it all like a duck to water.'

'Well,' I said, not wanting to let her praise go to my head. 'I have volunteered before, haven't I? I did have an idea about what I was letting myself in for.'

'But it's Christmas,' she said, deftly stepping in to stop an argument over the last red sweet, 'it's in a league of its own, isn't it?'

I didn't have the chance to answer as Beamish stuck his head around the door, inhaling theatrically.

'Haven't you finished baking my biscuits yet?' he asked the children. 'This lovely smell wafting through the school is making my belly rumble.'

'They're not for you!' the group bellowed, and not for the first time. 'These are all for us!'

They seemed to take great relish in seeing his face drop, especially when he pretended to wipe a tear from his eye.

'And what's the state of that classroom floor like this afternoon?' he asked Mrs Newton. 'I hope you haven't let Hattie loose with the glitter tub again.'

There had been an unfortunate incident with the highly coveted tub of gold glitter the day before, but personally I thought the carpet looked a little more festive with a sparkly dusting.

'It's immaculate,' said Mrs Newton.

'Well, almost,' I laughed.

'There's a delivery for you in the staffroom, Hattie,' Beamish then told me.

'A delivery?'

'Yep, and given the size of it, I think I'd better run you and Dolly home in the truck tonight.'

'Oh,' I said, 'right.'

I had no idea what it could be. I hadn't ordered anything online and even if I had I would have arranged for delivery to Dolly's, not the school.

'I'm intrigued now,' I frowned.

'I thought you might be,' Beamish grinned. 'By the way, you are still all set for tonight, aren't you?'

'Tonight?'

'Late-night shopping,' he reminded me. 'First of the month and we promised Dolly we'd drive round and see the lights, remember?'

'Of course,' I fibbed, only now remembering those two particular things she had added to the Wish List.

In my tired-out state, all I had earmarked for the evening was a long hot soak and an early night in preparation for the school fair the next afternoon, but as ever, Dolly and Beamish had other ideas. At least I could tick the Christmas lights tour off the Wish List and looking at the tray of cooling biscuits lined up on the table, I could probably strike out festive baking too. I wasn't sure if Dolly realised it but so far, her plan to make me fall back in love with Christmas had felt like jolly hard work.

The mystery delivery turned out to be a huge bouquet of stunning winter flowers. A hand-tied mass of cream-coloured chrysanthemums, deep red roses and an excess of greenery interspersed with little woven willow stars which had been sprayed gold.

'My goodness,' gasped Rose as she came into the staffroom after releasing her class at the end of the day. 'What have you done to deserve those, Hattie?'

I didn't need to open the card to know that they were from Jonathan and would have been sent by way of apology after our argument. This was just the sort of gesture he went in for and as lovely as the flowers were, I felt really rather rotten that he had sent them. Surely, I should have been the one sending something to him? And more to the point, how had he known to have them delivered to the school? I was certain I hadn't let slip about my plans to volunteer because I knew he would have objected and said I should be resting as I was on holiday.

'So,' said Beamish, wandering in and joining in with the conversation. 'Who are they from?'

'One of Hattie's *many* admirers,' said Dolly with emphasis.

'You didn't think you were the only one, did you, Beamish?' laughed Rose.

Poor Beamish turned bright red and disappeared again.

'What did you mean by that, Rose?' I asked, still puzzling over the choice of delivery destination.

'Isn't it obvious?' she replied, sniffing the pint of milk which had been left out of the fridge all afternoon before deciding to risk it.

Whatever she was getting at, it wasn't obvious to me.

Chapter 8

Before we left school that evening, I made use of the ICT suite to check my emails. Jonathan had already mailed me and attached lots of photos of the apartment he favoured most and where we would hopefully be living in just a few short weeks. His photos were far better than the agent's and I was in complete agreement that he had picked the perfect place for us. I took my time, admiring the high spec, stylish details and cloudless blue sky beyond the windows. It didn't look all that dissimilar to the flat we shared now, but this one would be ours, as opposed to Jonathan's, from the off, and I couldn't help thinking it was us to a T.

I replied, thanking him for the flowers, but not mentioning the delivery address, and added my thoughts about our new abode, still wishing that I could have been there for the first viewing. Seeing where I was going to live on screen and imagining the life I would lead there, had put me back on track; my decision to go had been the right one. Wynbridge and Dolly's cosy cottage were wonderful for a quaint rural holiday, but the sleek images in front of me represented the kind of couple Jonathan and I were and I knew we were going to be very happy there.

'Don't worry,' said Dolly, placing a hand on my shoulder. 'You'll soon make it look like home.'

I hadn't heard her come in so I jumped, biting back the expletive on my lips when I remembered I was still at school.

'I think it already does,' I said, looking up at her.

Her comment had made me feel a little defensive.

'Perhaps,' she said, cocking her head as she bent to get a better look, 'but a few cushions on that sofa and some houseplants dotted about the place might make it feel a bit cosier, or should I say hygge? That's one of the buzzwords for comfortable interiors now, isn't it?'

I wasn't sure hygge was a thing in Abu Dhabi and I wasn't sure how Jonathan would feel about the introduction of a spider plant or a cactus, but the cushions wouldn't go amiss.

'Perhaps you could even have a cat of your own,' Dolly added for good measure.

I closed the screen down.

'Because I'm such a big fan,' I laughed, 'No, I don't really think a cat, or a pet of any sort, will work for us out there and as lovely as the apartment is, we'll be spending more time out of it than in.'

'I hope you aren't planning on working all hours again, Hattie.'

'No,' I said, 'Not work necessarily. I just mean we'll be living a very different lifestyle to the one that you have here in Wynbridge.'

She didn't get the chance to start listing the virtues of a welcoming hearth or remind me that home should be where the heart is.

'Here you are,' said Beamish, 'Come on, you two. We need to going or we'll never get parked.'

'It's not even four yet,' I reminded him. 'Surely it's still too early to see the lights.'

'But we're shopping first,' he reminded me, 'and it's a dull old day. By the time we've got what we want in town the light tour will be getting busy.'

'He's right,' said Dolly, accepting his offer of help as she pulled on her coat, 'and I don't want to be too late to bed, not with the fair looming. It'll be bedlam in here tomorrow afternoon, it always is.'

Beamish had been right to chivvy us along because we weren't the only early arrivals in town and he was also right about the lights. The murky sky meant it was almost dark by the time we had stowed my bouquet safely in the truck and reached the market. The whole place was looking, sounding and smelling very festive and even I, who had so adamantly maintained that I wasn't all that bothered about Christmas, felt a brief flicker of excitement as I listened to the carollers in front of the huge tree and thrust my hand into the bag of hot roasted chestnuts Beamish had treated himself to.

'Does this count as Christmas food?' I asked Dolly as I munched my way through what was probably more than my fair share of the sweet yet earthy treats. 'Can I tick festive food off the list now I've eaten these?'

'What is this list you keep mentioning?' Beamish asked. 'You were on about it the other day.'

I wasn't going to tell him, but Dolly had no such qualms about sharing our secret.

'It's my secret weapon for making Hattie fall back in love with Christmas before she leaves these shores in the New Year,' she told him.

'And so far, it's been nothing but hard work,' I grumbled.

'Give it time,' Dolly said back.

'But you're going to Abu Dhabi, aren't you?' frowned Beamish. 'Christmas there's a bit different to here.'

'I know,' I told him. 'I have been before.'

'And did you like it?'

'Not really,' I said, wrinkling my nose, before quickly adding, 'the Christmas bit, I mean.'

'Then surely this list is a bit mean, Dolly.' He frowned. 'Why would you want to send Hattie off with a hankering for all the things you're making her experience again when you know she won't be able to have them out there?'

I hadn't thought about it like that, but I wasn't too worried. She still had a long way to go before I was back in love with any of it.

'It's about giving her the chance to make some memories to take with her as much as anything else,' said Dolly, justifying her plan. 'I want her to look back on this time we spent together fondly and remember Wynbridge in winter for all the right reasons.'

'What might be the wrong ones?' I frowned.

Dolly didn't answer.

'In that case,' said Beamish, 'you'll have to show me this list. I might be able to help with it. I'm assuming you've put a kiss under the mistletoe somewhere near the top.'

'Funnily enough,' I tutted, 'kissing isn't featured any-where on the list at all.'

'Well,' he said, screwing up the now empty chestnut bag and grinning. 'We'll have to see about that, won't we? Or would your admirer not approve, Hattie?'

Jonathan most certainly would not approve of me kiss-ing someone else, even with a bunch of mistletoe in the vicinity.

'Right,' said Dolly, before I could answer. 'Why don't we split up, that way we can buy our presents in secret? Let's meet back here in an hour and then we can get going with the tour. Unlike the mistletoe, that's definitely on the list.'

Whereas at the switch-on I had felt a little out place being among everyone who knew each other, I now found a few more familiar faces among the throng and there were plenty of people who knew me, even if I didn't know them.

'How did you like your flowers?' asked the woman on the fruit and veg stall as I walked by. 'I knew you were working at the school so I thought it best to take them there rather than leave them shivering on the doorstep at Dolly's which is where they were supposed to go.'

'They're beautiful,' I said, stopping to answer and feeling relieved to have that little mystery cleared up. 'Thank you. Did you arrange them?'

'I did,' she said proudly. 'I'm Marie Dempster. I'm a florist by trade but I'm helping my husband and son out on the stall tonight as it's so busy.'

'Hello, Miss,' said a voice behind me and I felt a firm tug on the hem of my jacket.

'Hello, Thomas,' I said, turning around. 'Are you Christmas shopping?'

'Dad is,' he said, pointing at his father.

'You must be Hattie?' His dad smiled. 'Thomas tells me you've helped him make something special for the fair tomorrow.'

Thomas's bauble was positively groaning with glitter and sequins and I'd had to reinforce his ribbon to stop it weighing down the branches of Dolly's old tree.

'I have,' I smiled, winking at Thomas. 'But it's a secret, isn't it, Thomas?'

He nodded enthusiastically.

'I'll see you tomorrow then,' said his dad as they moved off.

'Alison was telling me you've been a godsend already,' said Marie, picking our conversation up again. 'Poor Mrs Newton was frazzled before you arrived.'

So was Mr Patterson, but I didn't think it would be appropriate to say as much.

'I've only been there a couple of days,' I said instead. 'I can't have made that much difference.'

'You'd be surprised,' she laughed. 'Now, what can I get you?'

I didn't want to buy anything from her stall, but she very kindly directed me to the Cherry Tree one where I spent much of my shopping time looking through the pretty makes which Lizzie Dixon had put together. I hadn't really expected to buy anything from there either, but was soon seduced by what was on offer.

I found a floral-patterned quilted knitting bag for Dolly, which Ruby, the young woman running the stall, told me Lizzie had made herself and then I crossed the road to the gallery where I found the perfect supersized chunky scarf for Beamish which was also locally made. He would be able to wind it around his neck and have yarn to spare.

As I stowed my purchases out of sight, I couldn't help thinking that picking out my presents and chatting to the sellers had been far more pleasurable than clicking a few buttons and loading up my PayPal account when I was home alone.

'What did you get?' asked Beamish who had crept up in full stealth mode behind me.

'Jeez!' I jumped. 'About three years knocked off my life expectancy, I reckon.'

He laughed and tried to look into the bag.

'No peeking,' I told him firmly, nudging him to one side. 'What did you buy?'

He had far more bags than me, but then he no doubt had more folk to buy for. He certainly seemed to know everyone.

'No peeking,' he mimicked, nudging me back. 'But our time's up. Let's go and meet Dolly. I know she's desperate to see these lights.'

As we drove around the little town, the map from the Wynbridge tourist information representative guiding our way to the illuminations, I could sense Dolly's excitement to see how everyone else had decorated their homes.

There were plenty of garishly adorned front doors, tinsel toting fence posts and lavishly lit facades and I knew Jonathan would have hated them all. He would have berated everything on display and I realised that my 'tacky Christmas tat' comment had indeed come straight from his phrase book, not mine. I would have to watch that. I might not have been a huge fan of the flashing lights and inflatables myself, but my own opinion was nowhere near as harsh as my other half's, so why express it?

'I've saved the biggest for last,' said Beamish as we drove out of town. 'This one is definitely the most spectacular.'

After a mile or two he turned off the narrow twisty road and onto an even more twisty and potholed drive.

'Oh, my goodness,' I gasped, my breath catching in my throat as we turned the last corner and were faced with what looked like a stately home. 'That's incredible.'

'That's Wynthorpe Hall,' smiled Dolly.

The hall was lifted straight off the pages of a fairy tale and we weren't the only ones who had turned out to take a look at it. I could see lots of people milling about. The entire house was draped in the warm white lights I had mentioned to Dolly, and was definitely worthy of the coveted front page of a glossy magazine. Noting the rapture on Beamish's face, I got the impression that he wasn't likely to tease me about tasteful decorations on this occasion.

'You introduced me to the owner, didn't you?' I said to Dolly as I leaned between the seats to get a better look.

'That's right,' she nodded. 'Catherine Connelly. This place has been in her family for generations but, like the town, its undergone quite a transformation in recent years.'

'Her husband, Angus,' Beamish laughed, 'is mad keen on Christmas. He's the one behind the Winter Wonderland.'

Perhaps a sleigh ride around the grounds might not be such a bad idea after all and perhaps I shouldn't grumble about the work Dolly's list involved if visiting places like this also formed a part of it. I could well imagine that the memory of Wynthorpe Hall in winter, recalled while lying beside an infinity pool, under a cerulean sky, would help me cool off if nothing else.

'I know you weren't too keen when Catherine mentioned the event . . .' Dolly said to me.

'Yes, about that,' I quickly cut in. 'I think I might have been a bit hasty.'

Dolly said she would add it to the Wish List and she might even telephone Catherine and ask if there was any chance of a private tour of the hall.

'I'd love to get a look inside,' she said, taking in the prettily lit windows, 'and see how they decorate the family rooms. I love my little cottage,' she added, 'but it would be exciting to see how the other half lives, wouldn't it?'

I knew Dolly had maintained that she always did everything she wanted at Christmas, but clearly she was keener to make some extra special memories for herself than I first realised and even if she didn't succeed in making me fall back in love with Christmas, I was going to make more of an effort to make sure that she ticked off everything she wanted to achieve.

After unloading the truck and making sure Dolly had a cup of tea, some biscuits from Jonathan's hamper and a well-stoked fire, Beamish asked if I would like to go back into town with him.

'I'm not going to be long,' he said. 'I'll need a decent night's sleep ahead of setting up for the fair in the morning, so you can't use me dragging you out for a late night as an excuse not to come.'

'It would do you good, Hattie,' Dolly agreed.

'All right,' I said, 'thank you, Beamish.'

Truth be told, I wouldn't have minded being dragged out for a late night. It had been a while, although going to the pub with Beamish was going to be a far cry from going out with Jonathan. That would involve hours of preparation; selecting the right outfit and applying flawless make-up. Heading out with a speedy slick of lip gloss and my hair in a messy bun was a completely different kettle of fish.

If Jonathan had landed on Dolly's doorstep then, I wasn't sure he would have recognised me, but it felt good zipping out again without having to put in so much effort. I hadn't let my cleanse, tone and moisturise routine slip because that was plain good sense, but it was nice to forget the rest for a few weeks. I knew that working in an Abu Dhabi hotel would require the whole pristine package, so this downtime Dolly had bestowed upon me was quite a luxury.

'So,' said Beamish, after we had arrived at The Mermaid and he had introduced me to the owners, Evelyn and Jim, 'tell me some more about how you met Dolly. She said she used to come and stay in the most amazing hotel where you worked.'

'The hotel was amazing when Dolly used to visit,' I agreed. 'It was run by the Lucca family and they were the most wonderful hosts.'

I told him all about the little finishing touches the Luccas had considered so important, how the place had been a hit with families and how lots of customers, like Dolly, came back year after year.

'It was a wonderful place to work then,' I sighed.

'But not now?' Beamish questioned. 'I mean, I know Dolly said you'd been made redundant but the hotel had changed hands, hadn't it?'

'Yes,' I said, 'the Luccas sold up a few years ago and it's completely different now.'

As I described to him all the changes which had occurred since the Luccas left, and how the place had gone from comfortable to corporate, I realised just how much I had changed too.

The person I was in that moment, sitting opposite Beamish in jeans, drinking a lager, was far more like the person I had been when the Luccas were in charge, but that version of me rarely put in an appearance now. She was the Hattie which Dolly had been hoping to find, but before I knew it, I would be boarding a plane and leaving her behind for good.

'So, what's next?' Beamish asked, pulling me out of my reverie.

'What do you mean?'

'Well,' he said, 'it seems to me that you're absolutely loving your time volunteering in the school.'

'So?'

'So, is that what you're going to do in Abu Dhabi? Have you got a job lined up in a school?'

'Oh no,' I said, 'absolutely not. I haven't got anything lined up, but I'm not thinking about schools. I'm going to be looking for another hotel position.'

I had worked hard to gain my promotion and glowing reference and I was good at my job. There would be no point in letting all that go to waste.

'I might even try for management,' I told Beamish,

lifting my chin a little. 'I'm still young enough to be considered for an in-house management training programme.'

'Crikey,' said Beamish, draining his glass of Coke.

'What?'

'Nothing,' he shrugged. 'Fancy another?'

I watched him chatting to some of the other customers while he waited to get served. He was the perfect fit for the place, and I didn't just mean the pub. Beamish was the ideal fit for Wynbridge. I hoped I would look even half as at home in Abu Dhabi after I'd had time to settle in.

'I hope you don't mind me asking about this again,' Beamish said when he came back, 'but have you given any more thought to getting back in touch with your parents?'

He was certainly full of questions and I couldn't remember the last time I'd spent so long talking about myself.

'I have,' I told him, wholeheartedly wishing that was the one question he hadn't asked, 'and I'm not going to.'

'Oh.'

'I'm not going to go into it all,' I went on, 'but like I told you before, it's a whole lot more complicated than you know and I just don't think contacting them now would be the right thing to do. I know you said you have regrets, but . . .'

'But my situation was complicated too,' he cut in. 'And it's the fact that I didn't work through those complications when I had the chance that make my regrets even harder to live with.'

'Complicated in what way?'

Beamish bit his lip.

'Sorry,' I said, 'you don't have to answer that.'

It was hardly fair that I should expect him to explain his situation to me when I had just told him I wasn't prepared to go into the details of mine.

'My father was a monster,' he shocked me by saying. 'He was a manipulative bully who made my mother's life an absolute misery.'

'Oh god, Beamish . . .'

'He was a control freak,' he said angrily, 'everything had to be done his way or not at all.'

I didn't know what to say. I was completely taken aback by his words and bitter tone. He didn't sound anything like the good old Beamish I had gotten to know at all.

'I begged Mum to leave him for years,' he carried on, distractedly running a hand through his hair, 'but she wouldn't. She said she knew he wasn't the easiest man to live with, but she loved him and that compromise was all part of being married.' He shook his head. 'But there was no compromise from him. Everything was always about him getting his own way.'

'Had he always been like that?' I asked, unsure I wanted to hear his answer.

Beamish was quiet for a moment.

'No,' he said eventually. 'No, I don't think he was, but from what I can remember, there was always an element of jealousy in him. He would accuse my mother of ridiculous things and god forbid if any man wanted to talk to her.'

I shifted in my seat, suddenly wishing he'd stop.

'Sometimes there would be a big blow-up and I'd think that was it, she'd leave, but she never did. She always believed his promises that he'd change, but before long something else would trigger him and then it would all start to build up again. In the end, I left them to it.'

I didn't want to hear any more. Some of what Beamish had said reminded me a little too much of the 'big blow-up' I'd had with Jonathan but at least enough time had passed now to ensure that I could be certain he would stick to the promises he had made me.

'I know the situation with your parents is completely different,' Beamish finished up, 'but the reason I've just told you all this is because I really don't want you to end up like me. I should never have left the situation as it was. I'll never forgive myself for not doing more for Mum, for not making her see sense.'

'I'm really not sure you would have been able to do that,' I said softly. 'You can't blame yourself, Beamish.'

'Perhaps not,' he said, 'but the point I'm trying to make is that I still wish I'd tried harder, I shouldn't have wasted the chances I had. I kept thinking there would be more time but before I knew it, it had run out.'

His words were doing nothing to reinforce the lid on the emotional box marked 'do not open' I'd already almost let my parents escape from.

'I'm guessing the rift with your parents runs pretty deep, Hattie, but I hate the thought of you letting it get in

120

the way of trying to make things right.' He drove on. 'If something happens to either of them when you've moved and you haven't even tried to make contact, you'll be filled with regret for ever. This time, right now, is the perfect opportunity for you.'

Deep down I knew he was right.

'Whatever it is that's holding you back,' he said forcefully, 'please don't let it.'

Chapter 9

I went to bed knowing I needed a decent night's sleep ahead of the Christmas fair, but it took me hours to nod off. I had worked hard in school and enjoyed the evening taking in the many and varied Wynbridge illuminations, but my time in the pub with Beamish had been tough, not that he knew it. Surprisingly, it wasn't the thought of getting in touch with my parents which kept the sandman at bay, but what he'd told me about his.

Listening to what he had to say about their relationship, how his father had accused his mother of silly things and been jealous of other men, had reminded me a little too much of the argument with Jonathan which had sent me running, albeit briefly, to Dolly.

Other than the most recent show of clinginess, there hadn't been a hint of anything untoward since it had all been sorted, and I was certain there wouldn't be in the future either, but I was feeling edgy nonetheless. I had made a point of not mentioning

Beamish during any of the conversations I'd had with Jonathan since I arrived in town and that suddenly didn't strike me as the rational behaviour of someone in a happy relationship.

As my alarm began to sound, I swung my legs out of bed, reminding myself that my decision to keep my friendship with Beamish to myself was *my* decision. It wasn't fair to assume that had I told Jonathan about it he would have reacted in any way other than appropriately. This was my problem, not a problem resulting from anything Jonathan had done recently and I needed to find a way to fix it.

'Morning, Dolly,' I yawned as I came down the stairs and found my friend sitting at the table looking through the Wish List. 'What do you fancy for breakfast? I'll make it this morning.'

'Something fortifying,' she said, pushing the list to one side. 'We're going to need it, and you might want to refresh the tea.'

I lifted the cosy and felt the pot. It was stone cold.

'How long ago did you make this?' I asked, taking it to the sink to swill it out. 'Couldn't you sleep? I didn't wake you when I came in last night, did I?'

'No,' said Dolly, getting up a little stiffly from her chair, 'you didn't wake me. I was just up early, that's all.'

She joined me at the worktop and we ended up making breakfast together even though I had offered to do it.

'Did you have a nice time in the pub?' she asked. 'Was it busy?'

'I did,' I told her, deciding not to go into too much detail, 'and yes, it was.'

'It's a popular place,' she said. 'I sometimes pop in for coffee on a Saturday myself if the Cherry Tree hasn't got a table.'

'That's another popular place,' I smiled.

'Indeed,' she agreed, setting out the cutlery. 'Did you get to meet any of Beamish's rugby buddies? They're quite a crowd.'

'No,' I said, 'not last night. It was just the two of us but it was lovely nonetheless,' I continued, thinking of the earlier part of the evening. 'I can't remember the last time I spent so long talking about myself.'

'I daresay living with someone like Jonathan you don't get the chance to all that often.'

'What's that supposed to mean?'

'Just that half the time he's too keen on his own voice and opinions to let anyone else express theirs,' she said with a wry smile.

Had she not finished her sentence with a smile, I would have assumed she was being a bit mean.

'He just has a lot to say, that's all.'

'Indeed,' Dolly sighed. 'I was on the receiving end of his runaway mouth last night.'

'What?' I gasped, dropping the butter knife on to the flagged floor where it landed noisily and of course, butter side down.

'He called here,' said Dolly, 'not long after you and Beamish had left for the pub.'

Suddenly, I didn't much fancy the toast I was buttering. I swallowed down the bile which shifted as I bent to retrieve the knife and set it to one side before getting another one.

'Did he want to speak to me?'

'Well of course, he wanted to speak to you,' Dolly chuckled.

It wasn't like him to ring the house phone.

'But he wanted to speak to me too,' she added. 'He wanted to know if I liked the hamper. He said the biscuits were a particular favourite of his and that the coffee was his preferred blend.'

It all sounded innocuous enough I supposed, even if it was devoid of any of their usual sparring.

'I told him I hadn't tried the coffee yet because I haven't got a cafetière thingy and he's promised to send me one of those as well. I wasn't quite sure what had gotten into him, to be honest. He couldn't have been more amenable and was in no rush to let me go.'

Ordinarily I would have been absolutely thrilled to hear the pair had been getting along, but I was more concerned about how Dolly had explained my absence.

'Where did you say I was?' I croaked, keeping my eyes on my buttering and ignoring the heat prickling the back of my neck. 'Did he say he'd tried my mobile?'

Because of the lack of consistent signal, I hadn't bothered to keep it turned on.

'He said he was sick of not being able to reach you on it, so that was why he'd rung the house instead and,' she paused, 'I told him you were already in bed.'

Even with the time difference that was still a bit of a push. It would have been a very early night for me and I didn't feel all that comfortable that Dolly had felt obliged to lie.

'Did he believe you?' I swallowed.

'Of course he believed me,' she tutted, taking away my knife. 'You'll be through to the other side in a minute. I told him you had a headache and we carried on talking until he had to go. He sounded very excited about the apartment. He even mentioned a spare room if I ever fancied visiting.'

I felt my shoulders drop and my stomach unclench. It seemed we'd got away with it. Or Dolly had.

'OK,' I nodded, letting out the breath I didn't realise I'd been hanging on to. 'Excellent. That's great.'

'Oh yes,' said Dolly. 'It's brilliant, isn't it?'

She didn't sound anywhere near as pleased or relieved as I was.

'What?'

'Well,' she said, 'like you just said, everything is obviously great. I mean, that startled fawn look you've just demonstrated is the ultimate indicator of a happy relationship. And of course, it's perfectly natural that I should think to lie to your husband-to-be rather than tell him the truth.'

'Why did you lie?'

'Let's just say my gut feeling was that you hadn't mentioned Beamish so I thought it would come as quite a surprise to Jonathan if I said you were down the pub with him.'

'I'm so sorry,' I said, abandoning my toast and dumping myself down in Dolly's chair. 'And your gut was right. I haven't mentioned Beamish.'

She didn't give me the chance to explain that I knew I was in the wrong.

'But why ever not? If everything is as good as you say it is with Jonathan now, then what possible reason can you have?'

'Everything *is* good between us,' I insisted. 'It's not Jonathan, it's me. I am going to tell him; I've just been working out how.'

Dolly didn't look convinced.

'Beamish is a good-looking guy,' I rushed on, 'and I suppose I've been worried that it might complicate things if I mentioned him.'

Dolly shook her head. Apparently, I was completely incapable of finding the right words to justify my silence about my new friend.

'I'm certain you could have talked about him without bringing up his rugged good looks and Chris Evans dimensions,' she tutted.

'Oh Dolly.'

'Look,' she went on, 'Jonathan went to great lengths to make amends for what he did and you've never mentioned him showing his temper since.'

'He hasn't shown it,' I insisted.

Getting annoyed about me wanting to contact Mum and Dad didn't count in this situation. To be honest, his reaction had been more than justified.

'Then perhaps you do him a disservice,' Dolly said brusquely, surprising me by springing to Jonathan's defence. 'How will you ever know if things really are as they should be if you go about hiding your friendships . . .'

'I'm not hiding my friendships,' I said, sounding more pathetic by the second. 'I just haven't mentioned this one yet.'

'If Jonathan really has given you no reason for concern,' Dolly continued, 'and I can't imagine that he has, given that you're moving to the other side of the world with him, then you need to have a long hard think about the reason why you are keeping quiet, Hattie.'

I'd already laid awake most of the night thinking about exactly that. It seemed I had some psychological readjusting of my own to do because I had, as Dolly had just so adroitly pointed it, done Jonathan a very grave disservice indeed.

That said, it wasn't easy to banish the image of him bursting into my evening during a hotel training course and punching a colleague with whom I was having a drink. His aggressive outburst had been the reason behind my last trip to Wynbridge, but his heartfelt apology, prolific promises and appeals to move into the flat with him had soon drawn me away again . . .

'I know I do,' I said, shaking my head. 'It's just that this situation with Beamish . . .'

My words trailed off.

'What situation with Beamish?' Dolly demanded.

There was no way I could say out loud the words which were whirring around in my head. How could I tell Dolly that he made me feel good, made me laugh, put me at ease, drew things out of me, asked me questions and listened to my answers, without inferring that I was developing too strong a fondness for our rugby-playing friend.

If I gave voice to all those things, it would suggest that Jonathan, the man I was about to move to the other side of the world with, didn't do any of those things to or for me, and that simply wasn't true. Was it?

'I haven't mentioned I'm volunteering at the school either,' I blurted out instead.

'Hattie . . .'

'Look,' I said pointing up at the clock and avoiding her gaze, 'it's almost a quarter to and we still haven't had a bite to eat yet.'

The school fair that afternoon was the perfect distraction from my muddled thoughts and every bit as busy as I had imagined it would be. Even with the heating on the temperamental boiler turned to low, (much to Beamish's consternation as he was going to be the one responsible for trying to fire it back up again), the classrooms and the hall were still sweltering.

'How are you getting on?' Rose called above the din as she tried to keep track of her class.

'It's mad!' I called back, 'but we've sold practically everything already.'

There were just a few bags of biscuits left, but they were fast disappearing and I was pleased I'd had the chance to make some extras. The parents loved the baubles and I could well imagine them adorning the family trees for many years to come. I knew my mum still had two of the angels I had made when I was in primary school. Well, she had the last time I saw her at Christmas. They had still merited pride of place on top of the tree then, even though they did look somewhat out of place with all her other decorations.

'We should do this on a Saturday,' puffed Mr Matthews as he rushed around, trying to keep tabs on the children whose parents hadn't been able to come because they were at work.

'Yes,' I agreed. 'I'm sure it would be much easier if the children came and went with their families on a weekend afternoon.'

'And it would be much more convenient for those who can't get the time off during the working week,' he added. 'Unfortunately, though, unless I have all staff willing to come in, then it's out of the question I'm afraid.'

'Perhaps the PTA could fill any gaps?' I suggested.

'Perhaps,' he said, checking the time on his watch. 'Not long now. Don't forget to man an exit when the bell goes, Hattie. I'm only letting children out of the main door today and they all have to be ticked off their class lists and with a family member before they go.'

'Unless we've had written confirmation of other arrangements,' I added.

We'd all been well drilled about how to let the children go at the end of the day and I wondered if it was a responsibility any of the parents even thought about when they were in a rush to get home.

'Have you got the bauble for Peter Patterson?' Beamish asked, as he pushed his way through the throng with a little girl with blonde bunches in his arms.

'Yes,' I said, taken aback by the sight of him in the role of childminder.

He was obviously very relaxed in the part. In fact, I'd yet to find a role that he wasn't relaxed in. Clearly, he had carried this little one about before. She had her arms draped loosely around his neck and was enjoying the view from her elevated position.

'It's here.' I said, tearing my eyes away, as I pointed to where I'd stored those belonging to any children whose parents couldn't attend. 'I've put them to one side so they don't get sold by mistake and I've put some extra biscuits with them too.'

I didn't think it was very likely that someone would buy a Christmas decoration with a random child's photo in it but I wasn't taking any chances. My class had put in a lot of effort to create their bespoke baubles and I didn't want any of them to go missing.

'I'll take his now if that's all right?' said Beamish, easily transferring the girl from one arm to the other as he reached into his jeans pocket and pulled out a rather crumpled five-pound note. 'Peter's going home early,' he added.

'Is he?' I frowned. I couldn't remember hearing anything about a doctor or dentists' appointment.

'He's in the medical room with his mum and Mrs Newton,' Beamish explained. 'He's been sick.'

'He seemed fine earlier,' I said, swapping the money for Peter's bounty.

'Too many sweets!' said the girl with relish.

131

'This is Isobel,' said Beamish, jiggling her about a bit. 'Peter's sister.'

'Mummy's had to leave work so she picked me up from nursery first and then we came to get Peter. She's not very happy.' Isobel pouted.

'I'll bet,' I said.

I was tempted to give her another bag of biscuits, but given the circumstances, thought better of it.

'Beamish plays rugby with my dad,' she told me seriously.

'Does he?'

'Yes, and sometimes he goes to the pub with him as well.'

I wasn't sure why she felt the need to tell me that.

'And when they come back a bit wobbly, Mummy always says . . .'

'Right,' said Beamish as I started to laugh, 'let's go and find her, shall we? I'll see you later, Hattie.'

At the end of the afternoon, after the children had all safely gone home, there wasn't an awful lot of tidying up left to do and there was very little left which hadn't been sold.

'Anyone recognise these?' shouted Rose holding aloft a pair of brightly knitted gloves as we dismantled and tidied. 'They were on the floor near where the Bees class were set up.'

Mrs Anderson, the receptionist, wandered over for a closer look.

'Sutton's,' she said, 'the youngest boy. He was in the pushchair when they arrived and he was wearing these. His sister, Emily, is in Bees, you could send them home with her on Monday or I could keep them in the office. Her mother's bound to ask.'

'How did she know that?' I whispered to Rose after Mrs Anderson had gone back to reception, taking the gloves with her. 'How could she possibly know?'

'She knows everything,' giggled Rose. 'I once found a milk tooth in an unmarked envelope in the music room. It was in a tambourine. I took it to reception and she knew who it belonged to.'

'She never did!'

'True as I'm standing here,' Rose told me. '"That'll be Harry Tompkins's" she said. "He had a tooth fall out a couple of weeks ago and his class get changed for PE in the music room. He'll have no doubt left it behind."'

'And was she right?'

'She was.'

'Wow,' I gasped, 'that's some kind of amazing.'

Beamish was walking up and down, cleaning the floor with a massive sweeping contraption which opened up scissor like and had a sort of elongated mop head.

'Standard sweeping technique,' he winked with a swagger, 'all in the caretakers' handbook of efficient cleaning.'

'Not you, you idiot,' I laughed and he pretended to look offended. 'I was talking about Mrs Anderson being amazing, not you.'

'Oh well now,' he said, making one last lunge into the nearest corner, 'she really is amazing. I couldn't even hope to compete with her levels of brilliance. What's she done now?'

'Glove identification procedure,' I said, mimicking him. 'All in the efficient school receptionist's manual.'

'She wrote that,' Beamish laughed.

'You're a hotel receptionist, aren't you, Hattie?' asked Rose.

'I was until I was made redundant.'

'You don't fancy a move into education, do you?'

'No way,' I told her. 'I couldn't hold a candle to your Mrs A. I couldn't cope with all that early morning parental pressure.'

'I think Rose was meaning a move into the classroom, Hattie,' said Beamish. 'And I still think that should be your next move too. I believe I might have mentioned it before.'

He had of course and I had managed to successfully sideline the suggestion, but now Rose looked poised to join in too.

'I'm there already, aren't I?' I joked, looking about me.

'I mean permanently,' said Beamish seriously. 'You're wasted working in a hotel. You should forget about management training and look for a job in a school.'

'After I've moved to Abu Dhabi you mean,' I reminded him.

'Yeah,' he said, 'why not?'

'I'm not sure how things like that work out there,' I told him. 'I've hardly got a wealth of educational experience or teaching qualifications to draw on and I daresay it's nowhere near as easy as you're suggesting.'

'Then perhaps you should find out,' said Rose, moving to stand next to him. 'You're a natural in the classroom, Hattie, and it would be a real shame to let a talent like yours go to waste.'

'That it would,' Beamish wholeheartedly agreed. 'That it would.'

Chapter 10

After the school fair Dolly was desperate to get the decorations up in the cottage, and as Beamish was going to be putting her spare tree back in the loft, he kindly offered to get down the rest of the boxes so we could set to work that weekend.

'I'd usually wait until the weekend of the tree auction,' Dolly told me at first light on the Saturday morning, 'but that's a whole week away so I'll make do with my other artificial tree this year.'

She sounded every bit as excited as the children at school.

'Or we could put everything else up and do the tree next weekend?' I suggested. 'That way you won't have to miss out on having a real tree.'

'No, no,' she said, checking the road again to see if Beamish was in sight. 'I want it all done today.'

'OK,' I nodded, 'whatever you say.'

'Although you can't beat the smell of a real tree of course,' she wistfully added, 'and that's probably something you should add to the Wish List, Hattie.'

'Tree sniffing?' I laughed.

'Scents of the season,' she smiled back. 'Cinnamon, orange, nutmeg and gingerbread . . .'

'Oh stop,' I interrupted, 'you'll set my stomach growling if you carry on.'

'Oh,' she said, abandoning her station at the window and heading for the door. 'Here he is. You'd better get the kettle boiled again, Hattie dear. Decoration box distribution is hard, thirsty work.'

I went to fill the kettle at the sink thinking that so far pretty much everything on the list had been hard work, then I heard Dolly gasp.

'How's that?' I heard Beamish ask. 'Will it do?'

'Oh Beamish,' she cried, opening the door further and letting in a glacial blast of Wynbridge winter air, 'it's perfect, but wherever did you get it? The auction isn't for another week. I didn't think anything had been delivered yet.'

'Well,' he said, sounding well pleased by Dolly's reaction, 'I have my sources and I didn't think you'd really want Hattie's last Christmas in the UK spent looking at an artificial tree. They just don't smell the same, do they?'

'Come and see, Hattie!' Dolly called, even though I was only a few feet away. 'Look what Beamish has brought for us. You'll have to let me pay for it,' she added. 'Now, where's my purse?'

But Beamish wouldn't hear of it.

'It's a gift, Dolly,' he said. 'Although not from me. The

person who sent it said to consider it an early Christmas present. What do you think, Hattie?'

'I think it's the most perfect tree I've ever seen,' I beamed, taking in the beautifully balanced branches and drinking in the heavenly fresh pine scent my friends were so keen on. 'What a generous gift.'

Beamish's smile grew even broader.

'You still haven't said where you got it from,' Dolly reminded him. 'I can't imagine the garden centre have beauties like this. Look, Hattie, we're going to be hard pushed to get the angel on top. It's almost touching the ceiling.'

I couldn't help but giggle, her excitement was contagious.

'I popped down to Wynthorpe Hall last night to see Catherine and happened to mention that you were putting your decorations up early this year, in spite of the fact that you had no tree and Angus, eager as ever, had taken early delivery of a few extras to set up around the Winter Wonderland trail.'

'That man,' Dolly chuckled. 'I've heard the event is going to be even bigger this year.'

'Given what I saw,' Beamish told her, 'I think you heard right. Anyway, Catherine said he could easily spare this one and insisted that I took it for you.'

'That was very kind of her,' I said.

'The Connellys are always very kind,' said Dolly.

'And generous,' Beamish added. 'And,' he went on, standing taller than I thought I'd ever seen him, 'you'll be pleased to know that Catherine will be more than happy to offer you a tour of the hall, Dolly.'

'What?'

'When we went to look at the lights you said you fancied seeing how the other half lived, didn't you?'

'I did.'

'So, I went down there to see if that might be possible.'

'Oh Beamish,' Dolly clapped her hands together and I swallowed down the lump in my throat.

'In view of their expanding plans for the Winter Wonderland they're also decorating early this year so even though your trip is arranged for before the auction in town, the hall will be all dressed for Christmas too.'

'I don't know what to say,' Dolly sniffed.

She looked and sounded absolutely delighted and I couldn't help thinking what an honour it was to witness such an act of kindness. It was incredibly kind of Catherine to agree to open up her home but it was equally kind of Beamish to remember Dolly's wish and go to the trouble of arranging it all.

'It's next Thursday,' Beamish explained, also now sounding a little choked. 'After school. Dorothy, the hall cook, said she'd lay on an afternoon tea and I said I'd run you there and back. You've been invited too, Hattie.'

'Oh, my goodness. Thank you so much,' I said, feeling genuinely touched to be included, 'that's really very kind.'

'I thought it might be something you could both tick off the Wish List,' he smiled, clearing his throat and sounding more like himself again. 'There's little in the Fenland countryside more quintessentially English than Wynthorpe Hall and at Christmas time the place is pure perfection.'

'Now I'm even more excited!' I laughed.

'Well done, Beamish.' Dolly winked. 'You've got Hattie's Christmas spirit stirring!'

By the time I had made us all breakfast and Beamish had carted all the boxes Dolly wanted out of the loft and set up the tree in a special stand and positioned it in the best spot, he was running a little late.

'I wish I could stay,' he told us. 'But it's a big match today and the coach has insisted we've all got to turn up early. Not that I am that early now.'

I couldn't think of anything worse than running up and down an almost frozen expanse of grass in shorts and getting the stuffing knocked out of me, but I wouldn't have minded cheering from the sidelines if I was well wrapped up. These rugby types were made of stern stuff.

'Well you be careful,' said Dolly. 'You're only just getting over that last knock.'

'It was touch and go whether I'd be allowed to play at all,' he said, rubbing his eye and the bruises which were now more yellow than black, 'but as I didn't get knocked out, the doc has given me the all-clear.'

'Don't go breaking anything,' I said. 'We'll need your support on the rink tonight. I don't know about Dolly but I've never quite mastered the art of standing on ice, let alone skating on it.'

One of Dolly's Wish List additions had been to go ice skating, so Beamish was driving us over to a rink in Peterborough after his match. I wasn't looking forward to it at all.

'I hope you aren't really expecting me to skate, Dolly?' he said imploringly. 'I'm no better than Hattie.'

'You'll soon get the hang of it,' she said, with a wave of her hand, 'it's like riding a bike. You never forget.'

'But what if you never grasped it in the first place,' I began, but quickly stopped.

The look on Dolly's face told me protesting was pointless. I was going to have to face my fear of losing my fingers and if I was going down, then I was taking Beamish with me.

'Oh, we'll be all right,' I said, announcing my change of heart to Beamish, who was looking stricken. 'How hard can it be?'

'That's the spirit,' Dolly chuckled.

Once he had gone, Dolly and I began to look through the boxes of decorations and work out if she had enough to dress the tree which was somewhat larger than what she was usually used to.

'I thought Tiddles might have sprung into action and pulled it down by now,' I said, beadily eyeing the cat who was fast asleep next to the fire even though it wasn't lit yet. 'I hope she isn't waiting until we've finished making it look beautiful.'

'I don't think we need to worry,' said Dolly, handing me a box full of old-fashioned glass baubles. 'She's got about as much go in her as I have these days.'

'If that's supposed to set my mind at rest,' I laughed, 'it hasn't. You do all right Dolly and you're taking to the ice tonight. I think you're a darn sight more sprightly than your pensionable cat.'

'That's true,' she agreed. 'Now, I think we'd better start with the angel, don't you?'

Precariously balanced on top of a dining chair I couldn't help wishing that we'd thought to ask Beamish to position the angel for us even though there wasn't much height difference between us, but with one final stretch she was in situ, if not sitting entirely straight.

'She's a beauty,' I said when my feet were back on the floor. 'Where did you find her, Dolly?'

'Oh,' she said, 'she's been in the family for years. She's probably from the sixties and I daresay she came from Woolworths. She wouldn't have cost much.'

'I bet she's worth a fortune now,' I said, gazing up at her angelic expression and slightly battered wings. 'Did she come in a box?'

'Probably,' Dolly shrugged, 'but that's long gone. Now, come on. We better get cracking otherwise we won't be finished before Beamish comes back to take us skating.'

Decorating Dolly's little cottage was nowhere near as heavy going as the things I'd ticked off the Wish List through sheer hard work at school and I thoroughly enjoyed helping with the transformation. It had been a long time since I had decked anything and it was a pleasure looking through the boxes of treasures. Dolly's array of decorations spanned decades and were an eclectic mix but looked fittingly festive nonetheless.

Dolly insisted that pretty much everything made it out of the boxes and I let her run with her over-the-top attitude to decking her halls because I knew she was doing it more for me than her. Her 'making memories' ethos was in full swing and I had no intention of trying to temper her enthusiasm.

'You're well ahead this year,' commented the postman who had knocked mid-morning to deliver a couple of parcels which needed signing for.

'That I am,' said Dolly, scribbling her signature on the screen. 'That's nothing like my writing,' she said, handing the contraption back.

'They never work properly,' tutted the postie. 'Don't worry. It'll do. Your lights look lovely by the way,' he called back as he reached the gate.

'Thank you,' Dolly called after him. 'That timer must be on the blink,' she said to me. 'They shouldn't still be on, but then it's so dark today they do offer a little cheer, don't you think?'

'Definitely,' I agreed. 'You'll have to get Beamish to check the setting though. What do you think these are? Early presents to go with your early decorations?'

It turned out I wasn't far off, with one of them anyway. As promised, Jonathan had sent Dolly a cafetière so she could try the coffee from the Fortnum's hamper.

'Whittard,' said Dolly, sounding impressed, as she tore into the packaging. 'Very fancy.'

It certainly was and he'd added even more coffee to the order.

'Let's try it out with our late lunch, shall we?' I suggested.

Dolly was all for that and saved the other parcel until we

were sitting down to eat. She had also taken delivery of her monthly meat order from the local butcher and insisted we had a hot meal.

'You'll need some sustenance for tonight,' she said, sliding the delicious-looking hand-raised chicken pie into the oven to warm. 'And you can't go wrong with these.'

The second parcel was a prettily wrapped box of locally designed Christmas cards from the Cherry Tree gallery.

'I would have picked these up, Dolly,' I said, looking through the selection. 'Saved you the postage.'

'I didn't pay for postage,' she explained. 'Lizzie Dixon asked if I wouldn't mind having them delivered, free of charge. They've had a problem with their courier apparently and wanted to send out a few orders by good old Royal Mail to regular customers to see if they fared any better.'

'I see,' I said, picking up a card sporting a very feisty look-ing Robin. 'This one is rather nice.'

'Isn't it?' Dolly smiled. 'He's certainly got a lot of char-acter! A young woman called Hayley, who happens to be the Wynthorpe Hall housekeeper, designed these. You'll no doubt meet her next week when we take the tour.'

'She has an amazing talent,' I said, taking in the finer details. 'And I have to say I'm rather intrigued by the hall as well as the people who live there. It really does sound like a magical kind of place to me.'

'It's certainly that,' said Dolly with a wink, 'you'll see. Now, while that pie's warming, I'll ring Lizzie and let her know these have arrived and,' she craftily added, 'you might want to have a proper sort through and see if you can find a card you'd like to send to your parents.'

It was almost dark when Beamish arrived late that afternoon, but even before he'd stepped into the light in the cottage, I could see he was looking a bit rough around the edges again.

'My goodness,' he laughed, looking around him. 'You two have been busy, haven't you?'

'Dolly wanted the decs up,' I told him, 'so that's what she's got.'

'With bells on,' he laughed again, his gaze taking it all in. 'It looks fantastic.'

Just a few days ago I would have most likely disputed that description but since Dolly had plunged me into a vat of festive feeling, I felt rather more inclined to agree. I couldn't help thinking that my seasonal spirit was finally beginning to wake up and there was nothing offensive about the abundance of sparkling tinsel and gaudily coloured garlands at all.

'Thank you,' I smiled, appreciatively accepting his praise before taking a closer look at his face, 'but never mind our decorations.' I frowned. 'What's happened to you? It must have been a brutal game, either that or you just aren't very good at keeping out of the way.'

'Bit of both actually,' he admitted, shoving his hands in his pockets and looking rather sheepish. 'I couldn't seem to stay focused for some reason.'

'Even though you had a pack of guys the size of rhinos charging towards you?'

'Even then.'

He locked his eyes on mine and I had to look away.

'That's not like you,' said Dolly who had been upstairs when he first arrived. 'What's got you in such a tizzy that you can't concentrate on your game?'

'I don't know,' he shrugged, shifting his gaze from me to her. 'Does it matter?'

His cheeks, I noticed, when I looked back, had turned an interesting shade of red.

'If you're Coach Hudson,' Dolly pointed out, 'then yes, I would imagine it matters a great deal.'

'Yeah,' said Beamish, now rubbing the back of his neck, 'yeah, he did say it mattered to him actually.'

'I'll bet he did,' Dolly tutted, 'and I daresay he said a whole lot more besides. Are those actual stitches this time?'

Thankfully, Beamish didn't go into detail about either his coach's choice of words or what the medics had used to put him back together, but instead set about confirming that he could still take to the ice before demolishing the pie Dolly had saved for him. I guessed the air had been a bit blue after the whistle had called full time.

'Right,' he said, when he'd finally worked his way down to crumbs, 'let's get going. I was lucky to get these tickets at the last minute and if we don't get a wriggle on, we won't make it.'

'That's fine by me,' I smiled, pulling my woolly hat over my ears.

Dolly swatted me with her scarf.

'I'm looking forward to this,' she reminded me, 'and as Beamish just said, he was lucky to get the tickets.'

'Sorry,' I said, following her outside, 'I'm only joking.'

'No, you're not,' Beamish unhelpfully added with a smirk.

As Beamish and I watched Dolly take to the rink it was immediately obvious why she had been so keen to literally get her skates on and not miss a single second of her allotted time on the ice.

'Did you know?' Beamish asked, agog.

'Not a clue,' I answered, open mouthed.

By the time she had finished her first circuit, Dolly was up to speed and attracting a fair few admiring glances. Elegant and graceful she cut a path through the wobbly-legged and I banished all prior concerns that she might fall and break a hip. I was now far more worried about my own bones than hers.

'Come on,' said Beamish, reaching for my hand and pulling me to my feet in one swift movement, 'we can't put it off for ever.'

His fingers touching mine set off the same tingle as the first time we had held hands and under any other circumstances I would have let go of him straightaway, but I was so scared of falling that I kept a tight grip, trying not to admit to myself how much safer I felt with his large hand clasping my smaller one.

We made it on to the ice and, when he eventually prised

me away, I clung to the side, too unsteady to worry about how much of an idiot I looked. I braved a quick glance around and found I wasn't the only one hugging the barrier.

'Here you are at last,' said Dolly, coming to a steady and controlled stop next to me.

'You're a dark horse, aren't you?' I said.

'You're amazing, Dolly,' Beamish added, tentatively testing out his balancing skills and grinning when he didn't end up on his backside.

Dolly gave a little curtsy.

'My father taught me.' She told us. 'He was a champion skater. He used to compete when the Fens froze over.'

'I didn't even know that was a thing,' I said.

'Oh yes,' she said, turning to glide away again. 'It was a regular thing once. That was when we had proper winter weather, mind you.'

'Well I never,' said Beamish, still wearing his grin, 'lives and learns.'

'It must be in her genes,' I said, looking enviously after her, 'whereas I seem to have a fear of losing my fingers instilled in mine. I think I'll just stay here and watch.'

'Oh no you don't,' said Beamish, as he tried to release my fingers from the side, 'come on. We'll go together. I'll look after you and your lovely digits.'

I screwed my courage to the sticking place and let him, well, pull me around the rink, would probably be the best description of how we moved. Dolly whizzed by at least twice for our every one circuit, but I hardly registered her, because I was too busy focusing on my feet and, when I was on my bottom, everyone else's blades.

'Try and relax a bit,' Beamish advised, as he moved behind me and placed his hands lightly on my waist so he could push me along.

Oh yeah, that was going to help. The feel of his hands, even though cushioned by the layers of clothes, and his breath on the back of my neck, set my knees trembling again as the real reason for not telling Jonathan about my new friend became more obvious with every passing second.

'Better?' Beamish asked, his voice was deep and so close to my ear it made me shiver, but not with the cold.

'Yes.' I squeaked. 'Great.'

The set up didn't work particularly well because I was as rigid as an ironing board. With Beamish's hands on me, there was just no bend in me at all. He changed position again.

'Sorry,' I said, shaking my head.

'You're doing really well,' he said kindly as he unravelled his scarf.

I really wasn't but he was too much of a gentleman to say otherwise.

'Here,' he said, 'try hanging on to the end of this.'

'But then I won't have hold of you,' I swallowed.

I didn't much like the idea of relinquishing my safety blanket.

'Trust me,' he smiled, his uninjured eye imploring me to believe in him.

So, I did.

And we had almost made it around, a little faster now, with him towing me along before I fell in a heap for the final time and a buzzer announced that our time was up.

'Did you enjoy that?' I asked Dolly once we had returned our skates and had a warming mug of marshmallow-topped hot chocolate and a ringside seat.

It was a silly question. Her glowing cheeks and bright eyes were testament to the wonderful time she'd had. By contrast I was as white as a sheet and having a job to stop my legs from shaking. It hadn't been that long since I'd stretched my muscles, surely?

'I felt about fifteen again,' she breathed. 'I felt just how I used to when I was a girl.'

'You were amazing,' said Beamish. 'So elegant, Dolly. You cut quite a figure out there.'

Dolly nodded and wiped away a tear which Beamish and I pretended we hadn't seen.

'That's one wish from the list well and truly fulfilled,' I told him with a gentle nudge. 'Thank you, Beamish.'

'You're very welcome, Hattie,' he said, nudging me right back.

Chapter 11

It felt good to wake up in Wynbridge without that heavy weight on my chest, but the morning after our skating session it was more than obvious that the pain had simply transferred further down my body. My legs felt as though they had been struck by the *Harry Potter* Leg Locker curse and for a while, I didn't think I would ever be able to move them again.

I shuffled, rather than walked, to the bathroom, all the while wishing Dolly had added something slightly less physically demanding to our Christmas Wish List. But that said, at least focusing on the physical pain was distracting me from the mental turmoil which was beginning to build. So much for my relaxing holiday, I hadn't felt this stirred up in a very long time.

'You're up at last,' Dolly called up the stairs when she heard me whimpering. 'Come and see what I've found.'

Listening to her pottering about and humming along to Festive FM, or whatever channel she'd tuned the radio to, it was obvious that she wasn't suffering anything like I was. I wondered if Beamish was feeling the strain this morning. Probably not. His strapping thighs were used to a regular workout on the rugby pitch.

'Are you all right?' Dolly frowned as I inched my way stiffly and straight-legged down the stairs. 'You look a little flushed.'

'No, I'm not all right,' I told her.

'I hope you aren't coming down with a cold. Your cheeks are quite pink.'

'Never mind my cheeks,' I grimaced, knowing the flush was more the result of my thoughts of Beamish's thighs than any bug I might have picked up, 'I'm more concerned about my legs.'

'Why?' she frowned, scrutinising my pins, 'what's wrong with them? They look all right to me.'

I gingerly lowered myself into a chair and let out a sigh.

'They're stuck rigid,' I told her, 'I really don't think ice skating agrees with me.'

Dolly chuckled and poured me a cup of tea.

'Perhaps if you'd relaxed into a bit more,' she advised. 'Had you not been so tense you and Beamish would have been whizzing around in no time.'

I wasn't sure if that made me feel better or worse. Feeling his hands on my waist was the real reason I hadn't been able to loosen up.

'You two look good together,' Dolly continued, making my face burn even brighter. 'You're well matched.'

'Only because we're practically the same height,' I told her.

Jonathan and I were the same height too, but Dolly had never said we looked good together, but I knew that we did. The photographs taken at his work's summer ball earlier in the year were proof enough of that. Jonathan's physique was made for fine tailoring and his thighs, although not as wide as Beamish's, were every bit as impressive. I needed to remember that, amongst other things.

I was spending far too much time with the Good Samaritan of Wynbridge, and what with it almost being Christmas and everything, his kind deeds were turning my head. I had to nip this silly crush, if that's what it was, in the bud. I was in love with Jonathan, practically his wife, and all set to move to the other side of the world with him in almost no time at all. I hoped he would call again soon so I could tell him properly how much I had loved the photos of the apartment.

'Anyway,' I continued, quickly bursting the Beamish filled bubble with a Jonathan shaped pin, 'did you tick skating off the list?'

'Yes,' said Dolly, with a sigh, 'although personally I wouldn't have minded another few laps around the rink.'

'Well there's still time,' I told her. 'I think it's going to be set up into the new year. Perhaps we can arrange for you to go back again.'

She didn't answer and when I looked up from stirring my tea, her face was wearing the strangest expression. I couldn't put my finger on what it was, but it scared me a bit.

'Couldn't you, Dolly?' I prompted when she didn't comment. 'You could go back again?'

'Hattie,' she said, her voice catching, 'there's something . . .'

Her words trailed off but she still looked a little odd. I hoped having me here wasn't proving too much for her. Having watched her glide over the ice and running rings around the children at school, it was all too easy to forget how old she was. She was such a generous hostess. She'd barely let me lift a finger since I'd arrived.

'What is it?'

Her eyes darted to the front window and I heard the gate creak open.

'Oh, now here's Rose,' she said, sounding completely normal, 'and I haven't got all the albums out yet. Can you give me a hand, Hattie, please? Assuming of course you can bend that far.'

After I had let Rose in and taken her coat, scarf, and gloves all thoughts of what it was that Dolly might have been going to say were forgotten.

'I can't help thinking it looks like snow,' Rose said glumly.

'I thought you'd be all for a bit of the white stuff,' I told her. 'What with you and the rest of Wynbridge being so mad keen on Christmas. I bet the Connellys at Wynthorpe Hall will be thrilled with a white Winter Wonderland.'

'Angus has got a snow machine for the grotto should the weather not come up trumps,' Dolly laughed.

That didn't surprise me. I hadn't met him yet but I couldn't imagine that a little thing like Mother Nature

153

would get in the way of him creating the right ambience for his visitors.

'And I am all for the white stuff,' Rose told me. 'I'd just rather it arrived after we've broken up for the school holidays. The last thing we need is that bloody boiler putting its parts on and us having to close. It's the play on Wednesday.'

'Don't worry about that,' said Dolly stoically, 'Beamish will keep it going.'

Good old Beamish.

'What was it you wanted me to get for you, Dolly?' I hastily asked, keen to pull her thoughts away from our local hero again. 'Did you say albums?'

It was a job to kneel, but I managed it. In Dolly's large sideboard there were collections of photograph albums dating back decades.

'This is my father,' Dolly said proudly, once she pored through them looking for what it was Rose had come to borrow. 'This was the first year he was crowned champion.'

The photograph she was holding up showed the Fenland landscape gripped in what looked like Arctic conditions. Even though it was in black and white and a little blurry you could tell from her father's pinched features just how bitingly cold it was.

'This was the real weather you were referring to at the ice rink last night, I take it, Dolly?'

I was surprised she hadn't shown me the photographs before.

'Yes,' she said. 'We had snow every year then and the

deepest wind-driven drifts and the River Wyn was always frozen solid.'

'These are perfect,' said Rose, picking out some other images of children building snowmen and old cars being pulled out of ditches. 'They're the perfect snapshot of the time. Can I take these and copy them?'

'Of course,' nodded Dolly. 'I'm delighted you've found a use for them.'

'What are you using them for?' I asked Rose as I picked out one of Dolly looking adoringly up at her father as he held up his trophy, her cheeks rosy from the Wynbridge wind.

'They're going to be writing prompts for the year three class,' Rose explained. 'Mr Matthews is keen for the children to feel a connection to the Fens and its unusual landscape. We're going to use these to show how different the winter was when Dolly was their age and encourage them to come up with a piece of writing or a poem which captures the Wynbridge winter as it once was.'

'That's a big ask, isn't it?'

'You'd be surprised,' she smiled. 'There are some extremely creative young minds in that class and you're going to talk to them, Dolly, aren't you? Just to help them along a bit.'

'Yes,' said Dolly. 'I'm looking forward to it.'

'I think it sounds like a wonderful idea,' I added.

'It's going to be something they can dip in and out of for the next couple of weeks,' said Rose. 'The last few days are always disrupted with play rehearsals and concert practice and with their minds on their Christmas stockings instead of their lessons it's far easier all round to just go with the flow.'

'And talking of Christmas stockings,' said Dolly as she went to check the oven. 'Have you finished your shopping, Rose?'

'Almost,' she answered, as Dolly opened the door and the air was filled with the most delicious smell. 'I've just a few bits and pieces left to get. What are you cooking, Dolly? It smells divine.'

'A nice piece of brisket,' she said, 'it's been in since first thing.'

'Are you doing Yorkshire puddings to go with it?' Rose drawled.

'Of course. You can't have beef without puddings, can you?'

'And proper gravy.'

Dolly nodded.

'I don't know why I'm torturing myself,' Rose tutted. 'I better go.'

'Everything sorted with your sister?' Dolly asked as we gathered the pile of photographs back together.

'Oh yes,' Rose smiled. 'It was just a silly misunderstanding. I'm so relieved she and mum are talking again. I was dreading Christmas with the family torn in two. If there are arguments and differences to be settled, then now's the time to do it. Nothing should come in the way of being with family at Christmas, don't you agree?'

'I do,' said Dolly firmly. 'I certainly do.'

*

After Dolly's delicious Sunday dinner, I insisted that she let me deal with the dishes so that she could sit and write her Christmas cards.

'It will do my legs good if I stand up for a bit,' I told her. 'They're still as stiff as anything.'

She took some convincing but I won her around in the end.

'You said you wanted to get them in the postbox tonight,' I reminded her, 'and if you don't start writing now you won't be finished before church.'

As I washed and dried, Dolly's pile of envelopes, filled out in her beautiful cursive handwriting, steadily grew.

'Do you send cards to everyone at school?' I asked, when I eventually joined her at the table, wincing as I sat down.

'Not as a rule. Generally, I just send them to the staff and my class but this year I've got extra packs of charity cards so everyone will get one.'

'That's a lovely idea,' I smiled.

'Well as it's my last Christmas I thought I should make an extra effort.'

I knew she was talking about working in the school, but I wished she wouldn't put it like that.

'Your last Christmas at work, you mean,' I corrected her. Dolly smiled.

'I've saved this card with the robin on that you were so fond of.'

'Thank you,' I said, taking it from her. 'What are you going to write in it?'

'Nothing,' she laughed. 'I didn't mean I was going to write it to you, I meant I had saved it for you to send.'

'Oh,' I said, looking at it again. 'I see.'

'You will send it, won't you?' She frowned. 'To your parents.'

'Oh Dolly,' I said, feeling even more confused as Rose's talk of family mingled with Beamish's insistence that I shouldn't waste time and Jonathan's not surprisingly negative reaction to the idea. 'I don't know. I still haven't made up my mind.'

'It'll be too late soon,' she said, wagging a finger. 'And then you'll be wishing you had.'

Would I?

'Look,' she said, pushing a pad of Basildon Bond notepaper across the table, 'why don't you write them a letter?'

'What?' I gasped, aghast. 'I don't think I'd even know what to put in a card, what makes you think I could write a whole letter?'

'I bet, if you put your mind to it, you could come up with a hundred and one things that you would like to say to your mum and dad.'

'Not quite a hundred and one,' I admitted once I had given it some thought, 'but perhaps a couple of dozen.'

'So, write it all down,' she said, handing me a pen. 'You don't have to send it. I bet that just writing it will make you feel better, get it clearer in your head and by the time you've finished you'll know whether or not posting the card will be the right thing to do.'

I wasn't sure that what she was suggesting made much sense, but once I had got over the first few sentences the words began to flow and before I knew it the cramp in my hand matched my legs and I had filled almost four sheets of paper.

'There now,' said Dolly as I sat back and rubbed my hand. 'Cathartic, isn't it?'

'Maybe,' I shrugged.

It was too early to tell. My eyes flicked over the pages again. I hadn't planned to hark back to old hurts but I knew that if we were going to end up making amends before I moved, then it was important to bring everything out into the open.

'Did you write about, David?' Dolly asked.

'Yes,' I said huskily, 'and the baby.'

Dolly nodded.

'Thank you for helping me through all of that, Dolly,' I whispered, remembering how she had insisted that I kept the channels of communication with my parents open after my world had been blown apart and I had moved into the hotel.

'I only did what any friend would,' she said gently.

The moment my parents had discovered that, at just seventeen I was secretly seeing an older man, they had tried to put a stop to it. Headstrong and in love, I of course could see nothing wrong and had done everything in my power to keep the relationship going. However, discovering I was pregnant was a huge shock for all of us and I could understand now why they had been so horrified. Although not nearly as horrified as when my father tracked David down and discovered he was a married man.

'I used to say,' I said, smoothing the letter out in front of me, 'that first I lost David and then I lost the baby, but I suppose he was never mine in the first place, was he? David, I mean.'

I winced as I recalled the blazing rows I had about him with my parents. I blamed them for ruining everything after they threatened to tell his wife and then when I miscarried, I blamed them for taking the baby too. Had I not moved into the hotel I didn't know where I might have ended up.

'You know I admire you, Hattie,' said Dolly.

'Why?'

'For finding the courage to forgive your mother.'

'I'm not sure I have forgiven her,' I told her, 'but you know,' I mused, 'sometimes, I struggle to believe she really did say that she was pleased I'd lost the baby.'

I knew she and Dad had been disappointed when they discovered my affair and devastated about the pregnancy, but Mum wasn't cruel. She hadn't wanted me to move out after the miscarriage, she had wanted to look after me and so her spiteful words, coming years later, were even more of a shock.

Dolly nodded and bit her lip.

'But the look on Jonathan's face when he told me ...' I carried on, 'well, let's just say, I knew he had to be telling the truth.'

'And the way he said they both used to talk to him when

you weren't around,' Dolly went on, 'that was a shock too, wasn't it?'

'It was,' I sighed, 'we didn't visit all that often and he always tried to play it down but whenever we left, I could tell there was something wrong, something eating away at him and I would eventually drag it out of him. He knew my relationship with them was fragile, and that's why he never wanted to tell me.'

'But he did in the end.'

'Only because I made him,' I said, slumping back in my chair as the memories and cold hard reality came flooding back. 'Oh Dolly,' I sobbed, 'is sending this going to be a mistake?'

'Only you can decide that,' she said.

I swallowed away the lump in my throat and blinked away the gathering tears.

'Get the card written and stick it all in the envelope,' she encouraged, 'and then, if you do decide to go ahead, it'll be done. You really haven't got much longer to decide you know.'

I did as Dolly instructed and put it next to, rather than on top of the pile, with all the others, but I had no intention of sending it, not the letter part anyway. And even if I had wanted to send the card, given the conversation we'd had, I knew it wouldn't be fair on Jonathan. I sat there and stared at the envelope thinking Dolly had been wrong to assume I'd feel better for getting it all out of my head because if anything, I actually felt worse. The best thing I could do was forget about it. Bin the card when Dolly wasn't looking, squash all my emotions back into their assigned box and cram the lid firmly on.

'Done,' Dolly announced a minute or so later, plonking her pen down with a flourish and putting her cards for school in a separate bag as they wouldn't need sending. 'They're all ready to go. It didn't take as long as I thought it would,' she added, looking over at the clock, 'but then when you get to my age there are fewer and fewer to write each year.'

'Dolly,' I frowned.

'What?' She shrugged, 'it's true.'

It may well have been true, but it made me feel uncomfortable nonetheless.

'How are your legs?' she asked. 'Up to an hour in church?'

We decided they really weren't and Dolly offered me what she said would be, if not a miracle cure, then a definite help.

'Just add a few drops of this to your bath water,' she said, handing me a small blue bottle, 'and then sit in it for at least half an hour.'

'What's in it?' I asked, removing the stopper and taking an exploratory sniff.

It wasn't unpleasant, but it wasn't Radox either.

'I'm not sure exactly,' Dolly frowned, 'there's definitely marjoram and rosemary but beyond that . . .'

'Where did you get it?'

'From Molly at Wynthorpe Hall.'

I hadn't heard mention of a Molly before.

'How many people actually live in that place?' I laughed.

'She doesn't live in the hall. She has a cottage in the woods. She makes all sorts of remedies.'

'Is she a witch?' I joked.

'Yes,' said Dolly, pulling me up short. 'I suppose she is. Of sorts. Anyway, whatever she is, she knows her stuff. A few drops of that and a decent night's sleep will set you to rights.'

I didn't ask for further explanation and made sure I was firmly ensconced in the bathroom with my phone playing some soothing music well before Beamish arrived to take Dolly to church.

'I'll lock the door,' she called up to me. 'See you later.'

'Bye!' I called back.

I was surprised that I felt disappointed to be missing out on singing a few carols and seeing the second advent candle lit, but I thought it best to put some distance between me and Beamish, at least until I had turned off the little torch I had started to shine for him.

I had just started to nod off when my phone began to ring and I jolted upright, sloshing water over the sides of the bath. It was Jonathan, requesting a video call.

'Where are you?' he laughed once I had propped the phone up on my towel which was on the chair next to the bath.

'Can't you see me?' I asked, leaning in a little.

'Oh yes,' he grinned. 'Hattie, are you in the bath?'

'Yes,' I giggled, then remembering where he was added, 'You aren't out in public somewhere, are you?'

'No,' he said, 'I'm in the hotel and I'm rather pleased I called your mobile rather than trying the house phone now.'

163

'Don't get any funny ideas,' I told him. 'I just wanted to make sure no one was likely to look over your shoulder, that's all.'

He laughed again, his whole face lighting up.

'I've really missed you today,' I told him, leaning even further forward so I could properly see his face.

'Have you?'

'Yes,' I said. 'I could have done with a hug.'

'A hug?'

'Amongst other things,' I sighed.

'Are you thinking about that bath in Iceland by any chance?' he said huskily.

'The one with all the bubbles,' I dreamily added.

'That's the one,' he said. 'That was quite something, wasn't it?'

'Oh yes,' I agreed.

We'd enjoyed the luxurious bath during the most lavish trip we had ever taken. The temperature was a stark contrast to Abu Dhabi but we'd found ways to keep warm while lying beneath a glass-topped dome. The memory of those nights could still melt my insides.

'Anyway,' I said, 'don't get me all riled up when you're so far away.'

He raised his eyebrows.

'I actually wanted to talk to you about the apartment.'

'You are happy with it, aren't you?' he asked, sounding concerned. 'You seemed pleased in your email and I would have called again sooner, only—'

'I love it,' I interrupted. 'I only wish we were moving in this year instead of next.'

'Me too,' he sighed. 'But it's not long now. And the place has the most amazing views. We were really lucky to get it.'

I could believe that. Property was fast becoming as hot as the temperature in Abu Dhabi. We chatted about the location, aspect of the rooms and of course, the laundry service.

'And what have you been up to this weekend?' Jonathan then asked.

I knew it was impossible to tell him about my letter-writing exercise and as nothing was going to come of it anyway, it would have been pointless. More likely than not mentioning my parents again would have caused an argument, so instead I told him briefly about the skating and how amazing Dolly was on the ice and thanked him for the cafetière and extra coffee.

'She's feeling very spoilt,' I said.

'Well I'm trying to make more of an effort.'

'She told me you chatted for ages the other night,' I felt myself go hot as I remembered that the conversation had included a lie Dolly had told for me.

'We did,' he said, 'and I'm pleased she's liked her presents.'

It wasn't lost on me that Jonathan had used material gifts to win Dolly around, while certain other folk had gone out of their way to set up experiences and trips out. Memories rather than stuff.

'So, what are your plans for tomorrow?' Jonathan eventually asked after spending ages giving me the lowdown on his weekend – fine dining in a swanky restaurant, followed by an overnight stay on a friend's yacht made his couple of days sound far fancier than mine.

I told him about the photos Rose had picked up and how busy she had said the school was. I also mentioned that it was a bit much for Dolly, which wasn't strictly true but led me nicely into telling him that I was occasionally helping out a bit myself, just to share the load.

'Well, don't tire yourself out,' was all he said, 'you're supposed to be there on holiday, remember?'

I was surprised by his lack of reaction, but grateful for it and promised I wouldn't overdo things and that I would be fighting fit for when I saw him again.

'I better go,' I said eventually, standing up and giving him a glimpse of my bare skin before I wrapped myself in the bath towel. My legs were feeling much more relaxed than before. 'The water's going cold.'

'I could tell,' he drawled. 'You look like you've got goosebumps.'

'Well don't zoom in,' I laughed, not even sure if that was possible.

'I don't have to,' he grinned.

'I'll speak to you in a few days.'

'All right,' he said, leaning forward to sign off. 'Have fun at school.'

'I'll try.'

'Love you.'

'Love you too.'

I was feeling as light as air by the time I finished dressing. Thoughts of the card were banished and it was a relief that Jonathan knew I was working in school. Now I wouldn't have to be guarded about letting anything slip whenever we spoke. I had been wrong to think that he would object. I really hadn't been giving him enough credit recently.

I waited upstairs until I heard Dolly come in and made sure Beamish was gone before I went back down.

'How was your bath?' she asked. 'You certainly look better.'

'I feel it,' I yawned, stretching my hands above my head. 'And Jonathan called.'

'While you were in the bath?'

'Yes.'

'Whatever next,' she tutted.

I didn't tell her we'd Skyped.

'How was church?' I asked, moving a few things on the table so I could set it.

'Lovely,' Dolly smiled. 'There were—'

'Dolly,' I cut in.

'What?'

'Where are the cards?'

'The cards?'

'The Christmas cards,' I all but shouted. 'Where are they?'

'In the postbox,' she said, not catching on. 'Beamish stuck the stamps on while I was getting ready and we posted them on the way.'

'All of them?'

Her eyes darted from mine back to the table as she realised what had happened.

'Oh, my dear girl,' she tutted. 'I'm so sorry, but it's gone.'

Chapter 12

To say I was distraught didn't come close to expressing the emotions coursing through my veins. Not only had the envelope containing the jolly robin card entered the postal system, but the letter inside it had gone too. If this was Dolly's idea of helping me ignite my seasonal spirit and make some happy memories, then she was failing dismally. The only thing alight was my temper.

'Well I can't just leave it,' I wailed. 'That letter . . . I would *never* have sent that. The card perhaps, but not the letter.'

'I'll call Beamish,' said Dolly, realising I was no more capable of accepting the situation than I was able to fly to the moon.

I didn't see what good it would do, but I let her go ahead.

'Can you come back?' I heard her asking him as I circled the table, alternately checking the envelope hadn't slipped underneath and tearing at my nails. 'There might have been a mix-up with my Christmas cards.'

'What did he say?' I demanded, the moment she ended the call.

'That he's on his way, but he doesn't think there could have been a mix-up because he posted the lot.'

'Oh my god,' I wailed again, stuffing my hands in my pockets. At this rate I wouldn't have any nails left.

Jonathan was going to go berserk and I could hardly blame him. Why had I listened to Dolly? He had accused her of meddling before and I had defended her, but I couldn't now, could I? I tried to console myself with the thought that perhaps my parents would put the card and the emotion-laden letter in the bin unopened, but knew I was in for a tense few days waiting to find out.

'Where's the fire?' Beamish beamed, bursting in. 'I didn't even have time to get my coat off.'

I looked at him and narrowed my eyes.

'This is your fault,' I began, but Dolly cut me off.

'No,' she said sternly. 'It most certainly is not.'

'Yours then,' I bit back.

'Hey,' Beamish frowned, coming further into the room. 'That'll do.'

I bit my lip, too wound up to apologise. I was hell-bent on blaming someone for the mess and determined to find someone else to fix it.

'Now,' said Beamish, 'tell me what it is that I'm supposed to have done.'

Dolly explained again, this time paying particular attention to my card which hadn't been on the pile.

'I definitely took the lot,' said Beamish, 'I told you that on the phone, Dolly. I assumed that the separated card must have slipped off the top and, as there were exactly the right number of stamps for them all, I posted that one with all the others. I take it, it wasn't meant to go?'

'No,' I sniffed, feeling some of the fight leave me, 'no, it wasn't.'

Not only were my legs now seizing back up, but the rest of my body felt as tight as a coiled spring. It would take more than Dolly's herbal potion to ease the kinks out of this one.

'It was to my parents,' I explained. 'Dolly's idea of a cathartic greeting card and a very emotional letter to go with it.'

'And you really didn't mean for it to be sent?'

'No,' I swallowed, 'I really didn't.'

'But after our chat,' he said, 'I thought you still might be thinking about getting back in touch with them.'

'Yes, well, thinking and doing are two very different things, aren't they?'

Beamish nodded.

'I might have let the card go,' I told him, 'but not the letter.'

'Well,' said Dolly, trying to make the best of things and failing, 'think of it this way. You've been more than willing to let fate lend a hand in your future recently, perhaps you should let it lead the way through this situation, too?'

I shook my head.

'No,' I said, 'this isn't fate. This doesn't feel like fate. This is one almighty cock-up.'

'Look,' said Beamish taking in my sorrowful expression, 'I have a mate who's a postman. I'll go and see him. Find out if he's opening the boxes in the morning and ask if there's any way we could get the card back?'

'Could you do that?' I asked, jumping back up again in spite of my protesting legs. 'Could you take it back do you think?'

'I have no idea,' Beamish told me, 'but I promise I'll do what I can.'

'You can't ask for more than that, Hattie,' said Dolly.

She was right, I couldn't, but if anyone could have quickly found the formula to turn back time I for one would have been more than happy to be the guinea pig to have first dibs on giving it go.

It was stomach churning walking past the postbox the next morning, especially when I read that the first collection wouldn't be happening until nine. That meant the card and letter was still sitting there, mere centimetres from my fingers and there was nothing I could do about it.

'Come on,' said Dolly. 'There's no point loitering. We'll be late if we don't get on.'

'But this says the collection isn't until nine,' I said accusingly, 'and there wasn't one at all last night so I don't see why you were in such a hurry to get your cards gone.'

Dolly didn't comment.

'If you'd left them until this morning,' I muttered on, 'then none of this would have happened.'

I knew it wasn't fair to keep niggling at her, but I couldn't let it drop.

'Don't you think I haven't laid awake most of the night thinking that very thing myself?' Dolly snapped back. 'But as they were done, I wanted them posted. One less thing to have to worry about.'

I couldn't imagine she had all that much to worry about, but I did feel bad that she'd had a restless night. It wasn't like her to snap. Lack of sleep was the last thing either of us needed while we were preparing for the school performance on Wednesday.

'I know,' I said, taking her bag and linking my arm through hers. 'I'm sorry.'

I didn't catch sight of Beamish until morning break and as he came over to where Dolly and I were checking costumes for the dress rehearsal I could see he wasn't carrying an envelope.

'I'm so sorry, Hattie,' he sighed and I knew he hadn't managed it.

There was no suggestion of a double bluff, no envelope tucked into his back pocket to be produced with a flourish. Wynbridge's answer to Ironman wasn't infallible after all.

'I did try, but my mate wasn't on shift and the guy who was wouldn't help. He said it was more than his job was worth.'

I nodded and tried to swallow away the lump in my throat. This trip to Wynbridge was turning into a total disaster.

'Oh well,' I said, knowing I would have to resign myself to what had happened and feeling the tiniest glimmer of relief that if there was a response it would come to Dolly's cottage or my inbox, rather than the flat. 'It's done. It doesn't matter.'

'Actually, 'said Dolly, rubbing my arm before ticking the third set of sparkly angel wings off her checklist, 'it might turn out to matter a great deal.'

Luckily for me, Jonathan messaged to say he was inundated with work and wouldn't be able to call until later in the week. It was a huge relief because I didn't think I would be able to stop myself from telling him what had happened. Following his staunch work ethic, I threw myself into helping at school and did what I could to ensure that the performance on Wednesday, in which every child had a part, (even if they were only a sheep present at the birth of baby Jesus), ran like clockwork.

There was no job I couldn't turn my hand to. Whether I was reattaching elastic on masks, adding sequins to hem-lines or painting scenery, I was up for it. Anything to stop me imagining that card and letter winging its way across the country, but I was hard pushed to eradicate it completely from my thoughts.

Sometimes my head was filled with an *Indiana Jones* style map, complete with theme tune. You know the ones they use in the films to plot his progress across continents in a hot air balloon or something. I pictured a robin, just like the one on the card, with the envelope clasped tightly in its little beak, battling blizzards to make sure it reached its destination and was delivered right on time.

'You're still thinking about that card, aren't you?' Beamish asked as he took in my faraway expression. 'I really am sorry about it, you know.'

It was the night before the play and, having got my crush for him (helped in no small part by his cock-up with the card) under control, I had agreed to stay late to help him with some last-minute tweaking to the new stage lighting. The money for it had been raised by the PTA and, as this was to be its debut performance, it had to be impressive.

'If it's any consolation, it won't have arrived yet,' he said, climbing the ladder to position the spotlights above the recently repaired stage. 'Not at this time of year.'

'Don't you think?' I asked, squinting up at him and momentarily blinding myself.

'Don't look at the lights, you idiot,' he laughed as I grimaced and rubbed my eyes. 'Just stand there so I can see where to angle them.'

'It might be there tomorrow though, mightn't it?' I said, unable to let it drop. 'I can't imagine it will take longer than three days.'

Beamish didn't answer and I tried not to think about Mum and Dad reading what I had written.

'Oh, blast,' I said, rushing across the stage and out of his pool of light.

'What?'

'The manger,' I called up to him. 'I was supposed to paint it this afternoon but got asked to do something else. It completely slipped my mind.'

'Does it need painting?'

'It's a cardboard box from the supermarket, with twelve bottles of Merlot stamped on the side so I would say yes, it definitely needs painting.'

Beamish chuckled and climbed back down the ladder.

'Do you want a hand?' he offered. 'I'm all done here and I can't lock up until everyone's gone.'

'I think it's just us now,' I said, looking out into the empty car park.

'Come on then,' he said, scooping up the doll which had been drafted in to play the starring role. 'Let's leave Jesus and his bed of straw here and get this done. I might even be able to give the paint a knotty wood finish.'

'Oh my,' I said, following him out of the hall, 'fancy.'

Beamish, of course, was as good as his word, and after we'd waited for the first coat of brown paint to dry, he then expertly added some knots and bark embellishments in a darker shade which, from a distance looked more or less like the real thing.

'Well, well, well,' I said standing back to admire his handiwork, 'you really are a man of hidden talents, aren't you?'

'You'd be amazed,' he winked and I felt my face flush.

Gestures like that weren't going to keep my crush at arm'slength for long.

'In this job,' he went on, thankfully unaware of my change of colour, 'you have to be able to turn your hand to pretty much anything and everything.'

'For someone with such huge hands,' I stupidly carried

on, making the situation a gazillion times worse, 'you have a very gentle touch.'

What the hell possessed me to say that? And to make the situation worse, all I could now think about was the way his fingers had rested on my waist at the ice rink.

'What I mean is,' I crashed on, 'is that you're good with your hands.'

He looked at me and raised his eyebrows.

'No,' I said, 'I don't mean like that.'

'What do you mean then?' he asked, a smile pulling at his lips.

'I mean . . .'

'Oh, never mind,' he laughed, 'let's just leave it, shall we?'

More than embarrassed, I nodded and gathered the brushes together to wash them. He came to stand next to me, emptying the jam jars of murky water into the sink as I turned on the tap to start rinsing everything off. The water pressure was not what I was expecting and it came spurting out in a series of short bursts, covering us and everything else within a metre radius.

'Oh my god,' I gasped. 'It's freezing! Why won't it stop?'

Beamish leant over and grabbed the tap, managing to turn it off. He went to say something but caught sight of my face and T-shirt and started to laugh instead. I looked up at him and laughed back. We were both soaked and covered in splatters of thick brown paint.

'I better add this to my list of urgent jobs,' he said, reaching around me for a handful of paper towels. 'Here,' he said, 'this'll get the worst of it off.'

We mopped up as best we could and I was about to make a second attempt to clean the brushes when I felt him closing the gap next to me.

'What?'

'You missed a bit,' he said, gently sweeping my hair aside and pressing the towel against my cheek. 'It will probably stain if you don't get it off and how good will that look for the parents tomorrow?'

'They'll probably just think I've thrown myself into my work,' I said, turning to face him as he cupped my face with his other hand and tilted it up to the light.

Just for a second, he took his eyes off the splodge of paint and looked into mine. I knew I should look away, but I couldn't. It was as if there was a magnetic field pulling me towards him.

'Hattie,' he said, his eyes flicking to my lips as I leant further in, 'what are you doing?'

For a second, time stood still and then I came to my senses.

'Returning the favour,' I said, somehow managing to stop myself and reaching to grab another paper towel, 'you've missed a bit too.'

He took the towel from me and I quickly turned back to the sink.

'How's that?' he asked, once he had scrubbed at his face.

His complexion was almost as red as mine, but I couldn't tell if that was because he'd rubbed too hard or was feeling as hot under the collar as I was.

'Great,' I said, 'all gone.'

'I'm just going to check on the boiler then,' he said, 'and then we should really get going. It's a big day tomorrow.'

I watched as he rushed away, my face burning again. What the hell was wrong with me? I was an almost engaged person and I had very nearly just kissed another man.

Chapter 13

Had it been any other school day, I would have phoned in sick, actually I would have done anything on any day to avoid having to face Beamish again, but it wasn't any other day and I knew as soon as I opened my eyes that I had no option but to just get on with it. After all, it could have been worse, I could have actually kissed him, rather than *almost* locked lips.

As soon as I crossed the school threshold, I became aware of a change in atmosphere. There was a sense of excitement and expectation and from every classroom came the chorus of a different carol, someone noisily practising their lines, or someone else wailing that they'd forgotten theirs. The change in mood was a godsend. We were all rushed off our feet and, thankfully, it was nowhere near as difficult to avoid Beamish as I had imagined.

'What on earth's the matter with you this morning?' Dolly asked me during morning break when she brushed by and I jumped almost as high as the ceiling. 'You're like a cat on a hot tin roof.'

I had thought I'd been playing it rather cool, but apparently not.

'This is no day for being distracted,' she said handing me a mug of coffee.

'I know,' I dithered, in spite of my best intentions not to. 'I'm just so tense about this afternoon and, added to that the thought that right now Mum and Dad could be reading my letter, it's all a bit much.'

Obviously I couldn't mention the near-kiss which was also playing havoc with my head.

'Fear *and* excitement,' Dolly tutted, gazing off into the distance and looking more Miss Marple than ever. 'Now that is a heady mix.'

'It is,' I agreed, blowing into the mug to cool my coffee.

'And completely understandable,' she continued as I took my first searing sip, 'but it doesn't explain what Beamish said.'

I hastily swallowed the liquid down and felt it blazing a trail to my stomach to join the butterflies.

'What do you mean?' I spluttered. 'What did Beamish say?'

'Well, he's a bit all over the place this morning too,' Dolly elaborated, 'and when I asked him what was the matter, he said that I had to ask you.'

'Oh,' I said, my heart thumping, but not because of the caffeine.

'Did something happen last night?' Dolly asked.

'What?' I squeaked.

'When you stayed late, was there some problem with the stage or something? We can't have children pitching off the front again.'

'No,' I said, taking another mouthful of coffee and thinking on my feet. 'There was nothing wrong with the stage or the lights, but we did have to quickly paint the manger. I daresay he was just worried that it hadn't dried.'

Dolly opened her mouth to say something else but I didn't give her the chance.

'In fact,' I said, tipping the rest of my still too hot coffee down the sink, 'I better go and check on it before the bell goes.'

The hall that afternoon was packed. It seemed that practically every parent, grandparent, sibling and cousin had turned out to watch the performance of the year. In fact, it was so full that I thought there were going to be fisticuffs over the last chair but as Beamish dimmed the lights and the music began, everyone settled down and a hush fell over the audience.

I hovered in the wings making running repairs to costumes, handing out props and jollying along those who looked as if they were about to deliver something other than their lines. Mr Patterson didn't miss a beat at the piano and by the final rousing chorus of 'We Wish You a Merry Christmas', there was barely a dry eye to be seen.

The painted manger had pride of place centre stage and

the spotlight shining on it made my face flush all the more as I thought about what had almost happened after its make-over. I wondered if Beamish was thinking along the same lines, but hidden behind the lights his face was in shadow so I couldn't see, which was probably just as well.

Mr Matthews stood up and made a wonderful speech thanking the children for their enthusiastic performances and the staff for putting in so much effort to make the after-noon one to remember. He was keen to remind the audience that everyone had gone above and beyond this academic year and that the perceived lengthy school holidays were often anything but for the staff when there was so much work to do behind the scenes before and after the official term dates. His speech raised a few parents' eyebrows but the staff looked delighted to have their efforts so publicly acknowledged.

'And as it's not too early in the afternoon,' Mr Matthews announced, closing his speech, 'if you would like to wait in the usual place outside, we'll get the children changed and let them out to you straightaway.'

A cheer went up from the children who were still assem-bled on the stage and I knew there would be a mad rush to see who could be out of the door and home first.

'How are you getting on?' Rose asked, as she popped into class a little while later. 'Everyone gone?'

'I've just let the last one go,' I told her, as I folded up the few remaining pieces of costumes which had been left behind in the push to get out the door. For a few minutes it had been bedlam, the classroom caught up in a maelstrom of discarded clothes and mismatched shoes. 'Poor Daisy had to wait until three fifteen because her parents couldn't get time off work to come.'

'Such a shame, isn't it?' said Rose, 'but at least we've recorded it this year. We couldn't last year because we had one child we couldn't film or photograph. It was a shame, but we couldn't risk catching him in shot.'

'Couldn't you have edited him out?'

'Possibly, but we decided it wasn't worth the risk. Come down to the staff room when you're done. We're having mince pies to celebrate the afternoon's success.'

'All right,' I said, my attention returning to an abandoned shepherd's outfit as I spotted Beamish loitering in the corridor.

'How's it looking in here?' he asked, once Rose had gone.

'Not too bad,' I said, looking around. 'You won't bother cleaning tonight, will you? It's the party on Friday so it hardly seems worth it.'

I knew he was rushed off his feet as the two cleaners who usually took care of the vacuuming had both called in sick and he was having to pick up the slack. The poor chap. He really did have his hands full in the run-up to Christmas.

Best not to start thinking about his hands again . . .

'I'll vacuum reception and the main corridor, but that's it,' he said, coming further into the room and closing the door. 'Hattie, look I know you've been avoiding me today.'

'No, I haven't,' I lied, moving to the other side of the room. 'I've just been busy. As have you, along with everyone else for that matter.'

'Well, whatever,' he cut in, 'but I need to talk to you about last night.'

Oh god.

'Did you fix that tap?'

'Bugger the tap,' he muttered. 'You know what I'm talking about.'

I fiddled about with the shepherd's head gear and pursed my lips. He was obviously well aware that I had been on the verge of kissing him, but given my new-found gift of making situations a hundred times worse since I'd arrived in Wynbridge, I decided to hear what he had to say about it all before I added my two pennies' worth.

'You were going to kiss me, weren't you?' He blurted out.

Damn. I bent down to ostensibly retrieve a coat hanger but really, I was buying time.

'And had you not been about to fly off to the other side of the world, Hattie,' he carried on, 'I would have definitely kissed you back, but—'

I didn't need to hear that.

'Beamish,' I said, a little louder than I meant to. 'I don't know what made you think I was going to kiss you, but I definitely wasn't.'

'But you leant in.'

'Because you had paint on your face and you needed to get it off before it dried.'

185

He ran a hand distractedly through his hair.

'You really weren't leaning in for a kiss?'

'No,' I laughed, 'of course not! Were you when you wiped my face?'

'No,' he insisted, 'no.'

'There you are then,' I said, even managing a nonchalant shrug.

'Oh god,' he groaned, running both hands through his hair this time. 'I really thought ... oh my god, this is so embarrassing.'

'It's fine,' I said, feeling a sharp prickle of guilt.

It really wasn't fair to turn the tables on him, but I didn't know what else to do.

'No, it's not,' he said, sounding mortified. 'Whatever must you think?'

'Nothing,' I shrugged again, hanging the shepherd on the rail. 'It was nothing, just crossed wires. Forget it.'

'I'm an idiot.'

'No,' I said, 'you most definitely are not.'

'Well,' he said, clearing his throat, 'I'm sorry. I was wrong and I hope I haven't made you feel awkward. That was certainly not my intention.'

'You haven't,' I said, 'it's fine. I promise. Let's forget it.'

'Are you sure? You must think I'm a right arrogant prick.'

'I really don't,' I said, as the door began to open, 'let's say no more about it.'

'Now here you two are,' said Dolly, stepping into the

room and eyeing us curiously. 'We were wondering where you'd got to. If you don't hurry up there won't be any mince pies left.'

Dolly and I weren't expected in school the next day and it was a relief to think that I would be able to go to bed and not have to set an alarm on a weekday. Don't get me wrong, I was enjoying my time in school, in spite of the incident in the art room, but getting up in the dark during my holidays was not my favourite thing to do.

'The play was wonderful, wasn't it?' I said to Dolly that evening as I replayed some of the most memorable moments out in my head.

'A total triumph,' she agreed, as she settled down with her knitting. 'But given the amount of work which went into it, it couldn't have been anything but. I don't think I can remember a more intense year of planning and preparation.'

I wasn't sure if it was all that different to any other year, or if my friend's advancing years were catching up with her. She had certainly yawned more than I had that evening and I was feeling pretty zonked myself.

'And how are you looking forward to the tour of Wynthorpe Hall tomorrow?' I asked, picking up the Christmas Wish List.

We still had a way to go to complete it, which was just as well given my seasonal spirit was still struggling to burst into flame. The play had produced another spark, but with so many other things to worry about crammed into my head, it hadn't caught light yet.

'I can't wait,' she smiled. 'I bet it's going to be amazing and I've heard that Dorothy's afternoon teas are legendary so we won't have to worry about cooking dinner tomorrow night.'

'I'm looking forward to meeting the folk who live there as much as getting a peek inside the place,' I told her, which was true. 'What time will we be leaving?'

'Not until after school,' she said. 'Beamish will come and get us as soon as he's finished for the day and in view of the fact that we don't have the usual early start tomorrow, I think I'll have a lie-in.'

My eyes flew from the list to Dolly's face.

'Well I never,' I gasped, feeling as if the world had slipped a little on its axis.

That wasn't like her at all. Dolly was always up with the lark, even when she had stayed at the hotel, but her unchanged tone didn't suggest it was anything for me to be worried about.

'Well, that's the plan,' she said, now frowning as her needles clicked at speed, 'so I daresay I'll be awake even earlier than usual because I haven't got to get up, won't I?'

'Yes,' I agreed, 'in my experience, that's usually the way of it.'

'And what have you got planned for tomorrow?' she asked me.

'Same as you most likely,' I sighed. 'I wouldn't mind

staying under the eiderdown until there's a hint of daylight peeping around the curtains.'

I didn't add that I was planning to telephone Jonathan and tell him about the Christmas card fiasco. I wasn't going to mention the letter which accompanied it, but as I was feeling so guilty about that *and* the near-kiss, I had to come clean about something.

It wasn't a call I was looking forward to but it didn't feel right, preparing to head off for a new life in another country with the man I loved while stowing away an extra suitcase full of secrets. That said, I wouldn't be mentioning Beamish. There was no need to test Jonathan's resolve about my friendships with the opposite sex just for the sake of it.

'I'll bring you breakfast in bed, if you like,' I told Dolly.

'Oh now,' she smiled, 'that would be a treat. I can't remember the last time I had breakfast in bed. Certainly not since I lost my Stanley,' she mused. 'It's just not the same, getting out of bed to make it and then getting back in again, is it?'

'I suppose not,' I smiled back.

Dolly rarely mentioned her husband who had died young, far too young judging by what she told me. They had had no time to start a family and Dolly had never looked for another partner to share her life with. '*When you've drunk vintage champagne,*' she had said, '*there's no desire to sup second-rate fizz.*'

'Did Stanley used to bring you breakfast in bed often?' I asked.

Heidi Swain

'Special occasions,' she said wistfully. 'Birthdays and anniversaries. Not that we shared enough of them. So yes, breakfast in bed tomorrow would be lovely, Hattie. Thank you.'

At least I could go to bed knowing that I was going to be starting and ending the next day nicely, even if the bit in the middle did feel destined to go a bit belly-up.

Chapter 14

Snow was something Dolly and I had decided not to include on the Christmas Wish List.

'It's too chancy,' she said, when we discussed it. 'I only want you to add the things that are dead certs and as lovely as snow would be, it's just too far beyond our control and it generally arrives in Wynbridge after Christmas these days anyway.'

However, I knew the moment I opened my eyes and glanced from the window to the bedside clock, that the local TV weather forecaster had underestimated the potential 'odd flake' she had hinted at and that this year was the exception to Dolly's rule.

The light was just a little too bright to match the time and sure enough, when I looked out, everything was covered with a pretty dusting and the clouds looked very much like they had more to offload. I was surprised to discover I was rather excited by the sight.

'Good morning, Dolly,' I greeted her a good while later with a laden breakfast tray and the newspaper. 'Are you ready for room service?'

Dolly smiled and hitched herself further up the bed. She looked tiny in the double divan as she plumped the pillows and rested her head back into the snowy white cases.

'Is it too early?' I quietly asked. 'Do you want me to come back in a bit?'

Personally, I was surprised she was still in bed at all, but looking at her I felt sure she could have carried on snoozing all day.

'No, no,' she said, her first words were a little croaky. 'This is perfect, thank you, Hattie. I never meant to lay so late. Whatever time is it?'

'Well after eight,' I said, setting the old-fashioned tray with its legs down, over her lap.

'It's light for eight,' she frowned, picking up on the same clue to the weather that I had spotted. 'It hasn't snowed, has it?'

'It sure has,' I told her, pulling the curtains open. 'It's not particularly deep but everything's covered.'

'Well I never,' she smiled, sitting up straighter. 'That young woman on the weather last night said it wouldn't reach as far south as here. Can you move the tray, my dear? This I have to see.'

'No, you don't,' I said, pulling my phone out of my dressing gown pocket and snapping a few shots of the view. 'You stay where you are.'

Dolly looked at the pictures and tucked into her honey-covered toast while I poured us both cups of tea.

'I'm rather pleased I'm not at school today,' she said, no doubt thinking of the slippery walk to work. 'Although it's a shame to miss the children's excitement.'

'But not Beamish's concerns about the boiler,' I reminded her. 'I bet he'll be like a bear with a sore head.'

'Now, Hattie,' she tutted, 'when have you ever known him to be anything other than an affable young man? Nothing fazes him. Although,' she added, looking again at my phone, 'there'll be plenty of extra jobs for him to do today, what with gritting the paths and checking the water pipes.'

My mind flitted back to the dodgy tap in the art room which had very nearly been the instigator for more than a wet shirt.

'But I'm sure he'll manage,' Dolly sighed, 'and still be on time to take us to the hall.'

'Oh yes,' I agreed, dismissing the thought of our drenching. 'Wynthorpe Hall is going to look even more perfect now, isn't it?'

'Yes,' she said, her pale cheeks gaining a little colour. 'Let's hope it hasn't all melted away by the end of the day. Was that the post?'

Her mention of the rattling letterbox reminded me of my morning's task. It was now four days since my Christmas card to my parents had set off on its unexpected journey.

'I'll check,' I told Dolly, standing up, 'and would it be all right if I used the house phone to call Jonathan? I promise I'll reimburse you when the bill comes in.'

'Of course,' she said. 'You should know you don't have to ask. And don't worry about bringing the post up, but if you could take the tray down that would be most appreciated. I'm rather comfortable in here so I don't think I'll get up just yet.'

I wasn't sure if she was tactfully staying out of the way while I made my call or if she was genuinely enjoying her lie-in. Either way, I valued the privacy her reluctance to get up afforded me.

'All right,' I said, as I backed out of the room and pulled the door to with my foot. 'I'll see you in a bit.'

Downstairs I picked the post up off the mat – checking there was no missive for me – and then fiddled about with the breakfast things before making myself a strong coffee. For someone who was so keen to come clean, I was certainly dragging my heels. I glanced up at the clock to work out the time difference. It would be after lunch for Jonathan and the last thing he probably needed was an interruption from me. Perhaps I should leave it until later, when I could be certain that he wouldn't be at work? No, I couldn't. I would end up tying myself in knots all through my visit to Wynthorpe Hall and I didn't want anything to mar that.

I might have still been feeling rather sceptical about what Christmas and all its associated traditions and rituals really meant to me, but now, thanks to the Wish List and the school and the snowy scene beyond the window, I could sense that little spark was starting to consistently burn a tiny bit brighter. Had I not made such a mess of a few things it might well have been roaring away, but what I had so far was better than nothing and a darn sight more than I would have had had I decided not to come.

'Jonathan?'

'Hattie, is that you? Is everything all right?'

'Yes,' I said, swallowing down the lie. 'Yes, I just wanted to talk. I've missed you this week and I have something . . .'

'Look, my darling, I'm sorry to cut you off, but I'm just about to go into a meeting. Can I call you back?'

'Of course.'

'Are you sure everything's all right?'

'Yes,' I said, 'sorry. I shouldn't have rung now.'

'It's fine.' He said. 'I'll ring you back in a bit, on the cottage phone, yes?'

'Yes,' I said again, 'that would be great.'

I had known it would be awkward for him to talk during the day and I hoped I hadn't got him into trouble. Taking personal calls was most likely frowned upon, but I just couldn't have put it off any longer.

By the time he called me back the single knot I'd tied myself into had turned into an entire tangle. Thankfully there was still no sign of Dolly and no sound of creaking floorboards overhead so I guessed she must have fallen back to sleep. I was rather pleased she was retiring before my move. A lady of her age deserved to sleep in every now and again.

I snatched up the phone before it had finished its first ring.

'Jonathan?'

'Yes, it's me. I'm sorry about before.'

'That's all right,' I said, sitting in the chair next to the fire which, in view of the chilly weather, I'd already cleaned out, messily remade and fumblingly lit. 'I knew it probably wasn't a good time, but I wanted to talk to you.'

'How's the weather?' he asked before I had a chance to elaborate. 'I checked the forecast first thing and it looked like you might be getting some of the white stuff.'

'Yes,' I confirmed, 'everything was white when I got up this morning and actually,' I added, looking over to the window, 'it's coming down again now.'

'That's something you won't have to worry about over here,' he said and I could hear the smile in his voice. 'It's twenty-seven degrees today.'

'Wow,' I said, trying to imagine the warmth on my skin and the hot breeze caressing my bare legs even though my calendar was flipped to December. 'That sounds wonderful.'

'It is,' he said. 'So, are you home alone then? I'm guessing Dolly's in school. I thought you were going in with her? You aren't sick of all those screaming kids already are you?' He added with a chuckle. 'Have you abandoned ship? I wouldn't blame you if you had.'

'No,' I told him, feeling a little riled. 'Dolly and I have a day off.'

The children at school didn't scream, well not indoors anyway, and I wasn't sick of helping out at all. Far from it, in fact.

'She's still in bed actually.'

'What, at this time? She isn't ill, is she?'

'No,' I said, biting back my annoyance when he was so obviously concerned about my friend. 'She's just tired.'

'That's all right then. I don't want you playing nursemaid as well as childminder during your holiday.'

My irritation began to prickle again. He wasn't quite so concerned about Dolly then, just unhappy about the thought of me pandering to someone other than him. I decided it was time to pull the conversation back to the original reason for my call before I ended up not telling him about the card at all.

'Look, Jonathan,' I began, 'there was a reason why I was ringing.'

'Yes,' he said, 'you did say there was something. What is it?'

'Well,' I said nervously, the words unhelpfully sticking like treacle. 'It was never meant to happen. And I'm so sorry that it has.'

I felt my eyes fill with tears which were of no help at all and my voice caught in my throat.

'Hey,' said Jonathan, 'Hattie. Don't cry, not when I'm so far away. Whatever is it? It can't be that bad.'

'It is,' I sniffed.

'Come on,' he said, 'tell me what's happened and let me decide if it's the disaster you're imagining. I'll bet it isn't.'

'All right,' I said, taking a deep breath. 'You know how I said a few days ago that I was thinking about getting in touch with Mum and Dad.'

'And we decided that you shouldn't.'

'Yes,' I whimpered. 'Well, the thing is. I wrote them a Christmas card. And I had no intention of sending it. Absolutely no intention at all, but . . .'

'But?'

'But,' I said, forcing the words out and cursing over why I had ever thought telling him was so important, 'but it got muddled up with Dolly's pile of cards and was sent in error.'

The other end of the line was suddenly deathly quiet.

'I'm so sorry, Jonathan. It was an accident . . .'

'And have your parents been in touch?'

'No,' I said quickly. 'No. I haven't heard a thing.'

I didn't remind him that the postal service in the UK was stretched to the limit at Christmas and it might not have even arrived until today.

'You're angry, aren't you?' I carried on, filling the gaps where he should have been talking. 'And you've every right to be, especially after we'd discussed it and decided it was a bad idea.'

'I have no idea why you'd even think to write the card in the first place,' he said finally.

It would have been so easy to tell him that it had been Dolly's idea, but I didn't think it would go any way to improving their relationship. It was all very well chatting on the phone and Jonathan sending lavish gifts, but I needed the pair to get along in real life too and if he knew of the part my friend had played in the disaster then that was never going to happen.

'Me neither,' I whispered.

'But that's neither here nor there now, is it?' he carried on. 'And if it's gone, it's gone.'

'But aren't you angry?'

'Well I'm not best pleased,' he said, the disappointment in his voice making me feel even worse, 'but there's no point blowing up about it, is there?'

I felt another rush of guilt as I realised that was exactly what I had been expecting him to do.

'I really am so sorry,' I said, apologising for more than an errant card, even though he didn't realise it.

'I know,' he said, 'you sound utterly miserable and I daresay you're feeling even worse because your parents haven't bothered to respond.'

I hadn't really thought about that, assuming delivery was most likely delayed, but I was relieved that he had taken the news so well.

'Let's just forget about it,' he said. 'You've got more to be thinking about than that.'

'Thank you for being so understanding,' I told him. 'I know it was a silly thing to do and Beamish did try his very best to get it back. He even tried to convince the postman to take it out of the box and give it back to him.'

'Who's Beamish?'

'Sorry,' I said. 'What?'

'You did say Beamish, didn't you? Who's that? It's an unusual name.'

'Oh,' I said, chewing my lip. 'He's a friend of Dolly's. She

told him what had happened and as he knew the local postman, he thought he might be able to help.'

I was talking ninety to the dozen.

'But he couldn't?'

'No,' I sighed, purposefully slowing my chatter down.
'Unfortunately, not.'

'Oh well,' said Jonathan, 'I daresay it was worth a try. Is
this friend of Dolly's an old acquaintance? I don't think I've
heard her mention him before. You wouldn't forget an unusual name like that, would you?'

'I think she's known him a while.' I told him, then added,
'he's the school caretaker.'

It wasn't the sort of job Jonathan would have thought
particularly highly of and I was certain he couldn't imagine
a very young man in the role.

'Right,' he said. 'Well, like I said before, there's really nothing
to be done about it now, so please don't worry. You'll be here
with me before you know it and you'll forget all about your
life back in the chilly UK when you see these blue skies again.'

'I'm really looking forward to it,' I told him.

Some blue sky would be wonderful, but I didn't think I
was going to forget about my life in the UK, especially the
Wynbridge part of it.

'Look,' he said, 'I have to go. I need to get back to work,
but I'll be in touch again soon, OK?'

'OK,' I said, 'I am sorry, you know.'

'I know,' he said back, 'but let's just forget about it now.
Give my love to Dolly.'

'I will, love you.'

'I love you too, more than anything.'

I put the phone back in the cradle as Dolly came slowly down the stairs.

'I wasn't eavesdropping,' was the first thing she said.

'I know you weren't,' I smiled. 'I didn't wake you, did I?'

'No, no,' she said, 'I was already awake. How did he take it?'

I knew then that even though she hadn't been purposefully listening in, she'd heard my side of the conversation.

'Very well,' I said, letting out a sigh of relief. 'He was very good about it, considering.'

'Well that's a relief,' she nodded. 'Perhaps he is a changed man after all.'

'Yes,' I said, smiling, 'perhaps he is.'

Chapter 15

Throughout the rest of the day, the snow showers continued to sweep across Wynbridge topping up the earlier covering just enough to look picturesque, but not enough to cause widespread panic. I knew that if the temperature dipped overnight it would be a different story in the morning, but for now it was picture perfect.

'It's not as cold as you might think,' I said, stamping my feet on Dolly's back doormat to shake off the snow having made an intrepid trip into the garden to replenish the bird table, 'and it's lovely and quiet.'

The blanket of snow had muffled everything and I watched on, smiling, as Dolly hastily added snow to the Wish List, safe in the knowledge that she could tick it straight off again. The list was looking a little idyllic to my eyes now and I couldn't deny that, with the help of the white stuff, some of its charm was beginning to rub off on me.

Thinking over the outcome of my conversation with

Jonathan further lifted my spirits and I couldn't wait for the end of the school day when Beamish would be collecting us for our tour of Wynthorpe Hall.

In fact, I was feeling so much better for coming clean – albeit partially – that I thought the trip might be the perfect opportunity to tell him a little more about my imminent move, as well as who I was going to be making it with. If he knew about Jonathan, I reasoned, then he would be even more inclined to believe that our near-kiss really had been a figment of his imagination.

'He's late,' said Dolly, peering around the curtain the second Beamish was due, 'and he's never late. You don't suppose he's forgotten, do you?'

'Of course not,' I said. 'He was the one who arranged it so that's hardly likely, is it? And,' I quickly added pre-empting her next question. 'I'm sure there's nothing wrong at school either. You said yourself that, given the change in the weather, he'd have extra jobs to do. I daresay he's just checking the boiler or something.'

When Beamish did arrive, barely fifteen minutes later than his ETA, I could see that my soothing words to Dolly had been right; there was obviously nothing wrong at school because he had found the time to go home and change. Watching him walk down the path, I rather wished he hadn't.

'My goodness,' said Dolly, opening the door to let him in. 'Don't you look smart.'

'Thank you, Dolly,' he grinned, ducking his head, only on this occasion not to avoid the low doorframe.

I didn't say anything, but I did give him a surreptitious once-over as I pulled on my coat. He looked for all the world as if he'd stepped off the set of some photo shoot for supersized blokes. He certainly wasn't groomed to the max like Jonathan. Beamish was too rough around the edges to pull off that look, but the chunky jumper his broad chest was encased in would have certainly been comforting to cuddle up against.

I breathed him in, inwardly acknowledging that the woody scent of his aftershave ensured he was a treat for all the senses before realising that my silly crush was springing up again, leaping around my feet like an over-excited puppy demanding a fuss. I pushed it away before it stood to attention.

'Right then,' he said, clapping his hands together and helpfully breaking the spell, 'are we all set?'

'Absolutely,' said Dolly, gathering up her handbag and a Christmas bag with a card and a couple of presents in it. 'I've been wishing the time away all day.'

The lights covering the hall were already lit and as Beamish drove slowly along the drive, Dolly found it hard to contain her excitement. Beamish smiled at me in the rear-view mirror and I smiled back. It was impossible not to.

'Here's Gabe,' said Beamish, his eyes returning to the view ahead.

'And what's that he's got with him?' Dolly gasped. 'Some sort of bear!'

I leant forward to get a clearer look. Given what I'd heard about the hall, I wouldn't have been at all surprised.

'That's his dog, Bran,' Beamish laughed. 'He's an Irish wolfhound and the most placid creature on the planet.'

Both the man, Gabe, and his dog, were of impressive stature and given Beamish's bulk I was beginning to think there was something in the Wynbridge air or water which bred big, broad blokes.

'You can park right in front of the courtyard gate,' Gabe told Beamish as he pulled alongside him. 'And I've salted the path to the kitchen door so it's not slippery.'

'Thank you, young man,' said Dolly regally and I had to stave off a giggle.

The Wynthorpe Hall kitchen was like nothing I had ever encountered. It was vast, high ceilinged, warm, cluttered and full of smiling people, not all of whom I soon realised were family.

'We might not all be related,' said Catherine once she had introduced us to two of her sons and their partners, including Molly who actually was giving off a very witchy vibe, along with the cook, handyman and housekeeper, Hayley (the young woman responsible for designing that ill-fated Christmas card), 'but we're family nonetheless. Angus is about somewhere ...' she added, doing a quick head count.

'I think he's roped Gabe into doing something,' said Hayley, shaking her head.

Gabe was her partner and from what I could make out, Angus was forever getting him, and Mick, the handyman, into all sorts of capers.

'I'm sure he'll catch you up at some point,' said Dorothy, pointing at the clock. 'Now, would you like your tea before or after you've shown Dolly and Hattie around?'

It was decided we should have it after, even though it would be a little late, with Catherine in the morning room. Beamish went off with Mick to see if they could track down Angus and Gabe and Dolly and I went out the other end of the kitchen with Catherine and her soon to be daughter-in-law, Anna.

'Catherine tells me you're staying with Dolly for a few weeks,' she said to me as the two older ladies took the lead into the great hall.

'That's right,' I told her, gazing around at the beautiful wood panelling and vast tree which Dolly was making a beeline for. 'I'm moving to Abu Dhabi in the new year and wanted to spend some time with Dolly before I left. I'm going to miss her.'

'Well,' Anna nudged, 'you haven't gone yet.'

'What do you mean?' I frowned.

'I came here a few Christmases ago,' she explained, 'as a sort of companion to Catherine who was recovering from knee surgery. My contract was only for a few weeks ...'

'But you're still here.'

'I am,' she laughed. 'Within weeks my life was turned upside down by the Connelly clan. I had fallen head over heels in love with Jamie, given up my job and moved in for good. There's something in these Wynthorpe walls which draws folk in,' she said mysteriously.

'In that case,' I told her, 'it's probably just as well I'm staying in town.'

'Oh, I'm pretty certain it's in the Wynbridge air too,' she said seriously. 'You mark my words, Hattie, the longer you're here the harder you'll find it to leave. You're bound to fall in love with it.'

'But I have stayed before,' I told her, thinking that she was perhaps a little too besotted with it all. 'I've holidayed with Dolly at the cottage plenty of times and always managed to leave.'

'Something tells me that this time there's an added attraction.'

This hadn't come from Anna, but Molly who had swept in behind us, her feet making not a sound on the ancient wooden floor.

'Before there was a missing ingredient,' she said dreamily as Anna nodded in agreement. 'But it's here now.'

There was a sudden blast of freezing air as the huge door at the end of the hall was pulled open and Beamish wandered in, giving me a hundred-watt smile with Mick, the handyman, trailing behind him.

'Oh,' laughed Anna, as Molly drifted back in the direction of the kitchen again. 'Right on cue!'

I didn't have the chance to tell either of the two friends that I was already well and truly spoken for, and that I would be moving to Abu Dhabi with the love of my life, because Dolly was beckoning me over to admire the tree and the family decorations adorning it.

All of the decorations throughout the hall were every bit as outstanding as the impressive building and Catherine was kind enough to let us see it all, even the family rooms. The sitting room was my favourite with its squishy sofas, huge open fire and piles of magazines. The whole place was like a National Trust or English Heritage property, but one that was very much lived in. There were layers upon layers of Connelly family life and I loved it.

'Isn't it beautiful?' said Dolly, who had been in awe of everything.

'It is,' I agreed yet again to what had fast become her stock response to every new door that opened.

'It's like a fairy tale,' she told Catherine, who was delighted to have the opportunity to share her home.

'We're very lucky to have it,' Catherine told her, 'and it's such a pleasure to have found ways to let everyone else enjoy it.'

The Winter Wonderland wasn't the only event that happened here. There were other things going on throughout the year and Anna and Jamie ran a charity for bereaved under eighteens from the converted stable block. It didn't seem to matter where I turned in this part of the Fens, there were entrepreneurial folk reviving both the town and the countryside.

A gong sounded somewhere and Catherine cocked her head to listen.

'That'll be Dorothy,' she told us. 'It must be time for tea.'

Back in the morning room the table in front of the fire

had been laid with a lavish tea. There were tiny smoked salmon, egg and cress and cucumber sandwiches on the softest home-baked brown bread, exquisite cakes in pretty cases as well as warm scones and fragrant loose-leaf tea served from a silver pot which had its own little burner underneath.

A couple more dogs had joined the party, a spaniel and a chihuahua, and although the spaniel was giving the illusion of being asleep, the rapid darting of its eyebrows suggested otherwise. Any dropped crumb wouldn't besmear the carpet for many seconds.

'I really can't thank you enough for this wonderful experience,' said Dolly to both Catherine and Anna, once we had eaten and drunk our fill. 'It's been even lovelier than I imagined it would be.'

'I can't believe you've never been before,' said Catherine. 'It was a shame you missed coming with the Women's Institute. Dorothy laid on a wonderful lunch.'

Dolly shifted a little in her seat as I looked at her. I was surprised she'd missed the opportunity too.

'You were poorly, weren't you?' said Anna, sounding concerned.

'It was just a cold,' Dolly said dismissively. 'It's long gone now and to tell you the truth, I'm much happier having seen the hall dressed for Christmas.'

'Well, you are welcome to come anytime,' said Catherine, 'and please don't wait for an invitation. People are always dropping in here. It's how we like it, isn't it, Anna?'

'Definitely,' she agreed.

The sound of talking on the other side of the door stopped the conversation and Anna looked at me and smiled as she picked out Beamish's voice. I pretended I hadn't seen the look she gave me and focused my attention on the inside of my beautifully patterned teacup.

'So how are we getting on in here?' asked a man who strode purposefully into the room, and could only be Angus. 'Have you left a morsel for poor old half-starved me?'

He practically jumped out of his skin as Dorothy bustled in behind him.

'Poor old half-starved you nothing,' she tutted, 'you've just had yours with the boys in the kitchen!'

'Ah Dorothy,' he said, pushing his thumbs behind his braces, 'I didn't see you there.'

'Are you suggesting I haven't filled you up?' She frowned, 'When you almost couldn't manage that last sandwich.'

'No,' he blundered, 'no, of course not.'

'I should think not,' said Dorothy, winking at me before she rushed out again, 'half-starved indeed. The very idea.'

I couldn't help but laugh along as Catherine introduced me to her husband properly.

'Beamish tells me you and Dolly have created a Christmas Wish List,' he said after vigorously pumping my hand in greeting.

His eyes were shining and I could tell he was enthralled by the idea.

'That's right,' said Dolly before I had a chance. 'We've filled it with things Hattie would like to do before she heads off to sunnier climes in the new year.'

'What a wonderful idea,' he said wistfully. 'Catherine,' he added, turning to his wife, 'I wonder ...'

'Well I'd rather you didn't,' she cut in, not unkindly. 'Your wondering generally leads to something monumental, Angus, and I think we've got enough on our plates at the moment, don't you?'

'Perhaps,' he relented. 'Was your visit here today on your Wish List, Hattie?'

'It was,' I said, 'but it was Dolly's addition actually. She was secretly hoping for a private tour.'

'And Beamish arranged it,' smiled Angus as the man himself, Gabe and Jamie filed in followed closely by Bran.

The ample room suddenly felt fit to burst.

'I was hoping to end the visit with a sleigh ride for you,' said Angus, 'but it's still being serviced ahead of the Wonderland. You're more than welcome to take a turn through the woods and around the trail though.'

'That's very kind,' said Dolly, 'but I don't think I will today. It's a bit too cold out there for me and most likely slippery underfoot.'

'How about you then?' Angus asked me hopefully. 'Beamish knows his way around and I'm sure Anna will have some wellington boots you could borrow.'

'Of course,' said Anna, jumping up. 'Come with me,' she commanded, pulling me out of the chair. 'I daresay we're the same size and if we're not there'll be some here that'll more or less fit with a pair of boot socks.'

By the time Beamish and I set off it was rather dark, but it didn't matter as everywhere was so prettily lit. It was freezing though and I was grateful for the loan of a country tweed coat and thick gloves.

'Has Dolly enjoyed herself, do you think?' Beamish asked, striding ahead with me struggling a little to keep up.

We might have been matched in height but he could easily outpace me, especially over the ice.

'Sorry,' he said, slowing down and then, disconcertingly linking arms. 'It's not too slippery, but I'll keep you on your feet should you start to go over.'

'I'm certain she's had an amazing time,' I told him, ejecting the image of us landing in the snow together. 'She was just thanking Angus for the Christmas tree. It really was wonderful of you to arrange all this for her.'

'For both of you,' he said. 'I did it for both of you.'

'Well thank you,' I carried on, looking about me as we left the more formal part of the garden and headed over to what looked like the start of the woodland trail. 'I've had a great time too.'

'This Christmas Wish List was an inspired idea,' he said.

'It was,' I agreed, although I still regretted Dolly's addition about getting back in touch with my parents.

'It's all too easy to go through life not noticing things, isn't it? I mean, lots of things you've added to the list I take a bit for granted now, but having seen them through your eyes, I've appreciated them so much more this time around.'

'Really?'

'Yes,' he nodded. 'Really.'

'I guess it's the simple things in life that really matter, isn't it?'

'Absolutely,' he agreed. 'Accumulating stuff is all well and good for some, but personally I prefer to put my efforts into making memories and having experiences.'

I had surmised that much about him before. Jonathan and his love of material possessions, and how he always used them to try and either end an argument or make someone feel special, popped into my head again, along with my earlier determination to tell Beamish all about him, but now I found I didn't want to.

'Don't you agree, Hattie?'

'I do.'

If I had to choose between the presents Jonathan had showered me with or the excited expressions on the children's faces during the school fair or the thrill of seeing Wynthorpe Hall dressed for the festive season, then I was certain which I would go for.

'I'm sorry about the sleigh ride,' Beamish said, 'that would have been a great memory to take away with you. Perhaps we could come back at the weekend and look around the Wonderland together? By this time tomorrow everything will be in place and looking beautiful. This is where the reindeer are going to go,' he added, pointing to a fenced-off area.

'Reindeer,' I gasped. 'Really?'

'Oh yes,' he smiled. 'There are even polar bears in the grotto in the garden.'

'You're teasing,' I said, pulling my arm away from his, but he wouldn't let me go.

'No, I'm not,' he laughed, 'granted they're animatronic, but they're there. I'll show you on the way back, but the reindeer are real. I promise. Last year there was a calf too.'

'Oh, how lovely.'

Walking around the trail, the path lit to guide the way, I could well imagine just how enchanting it would all be and my own little festive flame shone brighter in the darkness as a result.

'I know it's the bake sale and auction in town on Saturday,' I said, 'but if you think there'll be time to come out here on Sunday, that would be wonderful.'

'I'm sure we can manage it,' said Beamish, 'and if not then, then perhaps the weekend after. Angus and Catherine decided last year that one weekend wasn't long enough, given the effort of setting up and dismantling, so this year they're going to open for two. They'll be stretched to the limit, but they'll pull it off.'

I was sure they would. What a truly wonderful place to live Wynbridge and Wynthorpe Hall was. I took back what I'd thought about Anna being too besotted when I first talked to her because I could see now exactly why she had fallen head over heels for it all. Had I been single . . .

I was shocked by the thought and hastily snuffed it out.

The sooner I saw Jonathan again the better. If I wasn't careful this place and certain folk who lived here were going to turn my head and I didn't want it turned. I was going to marry Jonathan and I was going to build a new life in Abu Dhabi. It was what we had decided, it was what fate had lined up for me.

'Where's that light coming from?' I asked, pointing ahead.

'Oh Hattie,' smiled Beamish, 'with your love of wishes, you're going to adore this.'

We carried on along the path, our breath streaming ahead of us and reaching the large clearing before we did. I could see the area hadn't been cleared on purpose, it was empty because the vast tree at the centre of it was taking up all the space. Lit from beneath, the beams of light illuminated the bare branches. Or were they bare?

'What is it?' I frowned, detaching myself from Beamish and moving closer. 'It looks like there are things tied to the tree.'

'There are,' he told me.

I circled the mighty trunk, spotting keys, letters, cloth flags and various trinkets, some of which looked like they'd been there for years. They moved gently in the breeze, some clashing together but making a melodious sound. I shivered, but not because of the chilly temperature.

'But why?' I whispered. 'What is this?'

'It's a wishing tree,' Beamish explained. 'People come here to make special wishes. Not for silly things like money or a new car, but for things that really matter, things that really mean something.'

'Money matters if you haven't got any,' I said, looking over at him, 'but I know what you mean. Do people think the tree carries some sort of magic?'

Given the peculiar feeling which had coursed through my system when I first stepped into the clearing, I couldn't deny that there was a certain something about the place.

'I guess,' said Beamish. 'Molly's the expert. You need to ask her really.'

I stopped next to him, gazing up into the branches and thinking how my time with Dolly was fast becoming a pilgrimage to wish fulfilment.

'A wishing tree,' I whispered. 'Have you ever made a wish?'

I turned to look at him, only to find he was already looking at me. There was such tenderness in his eyes that it made my breath catch in my chest. I wondered if I should wish he wouldn't look at me like that. I *should* have wished that he wouldn't look at me like that, but I couldn't bring myself to do it.

It suddenly dawned on me that he had wanted me to kiss him the other night. My forbidden feelings for him, if the look on his face was anything to go by and I was certain it was, were reciprocated.

'No,' he said, 'I've never known what to wish for, until now.'

I didn't dare ask what he had come up with.

'Do you really have to move, Hattie?' he then said. 'I mean, you seem so content here with Dolly and working in the school. I can't imagine that you could be any happier living anywhere else.'

'You sound like, Anna,' I smiled, trying to break the spell which held us entranced.

He shook his head.

'This is just a holiday, Beamish,' I said softly, 'this isn't forever.'

'But it could be.'

'No,' I said, 'it couldn't. This isn't real life.'

It certainly wasn't my life.

'But it could be,' he said again.

I shook my head. If I had stuck to my guns and talked about Jonathan this afternoon then Beamish wouldn't have been saying any of this. Knowing what I knew now, having seen the look in his eyes, he probably wouldn't have been talking to me at all.

'This isn't *my* life,' I told him, 'it's just a break until I . . .'

It was on the tip of my tongue to say until I was married to a man as yet unknown to him and we had moved half-way across the world, but Beamish was lowering his head. I ducked away just in time and heard him groan.

'You were going to kiss me,' I gasped.

'No.'

'Yes, you were.'

He scuffed the snow with the toe of his boot.

'Well, so what if I was,' he shrugged, shoving his hands in his pockets, 'you were going to kiss me first.'

'No, I wasn't,' I said sharply. 'I told you that you'd got that wrong and besides, you said you wouldn't have kissed me back because I was moving halfway around the world.'

'Yeah, well.'

'Yeah well, what?' I snapped.

I knew I had no right to sound so affronted but I was feeling even worse about keeping quiet about Jonathan now. All the while I had thought the crush I had developed for Beamish was one-sided I could handle it. Yes, I felt bad for feeling something for another man but now I knew that other man felt something for me, I realised I wasn't the only one at risk of being hurt and it made the situation so much worse.

'Yeah well,' Beamish carried on, 'seeing you standing there with your cheeks glowing and your eyes shining and your hair all messed up, it made me—'

'All right,' I said, self-consciously running my hands through my hair, 'I get the idea.'

I felt even worse that the version of me that Beamish had wanted to kiss didn't really exist anymore. He didn't know the real me. He was looking at the old version Dolly had been so keen to track down and who I would soon be banishing again.

'Just out of curiosity,' he asked, 'if I had have kissed you, would you have kissed me back?'

'No,' I said, 'of course not.'

'Because you're moving halfway around the world or because you wouldn't want to kiss me?'

Now it was my turn to kick up the snow. There were only so many fibs and half-truths I could get away with and I was fast approaching my limit.

'Actually,' he said, 'don't answer that.'

I turned to walk away feeling grateful he hadn't pushed me to reply.

'I hope I haven't ruined your day,' he called after me.

'You haven't,' I called back. 'Of course, you haven't.'

But he had.

Chapter 16

I decided it would be best to give the polar bears a miss.

'All right,' Beamish agreed. 'I suppose we have been gone a while. I'll show them to you when we come back to see the wonderland.'

'I'm not sure we should do that now,' I told him, slipping a little on the path but refusing the offer of his arm.

'Why ever not?'

Because my boyfriend wouldn't like it, because you make me feel things I shouldn't and I think you feel them too, because we can't seem to spend any time alone together without almost falling on each other's lips ...

'Not because of what just happened?' he said, stopping. 'I thought you said I hadn't ruined your day?'

'No,' I said, 'not because of what just *almost* happened.'

'What then?'

'I just don't want ...' I answered, thinking of the ideas Anna and Molly already seemed to have, 'anyone getting the wrong idea about us spending so much time together, that's all.'

'What does it matter what anyone else thinks?' He frowned. 'Besides,' he added, before striding off again, 'we're just friends and given the fact that we're both free and single how much time we spend together is no one else's business, is it?'

I felt my festive flame flicker in the wake of his words.

'But if it helps,' he said seriously, 'I promise I won't try and kiss you again. Let's put what just *almost* happened back there down as a moment of madness, nothing more. Let's say, I was simply seduced by the magic of the Wishing Tree.'

'All right,' I agreed, happy to let it drop. 'No more near-kisses and I'll come to see the wonderland with you.'

'Near-kisses?' He grinned. 'I thought there'd only been one?'

I put my head down and carried on walking.

I returned the clothes and wellies I had borrowed and after we had said our goodbyes back in the hall kitchen, and offered our truly heartfelt thanks for the wonderful visit, Beamish drove Dolly and me back to the cottage. I didn't have to worry about how I was going to fill any awkward silences because Dolly's excitement didn't allow for any. Her steady stream of reminiscing didn't require any input from either Beamish or me and I was grateful that she didn't ask if we had enjoyed our wander around the grounds.

'Are you expecting a parcel?' I asked as we pulled up at the cottage gate and I spotted something propped up against the front door.

'Oh yes,' said Dolly as Beamish helped her out of the truck. 'I'd quite forgotten about that. It's for you, Hattie.'

'Me?'

'Yes.'

'What is it?'

'An early Christmas present.'

'Another one,' I said, thinking of the advent calendar.

'Another one,' she smiled.

'Can I open it now?' I asked.

'No,' she said, 'it's for tomorrow. It's my contribution,' she explained, picking the parcel up as I unlocked the door, 'to ensuring that this Friday the thirteenth is memorable for far happier reasons than the last.'

'What happened on the last?' asked Beamish.

'The poor girl was made redundant from her job,' said Dolly.

'But don't forget,' I reminded her, 'that it was also the day I decided that I was going to move to Abu Dhabi.'

That wasn't strictly true, but the opportunity had presented itself then.

'Crikey,' laughed Beamish. 'That was fast work. You certainly didn't let the grass grow, did you?'

'No,' I frowned, 'I don't suppose I did.'

'I'm guessing it was something you'd been thinking about before you were made redundant?'

'Well actually,' I began, thinking I wouldn't get a better moment to explain.

'Never mind that now,' Dolly cut in, ushering me over the threshold. 'Get the kettle on, will you? I don't think we need worry about supper, but I could do with another hot drink.'

I had gone to bed that night feeling surprisingly excited about the next day. As well as the school Christmas dinner there was also the party in the afternoon. The children's excitement would be at fever pitch and I braced myself to deal with sweaty faces racing around the hall, the odd clash of heads and the prospect of at least one of them throwing up. What I hadn't been expecting were the contents of the present from Dolly.

'I admit,' she said, chewing her lip to stop herself from laughing, 'that it is a little unfortunate, but you have to wear it, Hattie. It's Christmas jumper day.'

'But I can't, Dolly,' I told her. 'As lovely as the gesture is, I can't possibly wear this. It's obscene and the fact that it lights up makes it all the worse.'

Dolly started to laugh and I wandered over to look in the mirror again. The jumper was covered with festive motifs and was very jolly, apart from the unfortunate, but most likely intentional, positioning of two Christmas puddings complete with flashing holly berries.

'The kids won't even notice,' she said stoically.

'It's not the kids I'm worried about,' I said, imagining

the laughs Beamish was going to get out of the situation. 'And you say they won't notice, but I bet some of the older ones will.'

'Perhaps if you put a cardigan over the top,' she suggested, proudly smoothing down her own jumper.

Hers featured a very tasteful Santa and also lit up, but nowhere where it shouldn't.

'If I wear anything over this, I'll absolutely bake. That hall will be stifling this afternoon.'

'And the kids will be so fired up they won't be interested in your jumper by then,' she pointed out. 'You'll be able to take the cardigan off after lunch. I'll see if I've got a thin one. I'm sure I've got a red one that will fit the bill somewhere.'

'If only you could turn the lights off,' I called after her as she went back up the stairs and someone knocked on the door.

'But where would the fun be in that?' she called back. 'Can you answer that?'

I hesitated for a moment and then decided that the reaction of the person standing on the doorstep would be a good indicator of the response I was most likely to get all day. I pulled it open with a flourish and found myself face to face with a giant knitted Rudolph complete with glowing nose.

I looked up as Beamish looked down and he started to laugh.

'Don't,' I said, stepping back to let him in. 'Don't say a word.'

'Well I don't know about your Christmas Wish List,' he smirked, 'but that was definitely on mine.'

'Oh thank you very much,' I said primly.

Given that I was trying to look as unappealing to him as possible after the Wishing Tree moment, lighting up my breasts wasn't the wisest of moves.

'What am I going to do?' I moaned, looking back up the stairs to where I could hear Dolly rifling through her wardrobe. 'This was Dolly's present, but I can't wear it, can I?'

'Well you can't offend her,' he whispered back. 'You'll just have to brazen it out. Perhaps the batteries will run out by the time the bell goes. That might help.'

I checked the time. It was still early so there was some hope.

'Perhaps,' I said, fighting down the urge to reach out and squeeze Rudolph's red flashing nose. 'Anyway, what are you doing here? Is everything all right?'

'I told Dolly that if there was any frost, I'd pick you up this morning. She said she wanted to go in early today and it's a bit dicey out there. Did she not mention it?'

'No,' I said, 'she didn't, but as you're here, you can help me with the breakfast.'

Thankfully Dolly's red cardigan did go some way to covering my embarrassment. In fact, I think I might have got away with it completely had Rose not drawn everyone's attention to the situation during morning break.

'Dolly tells me there's been a rather unfortunate pudding placement,' she laughed. 'Give us a flash!'

I gave everyone a quick glimpse to get it over with.

'Very eye-catching,' said Mr Matthews, who had just wandered in and turned rather pink.

'Hence the cardigan,' I explained, turning red myself. 'The jumper was actually a gift from Dolly,' I added, lest everyone assumed it was something which I had packed from home or purchased on purpose.

'Well I like it,' said Beamish, following in behind Mr Matthews.

'Of course, you do,' said Rose, rolling her eyes.

'What are you going to do this afternoon, Hattie?' Mr Matthews asked. 'You'll be far too hot serving dinners and supervising the party with that extra layer on.'

'I was rather hoping Beamish might turn the heating down a bit.'

'No chance,' he said, ducking out again. 'That thermostat stays exactly as it is and I'll know if anyone's been in the boiler room. I've got the place rigged.'

Mr Matthews was right. As the children excitedly took their place for dinner and pulled their crackers, the noise level as well as the temperature, began to rise. They were all much amused to be waited on by their teachers and TAs and by the time the main course had been served, I was sweltering.

'Take it off for pity's sake,' said Dolly when she spotted me fanning myself with a menu next to the serving hatch. 'No one's going to notice.'

I did as I was told and kept my arms folded until it was

time to clear plates and then I held the stack in front of me. I think my struggle made the meal even jollier for the staff but I was nowhere near as amused.

'We get extra play today, Miss,' said Charlie, one of the boys in my class, as I handed out the snowman-shaped ice creams.

'I know you do, you lucky things. That's so we can all have our dinner.'

'Will you sit in here, on these titchy chairs?' he giggled.

'We will,' I told him.

'However, will Mr Beamish fit on one of these?' he gasped.

'He'll break it,' joined in his neighbour. 'It'll never take his weight.'

I imagined there were going to be more than a couple of faces pressed up against the windows when it was time for us to eat.

'Come on, you two,' I said. 'The sooner you're done, the longer you'll have outside.'

As it turned out, Mr Beamish managed admirably on his chair with his knees peeping above the top of the table. I did notice him shifting a couple of times so he couldn't have been all that comfortable, but he didn't let on.

'Party time!' yelled the children as they were led back into school.

'Party time,' the staff responded, rather less enthusiastically.

By the time the support staff, including Beamish, had

hastily rearranged the hall, set up the snack table, fired up the candy floss machine (which in my opinion was pure madness), found an age-appropriate playlist and checked there were enough prizes for the games, Dolly was looking exhausted.

'Are you all right, Dolly?' I called over to her.

I tried to sound casual so she didn't think I was fussing.

'I'm done in,' she shocked me by saying and I wasn't the only one taken by surprise. A fair few heads swung around in her direction.

'In that case,' said Mr Matthews, sounding more authoritative than I had ever heard him, 'I've got just the job for you.'

Dolly readily accepted his suggestion and initially I wasn't sure if that was because he was the boss or if she was really feeling that tired, but on closer inspection, I decided on the latter.

'Do you think she's all right?' I asked Beamish as Mr Matthews fetched her a chair and sat her down next to the snack table which she was going to be supervising.

'On any other day I'd say yes, but she does look tired, doesn't she?'

'I'm beginning to wonder if having me to stay is a bit too much for her,' I frowned. 'She won't let me do a thing back at the cottage.'

'Oh no,' said Beamish. 'I'm certain that's not it. If any-thing, I think having you there has been a tonic. She was really quite unwell when she caught that cold.'

This cold which had plagued her had been mentioned before, but Dolly had never spoken about it directly to me and I couldn't remember any telephone conversations where she'd sounded bunged up.

'She kept herself shut away for a good couple of weeks,' he went on, 'and of course these last few weeks of term are always heavy going. You've been a great help, Hattie, and think about how energetic she was on the ice.'

That was true. She had positively whizzed around the rink putting many of the youngsters to shame.

'These next few months are going to be such a change for her,' Beamish continued. 'Not coming into school is going to take some getting used to, even if she does keep saying she's ready to give it up. It's all bound to take a bit of a toll.'

'And I should be with her, shouldn't I?' I said, biting my lip. 'That's when she's really going to need me and I'm going to be halfway across the world.'

'You haven't gone yet,' he smiled, nudging me. 'There's still hope.'

Thankfully, there was no time for me to try and work out if there was a hidden meaning behind that comment. Beamish went back to his chores and I didn't have a chance to talk to Dolly either as the hall doors were wrenched open and the children charged in, drowning out the requests from their teachers not to run amok.

'Every year I tell myself I'm calling in sick on party day,' said Rose, less than half an hour later, 'and every year I turn up.'

'It really wouldn't be fair to let everyone else take the strain, would it?'

'No,' she said, 'I suppose not, but my god it's tempting.'

'Here we go, look,' said Paul, who had been trying to get everyone's attention so he could set up a quiet game of pass the parcel, 'reinforcements.'

Three members of the PTA had kindly shown up to help out and just as Paul was on the point of shouting himself hoarse, Alison marched in from reception and gave three sharp blasts on a whistle. The children stopped in their tracks and we quickly corralled them into two circles.

'Run back to class and get my whistle would you please, Hattie?' Paul asked me, looking a little embarrassed. 'I should have thought of it earlier.'

The afternoon was exhausting, but great fun and the children weren't the only ones with sweaty face by the time three o'clock rolled around. Thanks to Dolly being in situ next to the snacks there were far fewer children feeling nauseous than I had expected, and the only injury was a grazed knee.

'Well if you will skid across the floor with bare legs,' I heard Rose saying to a tearful girl as she led her out.

'Not a single clash of heads,' Paul said cheerfully, as the children lined up to go back to class. 'I'd call that a success, wouldn't you?'

As far as I was concerned the whole day had been a success. I'd had a far better time than I imagined I would and I was looking forward to getting home with Dolly and ticking a few things off the Wish List. I was definitely in the swing of it all now; my festive memory slots were filling up fast and keeping busy was helping distract me from mulling over the unfortunate Christmas card incident, my crush on Beamish and my silence about Jonathan.

'How are you feeling?' I asked Dolly as I emptied the last of the snacks which had been subjected to so many hot little hands, into a bin bag.

'Much better,' she said. 'I've thoroughly enjoyed watching you joining in wearing that jumper.'

I'd forgotten all about my flashing boobs.

'I think we can safely tick Christmas clothes off the Wish List,' I laughed. 'And Christmas party.'

'Yes,' she smiled back. 'This wasn't quite what I had in mind when we added that one, but this afternoon just about covers it.'

'And tomorrow it's the bake sale and auction in town. I can't wait to see those.'

'Steady on,' said Dolly, still smiling, 'you're beginning to sound almost enthusiastic about it all.'

'I think she's found her festive mojo at last,' laughed Rose, who was sweeping nearby.

'And don't forget we're going to see the Winter Wonderland,' Beamish reminded me. 'I've got a match tomorrow afternoon, but after that I'm at your disposal.'

'Lucky Hattie,' said Rose, waggling her eyebrows.

'And there'll be another advent candle lit on Sunday,' said Dolly, ignoring Rose. 'And the carol concert Monday evening.'

'Well, there you are then!' I laughed. 'You lot are positively smothering me in all this festive cheer, so it's little wonder I'm finding my Christmas spirit, is it?'

Chapter 17

I slept from the moment my head made contact with the pillow that night until Dolly came in with a cup of tea the next morning.

'Morning, Dolly,' I yawned, snuggling down even deeper into the warm, soft bed. 'What time is it? Have I overslept?'

'Not really,' she told me, kindly keeping her voice low so as not to pull me too far out of my delicious slumber. 'But I'll be leaving in a minute and I didn't want you to wake to an empty house.'

'Of course,' I said, 'it's the auction and bake sale today, isn't it?'

'Yes,' she confirmed, 'and I'm getting a lift into town to help get things set up.'

'You aren't going to be on your feet baking all day, are you?' I asked, finally opening my eyes properly.

As well as selling cakes, I knew that the town hall would be opened up to anyone who wanted to try their hand at a bit of festive baking and Christmas cookie decorating. I was surprised Dolly hadn't added it to the list as an event for me to take part in.

'No,' she said. 'Jemma from the Cherry Tree and her team are in charge of baking. I'm serving teas.'

Not baking then, but on her feet all day nonetheless.

'I bet it's going to be busy, isn't it?'

'Oh yes,' she nodded. 'It's hugely popular. Practically the whole town turns out today.'

'Please don't overdo it, Dolly,' I pleaded. 'Yesterday was hard work and you really should be putting your feet up today.'

She laughed and headed back towards the stairs.

'There'll be plenty of time for me to do that in a few days,' she reminded me. 'I'll see you later, won't I?'

'Of course,' I said, sitting up and turning on the bedside light. 'I'm very much looking forward to it. I wouldn't dream of missing out on all the fun. I'll even help serve teas with you if you like.'

'That would be very much appreciated,' she smiled, 'and if there's a space, you might even try your hand at transforming a cookie or two.'

The list wasn't completely forgotten then.

'And watch out for Beamish,' she added, 'he's on mistletoe duty this morning before his match. Apparently, it's been a bumper year!'

Dolly left a little while later and I indulged in a far lazier start to the day than usual while mulling over the best route around the square which could keep me furthest away from the greenery sale. Not that, given what he'd said, I was really expecting Beamish to attempt another kiss, but it was better to be safe than sorry.

I sang along with the radio as I made my breakfast, almost wishing it really could be Christmas every day, and then had a long bath. I had the feeling that this weekend was going to be the pinnacle of my stay in Wynbridge. Whether that was because there was so much going on, because I was feeling relieved that my parents hadn't responded to my card and I wouldn't have to tell Jonathan what they'd said about it, or because I'd finally rediscovered my love of Christmas, I couldn't be sure, but I was feeling happier than I had in a very long time.

Happily humming away, I styled my hair into a messy bun, piled on plenty of insulating layers, added a swipe of rose-tinted lip gloss, (more a concession to the Wynbridge wind than vanity), and was good to go.

'See you later, Tiddles,' I called over my shoulder as I grabbed my cottage key and bag and opened the door.

'I seriously hope that isn't a new nickname for Dolly,' said a voice I recognised.

'Jonathan,' I gasped. 'Oh my god! What on earth are you doing here?'

I couldn't believe my eyes. I stood, rooted to the spot and feeling rocked to my very core. I blinked, twice, and looked again. He was still there.

'Freezing on the doorstep at the moment,' he half smiled. 'Are you going to let me in?'

'Yes,' I said, taking a step back. 'Of course, yes. Crikey. Sorry. It's just such a shock to see you. I can't believe it.'

'A good shock, I hope?' He frowned.

I realised that I hadn't leapt on him, thrown my arms around him or smothered him in passionate kisses, each, if not all of which, were most likely the reactions he had been expecting, but the shock of opening the door and finding him standing there had halted me in my tracks.

'Of course, it's a good one,' I laughed, putting my key and bag back on the table and reaching out to him.

'I was rather hoping that you'd throw yourself at me,' he said, confirming my thoughts as he looked into my eyes and wrapped me in his arms, 'but I can see now that you obviously haven't got the energy.'

I wasn't sure what he meant by that and didn't try to fathom it out as I succumbed to a long and lingering kiss. I was deep in shock and my head was all over the place so I assumed that was why the kiss didn't elicit the knee-weakening, butterfly-awakening feelings I usually experienced when he swept me into his arms.

'You weren't really just going out, were you?' he throatily asked, sounding a little breathless and thankfully unaware of my somewhat passionless response to our reunion.

I wished I felt as seduced as he sounded, but then I supposed I'd come back to life in a minute.

'Yes,' I said, thinking of the market square and my promise to help with the teas. 'I was heading into town.'

'What, like that?' Jonathan asked, letting me go and

taking in my hair, face and clothes in one disparaging look up and down.

'What's that supposed to mean?'

'Sorry,' he said, unbuttoning his jacket. 'That probably didn't come out right.'

There was no *probably* about it.

'It's just that you don't really look like *you*, Hattie, that's all.'

'How do you mean?' I asked, looking down at my multiple layers of wind-defying clothes.

'Well,' he said, 'you're usually so smart. You never leave the flat, not even to buy milk, unless you've done your hair and make-up.'

So, it wasn't my well-padded figure he was referring to, but my face. I should have been offended, but having so recently decided that all the effort I used to put into getting done up to go out had been a waste of time, I knew he wasn't aware of my change of heart and shrugged his comment off. Now I would rather save the contents of my make-up bag for special occasions, as opposed to trips to Tesco Metro, but of course Jonathan hadn't been brought up to speed about that yet.

'I'm wearing lip gloss,' I pointed out.

'Sorry,' he said. 'I'm not criticising.'

His tone suggested he was.

'What are you doing then?' I remarked.

I suppose his surprise was only to be expected. The version of me standing in front of him, wasn't the one he was familiar with at all and given his preoccupation with style, labels and how he wanted the world to see him, us really, I supposed it was a bit of a wonder to find me on my way out looking like I'd made zero effort at all.

'Shall we start again?' he suggested. 'Unless you really are in a rush to get off somewhere?'

'I was,' I told him, taking off my coat again. 'But I'm not now.'

I was crushingly disappointed to have my plans scuppered and I felt incredibly guilty for feeling it. The man I was going to be spending the rest of my life with had just undertaken an extraordinarily long journey to pay me a surprise visit and I was smarting over missing out on serving some teas in the town hall.

'I'm still amazed that you're even here.' I said, trying to inject some enthusiasm into my voice. 'I thought you were staying in Abu Dhabi for at least another week.'

'That was the original idea,' he said, heading towards the stairs, 'but there's been a bit of a change of plan.'

'Right,' I said, 'I see. Well it really is lovely to see you.'

I hoped that didn't sound like an afterthought.

'Well, that's a relief,' he smiled, 'for a second when you answered the door, I thought you were going to close it again. Now, I'm just going to freshen up, so why don't you make us some coffee, the good stuff I sent, and then I'll tell you what's going on?'

'All right,' I smiled back, watching him awkwardly negotiate the narrow stairs and thinking how he didn't fit into the fabric of the place at all. Beamish on the other hand was double his width and yet moved freely within the confines of the cottage.

I had just finished filling the cafetière when I heard, rather than saw, Jonathan coming back down.

'Jesus,' he swore as his head made crunching contact with the beam at the bottom of the stairs. 'God, I hate this place.'

I didn't comment.

'I don't know how you've managed to stay here,' he groaned, rubbing at the vivid red mark across his forehead. 'You're almost as tall as I am. How the hell have you coped? It's so fucking cramped.'

I winced at his choice of word, remembering I had used it myself when I first arrived, before Beamish corrected me. However, I refused to feel offended by Jonathan's mean-spirited comment because in the past I had bumped my head plenty of times in the same spot, so I knew exactly how much it hurt.

'I've learned to duck,' I told him, setting the coffee down at the table.

'I take it Dolly isn't here?' he said as I set out two cups.

'No, she left early for town,' I sighed. 'There's lots happening here today.'

'You're not wrong,' he tutted. 'My stupid satnav took me around the market square and it was full of shouting yokels, dragging trees and bundles of holly about. The place was heaving. It really is a little bit country around here, isn't it?'

'That's because it is the country.'

He gave me a look, but didn't answer back.

'It's the day of the Christmas tree auction,' I explained, trying to curb my annoyance. 'It's a charity fundraising event and Dolly is helping out.'

'She's certainly a fan of the season, isn't she?' he said, looking about him, 'and that tat on the front lawn—'

I flinched again.

'Don't you like the decorations?' I interrupted. 'I helped her put them up.'

'You?' Jonathan burst out laughing. 'My tasteful Hattie was responsible for this tacky tinsel fest.'

I poured the coffee into the cups before I succumbed to the urge to pour it over his head. No wonder Dolly and Beamish had been so affronted by some of my comments when I first arrived in town. I had moaned about both the cottage and the decorations and now, hearing my own words echoed back to me, I could appreciate exactly how rude I had been.

'Yes,' I said, 'I was. I rather like it all actually.'

'Good god,' Jonathan spluttered. 'I knew this so-called holiday was going to be a disaster.'

'And you still think that, do you?' I asked peevishly.

I really wanted to feel pleased to see him, but he just kept rubbing me up the wrong way. My brief time back in Wynbridge had peeled off some of the pretentious layers which matched me to my other half and it was going to take me a little while to reattach them.

'Oh, come on, Hattie,' Jonathan laughed. 'You only have

to look in the mirror. Staying here with Dolly was one thing, but getting roped into working at the school well, that's clearly taken it out of you. This is exactly the reason why I don't want us to have kids. If you look like this after a few days of looking after other people's, can you imagine the state you'd be in if we had our own?'

'I see.'

'You can understand why I want it to always be just the two of us, can't you?' He said, reaching for my hand and stroking the back of it. 'Hattie and Jonathan against the world, that's always been the plan, hasn't it?'

Had it? I knew it had been his, but had it *really* been mine too? Looking at him, sitting there, in his expensive clothes and with his manicured hands and groomed hair, I wondered if I had simply been caught up first with the hotel changes and then in his world which matched them. Had I just gone along with his so-called plan because I had been so in awe of him?

I had been both astounded and flattered when he kept pestering me, of all people, for a date and I couldn't believe my luck when the relationship turned serious. For a long time, I had thought someone like him was out of my league, now for the briefest moment, I wished he had been. But of course, had he not arrived out of the blue, I wouldn't be feeling this way. If I had been able to prepare to pick up the threads of my life with him, I would have had my mindset as well as my messy hair back under control in plenty of time.

'Yes,' I said. 'That's always been the plan.'

Heidi Swain

I turned my hand over and grasped his.

'But you still haven't said what you're doing here,' I prompted, ignoring the fact that there was no tingle.

I couldn't help remembering that when he had come to the cottage after our big bust-up and begged me to forgive him and move in with him, he had vowed he'd never visit the place again and yet here he was. I had assumed he hadn't wanted me to visit Dolly again because of the bad memories he associated with my last trip here, but I must have been wrong.

'Everything at work is all right, isn't it?' I asked.

'Couldn't be better,' he grinned, letting go of my hand and picking up his coffee. 'I got through a tonne of work in the last few days and decided to come back early. I've missed you so much and since you said about working in school, I have to admit I've been worried about you. It must be tiring, Hattie.'

'It is,' I admitted, 'but it's also great fun.'

'I'm sure you think it is,' he said, 'but at this rate you'll need a holiday to get over your holiday and I need you ready for this move. There are going to be lots of people for you to meet when we get out there and there'll be parties to host and to go to.'

'I'm certain I'll be able to manage,' I said, giving him a genuine smile as my stomach bubbled with the first flicker of excitement at the thought.

Jonathan's 'just the two of us' ethos had often meant we were on our own but clearly that was all set to change and I rather liked the thought of making connections with other

242

folk as soon as we moved. They might even become a circle of friends who could help me in my quest to find another job.

'That's all right then,' he smiled back, 'and as I'm here in the UK again now, I thought you might as well come back to the flat with me. Take some proper time out to get over this so-called holiday before the move.'

'What?'

'I want you to leave with me, Hattie. Today.'

I put my cup down and stared back at him. For a second, I thought he was joking, but he sounded deadly serious and there was no smile on his lips now.

'We've still got to decide what we want to ship out with us,' he added when I didn't say anything, 'I need you at home and you did say you'd try and cut your visit short.'

I didn't much want to be reminded of that.

'But Dolly and I have things planned for next week,' I told him, thinking of the Wish List and Dolly's last few days in school. 'We still have things we want to do.'

'I'll speak to Dolly,' he said.

I really didn't appreciate his assumption that his pronouncement was a *fait accompli*.

'No,' I snapped.

'But—'

'No, Jonathan.' I snapped again. 'Look, I'm delighted to see you and everything but I really don't like you just breezing in here and thinking you can take over. I'm quite capable of organising these last few weeks for myself, thank you very much and I know exactly how I want to spend them.'

'But I just thought—'

'I'm not sure you thought at all.'

Jonathan looked a little stunned, as well he might, he wasn't used to me standing up to him quite so forcefully. I was a little surprised myself. Not all that long ago I would have gone along with what he wanted, convinced myself that I wanted it too, but not now. I had no intention of putting up with him waltzing in and bossing me about. Was this Jonathan's arrogant alter ego who had rocked up, the one we had banished, or was this how he always spoke to me? Either way, I wasn't going to put up with it.

'Look,' I said, trying to moderate my tone so as not to shock him further. 'I can appreciate that you want to get ready for the move and it really means a lot that you've been so worried about me.'

'It's only because I care,' he muttered, sounding a little sulky, 'because I love you so damn much.'

I was half expecting him to remind me that, given the mess I'd made with the Christmas card, I wasn't actually all that capable of organising anything, but thankfully he didn't.

'I know it is,' I nodded. 'And I love you,' I told him, 'but I'm not ready to leave yet. Dolly retires next week and I'm going to be here for her, OK?'

Jonathan didn't comment.

'I'm not going to miss that, Jonathan. It's the whole reason why I'm here.'

Still nothing.

'How about we check into a hotel?' I tried. 'How about

we go to a nice hotel in Peterborough for the weekend and make the most of the next couple of days.'

'I suppose we could,' he shrugged, looking about him. 'Anything would be better than staying here.'

I bit my lip and nodded.

'It would be cramped in here with the three of us,' I said tightly.

Four if Beamish turned up. Even just the thought of Beamish turning up made my stomach roll again, but not in a good way. I hoped there were enough trees in town to keep him occupied until his rugby match. The last thing I needed was him and Jonathan running into each other. Then I really would have some explaining to do.

'I'll get changed and grab a few things,' I said quickly. 'Then I'll go and tell Dolly what's happening and we can leave right away.'

Jonathan pulled his phone out of his pocket.

'I'll see if I can get us a room somewhere,' he said, still sounding a little sulky.

'You won't get a signal in here,' I reminded him, 'best wait until we're on our way.'

He threw his phone down on the table and huffed.

'I really don't understand what you see in this place,' he scowled. 'I just don't get it at all.'

Chapter 18

'Here you are, at last,' said Dolly, as soon as she caught sight of me. 'I'd all but given up on you. Did you get waylaid? I hope Beamish hasn't been making a nuisance of himself with the mistletoe.'

I wished she wouldn't keep mentioning Beamish and mistletoe in the same sentence.

'Is it busy out there?' she asked, tossing me a snowman patterned apron.

The town was busy and full of music and laughter. As I had rushed through the market square it had looked every bit as Hallmark Christmas Channel perfect as I had imagined it would, but I hadn't had the chance to take it all in or linger around the auction which I could hear was well underway.

Dolly looked up at me and took in my expression.

'What on earth's the matter?' she demanded, when I made no attempt to answer her questions or put the apron on. 'Are you all right? You look as though you've seen a ghost.'

'It's Jonathan,' I said huskily.

'What about him?' she asked as she lined up more cups and saucers.

I cleared my throat.

'He's here, in Wynbridge. He turned up on your doorstep just as I was about to come and find you.'

I supposed I should have been grateful that I had still been at the cottage. I could only imagine how much he would have hated having to try and find me amongst the throng of *yokels* he so clearly had no time for.

'Well, I never,' gasped Dolly. 'Out of everything you could have said, Hattie, that was the last thing I expected.'

'Snap,' I readily agreed.

'Is he coming in?' she asked, looking over my shoulder. 'He'll have a job to park. I hope you gave him the good coffee.'

Evidently, Jonathan's recent charm offensive had worked wonders on my friend and her attitude towards him had undergone a total transformation. When I had arrived on her doorstep a year and half ago, desperate and distraught, she had been justifiably furious with him, then guarded and suspicious when I moved into the flat but now, thanks to a fancy hamper and an appropriate reaction to my faux pas with a Christmas card, she was insisting he drank 'the good coffee'. I couldn't help thinking she would have given him a far warmer welcome than I had, had she been the one to open the cottage door. It was just as well she would never know what he had said about her lovely cottage and the town.

'No,' I told her, 'he's not coming in. Not today.'

'Are you sure you're all right?' she asked again as I handed back the apron.

'I think I'm just in shock,' I admitted, 'he really was the last person I was expecting to see.'

'I can imagine,' she laughed. 'He didn't happen to go down on bended knee when you opened the door, did he?'

'No,' I swallowed. 'Of course not.'

'Is he planning to stay long?'

'No,' I wasn't going to mention how he thought he could just breeze in and whisk me away. 'Just for the weekend.'

'In that case,' she mused, as she added milk to the cups, 'you'll have to nip round to the butcher. I don't think I'll be able to stretch the dinner to three. Go and see what Frank's got left and stick that chicken in the freezer, would you, Hattie dear?'

'There's no need,' I said, wishing there was an easier way to break it to her. 'We won't need dinner. We're going to a hotel.'

'A hotel?'

'In Peterborough most likely,' I said. 'But I'll definitely be back in time for school on Monday.'

'But what about today?' she said sadly. 'You're going to miss out on all the fun.'

'I know,' I said, stepping aside to let more people through, 'but I think Jonathan wants . . .'

She clapped her hands together and gasped; all trace of disappointment banished.

'Of course,' she grinned. 'Say no more. He wants some proper time for just the two of you, I understand. He's going to ... oh Hattie. I hope you've packed something lovely to wear.'

'You know I didn't think of that,' I told her.

'How could you not?' she scolded. 'It's obvious, isn't it?'

'Yes,' I said, 'yes I suppose it is now you've pointed it out. I better go,' I added, feeling a little numb, 'before he gets a parking ticket.'

'All right,' she said, happily waving me off. 'I'll see you Monday morning. Have a lovely time!'

I rushed back to the side road where Jonathan had parked feeling a little dazed and wondering if the next time I saw the market square I was going to be engaged.

'You're very quiet,' Jonathan commented as we joined the steady flow of main road traffic heading towards Peterborough. 'Did Dolly give you a hard time?'

'No,' I said, 'of course she didn't. She was sorry to have missed you though. You will pop in and say hello when you drop me off, won't you?'

'Of course,' he said, smoothly changing up a gear. 'Besides, if you change your mind about coming back with me, I'll have to come in to help you with your things, won't I?'

'I'm not going to change my mind,' I snapped.

'I'm only joking,' he laughed, cutting me off before I launched. 'It was a joke.'

I took a sideways look at him. The tense set of his jaw suggested that it wasn't. I turned to look out of the window at the flat and far-reaching landscape. I really didn't want to argue. If only he would just lay off the silly comments long enough for me to fall back into step with him then everything would be fine.

We'd got on like a house on fire all the time we were messaging and Skyping so I couldn't understand why things between us felt so tense now we were face to face. Perhaps Dolly's assumption was right, maybe he was gearing up to propose and his nerves were getting the better of him. Not that Jonathan was usually prone to nerves but a proposal of marriage was quite a big thing.

'It's a godforsaken place, isn't it?' he said, following my gaze.

'You wouldn't say that if you'd seen the sunsets.'

'Well,' he said, 'whatever. Look, we'll be there in a bit. Do you want to fix your hair or something? While you were talking to Dolly, I managed to book us into somewhere really rather special and you might not want to turn up looking like that.'

I reached into the footwell for my bag and began going through the motions. It was hard work trying to keep my mouth shut but I knew it would be for the best in the long run. Apparently, my brief time under Dolly's roof and my banter with Beamish had brought out a feisty spark in my personality but I was going to have to tone it down a little if I wanted my relationship with Jonathan to steer a steady course on settled seas again.

'Not that you don't look lovely as you are,' Jonathan carried on, 'but, well, you'll see when we get there.'

Annoyingly, he was right. I wouldn't have wanted to turn up at the seventeenth-century luxury spa hotel looking windswept from Wynbridge. The grand exterior was imposing and dominated the landscaped grounds, and inside five-star indulgence awaited me.

'An entire suite,' I couldn't help grinning as Jonathan checked us in.

'And every spa treatment you can imagine,' he smiled back. 'I thought I'd start with a massage,' he added, 'to sort my spine and alignment after my collision with Dolly's low beam.'

The rooms were heaven – a huge canopied bed, extensive views, an open fire and a bath which was easily big enough for two – and it soon became obvious that Jonathan had one thing on his mind once we'd taken it all in.

'God I've missed you,' he groaned, looking down at my naked body after quickly relieving me of my clothes.

I ran my hands over the muscles of his back and wrapped my legs tightly around him, then pulled him down and into me in one smooth movement. His body was toned to perfection and the weight and warmth of him as he began to move promised an exquisite few hours to come.

'I've missed you too,' I gasped as he covered his mouth with mine and began to move faster.

An afternoon spent with a lover as competent as Jonathan would leave anyone feeling satisfied, but I couldn't help thinking, as I slipped out of the bed and went to run a bath, that there was something a little off. Some part of me that he hadn't reached. Sexually I was sated, but there was something else, something I couldn't put my finger on, but which left me feeling a little disconcerted nonetheless.

I crept back to where I'd dumped my bag and watched him sleeping. He was completely relaxed, his arm thrown across the bed and his chest rising and falling in long, deep breaths. He looked the same and physically he had felt the same, so perhaps it was me who was different not him. I quietly picked up my bag, pulled out my phone and went back to the bathroom.

There were missed calls and messages from a mobile I didn't recognise and I wondered if it was Beamish. Perhaps Dolly had given him my number and he wanted to confirm our Sunday plans to visit the Winter Wonderland. Had I thought of it I would have asked her to cancel the date on my behalf. I didn't dare check to see if my suspicions were right. Not with Jonathan asleep just metres away. Not that there was likely to be anything incriminating on my phone because I hadn't done anything wrong, but I would hate him to wake up and think I had snuck off to the bathroom to check my messages out of sight. I quickly turned the phone off and tossed it back into my bag before lowering myself into the bubble-filled tub.

'You all right in there, Hattie?'

I came to with a start and realised that I must have drifted off. For a moment I wasn't sure where I was and then I turned and saw Jonathan standing naked, with mussed up hair in the doorway.

'I'm very all right,' I said, 'thank you very much.'

'Room for a little one?' he asked suggestively.

'I suppose I could shift over a bit.'

I drained some of the water, refilled it with hot and added a few more bubbles. There was something very stirring about being in the water, but in spite of my best efforts to enjoy myself as much as Jonathan obviously was, I couldn't quite get there and ended up faking it. It was something I had never done before. He was certainly none the wiser, but I felt rotten.

'How about,' he suggested, as he laid back and watched me climb out and wrap myself in the biggest, fluffiest towel imaginable, 'we don't go down to dinner tonight. Let's have it served here.'

'But what about your massage? You haven't forgotten about that, have you?'

'What you've just done has pretty much sorted my alignment,' he grinned. 'I'll have it tomorrow instead.'

I was going to remind him that I didn't want to be too late heading back to Wynbridge and that there probably wouldn't be all that much time for pampering by the time we'd had breakfast but didn't want to spoil the moment. This, in spite of the unusually unsatisfactory sex, was the most it had felt like 'us' since I opened Dolly's front door and found him standing there. Surely it was better to nurture that feeling, than kill it dead?

'All right,' I agreed, 'but can we eat early? I'm absolutely famished.'

Chapter 19

Jonathan slept far better that night than I did, but in spite of that I could tell he was in a bit of a grump the next morning by the way he threw back the covers and disappeared into the bathroom. The proposal Dolly had predicted had still to materialise and I couldn't really imagine that he was going to ask me today, not if his less-than-sunny early-morning attitude was anything to go by.

'Are you looking forward to your massage?' I asked when he finally reappeared, his hair damp from the shower.

'What?'

'Your massage,' I said again. 'In the spa.'

'Oh yeah,' he shrugged. 'I guess.'

'I thought I might come with you.'

I didn't particularly fancy it to be honest, but if sticking together helped alleviate his bad mood then I would give it a go. Having me glued to his side was usually just how he liked things.

'What's wrong?' I asked when he didn't say anything.

'Nothing.'

'I daresay you're feeling a bit jetlagged.'

'It's not that,' he interrupted a little sharply.

So, it was something then. I waited for him to elaborate.

'I just wish we had longer together, that's all.'

'I'm sorry about that,' I told him.

I was still annoyed I hadn't thought to cancel my Winter Wonderland plans but was relieved that I had had the sense to factor in some wriggle room when I told Dolly I would be back in Wynbridge in time for school the following morning.

I supposed if Jonathan really put his parts on then I could extend our stay in the hotel for another night, so long as we left first thing in the morning and I was at the school gate before the bell went.

'I still don't see what's so important that it's stopping you from coming back to the flat with me today.'

I hadn't factored in *that* much wriggle room. I opened my mouth to tell him about the Wish List and Dolly's reason behind suggesting it, but stopped. Jonathan wouldn't understand. He wouldn't get it at all.

'Come on,' he said peevishly when I didn't answer. 'I'm starving. I want to go down to breakfast. Hurry up, will you?'

The breakfast was every bit as lavish as the rooms. One of the waiting staff ticked our room number off the list, showed us to a table and began to run through the help yourself set-up.

'We know the drill,' Jonathan grumbled.

I watched the young girl turn red.

'And I used to work in a hotel,' I told her with a supportive smile, 'so I know how these things work.'

She nodded, her cheeks flushed pink.

'It's hotel policy, to explain everything,' she mumbled, then took our drink order and scurried away.

'What did you have to say that for?' Jonathan demanded.

'What?'

'That you worked in a hotel.'

To make up for your rudeness, was what I wanted to throw back at him, but I didn't.

'Does it matter?'

It sounded very much to me like he was embarrassed that I had mentioned it. It hadn't bothered him before. Perhaps he didn't think working in a hotel matched his new and loftier position of employment.

'For all that poor girl knows,' I said lightly, 'I could have been manager of a whole chain of hotels.'

Jonathan looked at me, then pushed back his chair and stood up. I hoped he'd feel better with a few carbs whizzing around his system.

'If you want your eggs cooked differently,' another staff member said to me, as I dithered over the hotplates, 'just ask. Chef will be happy to cook whatever you fancy; however, you like it.'

Full marks to the staff for making the guests feel like a priority, our every whim was quite literally catered for. I was impressed.

'It's not that,' I said. I could see the eggs were poached to perfection. 'I just can't decide whether to have one or two.'

My plate was already modestly covered with crisp bacon, a very tasty-looking local sausage and grilled tomatoes.

'I'd have two,' the guy smiled, 'then give it an hour or so and swim it off in the pool.'

'That sounds like a very good idea,' I laughed, adding a couple of the eggs to my plate.

'What the hell are you doing?' Jonathan hissed at my side.

The waiter had fortunately turned to talk to someone else so didn't catch my companion's aggressive tone.

'Choosing my breakfast,' I said, 'I'm sorted now.'

Jonathan looked at my plate with a cold stare. He'd gone for muesli and a large glass of freshly squeezed orange juice. Just a few weeks ago I would have had the same. I blamed Dolly for my increase in appetite and love of a good cooked breakfast. This morning I thought I was likely to need it more than ever and was grateful she'd shown me the error of my ways when it came to knowing what to eat according to the schedule. Obviously, it wasn't something I tucked into too often, but it had become a firm favourite on heavier going days.

'Are you seriously going to eat all that?' Jonathan snapped, 'or were you just tempted over here by the pretty waiter who showed you some attention?'

I looked at him wide-eyed and realised that he wasn't simply hangry, it was the Jonathan from the dim and distant past who had woken up in the bed next to me. But where on earth had he sprung from and, more importantly, why?

'Of course, I'm going to eat it,' I said, quickly walking away in the hope that he would follow. 'You said yourself that you were hungry, well, so am I.'

My pot of tea and Jonathan's coffee were already at the table.

'When the hell did that silly girl bring this?' he barked, his eyes searching the room for the culprit. 'It's most likely cold now.'

It wasn't cold at all and I knew she would have rushed over with it to avoid having to talk to us again. I couldn't blame her. If I had the option, I would have avoided us, or at least one of us, too.

'I don't know how you can eat that,' Jonathan moaned as I tucked in. 'No wonder you've packed the weight on.'

I didn't think I had put any weight on. I'd hardly been sitting around twiddling my thumbs during my time with Dolly, but knew it was easier to let him rant than try and stop him mid-flow. I would just have to let him blow himself out and hope that the person administering his massage knew what they were about.

'I was going to suggest we had a swim later,' he said, when I didn't get upset about the weight jibe, 'but you'll sink if you go in after that lot.'

My prolonged silence seemed to do the trick, and I was pouring the last of the tea before he spoke again.

'Look,' he said, pushing aside the crockery and glasses so

he could hold my hand across the table. 'I'm sorry, all right. I know I've been a bit grumpy this morning.'

A bit!

'But I am tired from travelling and I thought that if you came back with me today, then that would be it. I wouldn't have to worry about anything other than work and packing and I certainly wouldn't have to drive out to the back of beyond again to pick you up.'

I sighed and let him hold my hand. This sudden re-emergence of the Jonathan of old was a direct result of him not getting his own way, the perfect example of a fully-grown man having a toddler tantrum. Doubtless he had been expecting me to say I'd go along with what he wanted when I woke up and was moping because I hadn't backed down.

I was more than disappointed that he wasn't keeping the promises he'd made, and that I'd been so sure of, the evening Beamish and I went to the pub, but there was no way I was going to be manipulated into changing my mind. I might not have been away from Jonathan for all that long, but I had already discovered I had changed quite a bit and he had better start coming to terms with the stronger, more independent version of me otherwise he was going to be stuck with a baby he didn't want. Himself.

'I have no more luggage now than when I came,' I told him reasonably, 'so there's absolutely no reason why you have to worry about making the journey again. I'm more than capable of getting myself back. I mean, I made it here all right, didn't I?'

Clearly, that was not what he was hoping to hear and I remembered how he had tried to sow those seeds of doubt about my ability to travel solo on the day I came to Wynbridge.

'I'm going straight to the spa,' he said coldly, withdrawing his hand and standing up. 'I'll see you back in the room.'

Safe in the knowledge that he was having his knots untied elsewhere, I locked myself in the bathroom, and turned my phone back on. I quickly scanned the messages, which were from Beamish, including one explaining that Dolly had told him I had decided to take myself off to explore more of the local landscape.

He thought it was an odd time to go, what with the auction and our plans to visit the Wonderland, but still kindly listed a few local landmarks he thought it would be worth my while seeking out. I wondered why Dolly had decided not to mention Jonathan when she explained my untimely disappearance from the town. Surely, it would have been the perfect opportunity to drop him into the conversation. But then, why should she? Jonathan was my partner, not hers. Perhaps, like me, she also felt it was a little too late to announce him.

Knowing Jonathan might not be much longer I quickly flicked to my email account. I gasped in surprise when I saw one from Mum sitting in my inbox. I stared at it for at least a minute and then, with shaking hands, sat on the floor, my back against the bath, and opened it.

I read it once, quickly, scanning the words and then,

because I thought I must have missed something, tried again. I took my time over each and every sentence two, three, four times, my breakfast churning in response. Surely this couldn't be right. There had to be some mistake. Lots of mistakes. Was this even from my mother? I could hear her voice narrating as I read it, but surely what she was saying couldn't be true?

> Darling Hattie, what a wonderful surprise it was
> to receive your card and letter. It didn't arrive
> until Friday and, knowing there was too little
> time to write back before Christmas, I rang your
> mobile and the hotel but having no success
> have decided to email instead.

Obviously, I wasn't contactable through the hotel now and Jonathan had insisted I took on a new mobile number when I changed my phone. I can't remember why he thought it was a good idea when I had considered it a right royal pain in the butt, but now . . .

> Your father and I are absolutely delighted to
> know that you and Jonathan are still together
> and have such exciting times ahead! We always
> hoped that once you had time to come to terms
> with things you would come back to us again,
> and although we didn't think it would take so
> long, we knew we had to respect your wishes

and leave you in peace if we wanted our Harriet back. Looking back, it probably was naïve of us to think that it had all been resolved. Thank goodness Jonathan put you in touch with his therapist to help you finally put your demons to rest.

The more I read, the less sense any of it made, unless . . .

It's a relief to know that you understand why we interfered (as you put it), in your relationship with David, but we're at a loss to understand some of the other things you wrote. The day Jonathan came and told us that the therapist had advised cutting yourself off from us for a while was a shock and I know the letter I sent back with him was . . .

'Hattie!'

I jumped almost out of my skin as Jonathan hammered on the door. My phone clattered to the floor, where it skittered across the tiles, but thankfully didn't crack.

'What are you doing in there?'

I retrieved the phone, turned it off and stuffed it back into my bag.

'Nothing,' I said, opening the door so he could see for himself. 'I was just about to brush my teeth. You were quick.'

'I changed my mind,' he scowled. 'Given the limited time we've got, I thought we'd best spend it together.'

Given what I had just read and realised, spending time with him was the last thing I wanted. I was more inclined to tear him limb from limb than cuddle up with him. There was no way I was going to suggest spending another night at the hotel now. I needed to get away, find some space to fully take onboard what I had just discovered.

'Are you all right?' he asked. 'You look a bit, pale, but then you did overdo it at breakfast, didn't you?'

'I'm fine,' I told him, sitting on the still unmade bed. My legs were wobbling every bit as badly as they had been the night I went ice skating. 'Actually, I'm pleased you've come back. I want to talk to you about something.'

He picked up the remote for the television and began flicking through the channels. The news blared out one minute, a music video on MTV the next. It was all I could to stop myself from launching across the room and wrenching the controller out of his hand, but I waited, a paragon of patience, until he decided to turn it off again.

'What?' he huffed, dumping himself heavily on to the bed next to me. 'What do you want to talk about?'

I twisted round on my knees so I was facing him and laid one of the pillows across my lap.

'My parents.'

'Have you heard from them?'

His tone was sharp, his brow furrowed and I knew why now. I knew the real reason why my mention of them would send him into a tailspin and it had nothing to do with protecting me and my feelings.

'No,' I lied.

I couldn't show my hand too soon. I needed to fully assimilate what I had discovered, and read the end of the email, before I presented him with it. For now, I simply wanted to gauge his reaction when my parents were mentioned and check the line he was taking about them.

'I just think it would be a good idea if we discussed what to say if they did get in touch, that's all,' I went confidently on.

He was quiet for a second, then his explosive temper, which had been bubbling away all morning, burst out of him like blistering lava pouring out of a volcano.

'You couldn't just leave it alone, could you?' he shouted. 'I wouldn't be surprised if you sent that fucking card on purpose!'

I had been braced for a reaction, but the sudden increase in volume made me flinch.

'Well, I didn't,' I rallied, recoiling as I gripped the pillow tighter.

'Don't interrupt!' he shouted, leaning across the bed, his face just inches from mine. 'Don't you dare interrupt.'

I didn't dare do anything other than breathe. I had seen him angry before, but nothing like this. If he wasn't careful, he was going to burst.

'Why can't you ever be satisfied with it just being us?'

Obviously, I didn't answer.

'I had the most amazing surprise planned for today,' he carried on; his volume dial still set to maximum. 'Did you know that? A massive surprise, just for you but then you came over all doe eyed in the dining hall and I thought—'

I wasn't having that.

'What are you talking about?'

'Flirting with that waiter and making yourself look ridiculous.'

Oh my god! Was he *really* going to do that? I looked over his shoulder, imagining each and every one of the promises he'd made me flying out of the open window and dissolving into the ether.

'And now you're back on about your bloody parents,' he raged on. 'Sometimes I wonder if I really know who you are at all, Hattie!'

Given what I'd just read and was now witnessing I could say exactly the same of him.

'They aren't interested in you,' he said cruelly. 'So, they won't be getting in touch, will they? And just in case you've forgotten, *you* were the one who made me go and tell them that you didn't want anything to do with them anymore.'

But how much of that entire scenario was actually down to him? If I had interpreted Mum's email correctly, then it was looking more and more likely that Jonathan had used the situation to suit his needs. He had set himself up as puppet master and we had all jumped when he pulled our strings. He had been feeding me one thing and Mum and

Dad something entirely different and we had lapped it up. He must have been in his manipulative element.

'If anything,' he spat, 'you've probably ruined their Christmas by sending that card, just like you've ruined what I've been planning for us today!'

'It wasn't me who woke up in a temper,' I said, swallowing my fear and biting back all the things I suddenly wanted to blurt out. 'Yesterday was fine—'

'Apart from the fact that you said you wouldn't come back to the flat, our home, with me.'

'I can't believe you're still smarting about that,' I shot back. 'It was never part of the plan.'

'Yes,' he said, smiling nastily, 'it was. Why do you keep pretending otherwise? You were the one who said you'd try and cut your visit short. I wonder how Dolly would feel if she knew you'd said that.'

I felt my face redden. I had only ever said it to placate him, but it was hardly the moment to highlight the fact.

'And anyway, what about *my* plan?' he raged on. 'My plan, to give a girl like you everything she could possibly want, that should be the only plan you're concerned about!'

'A girl like me?' I repeated.

'You know what,' he said, suddenly springing forward and snatching the pillow off my lap. 'Sod this. We're going home, right now.'

'No way,' I said, leaning back as far as I could without toppling off the bed. 'I'm not going to the flat with you, Jonathan.'

He lunged again, this time painfully grabbing me by the wrist and pulling me forward.

'What the hell are you doing?' I cried out.

He had never shown any sign of being physically aggressive towards me before. Words had been his weapon of choice but somewhere along the line he'd had an upgrade and I was scared. I tried to pull away but he had too tight a hold.

'We,' he said, talking slowly and emphasising every word, 'are going home. Now.'

'No,' I said, struggling to kneel up so I could stare straight back at him, even though it made me quake to do it. 'We are not and if you don't let me go, I will scream blue murder. Let me go, Jonathan.'

He ground his jaw for a second and then dropped my wrist. There were deeply pinched red marks where his fingers had been and it throbbed terribly. I rubbed it and looked at him. His breathing was shallow, the rise and fall of his chest rapid. He really was a man on the edge, but quite how he'd got there, I wasn't sure.

'I want you to take me back to Wynbridge,' I told him, my voice catching in my throat.

'No.'

'Yes, Jonathan,' I said, slipping off the bed so he couldn't reach me so easily. 'I'm going to pack and we're checking out. I'm going to tell Dolly we're on our way and you are going to drive me back to the cottage.'

I reached for my bag, but he snatched it up first.

'Give it back.'

'No,' he said, shaking his head, his expression more shocked than angry. 'We need to sort this.'

'There's nothing to sort. I ruined your big surprise and you're pissed off with me. I get it.'

Now I could see his temper had given over to the horror of what he had done, I felt stronger, more able to face up to him again.

'Give it a couple of hours and I'll have the bruises to prove it,' I added, holding up my arm so he was forced to acknowledge the evidence of his aggression. 'I'm going to call a taxi.'

He dropped to the bed, handed me back my bag and put his head in his hands.

'No,' he said huskily. 'Don't do that. There's no need. I'll drive you back.'

I noted that he didn't say he was sorry.

I knew it was a mistake getting in the car with him the second he re-joined the main road.

'Can you slow down, Jonathan, please?' I pleaded as he accelerated around the car in front, narrowly avoiding a motorbike in the oncoming lane.

'Why?' He shrugged. 'I thought you were keen to get back.'

I was keen, but I wanted to arrive in one piece. In the end I hadn't let Dolly know we were on our way because I didn't want her worrying in case Jonathan did something stupid and we didn't turn up. I didn't want her to have an inkling that there was anything wrong and I was going to make sure she didn't see the marks on my arm.

'You know,' said Jonathan, lifting his foot off the gas a little, but still not enough to settle my nerves, 'you really shouldn't talk to hotel staff like you talked to that guy at breakfast.'

'I used to be staff,' I reminded him, 'and I know the value of good customer interaction.'

'Is that what you call it?'

I ignored him. The last thing I wanted was to inflame an argument while he was behind the wheel, his right foot itching to break the current land speed record.

'And actually,' he carried on, 'I wanted to talk to you about your job.'

'I don't have one.'

'I know that,' he smiled, which I found more disconcerting than his frown, 'your next one. I think you should look for something different.'

'A different role in a hotel, you mean?'

The brief job search I had undertaken hadn't really inspired me at all and I wasn't much interested in hotel management anymore.

'No. Something completely different. You're a great communicator, Hattie.'

I couldn't believe the change in him. He was carrying on as if we were just idly chit-chatting, the abusive scene back in the hotel room completely forgotten.

'You're wasted in a reception role, even a senior one.'

The road ahead was too busy for another risky over-taking manoeuvre so I decided it was time for a little straight-talking honesty.

'You're right,' I said, throwing caution to the wind and saying what was in my heart as opposed to what he wanted to hear. 'And you know what, I'm loving working at the school. That's what I want to do next.'

'What?'

'It's something I used to think about a lot.' I carried on, my chest fluttering, the suggestion surprising me just as much as Jonathan. 'I think I just went along with the hotel thing because the Luccas looked after me. They offered me a refuge during a difficult time and the job was convenient.'

A bit like me accepting Jonathan's offer to move to Abu Dhabi. That had been a refuge from the shock of being made redundant, and it was convenient too, wasn't it?

'But what I should have done was carry on with my education and then look for work in a school.'

'Are you mad?' Jonathan asked.

Was I?

'You want to be Dolly,' he frowned, sounding almost disgusted. 'A teaching assistant at the lowest end of the pay scale.'

'Perhaps,' I said, 'I'm not sure. Money isn't everything, but maybe I could train as a teacher.'

'You *are* mad,' he confirmed, pressing his foot down again and pulling up to the bumper of the truck ahead. 'I was thinking corporate. Maybe banking or public relations, not wiping arses and mopping up sick.'

'There's not too much of that to do by the time the kids are old enough for school,' I corrected, my eyes trying to shut out the proximity of the registration plate in front.

Jonathan pulled back a little and was quiet for a mile or so.

'Are we OK, Hattie?' he eventually asked, as we reached the outskirts of Wynbridge in record time.

I shrugged, unwilling to appease him.

'I never meant to hurt you, you know?'

Wasn't that what all the people who abused those they allegedly loved said?

'And I can promise you, it will never happen again.'

That I knew was lifted straight from the handbook because I'd heard it before.

'I seem to remember,' I told him, 'you said something very much like that the last time I stayed in this town.'

He nodded, staring straight ahead.

'I know,' he said. 'I know. Are you going to bin me off, Hattie?'

'Not today,' I sighed, leaning forward as the church-yard came into view. 'You can drop me here. There's Dolly, look.'

My friend was tending to her late husband's grave and I was grateful that she was alone.

Jonathan indicated and pulled over a little distance away.

'What I am going to do,' I said, taking off my seatbelt and twisting around to face him, 'is have a good long think

271

about everything that's happened between us today and I don't want you to get in touch with me, Jonathan. I need some space. A week at least.'

My mind tracked back to the email from Mum as I imagined him saying something similar to her and Dad the Christmas before last.

'Oh, come on,' he said, slapping his hands on the steering wheel. 'That'll take us practically up to Christmas. It's a ridiculous request.'

'It might be to you,' I told him, 'but it's not to me.'

'I've just told you it won't happen again.'

It still hadn't occurred to him to say he was sorry, not that it would have made any difference to what I had decided I had to do.

'Open the boot and I'll get my bags,' I carried on. 'I'm guessing you aren't going to get out to talk to Dolly?'

The vein in his neck was throbbing and the temper which he had promised wouldn't be putting in an appearance ever again was already waving at the sidelines, demanding centre stage. I wouldn't have been surprised if he had decided to speak to Dolly, if only to tell my friend that I'd promised I'd cut my time with her short.

'No,' he said, flicking the boot catch, 'I won't be talking to her today.'

I climbed out, feeling relieved as Dolly straightened up, spotted me and waved. I waved back.

'I'll speak to you next weekend,' I told Jonathan, slamming the passenger door before he had a chance to say anything else.

I retrieved my things and the second I closed the boot he shot off. Dolly waved as he sped by and I walked up to meet her. My heart felt like a lead weight in my chest and my wrist was aching so much I had to swap my overnight bag to my other hand. I had no idea what I was going to tell her, but I knew it wouldn't be the truth. Not for now anyway.

Chapter 20

'I wasn't expecting you so soon,' Dolly called when I was in earshot. 'Where's Jonathan off to in such a hurry?'

I didn't answer. I didn't much want the whole of Wynbridge, even if it was only the dearly departed, hearing me shouting along the road, not that I had any intention of hollering out the truth.

'I hope he isn't expecting a dinner,' Dolly frowned. 'I put that chicken in the freezer because I thought it was just going to be me.'

'No,' I said, joining her at the graveside. 'You don't have to worry about that. Jonathan has had to go again.'

She looked at me, her eyes shrewdly taking in my face.

'What's happened?' she demanded.

I knew there was little point in saying nothing had happened. Dolly had some magical sixth sense where I was concerned and besides, she hadn't expected me back anywhere near this early. I had told her I'd be back in time for school on Monday.

'He had a phone call,' I said. 'He has to sort something at work.'

There was a certain irony that I was spinning out the same lie that she had used to explain why I had left the town so quickly after my last visit.

'On a Sunday?'

'I know,' I shrugged. 'I'm gutted. Some mix-up with a big contract or something.'

Dolly didn't say anything.

'But at least I'm not going to miss the third advent candle and I'll have had a decent night sleep ahead of the last week in school,' I said brightly.

Still nothing.

'These are pretty,' I said, indicating the flowers she had been arranging. 'Will they last in this weather?'

Dolly finally released me from her all-seeing stare and I let out a long breath, relieved that she had let me off the hook. I simply couldn't tell her what had really happened. She would be devastated if she knew about either my bruised wrist or what Mum had sent in response to my card. It was best I got it all straight in my own mind before I inflicted it on hers.

I heard a man laughing inside the church porch and turned around, my heart suddenly skipping merrily along, the horror of everything else that had happened that morning paling almost, but not quite, into insignificance.

'Is that Beamish?'

'Yes,' said Dolly, straightening back up again. 'He's been

helping the vicar with some staging for the concert tomorrow. He's going to run me home.'

'Hattie!' he shouted as he stepped outside.

Dolly and I exchanged a look and I wondered if she was thinking the same as me; that it was probably no bad thing that Jonathan had dropped me and run.

'Hey,' I called back.

'Well you weren't gone long.' His giant strides had closed the gap between us in seconds. 'We weren't expecting you back until tomorrow, were we, Dolly?'

'No,' said Dolly. 'We weren't.'

'I take it you didn't find the local landscape all that captivating then?'

'The what?'

'The flat Fens, the big skies?' he questioned. 'Oh, never mind,' he carried on, picking up my bag and Dolly's wooden flower trug. 'But you missed a great night in The Mermaid, and the auction was a record-breaker. I thought you were looking forward to it all.'

'I'm truly sorry I missed it now,' I said, thinking that a boozy night in the pub would have been far more fun than a night of five-star luxury with Jonathan.

'So why did you go?' he laughed. 'And yesterday of all days!'

I looked at his broad smile and kind eyes before he turned towards the gate and offered his arm to Dolly to keep her safe along the slippery path.

'I have absolutely no idea,' I sighed.

'Well, at least we can still go to the Wonderland this afternoon. If you fancy it?'

'Do you mind if we don't,' I said quietly. 'I didn't sleep well last night and I could do with a rest today.'

'Oh, all right,' he shrugged, 'no worries.'

Beamish didn't come in when we got back to the cottage. He said he was off to The Mermaid, but would see us at school tomorrow. I was suddenly very aware that I had been far more excited to see him emerging from the church porch than I had been to find Jonathan standing on the cottage doorstep.

'So,' said Dolly, once we had cobbled together a scratch lunch and made a pot of tea, 'how was your brief time with your beau? It was a bit of a surprise him just turning up out of the blue like that, wasn't it?'

'Just a bit,' I smiled.

'And I take it my assumption as to why he turned up,' she said, looking with emphasis at my bare ring finger, 'was a little wide of the mark?'

'Yes,' I said, thinking back to the bitter words Jonathan had thrown at me about ruining his big surprise. 'I think it might have been on the cards, but . . .'

'But then real life called and the plan was abandoned.'

'Something like that.'

'Well,' she said, pouring us both tea, 'I'm sorry it didn't work out and I'm also sorry to say that there was no post for you yesterday. I'm beginning to think I should never have nagged you about trying to get back in touch with your parents. I hope their silence hasn't upset you too much, my dear.'

Heidi Swain

Knowing how bad she felt, I couldn't lie about that as well as the real reason behind my early return, but I would have to hold back certain details, for now at least.

'Actually,' I told her. 'I did receive mail yesterday. Just not the sort that comes via the postman.'

'An email?' she asked, her face lighting up. 'From your parents?'

'From Mum,' I elaborated.

'And,' she carried on, 'what did she say?'

'Amongst other things, that she and Dad were happy to hear from me.'

'Oh Hattie,' she cried, clapping her hands together and almost making Tiddles stir. 'That's wonderful news! You'll be able to go to Abu Dhabi reconciled.'

'Perhaps,' I said, thinking more of Abu Dhabi than the family disharmony.

'You will,' she enthused, 'you'll be able to leave knowing that everything here is as it should be. I can't for one second imagine that you really intended to banish your parents for ever,' she rambled on. 'In fact, I can't help wondering . . .'

'What?'

'Oh nothing,' she said. 'Ignore me. You will tell Beamish, won't you?' She went on, sounding excited again. 'You must tell him. The poor chap has been feeling so bad about being the one who posted the card.'

'But it wasn't his fault,' I reminded her. 'It was just a mistake. We told him that.'

'I know,' she said, 'I know, but he also knows how upset

you've been about it. Not a day's gone by when he hasn't mentioned it.'

I was sorry that he had been worrying so much. I hadn't realised it had weighed so heavy on his mind.

'In that case,' I said, 'I'll definitely make a point of telling him.'

'I'm sure he would appreciate that,' she said, her tone changing from excitement to sadness. 'Dear Beamish.'

I knew that Dolly was extremely fond of her friend, as was everyone who knew him. He really was a gentle giant in the truest sense of the word and with a heart of pure gold to boot. I was fond of him myself, perhaps fonder than I should have been and, even though he didn't know it of course, grateful that our timely friendship had highlighted so many of the things that were wrong with my relationship with Jonathan.

I looked up and found Dolly staring at me. A shadow had fallen across her face and she looked anxious.

'What is it?' I asked, caught off guard.

'Nothing,' she said, hastily turning her attention back to her crackers and cheese.

I stirred my tea.

'As Beamish has come up in conversation,' I ventured after a few seconds had passed.

'Yes,' said Dolly quickly.

'I was wondering if you might have mentioned to him, who I went off with yesterday. I thought you might have told him about Jonathan.'

'Did you?' She nodded. 'Well I had been thinking about it, but something came up.'

She didn't say what.

'To tell you the truth,' she said, 'I'm surprised you haven't mentioned him to anyone yourself. Why haven't you?'

I thought back to the Christmas switch-on and what Rose had told me about how Dolly had explained what had prompted me to cut my last visit short.

'Well,' I said, 'I was going to, but Rose happened to mention that you'd told everyone that I'd had to rush back to work at the hotel after my last visit. You didn't tell them that I'd gone back to the guy with the bad temper even though they knew I'd arrived in town as a result of a row with him.'

Dolly shifted in her seat.

'You mean the guy who *used* to have a bad temper?'

'Yes,' I said, 'yes, the guy who *used* to have a bad temper.'

Picking up on my incorrect tense had enabled Dolly to momentarily sidestep the point I was trying to make.

'Did you think I'd made a mistake, Dolly?' I asked, going for the direct approach. 'In going back to Jonathan? Is that why you told everyone I'd had to go back to work at short notice?'

'I confess, at the time, I was concerned,' she admitted. 'I thought it was only a matter of time before something happened again and you came back. I thought keeping quiet might save you some awkward explanations in the long run.'

She sounded embarrassed to tell me the truth.

'Why didn't you say any of this at the time?'

'Because I was afraid that we might quarrel about it,' she explained. 'You had already cut your parents out of your life and I didn't want us to end up like that too.'

I could understand why that would have held her back.

'That said,' she added, 'I'm delighted to have been proved wrong and that everything has worked out.'

There was definitely no way I could tell her anything about the morning's drama now.

'However,' she carried on, 'I do think you need to tell Beamish that you aren't heading to Abu Dhabi on your own. I know everyone is aware that you're here to spend time with me before you go but I think it's only fair that you explain the situation properly, to him at least.'

'It's a little late for that now, isn't it?' I shrugged. 'And as we're just friends, I can't see that it matters.'

'Surely a friend would know if another friend was about to be married?'

'Are you suggesting that we aren't friends then?'

I was more concerned about her opinion of my relationship with Beamish than I was about the fact that I was no longer poised for matrimony.

'What I'm suggesting,' she said firmly, 'is that your friendship hasn't been built on a particularly honest foundation, and I know I am mostly to blame for that and that it was a mistake. An error of judgement on my part. I also know that Beamish is very fond of you, Hattie. Far fonder than he should be given that you're about to be married to someone else.'

I didn't know what to say, but my heart sped up a little in response. I wasn't ready to tell Dolly that my impending marriage was off thanks to Jonathan's abusive outburst and recently revealed treachery. I was still coming to terms with it all myself.

'Jonathan hasn't proposed yet,' I said instead.

'Don't be so flippant,' Dolly snapped, sounding cross.

'Sorry,' I hastily apologised.

Dolly rarely got cross and I was taken aback to see that she was seriously concerned.

'Has Beamish said something specific to you?' I asked. 'About me and him?'

I wondered if he had mentioned our near-kisses.

'No,' she said, 'but then he doesn't have to. There are just some things you pick up on and I can see it written all over his face. I hadn't bargained on that.'

'Hadn't bargained on what?'

'Never mind,' she frowned. 'But I know now that keeping quiet about Jonathan was a big mistake and you need to tread carefully, Hattie. The last thing that Beamish needs is a broken heart.'

'I hardly think—'

'That's half the problem these days,' she interrupted. 'Folk rarely do.'

The advent service that afternoon was all about joy, but I was far from feeling jubilant as I watched the third candle being lit. All I could do now was hope that Jonathan would respect my request to leave me alone. My mind might have been made up that we should part, but I wasn't ready to tell him yet because I wasn't sure how he would react. My wrist was a very painful reminder of just how explosive his temper could be.

My thoughts strayed back to Mum's email. She had said that the letter she sent back with Jonathan after he told them his therapist had said I shouldn't see them for a while was probably overly emotional, but of course I'd never received it so I didn't know.

> However, our concern for your mental health
> was, and still is, of paramount importance and we
> hope the therapy Jonathan helped organise was
> supportive in helping you move on from the past . . .

I had never had any therapy and the last few lines of the email revealed that my parents had never had a bad word to say about Jonathan either. The moments they had been alone together were not spent with them berating him as he had led me to believe, but with him telling them that I wasn't well, that I needed help, that it was best all round if they kept their distance.

Almost from the very moment I had confided in Jonathan about my affair with David and how it had fractured my relationship with my parents he had been cunningly crafting the tool to deliver the blow to split us apart for good. It had been his intention all along to set up an irrevocable rift so he could have me to himself and carve me into the shape he wanted. Clearly, he was the one who needed therapy, not me.

I was astounded by his behaviour and embarrassed that I had never seen through it. Thank goodness Beamish had sent that card and now I had the chance to set things right. However, the next few days stretched out in front of me and the demands of them were quite breath-taking – I needed to focus on composing a measured response to Jonathan, not break Beamish's heart, and help my darling Dolly adapt to a thoroughly different life to the one she had been living for as long as she could remember. And of course, there was also the Wish List to complete.

Before leaving the cottage for church, I had sent a brief text to the number Mum had included at the bottom of her email, explaining some of this. I kept the tone light, mentioning Dolly's retirement and how I wanted to talk to her and Dad face to face to properly untangle the wires which had been crossed. I promised we would see each other soon and that I would email as soon as I had a few more things settled in my head.

I was in for a tumultuous few days.

'Isn't this beautiful?'

I gave a little shudder as Beamish's breath tickled the back of my neck.

'Yes,' I agreed, my voice barely more than a whisper. 'Yes, it is.'

We were back in the church putting the finishing

touches to the preparations and decorations for the school carol concert. It had been heavy going in school. The children's excitement was almost at fever pitch and it was impossible to get any real work out of them. The teaching staff had succumbed to worksheets for most lessons. Festive-themed word searches for English and Christmas-based games in the ICT suite for maths, along with copies of Dolly's old photographs for writing prompts. It was all very noisy and hectic and the perfect antidote to help me forget my troubles.

'The candles along the window ledges are perfect,' I told Beamish.

'And high enough not to cause any trouble,' he grinned.

The altar and pew ends had been embellished with lengths of ivy left over from the greenery auction on Saturday and the place was a haven of calm and tranquillity. Or at least it would be until the children arrived. I hoped the sacred space would bring out their quiet side, or perhaps encourage them to dial it down a bit.

'By the way,' I said, as the first few families began to stream in, keen to get seats at the front, 'I have something to tell you. I didn't get the chance earlier, what with school being so busy.'

Beamish looked at me expectantly.

'Hattie,' beckoned Dolly, 'would you mind handing out the carol sheets? Rose has been slightly delayed.'

'Tell me after,' he smiled. 'I'm sure whatever it is will keep.'

I nodded and went to help Dolly, thinking how lovely it

was going to be to tell him that he didn't have to worry about the fallout from sending that card anymore.

There wasn't a spare seat in the pews and a few of us found ourselves on chairs right at the back. The choir sang their hearts out, enthusiastically bolstered by the voices of their parents, classmates and older and younger siblings. It was an idyllic rural scene, no doubt happening up and down the country and I was touched to be a part of it. I was half inclined to add it to the Wish List when Dolly and I got home. Of course, it would mean ticking it straight off again, but that wouldn't make it any less fulfilling.

As we sang the familiar carols my mind drifted off. I looked around at the upturned faces of the happy families – parents, grandparents and little ones – all preparing to spend the holidays together at this special time of year and my voice caught in my throat.

Jonathan had gone to the trouble of manipulating my life to ensure that I would never have what the folk filling the pews before me did. He had been so determined to have me to himself that he had twisted and tortured my already fragile family connections until they tore in two and because I had trusted him, I had believed every lie he had fed me without question. I had a kept a lid on my emotions all day, but the atmosphere in the church was too stirring to ignore. My poor parents.

I felt tears began to gather and slipped out of the church, into the star-studded darkness and out of sight of the door. There was little comfort to be found in the cold crisp air and

I let my tears flow unchecked, my hand covering my mouth to stifle noisy sobs.

'Hattie?'

I sniffed, but didn't answer. I didn't want anyone to find me like this.

'Hattie,' came the voice again, closer this time. 'It's me, Beamish.'

'I know it's you,' I snivelled, furiously wiping my face with the back of my hand.

'What are you doing out here? Are you all right?'

I shook my head and he pulled me into his arms. He didn't say anything, he just held me, safe from harm. Eventually I stopped crying and my body relaxed into his. I slipped my arms around him and squeezed tight. In that moment, wrapped in his all-encompassing embrace, it felt like the safest place in the world. I lifted my head from his chest.

'Sorry,' I swallowed, looking up at him and then at the tear-stained patch on his coat.

Not that he knew it, but I was apologising for so much more than crying all over him. He loosened his grip but didn't let go.

'Is this anything to do with what you said you wanted to tell me?' he asked.

I nodded.

'And there was me thinking it was going to be good news,' he tutted, now rooting about in his pocket one-handed for a packet of tissues.

'It is,' I said, taking the pack and breaking the contact between us. 'It is good news, just a bit overwhelming, that's all.'

'Go on,' he encouraged.

I blew my nose and took a deep breath.

'I've had an email from my mum,' I told him. 'She and Dad want to see me.'

Beamish laughed, the sound cutting through the chill air.

'But that's amazing, Hattie!' he grinned. 'Why on earth would you be crying over that? I thought you'd be over the moon.'

'I am,' I nodded. 'I am really. I suppose I'm just a bit nervous about it all.'

I wished with all my heart that I had told my new friend about the details surrounding my fresh start in the sun. How I wasn't some strong and independent young woman jetting off to begin a new life on her own, but that in truth, I was going to be flying off on the coat-tails of a man I now realised I couldn't trust.

I had grabbed the easy option Jonathan had laid temptingly out before me and now I had a whole heap of mess to untangle. Dolly had been right to be concerned when I went back to him and I had been ridiculously naïve to accept his miracle personality change and version of events with regards to my parents.

I felt more tears beginning to build and wiped my eyes again.

'I'm sure that's only natural,' Beamish told me. 'If I were in your situation, I'd no doubt be feeling nervous too and I'm sure your parents are, so you're all in the same boat really.'

'I guess,' I agreed.

'But at least you aren't going to end up like me, Hattie,' he carried on. 'You know the guilt and regret I carry.'

I nodded.

'So, have you decided when you're going to meet?'

'Not yet,' I sniffed. 'I haven't had a chance to email them back yet, but I've sent a text. I had been thinking about emailing from school but it's so busy.'

'Then you must make the time,' he said, reaching for my free hand as light began to pour out of the church and everyone streamed out, 'and you know, if you've changed your mind about moving, it's not too late. There'd be no harm in you not going if you aren't one hundred per cent sure that it's the right thing to do. I happen to know that there are plenty of folk around here who would be more than happy if you decided that Wynbridge was your fresh start, rather than Abu Dhabi.'

Chapter 21

When Dolly and I sat down to breakfast that Wednesday morning you could have heard a pin drop. I wanted to ask if she was all right, but it was obvious that she wasn't.

'It isn't too late to change your mind, you know,' I said instead, echoing Beamish's words to me in the churchyard as I reached across the table for her hand.

She looked back at me and smiled and I noticed how tired she looked. Perhaps retirement, proper retirement was the right idea after all.

'I could say the same to you,' she said, squeezing my fingers. 'I think out of the two of us, you might end up being the one more likely to have a change of heart about their future ...'

Her words stopped short and when I followed her gaze, I realised that the sleeve of my jumper wasn't quite covering my wrist.

'Hattie,' Dolly gasped, her face contorted with shock.

I tried to pull my hand free, but she held tight. For a woman of her age and slight build she certainly had a firm grip. She pulled my sleeve further back and the dark bruises, outlining Jonathan's fingers almost perfectly, were revealed in all their ugly glory.

'Oh no,' she cried.

'Don't . . .' I swallowed.

'Is this why you came back?' she demanded. 'Is this why you came back so early on Sunday?

I nodded. There was no point denying it. I would have looked a fool trying to make out those marks were anything other than the result of Jonathan's temper.

'He said he was tired from travelling,' I told her, then seeing the colour flood her face, very quickly added, 'but of course I'm not going to accept that as justification for what he did.'

'I should think not,' she said, sounding livid, 'and to think I had been seduced into believing that he really had changed.'

'You weren't the only one,' I told her. 'And up until recently he had.'

That said, I couldn't now deny that there had been a gradual build-up of comments that, had I picked up on them, would have been proof enough that not all was well in mine and Jonathan's very exclusive club. It had started soon after I was made redundant and I guessed that was the moment he thought he could tighten his stranglehold on me and make me even more reliant on him.

'Or so I thought,' I frowned.

I had assumed he was offering comfort and refuge but knowing how he had masterfully negotiated the estrangement from my parents I could see now that he had skilfully preyed on my vulnerability and bent me even further to his will.

'Whatever happened at that hotel?' Dolly asked. 'Please tell me this was a one-off. He hasn't been violent before, has he?'

'No,' I said reassuringly. 'Never. And up until the weekend he hadn't been verbally abusive since that other trouble either.'

'So, what kicked this off?' she said, nodding at my arm.

'It was brewing long before the weekend,' I told her. 'Looking back over the last few months, I can see now that he was becoming possessive again and then on Sunday he woke in a foul mood and accused me of flirting with one of the waiters at breakfast. It was almost as if he was looking for something to pick a fight about. I'm certain he wanted something to kick off.'

Dolly shook her head. She was taking it all in while I was letting it all go. I felt pounds lighter for telling her and decided not to stop there. While I was sharing, I might as well tell her everything.

'But it was mention of my parents that really put the cat among the pigeons,' I explained. 'I asked what he thought I should do if they got in touch and . . . well,' I said, nodding at my arm, 'he went ballistic.'

'Does he know about the email then?'

'No,' I told her. 'Having read it, I decided that it would

be best not to say anything. What Mum wrote was shocking and I dread to think how he would have reacted if he'd known about it.'

'Go on.'

I glanced up at the clock.

'I don't want to make us late, Dolly,' I told her, 'especially today.'

I might have been feeling heaps better for sharing, but I wasn't so selfish that I wanted to ruin her day.

'It doesn't matter,' she said. 'And besides, we won't be late if you hurry up and tell me.'

I could do better than that. At school I had printed Mum's email off for safekeeping. I watched as Dolly scanned the pages, her eyes growing wider with every word.

'So,' she said, her voice trembling a little, 'Jonathan was telling your parents that you hated them but that he'd try and do his best to talk you around and he was telling you . . .'

'That Mum and Dad hated him and were nasty to him every time they were on their own with him.'

'But what's all this about therapy?' Dolly frowned.

'He told Mum and Dad that I was having counselling, that some of what I said might not always make sense, which I guessed was a precaution on his part, and eventually that the therapist recommended I shouldn't see them. He fed me so many lies I snapped and told him to tell them I didn't want further contact with them.'

I don't know why I hadn't questioned why he had set himself up as the go-between before. I supposed he'd made such a good job of convincing both me and my parents that he had our best interests at heart. I would seriously have to think about nominating him for an Oscar because his acting skills were truly outstanding.

'And this letter from your mum?'

'He never gave it to me,' I confirmed. 'So, I have no idea what it said.'

'Well I'll bet she never said that she was pleased you lost the baby.'

I nodded in agreement.

'As soon as Jonathan knew my relationship with Mum and Dad was rocky, he started chipping away at it.'

'I can't believe it,' Dolly choked.

'Once I'd told him to tell them I was severing all contact he knew he'd won. His mission to create our exclusive club of two was accomplished, although he did say we'd be making friends and entertaining when we moved.'

'Of course, he did,' said Dolly scathingly, 'but you know it wouldn't have happened, don't you? And I bet he wouldn't have encouraged you to look for another job either. You can see that now, can't you?'

'Yes,' I nodded, 'yes I can.'

'You know,' Dolly mused, 'I'm surprised he tolerated our relationship.'

I didn't mention how he had tried to stop me from coming, how he had sulked when I refused to leave, or how he had hinted that Dolly's advancing age meant that she quite possibly wouldn't be a friend for too many more years.

'But then, whisking you off to Abu Dhabi would have put me nicely out of the picture, wouldn't it?' she said, puffing out her cheeks as I began to clear the dishes.

'Nothing could come between us, Dolly,' I told her.

'That's all right then,' she smiled. 'And how did he take the news when you broke it off? Is that why he roared off on Sunday?'

I didn't answer.

'You have broken it off, haven't you, Hattie?'

'Not exactly,' I admitted.

'What?'

'On Sunday I just wanted to get back here in one piece so I asked him to drive me home and then leave me alone. But don't panic,' I hastily added because she looked aghast, 'I'm going to tell him soon.'

'Good.'

'But I have to think carefully about how to do it. Don't forget all my possessions are at the flat. Granted I haven't got a lot, but I would like it all back.'

'Beamish could help with that.'

'No,' I shot back. 'I don't want Beamish knowing anything about any of this.'

I was feeling guilty enough for not telling him about Jonathan in the first place but now the thought had crossed my mind that I wouldn't ever have to tell him at all. I could just say that I'd changed my mind about moving and leave it at that. No harm done.

'I can sort it,' I carried on. 'I just need to do it gently. I might even try and find a way to convince Jonathan that it's all his idea to dump me.'

'I can't see that happening,' said Dolly. 'He's unhinged, Hattie.'

I chewed my lip.

'I know,' I said, 'I know he is, but right now he's doing exactly what I asked him to do, which is leaving me alone, and I'm grateful for that at least.'

I had thought he would start bombarding me with texts and voicemails, but so far, my phone had been silent.

'That is something I suppose,' Dolly nodded as I lifted the Wish List down from the mantel.

'And look at this,' I said, waving our notes about.

'I'm not sure it matters now,' she said.

'It does to me,' I told her. 'More than anything, and there are still plenty of things to tick off. I'm not going to do anything which will jeopardise us finishing this list, Dolly. Being here with you, and everyone at school and in town and at Wynthorpe Hall, has shown me what I'd be missing out on if I continued to think about the season how I did at the hotel, and as a result of adopting Jonathan's attitude towards Christmas as my own.'

'Do you really mean that?'

Yes,' I said, 'I really do. Christmas as it turns out, really does matter. And I'll tell you something else, even if Jonathan hadn't put his parts on at the weekend, there are things I've felt and experienced here in Wynbridge which were already making me question whether I was making the right decision or just going along with it because it was the easiest option.'

Dolly started to smile.

'And yes, I know you might have suggested that before,' I smiled back, 'but I suppose I just needed to work it out for myself, and being here has certainly helped me to do that.'

I wouldn't have been at all surprised if that had been the real reason behind her asking me to visit.

'Well that's something,' she said, taking my face in her hands, 'but what are you going to do now? Go back to your parents?'

I would have liked to say, stay with her in the cottage for the holidays, but I didn't. I daresay she was looking forward to some well-earned peace and quiet after the bell went at three fifteen today.

'Perhaps,' I said, 'but for now, I don't want to have to think about anything other than looking after you, Dolly.'

This comment was rewarded with a particularly stern look, the one usually reserved for the most disobedient children in school.

'And making the most of my time here to tick things off the Wish List,' I added to make amends.

There wasn't a dry eye amongst the adults in the hall that afternoon. Granted, the children were positively fizzing with festive excitement, but they were all aware of how strange school was going to feel when they returned in the new year and Dolly wasn't in it. She had been an educational and formative part of the lives of generations of families in Wynbridge and I couldn't imagine what it must feel like knowing you were loved and respected by so many people.

The presentation of gifts, cards and flowers continued long after the last bell of the term had rung out, with children lining up to present their tokens.

'I have a feeling of déjà vu,' Dolly kept joking. 'It feels like we've done this all before. You are very naughty to spoil me again.'

She had described to me, on many occasions, her first retirement assembly, and how much it had meant to her. Watching her from the other side of the hall, I knew there wouldn't be a third such time and there was a lump in my throat when Beamish wandered over.

'She's genuinely surprised by all this, isn't she?' he smiled.

'Yes,' I nodded. 'She is.'

'Everyone loves Dolly,' he said, rocking back on his heels. 'I can't imagine what it must feel like to be that loved.'

'Now you've surprised me,' I gasped, looking at him.

'Have I?'

'Yes,' I smiled.

It was funny to think that he had no idea of his own popularity amongst the great and good, the young and young at heart of Wynbridge.

'You might not realise it,' I told him, 'but you're pretty popular yourself, what with all your acts of kindness and gestures of goodwill.'

His expression said it all. He was every bit as selfless as

Dolly. He genuinely didn't have a clue what people thought and said about him.

'I just like to help out,' he shrugged.

'I know you do, and that's why folk love you too.'

'Well,' he said, looking embarrassed, 'I don't know about that. I better go and check the staffroom's all set up,' he stammered. 'Are you coming in for the party?'

'Of course.'

'And have you checked your emails today?' he asked. 'Any word from your parents?'

I had made a point of finding the time as he had suggested to email Mum and Dad back.

'I haven't had a chance to look yet, but I will before we go home.'

It was very much beginning to look as though I was going to be leaving Wynbridge having regained my family and lost a future husband but I didn't feel overwhelmed by the surprising turn of events at all.

Being in this beautiful little town had re-set my priorities dial and shown me the value of those relationships I should treasure as well as flagging up those which I could live without. What would have become of me, I wondered, had I succumbed to Jonathan's pleading and turned down Dolly's offer to visit?

Putting some distance between us had given me the chance to see exactly how reliant on him he had made me. He had firmly established himself as being the answer to my prayers rather than helping me look for my own. He had wanted to be my everything. He had wanted to have all the power but now I was taking it back and I was going to use that reclaimed strength to untangle myself from his clutches.

'Hattie?'

My gaze shifted back to Beamish and I realised he hadn't gone yet, but had carried on talking to me.

'Sorry,' I said, 'I was miles away.'

'You looked it,' he laughed. 'I said, I'm going to use one of the computers myself, so I'll leave that one switched on for you.'

'OK,' I nodded, 'thanks.'

During Dolly's party in the staffroom I was embarrassed to find the attention turning from her to me.

'We wanted to give you these, Hattie,' said Mr Matthews presenting me with a beautiful posy of flowers and a box of handmade chocolates. 'To say thank you for stepping in and helping out.'

'You've been a godsend,' said Mr Patterson.

'We couldn't have managed without you,' agreed Mrs Newton, my fellow TA.

It was a relief to know I hadn't stepped on her toes.

'And anytime you happen to be back in town,' laughed Rose, who was unboxing something on the table. 'Do feel free to come in and help again, won't you?'

'Of course,' I laughed back, 'and thank you all for making me feel so welcome and a part of the team. I know I haven't been here for long this time and it's been a bit manic in the run-up to the holidays, but I've absolutely loved it.'

I felt sadder to be leaving here than I had the hotel where I'd worked for over a decade. I'd been here for less than three weeks, but it had provided me with more than one lightbulb moment and I was most grateful for that.

'If any hours come up,' winked Rose, 'I'll get Dolly to send the details on.'

I didn't have a chance to tell her that I would be genuinely interested because she had turned her attention back to my friend, beckoning her over.

Everyone gathered around the table and, with a flourish she revealed a stunning cake which she had commissioned Jemma at the Cherry Tree Café to make.

'Would you look at that!' Dolly gasped.

'I thought you'd like it,' said Rose as we all crowded closer to look at the details of the decorations.

The blue and white iced two-tier cake was adorned with intricate snowflakes and balancing on top were a pair of ice skates, complete with blue satin laces.

'It's perfect,' said Dolly, dabbing her eyes with the lace hand-kerchief she always had in a pocket or tucked up her sleeve.

'How does Jemma do it?' asked Beamish, towering over everyone as he admired the creation.

'She's a cake-making goddess,' said Rose, handing Dolly yet another envelope to open. 'And Lizzie can match her in talent. She designed this card for you, Dolly.'

The card was every bit as beautiful as the cake and we all raised a glass to my dear friend who looked quite overwhelmed.

'I had a feeling you might say something in assembly,'

she said as Alison came in with a basket of beautiful winter flowers, 'but I wasn't expecting anything like this.'

'Well you deserve it,' said Mr Patterson. 'I honestly don't know how the school is going to carry on without you.'

'Oh, I'm sure you'll cope,' said Dolly, flushing at all the praise. 'I haven't been doing anywhere near as much as I used to.'

'But you're irreplaceable, Dolly,' sighed Mr Matthews. 'We're still looking for someone to take over your clubs. I don't suppose you'd change your mind about overseeing those until we find someone else, would you?'

Dolly shook her head.

'I'm sorry,' she said, 'I just . . .'

Mr Matthews put up a hand to stop her.

'No,' he said kindly, 'I'm sorry. I shouldn't have asked. Don't give it another thought, my dear, we'll find someone, and in the meantime, we'll juggle things between us.'

I was surprised Dolly didn't back down but was sure she had her reasons.

'Would you mind if I quickly went and used the computer before we go home?' I asked her a little while later. 'I just want to check my emails.'

'Of course not,' she smiled.

'I won't be long,' I said, slipping out as everyone got stuck into another slice of cake.

I hadn't seen Beamish for a little while but he had, as promised, left one of the computers turned on. According to what popped up on screen when I moved the mouse, I could see that he had been on Facebook, which came as something of a surprise. I didn't have him down as someone who bothered much about social media. I didn't particularly care for it myself. I did have a Facebook account but I rarely used it. I logged out of Beamish's user profile on the school system and into my own.

'Any joy?' he asked from the doorway a few minutes later.

'Yes,' I nodded, twisting around to talk to him. 'I've had another email from Mum. She replied to the one I sent almost straight away.'

'She's certainly keen,' he said, coming further into the room.

'She is,' I agreed. 'She wants us to meet before Christmas.'

'That's great.'

'It is.'

I was nervous about seeing her and Dad again, but excited too. They were both in complete agreement that it would be best to talk things through face to face. It wasn't a conversation I was looking forward to but once we had exorcised Jonathan from our lives, we could start afresh and that was a very happy thought.

'You do realise that Christmas is just a week away,' Beamish reminded me. 'By this time next week Hattie, you will have seen your Mum and Dad.'

'I know,' I said huskily, 'I can't believe it. Apparently, they're snowed under with work, but we'll sort something out.'

'Now that school's finished, perhaps you could travel to see them instead?'

'Perhaps.'

'I'm pleased it's all working out for you, Hattie. It would have been awful if you went away and still weren't talking.'

'It would,' I agreed, not that I was planning on going anywhere. 'But thanks to you,' I told him, 'I don't have to worry about that now. That card might have been sent in error, but I'm very grateful that it ended up in the postbox.'

Beamish nodded, but didn't look half as happy or relieved by my words as I hoped he would. Come to think of it, he didn't look anything like as cheerful as he had earlier on.

'Hattie,' he sighed, his change in tone making me sit up straighter.

'What?'

'Is there anything else you want to talk about?'

'No,' I said, 'I don't think so.'

'Are you sure?'

I chewed my lip. This could be the moment, the last opportunity to explain everything. He was offering it to me on a plate, but I couldn't do it. There was no point in doing it now my relationship with Jonathan was over, was there?

'Yes, I'm sure.' I nodded, swivelling back to face the screen, 'one hundred per cent.'

Chapter 22

There wasn't space to put down another thing in Dolly's cottage by the time we had finished unloading the contents of Beamish's truck. Flowers, cards, gifts and cake covered every available surface and if my friend joked again that 'Christmas had come early', she would have said it a hundred times since I arrived in town.

'I'm certain there's at least twice as much as when I retired the first time,' she said, shaking her head as she took the scene in.

'Yes, well,' Beamish reminded her, as he nudged things aside to set down one last vase on the dresser, 'you've added a fair few extra years of service on to the tally since then, Dolly.'

'I suppose you're right,' she yawned.

I tried to catch Beamish's eye but failed. Dolly's decision to leave school now, rather than in the summer, had definitely been the right one and I was certain he would agree.

'And now you can do all the things you've never had

time for,' I suggested. 'Perhaps you'll find another hotel to stay in that you'll come to love just as much as the Lucca's.'

'Yes,' she said, heading to fill the kettle, 'perhaps. If there's time.'

'I think she needs an early night,' Beamish said to me, then added in a whisper. 'I'll bring those bits round for you in the morning.'

'As long as you're sure it's no bother.'

I had come up with something else for the Wish List that I thought Dolly would love and Beamish had offered to collect what I needed to make it happen.

'Of course not,' he shrugged, 'I've already told you.'

He sounded almost impatient. Perhaps Dolly wasn't the only one who needed an early night.

'OK,' I said, 'well, thanks again.'

'No need to thank me,' he sniffed. 'A trip to the Cherry Tree Café isn't exactly a hardship.'

'Fair enough.'

I really wasn't sure how to read him. I'd never seen him without a ready smile on his lips and a warm remark to accompany it.

'It won't be a very early drop off though,' he said gruffly. 'I haven't got to go to bed tonight worrying about that blasted boiler, so I think I deserve to get up when I wake up, rather than when my alarm dictates, don't you?'

'Absolutely,' I agreed, pointing at Dolly who was now yawning again, 'and you aren't the only one.'

*

In spite of the very grown-up things that had happened over the last few days, waking up in the cottage on the first day of the Christmas holidays, I felt about ten years old. Dolly and I had a great day planned – baking at home, followed by tea in town and finishing with the Santa parade and the last opportunity to indulge in some late-night shopping. And I was still hoping there would also be time to squeeze in a visit to the Winter Wonderland before the Wynthorpe clan closed their doors at the end of the weekend.

I couldn't help thinking that the prospect of it all felt almost as exciting as the arrangements I had made for the previous weekend. I only hoped Jonathan didn't have plans to arrive and scupper these too.

For someone who had decided to end her long-term relationship I was hardly mourning its death. If anything, I felt better than I had in ages. It was as if Jonathan had been slowly poisoning me, then Dolly had rescued me and provided the antidote to draw him out. Her remedy, combined with my contrasting friendship with Beamish, Mum's revelations and Jonathan's show of aggression had completely vindicated my decision to break it all off and there was no way I was going to let him tie me up in knots and have me thinking what he'd done was my fault. I may have been facing the new year with no job and no roof over my head but, in the exciting build-up to Christmas, they felt like minor details.

All I had to do now was work out how to tell Jonathan that our relationship was over, but even that didn't feel quite such a daunting prospect with him so far away, and I certainly wasn't going to let thoughts of it ruin mine and Dolly's plans.

I could hear my friend moving about in the kitchen and threw back the covers, much to Tiddles disgust, and went down to join her.

'Morning, Dolly,' I smiled as she set the radio to Classic FM and the angelic voices of the King's College Choir filled the room. 'How are you feeling?'

'If I didn't know better,' she said, turning the volume down a notch, 'I'd say I was a little hungover.'

'Well,' I laughed, 'the fizz was pretty free-flowing yesterday afternoon.'

Dolly nodded and stirred some dissolvable painkillers into a glass of water. She must have been feeling rough. I don't think I'd ever seen her take medication before, not even when she broke her wrist the year we became firm friends.

'And how are you feeling about this exciting new phase of your life?' I asked. 'Has it sunk in yet?'

'No,' she said, grimacing as she took a swig. 'It just feels like the Christmas holidays as opposed to holidays for ever and no going back.'

'Oh, I'm sure you'll grace them with your presence at some point. What's in that bag?'

'Something for you,' she told me. 'It was propped up against the front door and there was a note pushed through the letterbox.'

Apparently, Jemma at the café started early and, as Beamish had woken even earlier than his usual time, he'd been and got the bits and pieces I'd asked for already. His note was brief, brisk almost, and given the strange mood he'd fallen into at the end of yesterday I wasn't surprised he hadn't slept.

'What is it?' Dolly asked, distracting me from wondering what might have caused it.

'Everything we need to tick off something I added to the Wish List after you'd gone to the bed last night,' I grinned, grabbing the list and handing it to her.

'Oh, how lovely,' she smiled back, her eyes shining. 'I haven't made a gingerbread house for years!'

'Me neither,' I said, opening the reusable shopper which was stamped with the Cherry Tree logo. 'Not since I moved into the hotel, but let's have some breakfast first. I've a hankering for a bacon butty this morning.'

'I think I'll stick to toast,' said Dolly, looking a little green around the gills.

After breakfast I cleared a space at the table and we set about following the list of instructions Jemma had included with the kit. Apparently, the houses had been a popular addition to the café's seasonal market stall and as we set to, I could see why. Everything was conveniently labelled and already weighed out so there was very little for me to mess up.

'Mum and I always used to make a house when I was little,' I told Dolly as I began to stir the ingredients together.

'And we would spend ages decorating it. It was never quite straight and there would always be one wall or one side of the roof which wanted to give up before the others, but we tried our best.'

'That sounds like a very happy memory,' Dolly smiled.

She was feeling a little brighter now the painkillers had worked their magic and she'd had something to eat.

'It is,' I smiled. 'And I've realised in the last few days, that I have lots of them. Ever since I had that first email from Mum they've been crowding in thick and fast.'

'I'm sure they've always been there.'

'I'm sure they have too,' I agreed, stirring faster, 'but all the time we were divided after Jonathan's meddling, I never allowed myself to think about them. I put both my parents and the happiest memories of my childhood out of my mind and never let them in.'

I would never be able to forgive Jonathan for that. When he came on the scene things between me and my parents were already fragile but he made sure he smashed the relationship we had left to smithereens and if he'd had his way, we never would have found a way to repair it.

'Just think if that card hadn't been sent,' I said, feeling a shudder run through me as I imagined myself accepting Jonathan's proposal and moving abroad.

'Best not to,' said Dolly, patting my hand and leaning closer in to check we were doing everything in the right order. 'Now come on, concentrate on the job in hand.'

I did my best, but it was hard work trying to banish

thoughts of my deceitful other half, and I wasn't the only one struggling to shove him out of the spotlight.

'You know,' Dolly said bitterly, as we carefully slid the tins into the oven, 'I can't help thinking he's made a fool out of both of us. He knew I had misgivings about him after he decked that poor chap, and he also knew I'd never voice them for fear of losing you. That said,' she added with a frown, 'I never would have suspected him of orchestrating you cutting your parents out of your life. Granted, some things might not have added up, but that was too extreme to be plausible. Or so I thought.'

'That's because you see the good in everyone, Dolly,' I told her. 'You're the sort of person who always hopes for the best in others as well as in life. I used to be like you.'

Her expression changed as she turned to face me.

'Don't you let what that man's done change that, Hattie.' She said sternly. 'There are still folk in the world with pure goodness running through their veins.'

'Oh, really?'

'Yes, she said, 'Beamish for a start. There's a man with not an ounce of malice in him.'

'All right,' I conceded. 'I'll let you have Beamish, but he's the exception, not the rule.'

Slowly the smell of gingerbread permeated every nook and cranny in the cottage and I was relieved the walls were going to need trimming so we would have plenty to nibble on as we shaped the framework of the house once it had cooled. There were also a couple of boiled sweets left over after we had crushed enough to make the stained-glass windows.

'More snow,' muttered Dolly, as she stood at the kitchen window.

'Really?'

'Yep,' she said, shifting over so I could see, 'look. There's not much to speak of yet, but if it keeps up . . .'

'I'll end up snowed in for Christmas,' I grinned.

I rather liked the thought of being cut off from the rest of the world. I could always find somewhere with enough signal to Skype my parents to wish them seasonal salutations and the Wynbridge wind could stir up deep enough snowdrifts to keep Jonathan at bay should he decide to try and make a return visit once I had told him what I had decided.

'You don't sound as though you'd mind being here a bit longer,' Dolly chuckled.

'Of course, I wouldn't,' I laughed. 'I can't imagine there's anywhere more perfect in the entire world than Wynbridge to spend Christmas in.'

'Well I never,' Dolly smiled, 'you really have had a festive turnaround, haven't you?'

'Just a bit,' I smiled back.

'In that case,' she said, 'I hope you know that you would be more than welcome to spend Christmas with me if you wanted to.'

'Really?'

'Really,' she confirmed. 'Unless you'd rather be with

your parents. I had thought about asking before, but didn't want you to feel obliged.'

'Obliged?'

I had no idea why she would think I'd feel that. I had assumed she hadn't mentioned me staying on because she was looking forward to having the cottage to herself again.

'Because I'm here all on my own,' she said, colouring slightly.

'You mean, you wouldn't want a pity guest staying under your pretty roof,' I teased. 'Someone who was staying because they would otherwise feel guilty about leaving you on your lonesome.'

'Something like that.'

I was trying to make her laugh again, but it didn't work. I hoped I hadn't offended her.

'Oh Dolly,' I said, pulling her into a gentle embrace. 'I've never known anyone with as many friends as you've got. I've barely ever seen you on your own, but none the more for that, I would *love* to spend Christmas with you.'

'Really?'

'Really.'

'But what about your parents?'

'Well,' I said, 'we're definitely going to see each other within the next few days and I'm really looking forward to spending time with them and getting everything straightened out, but I wouldn't want to put our first get-together under too much pressure.'

'That does make sense,' Dolly pondered, 'Christmas can

313

be tricky. Everyone has such high expectations and with everything else you've had going on between you.'

'Exactly.' I enthusiastically agreed. 'So, I'm more than happy to keep our first few visits brief. I'm sure everything will be fine but I don't want to force the situation and rush things.'

'That's fair enough. Very sensible actually.'

'I think so,' I said. 'And of course, that means I can spend Christmas with you Dolly, and we'll be able to add even more things to the Wish List, won't we?'

Dolly smiled again and I knew she believed that I was staying because I wanted to, not because I felt sorry for her, which was totally true.

'That's settled then,' she said, sounding as pleased as I was about the arrangements. 'And Angus will be over the moon about this weather,' she added, looking out of the window again as the snow began to fall faster. 'This is just what the Winter Wonderland needs.'

'I was so disappointed to miss my visit,' I told her.

'Well, we'll just have to see if you can get there this weekend,' said Dolly. 'I'm sure Beamish will be happy to take you.'

Given the funny mood he'd fallen into all of a sudden, I wasn't so sure.

'I'm certain he'd do anything for you, Hattie,' she said lightly.

My heart hammered at the thought.

I'd forgotten how long it took to make a gingerbread house, but spending the rest of the day shaping, constructing and decorating was a pleasurable luxury. The only thing I didn't enjoy was how my mind kept flitting back to Jonathan and how I was going to break the news of our break-up to him. I had been naïve to think that I could shut the imminent task out, even with the distraction of Christmas and the ever-growing Wish List.

'If I were you,' said Dolly as she took a step back to admire her creative skills with the piping bag. 'I wouldn't put it off much longer.'

'You're right,' I agreed. There was no need to ask what she was referring to. 'I'm going to do it tomorrow.'

'Good,' she said. 'I'm pleased. It will be a relief to get it off your chest and out of the way. It's one thing to have made the decision but now you need to act on it.'

'I know,' I said. 'And I can't imagine it's going to come as a complete surprise to him, can you?'

Dolly let out a long breath.

'Who knows?' she said. 'He's hardly predictable, is he? I mean, anyone in their right mind would be thinking that they'd cooked their goose, but this is Jonathan we're talking about and I'm not sure he knows what his right mind is.'

'He always thought the rules didn't apply to him, didn't he?'

There was no denying his arrogance. I had once considered it confidence, but now the scales had dropped I had recategorised an awful lot of his personality traits.

'At least he's stayed away like I asked. I told him to leave me alone and I haven't heard a peep out of him.'

It was out of character for him not to keep pushing and

doing what he wanted as opposed to what someone else had asked of him. Perhaps the marks he'd left on me had shocked him into submission.

'That's true,' said Dolly. 'And I'm certain however he reacts you'll feel better for having it all sorted. And remember; he can't reach you through the screen or down the telephone line. You have to be strong.'

'Yes,' I said, imagining what a relief it would be to have it ended, 'yes, I'm sure you're right. Now,' I added, keen to move our thoughts on, 'let's get ready to go, otherwise we'll miss our table at the Cherry Tree.'

Apparently, it wasn't unusual to have to book a table at the café at peak times now and, as Dolly and I climbed out of the taxi she had insisted on because of the snow, I could see that this particular evening was indeed a peak time for the town. It felt even busier than the night of the switch-on but that could have been because I felt such a part of the place and knew so many people.

We had barely taken a step before we stopped to talk to someone. Three weeks was all it had taken to integrate back into this warm and vibrant community which had welcomed me with open arms. I had no idea what my future now held, but I couldn't help wishing, as Dolly and I finally made it over the café threshold, that it would include Wynbridge or a town very much like it, assuming there were any others left.

'Welcome, ladies,' said Jemma as she came over to talk us through the menu she had put together for the evening.

The place was chock-a-block and yet she was the epitome of calm. Everything was running like a well-oiled machine and I admired her immensely.

'It's a set menu this week,' she explained. 'Makes our lives so much easier. Shall I give you a moment or would you like to order drinks now and I can come back for your food order in a minute?'

'Let's do drinks now,' said Dolly.

'And I want to thank you for the gingerbread house components, Jemma,' I smiled up at her. 'What an inspired idea to sell everything in kit form.'

'It's been so popular,' she laughed, 'I can't think why I didn't come up with it sooner. We've sold biscuit and cookie sets before at Christmas, but this has been the most ambitious so far and totally worth it. So many people have said they've never made one but the kits have encouraged them to have a go.'

'Well, it certainly made it easy,' I agreed. 'We're thrilled with ours, aren't we, Dolly?'

'Yes,' Dolly agreed. 'It's a total triumph.'

'I'm asking for photographs of the finished houses to pin up on the wall,' Jemma continued, nodding to where there was a vast cork board displaying community news and events. 'And next year we're thinking about adding a gingerbread house competition to the bake sale.'

'That's a lovely idea,' said Dolly. 'I'm sure you'll be inundated with entries.'

I didn't reckon much for the chances of some of them transporting all that well.

'Including yours I hope, Dolly,' Jemma went on with a cheeky wink. 'You'll be able to enter two now you're going to have all this extra time on your hands.'

'Now there's an idea,' I laughed.

'It's a shame you won't be here to take part, Hattie,' Jemma rushed on.

I was itching to tell her that I might come back to compete, but kept my lips locked.

'And if you do find yourself at a loose end, Dolly,' she continued, pointing at the board again. 'I'm in need of weekend staff.'

'Thank you, Jemma,' said Dolly. 'I'll keep it in mind, but I wouldn't hold your breath.'

Jemma grinned and headed back to the kitchen.

'You know,' I said, nudging Dolly as I leant forward to read the small print on the advert, 'when I grow up, I want to be like Jemma.'

'Don't we all,' Dolly laughed.

The Santa parade was a sight not to be missed. The pavements were lined three deep in some places as the Wynthorpe Hall sleigh made its way sedately around the market square pulled by a couple of stout ponies. I was fairly certain it was Angus Connelly at the reins but I couldn't be sure.

The lap ended under the huge Christmas tree and the adults began to line up, their children bouncing about them while they waited for their turn to be handed a gift from Santa himself. I was surprised I recognised so many of the rosy-cheeked little faces and Dolly and I waved enthusiastically back to a few who spotted us amongst the crowd.

'Hello, you two,' said Rose, who was queuing to see the big man with her family. 'How's the first day of the holiday been?'

'Perfect,' said Dolly. 'Hattie has had us baking a gingerbread house.'

'From a Cherry Tree kit?'

'That's the one,' I confirmed.

'We've used one too,' she smiled. 'Brilliant, aren't they?'

We chatted some more and then Rose said she had better catch up with her other half.

'Before you head off,' I said, catching her arm. 'I just want to say thank you, to both of you actually,' I added, looking at Dolly.

'Whatever for?' Rose asked.

'For press-ganging me into volunteering at the school of course. I know I was only helping for a short time.'

'But it's changed your mind about Christmas, hasn't it?' Rose interrupted.

'Oh yes,' I laughed, 'very definitely. You were right about the children's enthusiasm being infectious. I think I've caught a healthy enough dose of festive feeling to see me through and way beyond the season now.' Rose punched the air. 'But it's more than that,' I swallowed. 'It's made me think about my future too. Dolly, you know that in the past I had considered a career in education.'

319

'Yes,' she said, 'I did know that.'

'Well,' I said, 'my time at school has made me have a bit of a rethink about looking for another position in a hotel.' The idea had been a bit of a slow burner, but once I had blurted it out to Jonathan, it had taken hold and started to grow, in spite of his mean words. 'I'm not sure I want to teach, but I'm definitely going to think about a teaching assistant position.'

'That's wonderful news,' said Rose, clapping her hands. 'We've all said that you're a natural with the kids and I'm sure you won't have any problem finding work when you move. There must be plenty of schools in the UAE looking for English staff. But it's a shame though,' she added, sounding suddenly less excited.

'What is?' Dolly asked.

'That Hattie's moving,' she carried on. 'I've been in school today, all the teaching staff have, looking at budgets and things and Mr Matthews thinks he's found funding for a few hours. It's by no means going to be a full-time post, but it would have been ideal for you, Hattie. Are you sure you have to go? Have you really got your heart set on it?'

'Look,' said Dolly, waving madly and saving me from having to answer, 'there's Beamish.'

He caught sight of Dolly's windmill arms and wandered over just as Rose's family called her back to the queue for Santa.

'I better go,' she said, pulling me into a hug and kissing my cheek, 'you take care, OK?'

'I will,' I said, squeezing her back. 'I promise.'

Dolly looked at me over Rose's shoulder and winked. She didn't say anything. She didn't have to; first a weekend job at the Cherry Tree had been mentioned and now another in the school. My mind was whirring with possibilities, but were any of them feasible options when I had nowhere to live and a belly to fill? Perhaps not, but standing in the snowy square surrounded by the fine folk of Wynbridge, I was so happy and determined to live in the moment that I felt anything was possible.

'I wondered where you two had got to,' said Beamish, after Rose had gone.

'We ate in the café,' Dolly explained, 'and were lucky enough to get this spot to watch the parade.'

'Shall we go over to the pub?' I suggested. 'It's freezing out here.'

'I can't,' said Beamish, 'I'm meeting friends.'

His tone was as chilly as the temperature.

'Oh,' I said, 'right, no problem.'

It felt like he'd grabbed a giant pin and stuck it straight in the heart of my happy balloon. Clearly his mood hadn't improved even though he was on his holidays.

'I was hoping you'd come and see the gingerbread house this afternoon,' Dolly said to him, oblivious of my awkwardness.

'I've had no time,' he said, practically turning his back on me. 'I've been helping the service engineer with the boiler in school and working on a surprise for you, Dolly. It's something to do with the Wish List.'

'What is it?' she asked, her eyes twinkling.

'I told you, it's a surprise,' Beamish said again. At least he had a smile for Dolly. 'And I don't want you trying to suss it out either, so no more questions.'

'When is it happening?' I asked, trying to join in.

'Tomorrow,' he said, still looking at Dolly. 'You'll need to be ready at lunchtime and you'll definitely need layers. And wellies.'

'I'm sure I can manage that,' Dolly beamed.

'You can come too, Hattie, if you like.'

I was rather taken aback that he had asked me separately. Dolly and I had done everything on the list together. I felt almost spurned, an afterthought, rather than included in whatever it was that he had come up with.

'But don't feel obliged,' he added, shooting me a quick glance.

'But on second thoughts,' frowned Dolly, still oblivious of how Beamish was talking to me, 'I'm not sure about the wellies.'

'Don't worry,' he told her, 'I'll help you pull them off!'

Dolly laughed and tapped his arm.

'You really are a cheeky boy,' she told him. 'Is it the Winter Wonderland by any chance?'

'No,' he said, looking at me again, but still not offering me a smile, 'it's not.'

'Do you think we'll still be able to go together?' I swallowed. 'I really want to see it.'

'I went last week.'

'Oh,' I said, feeling even more foolish. 'Fair enough.'

'Right,' he said, rubbing his hands together and for once not reassuring me that he would find a way to make it happen. 'I better get on. The lads are waiting.'

'Don't stay out too late,' Dolly called after him.

'I'll see you tomorrow,' he called back. 'Don't forget, wear plenty of layers.'

'How exciting,' said Dolly linking arms once he was out of sight. 'I wonder what on earth it could be.'

I didn't answer. I was more preoccupied with wondering what on earth I'd said or done to upset him.

Chapter 23

That night my sleep was plagued with bad dreams featuring both of the men in my life. I didn't much mind that Jonathan was going to end up hating me, but being in Beamish's bad books was unbearable and that had translated painfully into my nightmare. All night I was either running away from Jonathan or reaching out to Beamish, through a thick, foggy haze. The second I was within reach he took another step away, his expression switching between sad, angry and repelled.

The following morning, I lay staring up at the ceiling long before there was even a hint of light creeping around the curtains, wondering if it was too early to call Jonathan and get the deed done. As loath as I was to look at him, I had decided that a Skype call, from Dolly's bathroom where the signal was strongest, would be best. I needed to have eyes on him when I told him I was breaking it off. I had to be as certain as I could be of his reaction when I explained what I had decided and why.

And as for Beamish, I was hoping the images of him, conjured in my dream state, were nothing more than a figment of my overactive imagination, rather than a true representation of how he was really feeling.

With a heavy heart, I crept into the bathroom and quietly closed the door.

'Hattie,' smiled Jonathan as his face appeared and filled the screen on my phone. 'I wasn't expecting to hear from you, especially at this time of day.'

'I'm not disturbing you, am I?'

I knew his routine better than my own. I certainly wouldn't have woken him. By my reckoning he would have just finished making his protein shake and would be pulling on his trainers, ready to run to the gym.

'Of course not,' he said, resting the phone where I could see a wider view of the pristine flat that I was now able to admit I had never really felt at home in. 'I was just getting ready to go to the gym.'

'I thought you might be.'

'But of course, I'd much rather be talking to you,' he quickly added. 'What have you been up to this week?'

The tone of his voice and his question sounded so natural. He talked as if we were picking up a conversation we'd already started and catching up on each other's news rather than having our first exchange since he had abused me, both mentally and physically. Everything about him, from his tone of voice, to his relaxed stance, told me that he had conveniently swept it all aside and was expecting us to carry on as if none of it had happened.

'I'm guessing school must have broken up for the holidays and of course Dolly has properly retired now, hasn't she?' he carried on when I didn't answer. 'Did she have a lovely party?'

My mouth opened and closed but no words came out. I must have looked like a goldfish. I certainly felt like a fish out of water. Even though I was feeling dog-tired I knew I would have been better able to cope with a confrontation than this mountain range of denial I now had to scale. I knew from former battles that if Jonathan didn't want to face up to something then he would refuse point blank to acknowledge its existence.

'Yes,' I said, finally finding my voice, 'yes, she did.'

'They're going to miss her—'

'Jonathan,' I interrupted. 'I really haven't called to chat.'

'It's fine,' he said, his eyes flicking to the clock on the kitchen wall. 'I've got time and I want to hear all about it. I've been so tempted to ring you this week. I've got so much to tell you about the move and I've been so desperate to hear your voice.'

That was funny, as Dolly had pointed out and I now realised I thought he preferred the sound of his own.

'But I didn't give in,' he said, his attention swinging back to me. 'I did as you asked, Hattie.'

Was that the paper he was going to use to try and cover over the cracks in our relationship? He hadn't called me for a few days ergo all was well. If it was, I didn't like the pattern, it didn't match mine and I wasn't going to settle for it.

'And I do appreciate that,' I told him, determined to keep my tone light and my hammer hidden until I was ready to deliver the final blow, and besides, I had appreciated his silence. It had given me time to think.

Jonathan nodded. Now was my chance. He was waiting for me to say something else but the blasted words wouldn't come.

'I know you were feeling rattled after our argument,' he said, eventually filling the silent void where my well thought through pronouncement on our relationship should have been, 'but I hope you've cooled off a bit now and have had time to think about what was said.'

I'd had plenty of time to play it all out in my head, but I wasn't sure I was feeling any cooler about it.

'I'm guessing you've called to apologise,' he carried on, his eyes crinkling at the corners as he smiled. 'And if that's the case, then I'm happy to just forget about it.'

In his thick head it was all catalogued just as I thought it would be.

'I take it, that is why you've called?' he frowned.

'Tell me, Jonathan,' I finally asked, just to be completely certain, 'what exactly is it that you're expecting me to apologise for?'

His smile slipped a little and he began to chew his lip.

'What is it that I've done that warrants an apology?' I asked again, my voice a little stronger now.

'Do you really need me to spell it out?'

I nodded.

'Yes, please.'

'Well for a start, you wouldn't cut your time in Wynbridge short, even though you know there's so much to organise ahead of our move.' he began. He didn't sound quite so good-natured now. 'I still can't believe you went in the first place, to be honest, and then there was the flirting at the hotel and your refusal to come home with me after that. Not to mention how you flew off the handle when I suggested that you should look for a job more suited to our social standing ...'

I zoned out as he got into his stride. If it wasn't some fantastical fabrication of his own making, his gripe was about a rare moment when I had stood my ground and he hadn't got his own way. What a waste of a call this was. I should never have asked him to spell it out for me, but at least his list of my alleged crimes was the proof, not that I really needed more, that I was doing the right thing.

'So,' I said, finally raising my voice to a level capable of cutting him off, but hopefully not waking my host, 'basically you're expecting me to apologise for things I haven't done but that you've dreamt up and for not toeing the line when you've told me to. Is that right?'

Dolly had been right. Now I was off and running I was feeling much braver thanks to the physical distance between Jonathan and me.

'Look,' he said, his eyes taking on that shark-like glaze

which had always warned me when trouble was looming, 'I know things got a little out of hand at the hotel—'

'A little!' I laughed, holding up my wrist so he could see the bruises he had inflicted.

They had spread further and were darker now and my wrist was tender to touch. It was going to take some time for them to fade both physically and mentally.

'But that was because I'm under so much pressure,' he carried on, ignoring the marks I brandished in front of him. 'I'm putting everything I've got into giving us a shot at an amazing new life. Things will be completely different once we're settled. Everything will be so much better when we've moved, Hattie, you'll see. You won't be stressed at all.'

I took a deep breath.

'I'm not stressed,' I told him, my eyes looking straight into his, 'and I'm not moving.'

'Don't be so ridiculous.'

'I'm not being ridiculous.'

'Of course, you are,' he spat back as if 'being ridiculous' was my default setting. 'You're just upset, that's all.'

'I *was* upset,' I calmly corrected him. 'I'm not now. Now, I'm clear-headed, rational and ready to move on.'

I didn't think I could have made it any clearer. I had planned to present him with what Mum had said in her email, read it aloud in fact, but there didn't seem to be any point now. My relationship with him was beyond salvaging and there was nothing to be gained from picking over the scrawny carcass.

'I think I better come and get you,' he carried on as if I hadn't said a word. 'You need to come home and start packing. Being with that bloody woman and fannying about over Christmas like you're some extra in a cheesy made-for-television film has made you lose focus. I daresay, deep down, you're just a bit jittery about leaving the country, that's all this is.'

Too deep down to trace as far as I was concerned.

'The only thing I'm leaving, Jonathan,' I said calmly, 'is you.'

'It's last-minute nerves.'

'It really isn't.'

I didn't know how I could possibly make what I was trying to tell him any clearer.

'It is, of course it is.'

'Look,' I sighed, 'I'm going now and I'm going to give you a couple of days to get your head around this, Jonathan, and then I'll call to make arrangements about collecting my stuff from the flat.'

'You'll change your mind,' he carried blithely on. 'In a day or so you'll be begging me to forget we ever had this conversation.'

I shook my head knowing I would never be able to match him when it came to selective memory skills and what was more, I didn't want to. I had been a fool to be flattered by him and think I'd fallen on my feet when he showed some interest in me. I had all too readily slipped under his manip-ulative spell, believing that he was too good for me, when actually, it was the other way around.

'You will,' he laughed, 'you'll be mortified by tomorrow and you'll be back here with me. You'll have to be. You're nothing without me, Hattie and you have no one—'

'Goodbye, Jonathan.'

Shivering, I made my way down the stairs and filled the kettle. Where I had thought there would be relief and a sense of release, there was a dull ache. Not because I regretted what I had done, but because I knew that Jonathan didn't believe that I had done it. I hoped he wouldn't follow through on his threat to turn up and try and take me away. I wouldn't put it past him. The man was so deep in denial he was a danger to himself as well as everyone else around him. I hoped he was going to use up the adrenalin our conversation had unleashed on the gym equipment rather than the gym staff.

'Did I hear you talking to someone, Hattie?'

'Morning, Dolly,' I said, smiling up at her as she slowly made her way down the stairs.

'Have we already had a visitor?'

'No,' I said, shaking my head. 'I wanted to get talking to Jonathan over and done with early and the only place where I can get a decent signal inside is in one corner of the bathroom. I hope I didn't wake you?'

'No,' she said, lowering herself stiffly into her chair next to the fire, 'you didn't. How did he take it? Dare I ask?'

'Much as you'd expect,' I shrugged.

'You mean he didn't believe you?'

'Got it in one. He's convinced I'll change my mind.'

I didn't tell her that he was threatening to come and get

me. I didn't want her worrying about him turning up and causing chaos. If he did arrive, I'd deal with him out of ear-shot of my friend who was still looking as tired as she had the night before.

'His arrogance knows no bounds,' she tutted.

'Apparently not.'

'I daresay he'll be turning up here at some point,' she said, 'trying to get you to go back to the flat.'

I gave her a wry smile.

'Best keep the door locked for today,' she added, 'and if he turns up later, we won't be here anyway.'

That was quite a comforting thought.

I was on edge all day and I couldn't wait for Beamish to whisk us away, even if he hadn't sounded as though he wanted to whisk me anywhere.

'Have you got your thermals on?' I asked Dolly as the time ticked slowly by. 'You know Beamish said you'd need layers.'

'I have,' she confided. 'A long-sleeved top and leggings. I feel the cold more than I used to these days.'

'I could microwave those handwarmer things you've got, if you like. I know you've got gloves, but you could slip them into your coat pockets just in case.'

'That's an excellent idea,' she agreed, looking at her hands.

I almost jumped out of my skin as someone rattled the handle and hammered on the door.

'That'll be Beamish,' said Dolly, rushing to turn the key.

I glanced at the clock and put up a hand to stop her.

'If it is him, he's early,' I noted. 'Let me just check.'

I peeped around the curtain and saw Beamish standing on the doorstep. The chink of light escaping on to the path alerted him to my presence.

'Are you going to let me in? It's freezing out here.'

'It is Beamish,' I said to Dolly, who then opened the door.

'Why was the door locked?' he frowned, letting in a blast of icy air as he stepped inside. 'You never have your door locked this early, Dolly.'

'We haven't been out,' she said lightly, 'so it's been locked all day.'

That was true enough but didn't explain why I had gone into stealth mode and checked who was outside before granting them entry. If Beamish thought anything was amiss, he didn't let on.

'All set then?' he asked. 'It's a bit of a drive so we need to crack on. Anna at Wynthorpe said you could borrow these, Hattie,' he added, holding out a bag.

It contained the wellies I had borrowed the day Dolly and I visited the hall.

'That was kind of her,' I said, taking the bag, 'and you.'

If he'd gone to the bother of sorting out some wellies, he couldn't really mind me tagging along, could he?

'It was Anna's idea,' he shrugged. 'Come on, let's go.'

I was more than happy to get out of the house but being unfamiliar with the area had no real idea where we were heading. Dolly, however, seemed to have more of an inkling.

'Something tells me,' she said, from her vantage point

in the passenger seat, 'that we're going to hear this surprise before we see it.'

Beamish shook his head and laughed.

'I can't keep anything from you, Dolly, can I?'

'I'm right, aren't I?' she asked and I could hear the smile in her voice.

'I think you might be.'

'What?' I asked, leaning between the seats. 'What is it?'

Dolly looked at Beamish and smiled back. Clearly, I wasn't going to be told what we would be hearing and seeing until the moment we arrived at our destination and, as it turned out, not even then.

'I bet you're glad of those layers now, aren't you?' Beamish said to Dolly as the three of us stamped on the spot, trying to keep warm.

'I am,' Dolly agreed, 'and the handwarmers Hattie microwaved.'

I wrinkled my nose and felt the biting cold tickling my toes. We had been warm enough walking from the truck to a large and crowded wooden hide but now the chill was finding its way in and it was only a matter of time before it reached my very marrow.

The hide was full of people as were the viewing platforms on either side. Everyone seemed very keen to get the best spot to look out over an expanse of empty water which was dotted with swaying reed beds and gently undulating islands. I hoped whatever we were here to see was worth risking pneumonia for.

'Is there any more coffee in that—'

Beamish put up his hand, his head cocked to one side.

'Shush,' he said, 'did you hear that?'

I opened my mouth to interrupt his interruption but then I thought I heard something too. It was distant and I had to strain to hear it but there was a distant 'honk' on the horizon.

'They're coming,' Dolly whispered, her eyes bright in the fading light. 'They're coming.'

The honking gradually increased in volume and was joined by what sounded like hundreds, possibly thousands of others. The noise was intense.

'Here they are!' someone who was standing outside shouted above the cacophony. 'I can see them!'

All eyes were now trained on the sky.

'They're pink-footed geese,' said Beamish, for my benefit. 'They come here to roost on the marshes. It's one of Norfolk's most stunning natural sights.'

'I hadn't realised we'd crossed county lines.'

'Well,' he said looking at Dolly, 'I can't offer her international travel but then, that wasn't on the list.'

Looking out as the geese poured in, their silhouettes filling the sky for almost as far as the eye could see, I wasn't sure if he was being sarcastic or not, but I wasn't prepared to let wondering about it mar the moment.

'This is amazing,' I said to Dolly.

'It certainly is,' she agreed.

Then, almost as quickly as it had started, the sound faded and the geese settled, each bird finding its own place for the night.

'Can we come back in the morning and watch them go, Daddy?' the young girl next to me asked the man she was with.

'I'm not sure even you can get up that early, my love,' he laughed, smiling at Dolly.

'I can,' his daughter insisted, bouncing on her toes. 'I will. There's no school now so we can sleep in the next day.'

'Perhaps,' he told her.

'Why did they make all that noise?' I asked Dolly. 'If this place is their nightly refuge, I would have thought they'd fly in quietly.'

'They're in family groups,' the little girl knowledgeably told me, 'and their honking keeps them together. It's their way of making sure they haven't lost anyone.'

'Oh right,' I said, 'I see.'

'It's really important that they all stick together, isn't it, Daddy?'

'Sure is,' he said, shoving her knitted hat back on her head. 'It wouldn't do to lose your family out there on the marshes, would it?'

'No,' she said seriously. 'They have to stick together to keep safe, just like us.'

She was right in more ways than one. Had I stuck with my family I would have been a damn sight safer than I had been when Jonathan had drawn me away. From now on I was going to make keeping my parents close a priority.

'Are you coming back again tomorrow?' the girl asked me.

'No,' I said, 'not tomorrow, but I will one day.'

'I can't imagine you'll have all that much time for ornitho-logical endeavours in Abu Dhabi,' said Beamish once we had walked back to the truck and Dolly was tucked into the passenger seat with warm blankets and a flask. 'But Dolly's pleased you came tonight.'

Wasn't he?

'She used to visit here with her father when she was younger, you know,' he carried on.

I hadn't known that.

'So, when I saw she'd included a coastal trip on the Wish List if felt as important as the ice skating to me.'

I looked at my friend through the truck window. She was staring into the darkness and I felt a sudden and uneasy prickling at the back of my neck. I didn't know what it was, but it was there nonetheless.

She had said she was fine to do the walk, but I could see the distance and slippery conditions underfoot had taken it out of her. I was going to have to put my foot down when it came to rushing about in the run-up to Christmas and felt even happier that I wasn't going to be leaving Wynbridge before the big day now. There was something amiss, some-thing niggling at the back of my mind about my friend but I couldn't pin down what it was.

'I see,' I said, turning to help Beamish stow our muddy wellies away in the boot. 'And I could tell she loved it, as did I.'

Beamish nodded but didn't comment.

'I really meant what I said about coming back to see it again,' I told him.

'Of course.'

'And as far as finding time to go birdwatching in the sun is concerned,' I continued, drawing in the biggest breath, 'that won't be happening now.'

'The birdwatching?'

'Any of it.'

'What do you mean?'

'I'm not going,' I told him. 'I've changed my mind.'

'Oh,' he said, 'right.'

'I'm staying with Dolly for Christmas and then I'll have a think about what I'm going to do and where I'm going to live in the new year.'

'You're not going back to your flat then?'

'No,' I swallowed. 'I'm not going back.'

He slammed the boot shut.

'We better get Dolly home,' he said. 'She'll need an early night after that long walk.'

I don't know what reaction I had been expecting when I told him about my change of plan, but I hadn't thought there would be no reaction at all.

Chapter 24

Another restless night stretched ahead and I couldn't help playing over Beamish's lack of reaction to my, what I considered, monumental news. It wasn't that many days ago that I'd been tethered and we'd had two near-kisses and multiple moments of prolonged eye contact. Now I was as free as a bird but not going anywhere and he didn't seem to care for me at all.

I wasn't looking to replace one man with another, but my friendship with Beamish (the way he listened when I spoke, respected and accepted my opinions even if he didn't always agree with them and was interested in what I had to say) meant the world to me and I wanted things between us to go back to how they had been before.

It was because of the man Beamish was that I had looked with fresh eyes at my one-sided relationship with Jonathan and come to the conclusion that it wasn't the healthiest, even before he had bruised my wrist. Beamish and I might not have been destined to end up together, but our friendship was priceless.

'What are your plans for today then?' Dolly asked when I went down to breakfast.

'I haven't actually got any,' I told her, warming my hands around the teapot, 'so I'll clean the fire out before I eat, if you like. It's chilly in here this morning.'

'What about the Winter Wonderland?' Dolly quizzed. 'I know you were keen to go. Didn't Beamish mention it last night?'

'No,' I said sharply, 'he didn't.'

Dolly didn't say anything and I felt bad for biting her head off. It was hardly her fault.

'How are we doing with the Wish List?' I asked, trying to make amends.

'All right,' she answered. 'There's still a few things to tick off but, by and large, I think we're getting there.'

'And with time to spare,' I said. 'I'm sorry I snapped.'

'It's all right,' she said kindly. 'I can't even begin to imagine how you're feeling right now. This isn't exactly how you expected your holiday here in Wynbridge to work out, is it?'

'No,' I told her, 'it isn't, but actually, I'm feeling far better about certain aspects of it than I expected to.'

Dolly looked rather pleased with herself and I wondered if my previous suspicions might have been right. Rather than simply asking me to stay to support her, I reckoned she had cleverly crafted this impromptu break and engineered my re-gaining of Christmas spirit, with a rather different motive

340

in mind. I knew she wasn't going to mourn the loss of my relationship with Jonathan, but what about my friendship with Beamish? If she had invited me with an ulterior motive, where, if anywhere, did he fit into her plan?

'Apart from . . .' I began but stopped.

'Apart from what?'

'It doesn't matter,' I said, crossing the room to retrieve the coal bucket.

'What is it, Hattie?'

I put the bucket back down.

'It's Beamish,' I told her. 'Something seems to have happened between us. Almost since the moment we met our friendship has felt like the easiest in the world but these last couple of days something's not felt right and I can't help thinking that it might have something to do with Jonathan.'

How it possibly could I didn't know, but that was what I was worried about.

'I didn't think it would matter now, but it feels deceitful that no one knows about him, even though he is out of the picture now. I don't like it.'

'Are you saying that you think Beamish has found out about your relationship with Jonathan?' Dolly asked.

'Perhaps,' I said, biting my lip. 'Although I don't s ee how.'

'Well if you're that worried about it, talk to Beamish and, if he hasn't found out, tell him anyway, tell everyone.'

'Surely it's too late for that now, and besides, I was under the impression that you thought I shouldn't.'

'I was,' she sighed, 'to begin with, but now I think that was a mistake.'

'I didn't think you made mistakes, Dolly,' I said a little bluntly.

She looked rather cross.

'What, because I'm old?' she frowned. 'Because I've seen a lot of life, you think I can't get things wrong anymore?'

'No,' I said, shocked to hear her snippiness matching mine. 'I'm sorry. That's not what I meant.'

'No, I'm sorry,' she said, throwing up her hands and letting them fall back into her lap. 'I had thought I was steering you in the right direction but I underestimated something.'

'What?

'The power of love.'

'What's that supposed to mean?'

Someone started hammering on the door before she could answer.

'It's all right,' she said soothingly as I flinched. 'It's my Christmas shopping delivery not your ghost of Christmas past. Give the driver a hand with the boxes, would you? We can sort the fire after.'

Once everything had been unloaded, the driver, who was one of the many locals to have been in class with Dolly during their formative years, accepted a mince pie and a mug of coffee.

'I shouldn't really,' he said, looking at his watch. 'I've got so many orders to get through.'

'You'll need to keep your strength up then, won't you?' said Dolly stoutly. 'Five more minutes won't hurt.'

She would brook no refusal when it came to keeping the chap's blood sugar topped up. She had told me more than once that the new delivery service was a lifesaver to many in the town. The local Co-op was happy to take orders over the phone from anyone who struggled with their weekly shop and the personal service was thriving as a result.

'Thank you,' he said, taking another pie. 'I suppose there's no harm really, is there? Are you coming to the film night tonight?'

'Yes,' said Dolly. 'We certainly are. I'm very much looking forward to it. I've seen both films at least a dozen times already, but never on the big screen.'

I wasn't sure a screen set up in the town hall warranted the title of a 'big screen', but it was going to be quite an occasion nonetheless. The early film was for family viewing. *Elf* was showing at half three and later on, the adults would have the opportunity for a romantic evening out watching *Love Actually*.

I hadn't been all that fussed when Dolly initially pointed out the posters advertising the first ever Wynbridge Festive Film event, but now I was looking forward to it. It would be interesting to see if my change in attitude towards Christmas extended to enjoying festive films.

'Are you going?' Dolly asked the lad as he washed down his last mouthful of pie with a slurp of still hot coffee.

'Yes,' he nodded, 'can't wait.'

'You'd better get on then,' said Dolly, her voice full of mischief. 'It would be a shame to miss the start because you were still out delivering those orders.'

*

The town hall transformation was perfect. There were seats to suit everyone, including beanbags for those fit enough to pull themselves in and out of them and a couple of squishy sofas which hadn't sold at the last auction. There was even a young woman dressed up as an old-fashioned usherette, selling sweets and treats from the tray she carried around her neck.

I spotted her the second we entered. Most likely because Beamish was standing right next to her, bending to say something in her ear, which made her hoot with laughter. Trying to ignore the uncomfortable sensation in my stomach that the sight elicited, I looked away.

'Dolly!' he called, pointing to the front row when he looked up and spotted us. 'Here! I've saved you the best seats in the house.'

Dolly and I walked up the aisle and I helped her off with her coat.

'Well now,' she smiled, 'these really are grand. Thank you, Beamish.'

'Some of the kids will be in front of you, Dolly,' he said wisely. 'I thought your presence might stop them chattering.'

'But you're forgetting I've retired,' she laughed.

'I don't think that will make the slightest difference,' I told her. 'They respect you, Dolly. We all do.'

'Exactly,' said Beamish.

On the one hand it was a relief to find him so relaxed but on the other I couldn't help wondering if the pretty usherette was responsible for his cheerful disposition and that didn't cheer me at all.

'I'm sorry about our trip to the Winter Wonderland, Hattie,' he said, finally looking at me. 'I was going to suggest we went today, but I got a call to say there were projector and electrical problems here and would I mind acting as electricians' mate.'

'Oh, that's all right,' I said, relief that he hadn't snubbed me on purpose making my stomach fizz rather than groan, 'I understand.'

'I had no idea it was so late until someone said it was an hour until showtime,' he added, turning back to Dolly. 'The day has flown by.'

'And between you all, have you fixed the projector?' I asked.

'Fingers crossed,' he said. 'It might need a bit of tweaking between films but I think it should be OK. Time will tell, I suppose. The electrics on the other hand . . .'

'I'm sure it will all be fine,' said Dolly, making herself comfortable. 'And if it isn't, you'll soon sort it.'

Clearly, she had great faith in the skills of the much-loved and most popular handyman in Wynbridge.

'And about what you told me last night, Hattie,' he said, dropping his voice a little, 'about your decision not to move . . .'

Dolly picked up her bag and opened it, ostensibly rifling for something to make it look as though she wasn't listening. 'Yes?'

'Well, I just want you to know that I did take it on board, even if it didn't seem like it.'

'Right.'

'I was just shocked,' he went on, 'still am, to be honest. Obviously, I don't know what prompted your change of heart and we've never discussed the circumstances surrounding your decision to go in the first place,' he said, fixing me with a penetrating gaze, 'but it was a surprise to hear you'd changed your mind.'

He still hadn't said whether he was pleased or not. The only emotion he had expressed was shock, but there was a look in his eyes which suggested there was something more going on in his head than feeling surprised.

'Right,' he said just as Dolly looked up from her bag brandishing a bag of sweets, 'I better get backstage or whatever it's called. See you later.'

'There,' said Dolly, when he was out of earshot, 'you were worrying over nothing.'

I don't know what she'd been listening to but it obviously wasn't mine and Beamish's conversation.

'Right as rain,' she beamed. 'Do you want a pear drop?'

The place had filled up in the time it took us to settle, and the noise level of excited chatter had reached fever pitch by the time the vicar stepped up on to the stage to address the audience, thank them all for coming and remind them that the evening was being laid on as a fundraiser for the church roof and that if it was a success, then the council would consider making it a regular event. His words were met with claps and shouts of approval and then the first film began.

I didn't pay much attention to Will Ferrell charging

around New York saving Christmas so it would have been hard to say if Dolly's determination to make me fall for all things festive had worked. My mind was fixed firmly on Beamish and the words I would use to explain to him about Jonathan.

Our strange exchange before the film had left me in no doubt that I had to do it and by the time the curtains had closed and the applause had died down I didn't want to wait a minute longer. It was now or never.

'Back in a sec,' I said to Dolly, who was selecting a bar of chocolate from the usherette who had kindly come over to her ahead of the queue which was forming in front of the stage.

The girl was even prettier close to and her kind-hearted gesture would have made her the perfect match for generous Beamish.

'Where are you off to?' Dolly frowned, but I didn't answer.

I wasn't going to let anything thwart my resolve to share my secret. There was an hour between the films and I would use that time to come clean and ask if we could start our relationship over again.

'Have you seen Beamish?' I asked Alison from school, who was waiting in line for the loos.

'He was heading towards the back room a minute ago,' she said, pointing over her shoulder, 'muttering something about the electrics in the kitchen. Are you OK? You look a bit flushed.'

'I'm fine,' I nodded. 'It's just a bit warm in here, isn't it?'

I slipped into the room she had suggested and could hear someone moving about. I closed the door behind me.

'Is that you, Mike?' Beamish called.

'No,' I swallowed, 'it's me, Hattie.'

'Even better.'

I was relieved he thought so.

'Can you give us a hand?' he asked, sounding agitated. 'I literally need another hand to see what's going on with this fuse-box. It's so damn dark in here.'

The room was badly lit with just a single dim bulb overhead. I ventured to the back of the room, around the corner and found Beamish precariously balanced in the near dark at the top of a ladder in a sort of cupboard.

'What on earth are you doing up there?' I gasped.

'What does it look like?'

'I don't know,' I snapped back, 'that's why I asked.'

'It's where the blasted fuse-box is,' he said, sounding strained. 'Something's blown in the kitchen and I need to see what it is. If that lot out there don't get their teas and coffees ...'

'There'll be a riot.'

'Exactly, so are you going to help or not?'

'I'll go and find the vicar.'

'No,' he said, sounding impatient. 'I don't need the vicar, I need you.'

'Oh,' I said, 'right.'

'You're lighter than he is.'

'What's that got to do with the fuse-box?'

Quite a lot as it turned out. With just the one ladder between us, Beamish thought it would be a good idea for me to climb up ahead of him and he would follow up behind, as it were. My job was to shine the torch at the fuse-box, leaving his hands free to fiddle about with whatever it was that needed his attention. It didn't sound like the safest of ideas but with the clock ticking I scaled the heights with Beamish hot on my heels.

'Am I squashing you?' he asked, once we were in position.

'A bit,' I said, feeling him lean into me. 'I hope this ladder is safer than it looks.'

'It's fine,' he muttered, pressing his body closer.

'Can you see anything?' I squeaked, trying not to look down for fear of feeling even giddier.

'I think so,' he said, stretching around me.

'Look,' I said, even though the timing was ridiculous, 'I really came to find you because I need to talk to you about something.'

'Do you?'

'Yes,' I said, shifting a little to give him better access to the box.

'Well do you think you can hang on to it for a bit?' he groaned, pressing me further into the rungs.

'I suppose so,' I gasped.

'For pity's sake, hold the torch higher.'

I didn't much care for his tone but stretched as far as I could. He was quiet for a few seconds and I hoped he was working on the problem.

'Hattie,' he whispered.

'What?' I gulped. 'Have you done? I don't think I can breathe like this for much longer.'

'What's that on your wrist?'

'Oh,' I said, jerking my arm back and almost dropping the torch. 'It's nothing.'

Out of all the details I had planned to divulge, my bruises were the one thing, especially given Beamish's family history, that I was going to keep quiet about.

'It looked like something to me.'

'It's nothing.' I said again.

'Look,' he said, squashing me even flatter as he flicked a switch, 'I've got my hands full right now, but—'

'That you certainly have!' shouted a voice from below, making us both wobble. 'What the hell's going on here, Hattie, Beamish?'

My heart was suddenly beating a tattoo and I could hear the blood rushing in my ears. It was a wonder I could keep hold of the torch because my palms were covered in sweat. I didn't need to shine the beam down the ladder to see who was standing at the foot of it.

'I said,' roared Jonathan's voice. 'What the hell's going on?'

'Good evening, Jonathan,' said Beamish as he climbed down and Jonathan thankfully took a step back. 'Hattie has been helping me sort a problem with the fuse-box.'

My legs had turned to jelly and I had to summon every ounce of courage I had to climb back down the ladder. I reached out to steady myself grasping Beamish's arm as my feet touched the ground.

'How do you know his name?' I stammered, fumbling to turn off the torch. 'How do you know who he is? How long have you known?'

I knew I was gabbling, but it was all such a shock. Not just Jonathan turning up when I had finally begun to think that he wouldn't, but both men casually dropping each other's names into the conversation as if it were the most natural thing in the world.

'Which one of us are you talking to?' sneered Jonathan.

Shakily, I pointed at Beamish.

'I've known about Jonathan for a few days,' he said, 'courtesy of your Facebook profile. I had been going to send you a friend request, but decided against it when I realised that I didn't know you after all. You need to check your privacy settings, Hattie,' he told me, 'if you don't want the world knowing your business.'

I shook my head, still not believing what was happening. His words, and the sad tone in which he delivered them, made my head pound.

'According to your relationship status and timeline pictures,' he carried on. 'Jonathan's been your boyfriend for quite some time.'

'Fiancé now, actually,' said Jonathan, pulling a ring box out of his coat pocket. 'I've come here tonight to ask you to marry me, Hattie. I know I should have done it earlier but with one thing and another the timing was never quite right.'

How could he possibly think that the timing, given that I'd already broken up with him, was ever going to be right?

'And how is it, that you know Beamish?' I asked Jonathan, my eyes darting between the two men who couldn't have been more different.

'You mentioned him, and his job one day and I tracked him down on the school website,' said Jonathan, as if it was the sort of thing any rational person would do. 'Initially I assumed the school caretaker would be some semi-retired grandad, but,' he added with another menacing sneer as his eyes returned to Beamish, 'apparently not.'

'Did you know who he was when you turned up here before?' I demanded, the puzzle pieces finally slipping into place as my brain began to unscramble everything.

Jonathan didn't answer, but he didn't have to. Of course, he had known then. I daresay his internet stalking was the real reason he'd turned up and tried to drag me away.

'Were you with him last weekend?' Beamish asked, pointing at Jonathan.

'Yes,' I whispered, feeling ashamed. 'Yes.'

'And did Dolly know?'

I nodded, unable to say it out loud.

'Right,' he said, making for the door. 'I see.'

Of course, he didn't see because I hadn't had the chance to make him. All he had in plain sight was the man from some staged, sunny online photographs brandishing a ring box and offering me a happy ever after. He had no idea what the sickening truth beneath the glossy veneer was.

'I'll give the pair of you some privacy then,' he said huskily.

'No,' I said, reaching out and grabbing his arm, 'please don't go.'

He looked down at my hand, my jumper had stretched back again and the bruises on my wrist looked even worse now they were lit by the bulb in the ceiling as opposed to the torch. Beamish looked quickly back at Jonathan and narrowed his eyes. I needed to think fast.

'Like I told you yesterday, Jonathan,' I said firmly, turning to stand between him and Beamish. 'I'm not moving with you, I don't want to be in a relationship with you, and I certainly don't want to be your wife.'

Jonathan shook his head and raised his eyebrows.

'Oh right,' he sneered, looking first at Beamish and then at me. 'I get it. You've moved on already.'

'Don't be so ridiculous,' I spat. 'Beamish is just a friend.'

'Oh really.'

'Yes,' I said, 'a real friend who has shown me what a healthy friendship looks like as opposed to the sick and twisted one that you turned ours and our relationship into.'

I was saying the words for Beamish's benefit, not Jonathan's. I wanted him to know how much I valued the time we had spent together but his stony expression when I glanced back indicated I wasn't reaching him at all. I couldn't blame him. Had I just discovered that Beamish had a partner tucked away somewhere, I would have felt deceived too. My reaction to seeing him casually chatting with the usherette was proof enough of that.

'I've told you a hundred times that things will be different

353

when we've moved,' Jonathan carried on. 'I admit I've been stressed, trying to organise everything—'

'And that warrants resorting to physical violence, does it?' growled Beamish.

The last thing I wanted was for them to start fighting. This was way beyond a Daniel Cleaver and Mark Darcy, *Bridget Jones* style scrap now.

'You think that using aggression will make for a happy marriage, do you?' Beamish carried on, his voice becoming louder with every word.

I knew that he had painful first-hand knowledge that it certainly wouldn't and that at any moment the situation could escalate out of all control.

'It really doesn't matter how you would answer that Jonathan,' I jumped in, 'because I know now that your treachery runs far deeper than any mark you could have left on me with your fists.'

'What's that supposed to mean?' he scowled.

'I know how you manipulated my relationship with my parents,' I said, lifting my chin in defiance. It felt easier to stand up to him with Beamish behind me. 'I shared my deepest secrets with you and you used them to get what you wanted. To pull me and my family apart.'

Jonathan shook his head and slipped the ring box back into his pocket.

'How is that love, Jonathan?' I sobbed. 'How can you possibly think that the lies you've told can have anything to do with love?'

He shrugged, his shoulders dropping a little and I hoped that meant my words were finally making an impact.

'You do understand now why I'm not coming with you, don't you?' I carried on. 'Surely, you can see that what you did was unforgivable?'

I held my breath, waiting for his answer.

'Are you really telling me,' he said, 'that you can't see beyond all that? That you can't appreciate how much better off you'd be without parents like yours?'

I shook my head. He was completely unhinged. I felt Beamish bristle behind me.

'Would you really rather stay in this crappy backwater, with the likes of him, than move with me to a life of five-star luxury where you'd never have to lift a finger or work another day in your life?'

'Yes,' I said resolutely, 'yes, I would. And I'll tell you why, Jonathan. Because, I don't want five-star luxury and I certainly don't want to give up my parents or my work, especially as I've only just decided what I want my next job to be.'

It was too much for him to bear and without warning he sprang forward and tried to catch my wrist again, but Beamish was too quick for him. Within a blink he had Jonathan pinned against the wall with his arm twisted behind his back.

'Jesus,' Jonathan groaned, crying out in pain as Beamish squeezed his arm harder. 'I could have you for assault!'

'And I could have you charged with that too, couldn't I?' I breathlessly reminded him. 'And much more besides.'

'I'm going to see you off the premises now,' Beamish said quietly. 'With no drama or fuss.'

His calm demeanour was far more powerful than any punch he could have thrown.

'And you're going to promise me that I won't see you in Wynbridge ever again, aren't you?' he added.

'You know what,' said Jonathan trying to push Beamish off, but failing. 'I wouldn't be seen dead in this dump and I'm beginning to think I've had a lucky escape. You're welcome to her, mate.'

'I'm not your mate.'

The look Beamish gave me as he spun Jonathan out of the room suggested that he didn't want me either. I might have finally been rid of Jonathan, but his eradication from my life had come at the highest possible price.

I gave it a minute before going back into the hall. There had been no shouting so I guessed Jonathan had gone quietly, but Beamish hadn't come back to find me.

'There was a guy looking for you in the interval,' whispered the usherette who was now standing behind the audience. 'Really good looking.' She grinned, blinking her long dark lashes. 'Did he find you?'

'Yes,' I said, 'he found me.'

'Is he a friend of yours?'

'No,' I said, ducking back to my seat, 'absolutely not.'

'Shame,' she laughed. 'I wouldn't have minded his number.'

'Where's Dolly?' I asked Jemma, who was now sitting in the row behind where I had left my friend.

'Alison has taken her home,' Jemma said, a deep frown knitting her brows as she leant forward to explain and the couple behind her grumbled about not being able to see. 'Dolly said she wasn't feeling well and that she didn't know where you'd gone, so Alison took her back to the cottage.'

I hadn't thought the evening could get any worse, but losing Beamish and my confrontation with Jonathan turned out to be just the tip of a very catastrophic iceberg.

Chapter 25

I grabbed my coat, told Jemma and her husband Tom to make use of the empty front row seats if they wanted them and rushed out, through the town and back to the cottage. My breath was sharp in my chest by the time I turned down Dolly's road and saw a car I didn't recognise parked up outside. The 'doctor on call' card displayed on the windscreen confirmed what Jemma had said, but Dolly had been fine when I left her to find Beamish. What on earth could have happened?

As I pushed open the gate, the front door swung open.

'I'll be as quick as I can,' I heard Alison say as she appeared in the pool of escaped light from inside, stuffing her arms into her coat.

A man's voice drifted out after her, but I didn't hear what he said.

'Alison!' I shouted, 'what's happened?'

She pulled the door shut behind her and rushed to meet me on the path.

'I was just coming to look for you,' she frowned. 'There's something the matter with Dolly, but I don't know what. She said she felt ill and asked me to bring her home and call the doctor. Now she's saying she has to speak to you before anyone else. It's all a bit of a mystery.'

Dolly wasn't one for melodrama and I began to feel scared.

'I best go in,' I said, but I didn't want to.

My feet stayed rooted to the path. I would much rather not have to cross the cottage threshold. I had a dreadful sense of foreboding that if I did then my life was going to be turned even further upside down.

'Go on then,' said Alison, giving me a much-needed nudge. 'She's waiting.'

The doctor was packing his bag when Alison and I went in and Dolly was in her usual chair next to the fire, which had been stoked and was bathing the room in a warm glow. I shivered nonetheless.

'You must be Hattie,' smiled the young doctor, holding out his hand which I tentatively shook. 'I'm Doctor Harris.'

I kept my eyes on Dolly.

'Yes,' I swallowed, 'I'm Hattie.'

'Dolly's all right now,' he said, pulling on his coat, 'and I've got to get off to another call, but she knows to ring if she wants me to come back later.'

'Right,' I said, trying to smile and failing. 'Thanks.'

'Can I give you a lift, Alison?'

'Yes,' she said, 'I better get back.'

'I'm afraid you'll have missed the start,' said Dolly.

Her voice sounded completely normal.

'Doesn't matter in the slightest,' said Alison, going over to squeeze her hand. 'It's not my favourite bit.'

'No,' Dolly smiled. 'Beginnings and endings are all right, but it's what happens in between that really counts, isn't it?'

I knew she was paraphrasing someone but couldn't remember who.

'I'll pop by again tomorrow,' said Doctor Harris, holding the door open for Alison.

'No need,' said Dolly.

He ignored her.

'See you in the morning,' he called over his shoulder, 'perhaps then I might get a cup of tea.'

Dolly tutted. Apparently, her GP was her mischievous equal.

'I'll let him get away with that,' she sniffed. 'He might only be a babe in arms, but he knows what he's about.'

'And what is he about?' I asked, squatting down in front of her so I could look at her properly. 'Dolly, what's going on?'

Dolly instructed me to make a pot of tea and fill a plate with sausage rolls and cheese straws before she would say another word and once it was all arranged, and the drink poured, I pulled my chair closer to hers.

'Hattie,' she then said, without any preamble whatsoever, 'I've got cancer.'

My cup wobbled in the saucer and she leant forward to take it from me and put it back on the little table.

'And I'm not going into details about which one. It doesn't matter, because I'm not going to have any treatment.'

I sat stock-still, not knowing what to say.

'According to Doctor Harris and the consultant at the hospital, fiddling about might give me a few extra months, but there's no guarantee and they'd be pretty miserable months at best, so I'd rather not.'

I folded my hands in my lap and stared at them.

'I might make it to spring, if I'm lucky,' she carried on, 'Hogmanay if not,' she chuckled.

My head snapped back up.

'Sorry,' she said, the smile fading from her lips.

I shook my head, sharp tears stinging my eyes.

'You'll have to forgive my brisk explanation,' she said kindly. 'It's how I'm dealing with it, I suppose and of course, I've had considerably longer to get used to the idea than the three seconds I've just given you. I didn't actually want you to know yet, but Dr Harris has said it's time I spilled the beans'

My heart felt as though someone had wrapped it in elastic bands and were pulling them tighter and tighter. This couldn't be happening. Dolly had only just retired. She had so much left to do, so many places to visit, so much life left to live. Her entire adult life had been given over to others and now she was telling me that there was nothing left over for herself. That couldn't be right.

'And before you ask if the hospital have muddled my notes with someone else's,' she said quickly, quashing my last hope, 'they haven't. This is definitely me that we're talking about, whether we wish it otherwise or not.'

'How long have you known?' I croaked. 'Exactly how long have you had to get used to the idea, as you put it, Dolly?'

She reached to the table again and handed me back my tea.

'I'd add another sugar to that if I were you,' she suggested.

I shook my head and she picked up her own cup before settling back.

'I had a feeling something wasn't right in the summer holidays,' she explained. 'Usually I find I'm back on form for the start of the new term, but this year I wasn't so I took myself along to see lovely Doctor Harris and the rest, as they say, is history, or it soon will be.'

'I'm so sorry,' I whispered.

I couldn't believe she hadn't told me before. That she'd lived with the knowledge all these months and not said a word. Why had she done that?

'Why didn't you say anything sooner?' I asked, then I realised. 'Oh Dolly,' I choked, 'you knew when you came to see me in September, didn't you? Is that why you came to find me at the flat the day I was made redundant?'

She nodded.

'And I was so full of self,' I said, hating myself for being so caught up in my own dilemma that I hadn't picked up on hers, 'that I never noticed.'

'What was there to notice?' She shrugged. 'I'd hardly gone out and had a T-shirt printed announcing the fact, had I? You weren't to know.'

'But why didn't you say anything after?' I cried. 'Why didn't you tell me when you invited me to stay?'

'Because,' she said with a heavy sigh, 'I wanted you to come for the right reasons and not with the knowledge of this hanging over you. I wanted to give you some time away from Jonathan with no strings attached. Some time to be free, if you like.'

'I see.'

'And it did the trick, didn't it?' she said, smiling again and sounding rather pleased with herself. 'You didn't know about my illness, so you weren't fretting about me and my failing organs.'

I couldn't help but flinch when she sounded so blasé.

'Coming to Wynbridge and making friends with Beamish opened your eyes and helped you make the decision to break things off with Jonathan, didn't it?'

'Yes,' I agreed, 'yes I suppose it did, in part.'

Then wasn't the time to tell her that keeping Jonathan a secret had ultimately cost me my precious friendship with Beamish.

'I have to admit,' she said, her eyes narrowing as her tone sharpened, 'Jonathan had me under his spell too for a while, what with that fancy hamper and his honeyed words.'

'Well, under the circumstances—' I began to say.

'Never mind the circumstances,' she cut in, 'we got there in the end.'

She sounded relieved and I guessed there were more loose ends that she wanted to tie up before too much sand slipped into the wrong end of her hourglass.

'And the Wish List,' I said, nodding to where it was pinned up next to the fire.

It was far lengthier than when we had first written it and ran to a full couple of pages, but most things were ticked off. Now, knowing about her illness, I could appreciate just what an effort it must have been for Dolly to glide around the ice rink and make the walk to see the geese. She'd never shown any sign, other than a little general tiredness, that anything was wrong, had she? Later I would trawl back over my time here, looking for clues I might have missed.

'That wasn't all about me, was it?'

'No,' said Dolly, with a wry smile, 'there were actually a few things on there that I wanted to do for myself but convincing you that you should do them too ensured you got to enjoy them. It was a little underhand, but . . .'

'No, it wasn't,' I smiled, thinking of the fun we'd had, especially putting up the decorations.

My amusement was tempered when I realised she had insisted they all went up because it the last time she was going to see them. Come to think of it, at one point, she'd even mentioned 'last Christmas' and then modified her words to make me believe she was talking about my last Christmas in the UK.

'It was clever,' I acknowledged.

Dolly smiled in agreement.

'Had I known that you were ill, I'd have gone about everything with a completely different mindset, wouldn't I?' I said.

'Yes,' she said, 'you would and so would I. I was looking for unadulterated joy with no sympathetic undertones and I got it.'

'I wish I could say the same,' I told her.

'What do you mean?'

'My time on the ice rink,' I reminded her, giving a little shudder as I remembered my fears and another as I recalled the feeling of Beamish's strong hands grasping my waist. 'You might have had the joy on that occasion Dolly, but I was looking for sympathy. That ice was cold and very hard!'

Dolly laughed at the memory.

'But, Hattie,' she said, the laughter fading as she reached for my hand, 'please don't convince yourself that I am simply ill, as you just said. I am dying. There is absolutely no doubt about that.'

'Aren't we all?' I said, looking her in the eye and trying to sound stronger than I felt.

'That we are,' she sighed, 'but some of us are going far sooner than others.'

We talked long into the night, about all sorts of things. Some related to what was going to happen to Dolly and others completely unconnected. One thing we did decide, was that I was going to stay at the cottage until ... well, you know ... and I would do my utmost to make sure Dolly stayed there too. She was adamant that she didn't want to go to the local hospice. She'd lived the best part of her life in the cottage and she wanted to leave there 'feet first' as she put it.

I couldn't help but admire her candid grasp on the situation, but like she said, she'd had far longer to get used to the idea than I had. She had told everyone she had shut herself away because she'd had a cold, bordering on flu, but that was all a ruse. What she had actually done was sensibly taken some time out to come to terms with her diagnosis. She explained that she had gladly gone through the whole anger, denial and self-pity process in complete privacy.

'So where did you slip off to earlier?' she asked as I eventually began to clear things away to go to bed.

I was surprised that between us we had worked our way through the seasonal snacks Dolly had suggested. All that was left were a few crumbs.

'I wondered if you might have gone to tell Beamish about Jonathan?'

What a wily old fox she was.

'I had,' I admitted.

'And how did he take it?' she asked, watching me closely.

'Well,' I said, puffing out my cheeks, 'it turned out there was far less for me to explain than I thought there might be.'

'Oh?'

'Let's get you settled in bed,' I told her, 'and I'll tell you what happened.'

'It can be my bedtime story,' she joked, then catching my expression added, 'it won't give me nightmares, will it?'

With Dolly tucked, disconcertingly without any insistence that she could manage on her own, under her eiderdown and with a mug of cocoa on the nightstand, I told her what had unfolded when I went to find Beamish and Jonathan had gatecrashed. Her eyes widened when I reached the part about the two men already knowing about each other, and Jonathan pulling an engagement ring out of his pocket, but she didn't interrupt.

'And how did you leave things?' she asked once I had finally reached the end.

'Well,' I said, 'I'm pretty certain that Jonathan has finally got the message.'

'And Beamish?'

I shook my head.

'Let's just say, I don't think we're friends anymore.'

Dolly looked appalled.

'This is my fault,' she said, plucking at a loose thread on the eiderdown.

'No,' I said, shaking my head. 'No. It's mine. I should have been talking about Jonathan from the off.'

'No,' she said, refusing to let me shoulder the blame. 'Like I said earlier, I underestimated the power of love and that was foolish of me.'

As a result of everything that had happened since, I'd forgotten she'd said that earlier.

'You do know,' she carried on, 'that Beamish has fallen in love with you, don't you, Hattie?'

'Of course, he hasn't,' I said, my temperature rising.

He might have liked me, even fancied me a bit, but he wasn't in love with me. How could he be when we'd known each other for less than a month?

'I should have realised it sooner,' Dolly tutted, 'but with everything else that's been going on I didn't spot the signs.'

'You're wrong,' I tried to tell her.

'And,' she carried on, talking over me, 'I think you've fallen in love with him.'

I shook my head. I knew now that the 'L' word wasn't one to casually bandy about. I would readily admit that there had been a spark of attraction, one that had led to our near-kisses, but it had been well and truly snuffed out now. The look of hurt on his face earlier was enough to confirm that we were done for. There was no room for even a hint of a friendship, let alone a loving feeling.

'If you had seen the look Beamish gave me when he left, Dolly,' I told her, 'then you'd be as sure as I am that the last thing he feels for me is love. He hates me for my deception and harbours no other feeling than that.'

'Rubbish,' said Dolly vehemently.

'It isn't,' I batted back, 'it's true and even if it wasn't, we could hardly do anything about it, could we?'

'Why not?'

'Well for a start I've just ended one relationship so I could hardly fall straight into another, especially with a man I barely know. It wouldn't be appropriate.'

Dolly was looking mutinous.

'Since when,' she demanded, 'has true love ever taken into account what's appropriate and what's not?'

Chapter 26

As I gradually drifted up through the layers of sleep, I realised I wasn't alone in the bedroom. I cautiously opened one eye and found Dolly standing next to the bed.

'What's wrong?' I panicked, sitting straight up and feeling instantly awake. 'What is it? Have you got a pain? Why didn't you wake me before?'

Dolly let me blow myself out before she said anything.

'Do you know what today is?' was her first question.

I took a quick mental jog around the calendar. I didn't think I'd slept right through to Christmas day, but I couldn't be sure. I'd felt emotionally wrung out by the time I crawled into bed so it wasn't beyond the bounds that I'd slept for days rather than hours.

'No,' I said, thinking it would actually be quicker for her to tell me than for me to try and work it out.

'It's the winter solstice,' she said. 'You need to get yourself up, organised and ready to go to Wynthorpe Hall. They'll be having the ceremony to celebrate it later.'

I wasn't sure why she thought that would have any significance for me. I hadn't much interest in the lengthening of days given our conversation the night before. If anything, I would rather have spent my time working out how to stop time. At least that way I might have my darling Dolly for a bit longer.

'If it's all right with you,' I said, 'I think I'll give it a miss. I'm not in the mood for getting in tune with my pagan side today.'

'No, it's not all right with me,' she tutted, tugging at the corner of the eiderdown. 'Beamish is going to be there. It will be the perfect opportunity for you to clear the air.'

I couldn't agree. I was pretty certain my former friend would far rather be left in peace. I would be the last person he'd want to have turn up and spoil his fun. Assuming a solstice celebration was fun.

'I think you're wrong, Dolly.'

'And I think *you're* wrong,' she interrupted. 'So, get yourself up. I've been told there's only so many times I can play my cancer card before it loses its power, but I'm playing it now.'

I looked at her aghast.

'You wouldn't want me to waste it, would you?' she asked craftily 'Surely you wouldn't dismiss a dying woman's wishes.'

'Really, Dolly . . .'

'Just don't tell him about my troubles,' she added as she walked out. 'I'll do that later when you come back here together for dinner.'

She had far more faith in my magical powers than I did. There was no way I would be able to get Beamish back to the cottage.

Catherine Connelly happened to be in the Wynthorpe Hall courtyard when the taxi I'd taken from Wynbridge dropped me off that bright but cold afternoon. I made a quick scan of all the vehicles I could see. Apparently, I wasn't the only one attending the gathering. My heart rate sped up to a gallop as my eyes came to rest on Beamish's truck. I had been hoping that he might have been elsewhere, but alas, no.

'Hattie!' Catherine called. 'How lovely to see you again. Are you here for the ceremony?'

'Um, yes,' I said. 'Dolly suggested I should come. Is that all right? I don't want to impose.'

'Of course, it's all right,' she said, opening the courtyard gate and letting the dogs rush over to greet me. 'The more the merrier. We're expecting quite a crowd, but we won't be starting for a while. Would you like to come in for a coffee?'

I wasn't sure what to do. For all I knew Beamish could be ensconced inside and it would be impossible to talk to him in a room full of people.

'Or you could take a turn around the Wonderland?' She suggested, reaching into the pocket of her skirt for something. 'Some of it has been packed away and I'm afraid Santa has vacated the grotto, but the reindeer are in their paddock and the trail is still set up.'

She unfolded what I could now see was a map.

'You're more than welcome to explore.'

'Oh yes please,' I said, taking the map from her and turning it what I thought was the right way up. I was pleased I'd decided to wear the borrowed welly boots now. 'I'll do that. I was sorry not to get the chance to come when it was all in full swing.'

'Maybe next year,' she smiled.

I didn't contradict her. Perhaps news of my changed plans had already reached the Wynbridge countryside.

'I'll tell Anna you're here. But don't get cold,' she added, pulling her shawl tighter around her. 'If you start to get chilly make your way back here to thaw out.'

'All right,' I said. 'Thank you, Mrs Connelly.'

'Catherine,' she said, clicking her fingers at the dogs. 'Please call me Catherine.'

I made my way to the front of the beautiful hall, thinking of the tour Beamish had arranged and the delicious tea. I could see from the map and a few scuffed patches on the gravel that this was where the refreshments had been set up, most noticeably the Cherry Tree Café mobile tea room. I wondered if the prettily painted vintage caravan on the map was an accurate representation. Knowing Jemma's sense of style, it most likely was.

Keen to get out of the wind, I hastily followed the arrows and the striped candy cane markers to where the path properly began. It was quiet among the trees, and truth be told, a little eerie, but I pressed on, admiring the listed features. My pace slackened as I heard voices ahead. Was I about to come face to face with Beamish? Part of me wished I was, if only to get the initial awkwardness over with.

'Aha,' said a woman as I turned a corner and stepped into a clearing.

My heart sank. There was no sign of Beamish.

'Could you possibly spare a moment to give us a hand?'

She introduced herself as Mags and the teenage boy with her, was her son, Ed. Between them they had been showing the owls they had rescued, to raise funds for the care of the growing menagerie of waifs, strays and injured birds and mammals which Ed tended to.

'He started with just birds,' Mags said fondly, 'but now we have all sorts.'

'We even had a fox for a while,' said Ed, as he handed me the corner of the canopy they had been struggling to fold in the breeze. 'But she was soon well enough to be released.'

'Would you like to hold one of the owls?' Mags asked. 'It won't take a minute to get one out again.'

'Oh no,' I said hastily, 'but thanks for the offer.'

I was more than happy to admire them from a distance.

'I'd better push on,' I said once the cover was stowed safely away. 'I'm really here for the solstice ceremony.'

'There's going to be quite a crowd today,' Mags nodded. 'Keep following the path and it will lead you to where you need to be.'

After briefly stopping to admire the three penned reindeer and their silky antlers, my ears picked up a musical sound I had heard before.

'The Wishing Tree,' I sighed.

There was no mention of it on the map and I wondered if it had been left off on purpose. Perhaps the Connellys didn't want it found or perhaps it was left for those who stepped outside the parameters of the paper to find. It was every bit as entrancing as before and I couldn't help but recall the first time I had seen it. How I wished Beamish was there so I could explain ...

'Hattie?'

I had barely made the wish and it had come true.

'What are you doing here?'

I turned and saw him sitting on a bench at the edge of the clearing. I hadn't noticed any seating before; my eyes had been firmly focused on the tree.

'Looking for you,' I said, taking in the biggest breath. 'Dolly was desperate for me to find you. She said I should explain.'

'And what about you?' he asked gruffly. 'Do you want to explain?'

'Of course,' I said, a lump forming in my throat as I took in the hard-set line of his mouth and the tension in his shoulders. 'Of course, I do.'

He shrugged and sat back, evidently determined not to make things easy for me and I could hardly blame him. Had the boot been on the other foot I wouldn't have wanted to be anywhere near him, let alone listen to anything he might have had to say. Taking a leap of faith, I walked over and sat, perched on the end of the bench, as far from him as it was possible to get without falling off.

'I know I should have mentioned Jonathan as soon as I arrived,' I blurted out.

'Yes,' he said, 'you should.'

'But to begin with,' I carried on, 'talking about him didn't seem relevant. I was simply in town to spend some time with Dolly before I moved. It didn't feel necessary to explain the intricacies of my private life.'

Saying those few words out loud made me feel uncomfortable. When I arrived, I was on the verge of becoming engaged and beginning a new life on the other side of the world. Surely, I should have been so full of it, it would have been impossible to shut me up. The fact that I had kept it all to myself, and not even consciously, said a lot about how I had really felt about my relationship with Jonathan.

'Did Dolly play any part in it?' Beamish asked.

'Yes,' I nodded, after I had thought about it for a second or two, 'yes, she did. She could see things in my relationship that I couldn't and she thought that, by bringing me to Wynbridge and giving me some space, I would be able to see those things for myself.'

At least that part of her strategy had worked.

'She also thought,' I bravely carried on, 'that if you and I became friends then I would rediscover what close friendships, relationships between adults should really be. An equal footing as opposed to the scales always being weighted in one person's favour.'

Beamish nodded.

'And her plan worked,' I carried on. 'My friendship with you did make me see everything that was wrong with my relationship with Jonathan. You landed in my life, just in the nick of time.'

'But not before Jonathan assaulted you,' said Beamish. 'Not before he physically hurt you.'

'I know it's probably hard to believe,' I explained, 'but the mental scars have run far deeper than the fading marks. Anyway, it doesn't matter now. He's gone. Finally, and I'm not living my life by his rules anymore.'

Had everything else not been such a disaster, I daresay it would have felt quite liberating.

'And what about us?' Beamish asked, turning to look at me properly for the first time. 'Did Dolly factor any feelings deeper than friendship developing between us into her plan?'

Now it was my turn to stare ahead.

'No,' I whispered. 'As far as I know, there was no contingency strategy to cope with deeper feelings. Dolly simply hoped that we would become wonderful friends.'

'But friends talk to each other, Hattie,' Beamish pointed out, sounding angry. 'Friends confide in one another. I told you about my parents and you even explained a little about yours. Surely that should have been the moment you mentioned Jonathan.'

He was right, that would have been the perfect time to come clean. Tears sprang to my eyes and I tried to blink them away.

'I do understand why you feel deceived,' I sniffed, 'and I know that all I've ever done is let you down, even though you've shown me nothing but kindness . . .'

The dreadful realisation of how I had treated the wonderful man sitting next to me hit me hard in the chest and I began to cry. What an idiot I had been to let Dolly talk me into coming here this afternoon and asking if we could still be friends. Her blasted 'cancer card' had a lot to answer for.

I let out a longer, unrestrained sob. How was I going to manage without her? How was I going to negotiate my way through my life when she was no longer in it? I felt Beamish shift closer. He wrapped an arm around my shoulder and pulled me into his side.

'Please don't,' I said, trying to move away. 'I'm not crying to make you feel sorry for me.'

'I know,' he said huskily.

'And I'm not crying about us,' I told him, determined to stick to the truth about everything. 'It's something else.'

'Oh . . .'

'I can't tell you what,' I carried on, 'but I am truly sorry about the way you've been caught up in my mess of a private life, Beamish. Had I known this was all going to happen, I never would have agreed to come to Wynbridge. Although,' I added, 'I am relieved to be rid of Jonathan and our poisonous relationship.'

Beamish didn't respond for a moment but then let out a long sigh and squeezed my shoulder.

'It's actually the poisonous part of your relationship with that man which has stopped me walking away from you for good.'

'What do you mean?'

'When I saw your Facebook profile,' he told me, 'and discovered that you were in a long-term relationship, I couldn't believe it. I was angry with you for keeping it from me. When I saw those pictures of the two of you together, my opinion of you changed completely. You weren't the person I thought you were and I felt hurt. But then . . .'

'What?'

'Seeing those bruises,' he said. 'Those marks on you, and meeting Jonathan in the flesh, it all got me thinking about my parents, how off-kilter Dad's manipulation skewed Mum's take on reality, and I began to wonder if under the circumstances and my understanding of them, if I could justify being so angry with you.'

I held my breath, not daring to interrupt.

'Those images online weren't representative of your real life at all, were they?' he went on. 'Come to think of it, very little of what anyone posts is actually the truth. It's just the filtered and edited shiny best bits, isn't it?'

I nodded.

'I can see that Dolly did have her heart in the right place. She knew you were living a lie and wanted to give you the space to see it. She genuinely thought she was doing the right thing, by you at least.'

'She was offering me an escape,' I whispered when he didn't say anything else. 'My time here and the Wish List have been all about rediscovering the person I was before I fell under Jonathan's spell.'

'And at least that worked,' said Beamish, his tone softer. 'And you know,' he added, 'we were great friends, weren't we?'

'Oh yes,' I agreed, 'the best. We might not have known each other for long, but something between us just seemed to click. I've never had a friendship like yours, Beamish, except perhaps with Dolly.'

I hated the thought of losing them both.

'Let's still be friends then,' he said, standing up and pulling me to my feet. 'Friends forgive each other, don't they? Why don't we start again?'

'Really?'

It was the very thing I had been wishing for but I hadn't thought it would be granted.

'Yes,' he said, 'unless you don't want to?'

'Of course I want to,' I told him. 'More than anything.'

'That's settled then,' he said, pulling me in for a hug. 'Let's forget about the bad bits and focus on the good.'

'All right,' I agreed.

I felt the weight of guilt lifting from my shoulders just as the sun began to peep through the breaking cloud and the sound of distant drumming met my ears. The solstice celebration was about to begin.

'I'd really love that,' I said, my eyes now shining with much happier tears.

'Life's too short not to, isn't it?' he grinned.

'It certainly is,' I swallowed, my thoughts tracking back to Dolly.

'Come on then,' Beamish carried on smiling. 'Let's go and welcome the return of the sun and the beginning of our re-formed friendship.'

We set off towards where the music was coming from and I knew I really couldn't have wished for a happier outcome.

I didn't understand everything that was said and done during the ceremony which was conducted by Molly and during which every member of the Connelly clan played a part, but I did enjoy searching for the yule-log which Catherine insisted I should choose and take back to Dolly.

'I know she will have no doubt made the chocolate equivalent,' Catherine smiled, 'but this is important too.'

I picked a smallish log that I would be able to manage to get into the taxi for the return journey.

'How did you get here?' Beamish asked as we made our way back towards the hall as the sun dipped out of sight and darkness began to settle around us.

'Taxi,' I said, tucking the log under my arm as I pulled my phone out of my pocket. 'I'm going to ring for one now to take me back, if I can get a strong enough signal,' I added.

I was keen to get back to Dolly and make sure she was all right.

'Don't be silly,' Beamish laughed, pulling the log out from under my arm. 'I'll run you back to town.'

'Are you sure?'

'Of course,' he smiled. 'That's what friends are for, remember?'

'Thanks,' I said, ducking my head as I put my phone away again.

I wondered how I was going to feel watching this particular friend going out on dates and forming 'friendships' with other girls. These next few months were going to be tough for so many reasons.

Beamish and I made our excuses from the lavish tea which had been laid on by Dorothy, thanked the Connellys for their hospitality and wished them all a Merry Christmas.

'Can you believe it's almost here?' said Beamish as he carefully reversed through the vehicles and turned on to the drive. 'By this time next week, it'll all be over.'

'Don't say that,' I groaned, thinking of all the effort that went into the preparations which would last for just a couple of days at best.

'Christmas Eve is always my favourite,' he grinned. 'The expectation of what's to come. I love it.'

I was just about to ask him where he would be spending Christmas Day but stopped as both my phone and his began to buzz and chatter.

'We must have found a signal hotspot,' he said, pulling up and cutting the engine again. 'Oh,' he added as he scrolled, 'I've been summoned. Dolly wants to see me.'

'Me too,' I said, showing him my screen.

I could only conclude that she had begun to doubt my ability to talk him into coming back with me and decided to add her influence to my endeavours.

'Is she all right?' Beamish frowned, stowing away his phone before starting the engine again. 'It isn't like her to be quite so bossy, is it?'

I wasn't sure if he was joking or not. Dolly had certainly had her moments in the last twenty-four hours, but given that she was running out of time, I could hardly blame her. No doubt she wanted to tell Beamish her sad news before it started to spread throughout the town. Which, in a place like Wynbridge, it would in no time at all.

'There's only one way to find out,' I told him.

Chapter 27

In spite of what I knew Beamish was about to be told, I couldn't help but smile as we drew up outside Dolly's cottage. It was picture perfect with the bright Christmas lights and Santa tethered to his sleigh looking as if he was poised to launch into the star-studded sky.

'I thought you didn't like it,' commented Beamish, when he noticed my rapt expression.

'You know I changed my mind,' I reminded him, my face warming as I remembered how I had arrived with fixed ideas about style and carefully co-ordinated decorations.

'You've changed your mind about a lot of things in the last few weeks, haven't you?' he said, passing me the yule-log as he opened the gate.

'That I have,' I agreed, thinking not only of Jonathan, but also the many things Dolly and I had added and ticked off the Wish List and which had now taken their rightful place in my festive preparations again.

Dolly was opening the door before we were halfway up the path and beckoning for us to hurry up, lest all the heat from the well-stoked fire escaped. She was thrilled with the yule-log and insisted I set it to the side of the basket so there was no danger of it getting muddled with the others and burned before she was ready to release its powers. Whatever that meant. I still wasn't sure I really understood the significance of it all, but I was delighted Dolly was so pleased to have her own yule-log nonetheless.

'Now,' she said, once the three of us were settled with tea and biscuits. 'I need to talk to the pair of you.'

Beamish looked at me questioningly and I had to look away. I knew that what he was going to hear was going to shake his faith in the world every bit as much as it had mine when I first heard Dolly say it. It was going to take some time for me to come to terms with what was going to happen and I had no real idea how much time Dolly had left. No one did, not even her.

'Thank you for your message, Hattie,' she went on, pointing at her phone. 'I appreciate you letting me know, but it's not going to be enough.'

I couldn't fathom what she meant. I had messaged to let her know that Beamish and I were friends again and I had thought she would be pleased, but apparently not.

'However,' she said, before I had a chance to question her, 'we'll get to that later.'

She returned her gaze to Beamish.

'Beamish,' she said, her tone softening as she sat back in her seat and prepared herself to say the words.

'I think I'll just freshen up,' I said, tears springing to my eyes. I couldn't bear to hear her say it again.

'There's no need,' she told me.

'I'll be back in a sec,' I said, putting down my cup and saucer. 'I just want to give you a minute.'

She didn't say anything else and I went upstairs into the bathroom and quietly closed the door. I perched on the edge of the bath imagining what the voices I could hear murmuring below were saying. I could hear the conversation was going back and forth and was then punctuated with longer silences.

When I felt certain that Dolly had relayed all she felt necessary I opened the door and slipped out on to the little landing.

'You can come back down,' she said as the creaking floorboards gave me away. 'You can come back now, Hattie dear.'

I slowly descended, resting my hand on Beamish's slumped shoulder as I brushed by to reach my chair. He placed his much bigger one over mine and sniffed before sitting upright. His eyes were damp and there was a definite trembling around his bottom lip and in that moment, I wanted nothing more than to kiss his hurt away.

'I can't believe it,' he said huskily as I picked up my tea again and drained the contents which were now lukewarm. 'Why now?'

'Why at all?' I said, sounding bitter on Dolly's behalf.

Beamish nodded in agreement, while Dolly looked entirely at ease.

'I've been through all of that,' she said, sounding resigned, 'in my own time and in my own way and nothing came of it. There was no sudden moment of enlightenment, it was just a waste of time. Precious time,' she reiterated. 'I suggest we all stop worrying about the whys and wherefores and focus on the here and now.'

Beamish sat up straighter and I returned my cup to its saucer. She was right of course and if that was what she wanted, then that's what I would do. In front of her at least; my private time would most likely be nowhere near as composed.

'Well,' I said, 'as you know, I'm not going anywhere for a while, Dolly. I'm going to stay in Wynbridge for as long as you need me.'

I couldn't bear to say until she was gone. I couldn't allow myself to think that far ahead, let alone, beyond that.

'And I'm only just a phone call and a short drive away,' said Beamish, backing up my good intentions. 'I can be at your beck and call twenty-four seven, Dolly. You needn't worry about that.'

'We're both here to do whatever it is you need,' I nodded vehemently, 'whenever you need it.'

Dolly nodded and I hoped our words were of some comfort to her. Whatever happened next, she was not going to be facing it on her own. Whether she had weeks or months, between us, Beamish and I would make sure they were as comfortable and as filled with as much wish fulfilment as Dolly could manage.

'Thank you,' she said, 'thank you both. That means so much to me and to be honest, I expected nothing less from either of you. I'm a very lucky woman.'

Beamish and I exchanged a look which spoke volumes.

'However,' Dolly continued, a frown forming, 'there is something else. Just one more thing.'

'Name it,' said Beamish and I nodded in agreement.

I would do anything to free Dolly of that frown and clearly, Beamish felt exactly the same way. Whatever Dolly wanted, if it was in our power to give it, then we would.

'It involves just you two actually,' she said, reaching for her phone again.

Beamish and I exchanged another quick look.

'Oh?' I swallowed.

'Yes,' she said, scrolling through her messages, 'this message you sent me Hattie, about finding Beamish and sorting everything out and reforming your friendship.'

'What about it?' I asked, feeling confused.

I had genuinely thought she would have been feeling as pleased about the situation as we were. It was a huge relief knowing that I wasn't going to have to edge my way around the cottage every time Beamish called in and I was certain that we were going to need each other to lean on as the coming days stretched into weeks and Dolly's illness became more obvious and difficult to deal with.

'Well,' she said, looking from one of us to the other, 'it's all well and good, but it's not enough, is it?'

'Isn't it?' asked Beamish, scratching his head.

'No,' she said firmly, 'it isn't.'

'In what way?' I said, 'I thought you wanted us to make amends.'

Dolly tutted. Clearly, we were missing the point.

'I think you'd better spell it out, Dolly,' said Beamish.

'All right,' she said, raising her chin. 'If you two really are as dense as I think you are, then I will.'

I held my breath.

'It's obvious to me,' she launched, 'more than obvious in fact, that the pair of you are going to get together, are meant to be together, as a couple I mean. As partners as well as friends. There's more than the spark of friendship between you and even though I might have been a little slow to real-ise it, I can see now that you had fallen headlong for Hattie, Beamish, the second you laid eyes on her.'

'Oh,' he blustered, 'well, I . . .'

'And you, Hattie,' she charged on, 'you also developed feelings for Beamish pretty smartish, didn't you? Even though you knew they were wrong and tried to pretend they didn't exist because you were tied to that ratbag, Jonathan.'

I couldn't help a laugh escaping my lips when I heard him described so unfavourably.

'She did go to kiss me first,' said Beamish with a grin.

That wiped the smile back off my face.

'I did not,' I protested.

Dolly looked at me and raised her eyebrows and I felt heat flood my cheeks.

'Exactly,' she said briskly. 'Just as I thought. So, there we have it. A mutual attraction which is going to ultimately, at some point, result in more than friendship.'

Beamish and I stayed quiet, not sure if we were supposed to confirm, deny or respond to what she was suggesting. I wasn't sure what his heart was doing, but the thought of having more than friendship with the man sitting next to me had got mine skittering along at a right old pace.

'However,' Dolly went on, 'what you both have to keep in mind, is that I haven't got a lot of time and I certainly haven't got a stretch left for pussyfooting about. By the time the pair of you have gone through the usual back and forth, the expected ups and downs and had the final will they, won't they Richard Curtis moment, I could be six foot under.'

'Dolly!' Beamish and I chorused.

'Well I could,' she said, laughing at our shocked expressions, 'couldn't I?'

'I suppose that is a possibility,' Beamish conceded.

I tutted but I knew there was some truth in what she was saying. Unfortunately.

'More than a possibility,' she said, shooting straight from the hip. 'So,' she continued, sounding a little breathless, 'I need the two of you to get on with it! I want the pair of you to be together, from this very moment. In fact,' she added, nodding to the Christmas Wish List which was in its usual spot next to the fireplace, 'if you look at the final page, you'll see it's my very last wish.'

I jumped up and reached for the list and sure enough, there it was, added in her familiar but now slightly shaky copperplate handwriting. I handed the note to Beamish but he didn't look at it. He threw it down on the table, jumped up, pulled me into his arms and kissed me passionately on the lips.

'There now,' I heard Dolly say, sounding suitably satisfied, 'we can tick that straight off!'

Chapter 28

Once Beamish had let me up for air and I had, laughing, grabbed him and kissed him back, Dolly was content that her work was done and announced that she was taking herself off for a bath and a very early night.

'There's only so much excitement I can handle,' she said, smiling, 'and I'm sure you two lovebirds would like a moment to gather your thoughts and catch your breath.'

I ran back up the stairs to draw Dolly's bath, adding the lavender salts she loved so much while Beamish made a light snack which she could eat in bed.

As soon as she was settled, we sat together on the sofa, Beamish tucked into the corner and me tucked into him with my feet curled under me. Our fingers were entwined as we watched the flames leaping up the chimney and the snow softly falling through the window in the garden. All was calm, all was quiet.

I twisted round to kiss him again, taking my time on this

occasion to enjoy the full-bodied tingling the pressure of his soft lips pressed against mine provoked. There were butterflies in my stomach and tongues of desire licking through my veins as his lips gently parted to deepen our kiss and my heart began to beat even faster. It was a heady concoction of feelings and nothing like I had experienced when kissing Jonathan, not even during the first flushes of our relationship.

'You OK?' Beamish asked, when we finally drew apart and I snuggled back down again.

'Oh yes,' I sighed, looking up at him. 'I'm very OK.'

He kissed the top of my head.

'Are you?'

'Oh yes,' he echoed the words back to me, smiling as he squeezed my fingers. 'I'm very OK, too.'

'Dolly was right, wasn't she?' I whispered, even though I knew she wouldn't be able to hear me. 'We would have ended up together, wouldn't we? We aren't just going along with this to make her happy?'

Beamish frowned.

'I mean,' I went on, 'it was just a few hours ago that we had decided to start our friendship over, and now here we are—'

'Hattie,' he cut in. 'Stop.'

'But—'

'Stop,' he said again.

'OK.'

'I do understand what you're getting at,' he said reassuringly, 'but no, we aren't just going along with this to make Dolly happy and yes, we definitely would have ended up together.'

'OK,' I said, feeling happier again.

'You might not realise it,' Beamish continued, 'but I knew the moment I set eyes on you on that windswept train platform that you were the girl for me, I just hadn't bargained . . .'

'On me having a belligerent boyfriend in tow.'

'That's one way of putting it.'

'I am sorry I never told you,' I said, pulling myself up a little so I could look at him properly again.

'It doesn't matter now,' he said. 'It's all worked out OK, hasn't it?'

'Yes,' I said. 'Yes, it has.'

'And like Dolly said, our friendship would have been very different if I'd known about him. I wouldn't have allowed myself to get so close to you and that would have meant that you weren't able to compare you and me with you and him.'

Dolly had said that was the main reason why she had never talked about Jonathan in front of Beamish.

'Things might have ended up very differently if she hadn't been a little bit deceitful about it all,' Beamish pointed out.

I wasn't sure that if Beamish had a secret girlfriend tucked away somewhere that he hadn't mentioned, I would have been so ready to forgive, but none the more for that, I was very grateful that he was.

'And Dolly's gut feeling was right about Jonathan, wasn't it?'

'Yes,' I said, 'it was. She knew he was no good for me but didn't want to risk our friendship by saying too much. She knew I was going to need her eventually and thought it best to just bide her time. I can't believe I was so blind to it all.'

'Well, they do say love is blind,' Beamish pointed out.

'It wasn't love,' I said, 'I thought I was in love with him but I wasn't. I know that now.'

'How do you know?'

'Because,' I said, stretching up and brushing my lips softly against his again, 'what I feel for you is completely different.'

'Oh really?'

'Yes,' I said, 'you're the real deal, Beamish. My feelings for you run far deeper.'

'In what way?' he asked, kissing me back.

'Well,' I said, 'for a start, I don't care if you've seen me with no make-up on and still in my PJs at lunchtime. I don't care if we bump into each other and I've got the wrong clothes on. With Jonathan it was all show, I was always on show. I was more of an accessory on his arm, one willing to accept his opinions rather than share and stick up for my own.' I stopped and bit my lip.

'It's all right,' said Beamish, 'I don't mind you talking about him.'

'It's not that,' I said, shaking my head. 'It's embarrassing, looking back and seeing how stupid I was, how easy to manipulate. I'm not a doormat, am I?'

'No,' said Beamish, pulling me back into his embrace. 'You're not. Jonathan was the problem, not you. Men like him are so convinced that they're the centre of the universe that they leave no room for anyone else to enter their orbit. The idiots.'

I snuggled back down, thanking my lucky stars and Dolly,

of course, for bringing me to Wynbridge and introducing me to Beamish.

'Anyway,' he said, tickling me and making me giggle, 'I know I said I didn't mind you talking about him, but I've heard enough for one day. I want to talk about you now, Hattie.'

'Me,' I said, 'what about me?'

'Well, for a start, are you still planning to visit your parents before Christmas? There's only a couple of days left now.'

'I know,' I said, 'the time has flown by and so much has happened. I'm going to email Mum again and explain everything, including what's going on with Dolly. I was hoping to travel up to see them but I can't right now. I'm sure they'll understand.'

'I could stay here with Dolly while you're gone,' Beamish suggested.

'No,' I said, knowing I would only worry the whole time I was away. 'It's fine. There's going to be plenty of time to see them now I'm not moving.'

'Which leads me on to my next question,' Beamish carried on, 'what are you going to do now, Hattie? What are you going to do, after . . .?'

His words trailed off and I was happy not to finish the sentence for him.

'I'm not sure,' I said, 'but for now, I just want to concentrate on giving Dolly the best ever Christmas and spending as much time with her as I can. I'll think about my future when the times comes.'

'That's fair enough,' he said, reaching for my hand again, 'and if I were you, I wouldn't worry too much about it. I have a feeling that everything's going to be all right.'

Once he had gone home and I had gone to bed, and in spite of his insistence that I shouldn't, I did begin to fret. The first few blissful minutes in my lovely warm bed were filled with remembering the kisses we had shared, and thoughts of how lucky I was to have friends such as Dolly and Beamish in my life, but then the fear of losing Dolly and the uncertainty about my future came flooding back.

What was I going to do long-term? Was staying in Wynbridge really going to be an option for me when I had nowhere to live and no income? I was going to have to force myself to put it all out of my mind, because the last thing I wanted was to be worrying about all of that while I was looking after Dolly. I would just have to bide my time and see what came along. Perhaps Beamish was right, perhaps things would be all right.

Dolly was up before me the next morning and looking very smug when I went down to breakfast.

'I can't begin to tell you how happy I am for you both,' she grinned, her cheeks positively glowing. 'The pair of you are perfect for each other and I know I barely gave you a second to patch things up like I would under normal circumstances, but with the grim reaper circling, these aren't normal circumstances, are they?'

I tutted and shook my head.

'Thank goodness you agreed to come and visit,' she carried on, bustling about in the kitchen, apparently oblivious to my reaction. 'I can't bear to even imagine what would have happened if you hadn't.'

'Me neither,' I said, with a little shudder as I thought how hard Jonathan had tried to cajole me into not making the trip.

Looking back, I realised I was relieved to be away from him right from the moment I left the flat, even though the journey had been a shocker and he had made me feel nervous about travelling alone. There were lots of things I had stopped doing on my own. Jonathan had always maintained that it was better for us to do them together but I could see now that he was trying to make me more reliant on him. He always had to be the one in control. There would be no fear of anything like that happening with Beamish; he was the kindest and most generous of men and an equal partner in every sense. And he was mine. Along with the school, the local community and every pensioner within a ten-mile radius, that is.

'So,' said Dolly, 'what are you plans for today?'

'That rather depends on you, Dolly. Is there anything I can do for you?'

'I don't think so,' she mused. 'Doctor Harris is popping in at some point and I have a couple of friends coming mid-morning. It's time I started telling everyone about my cancer so I've invited the two women I know who are most efficient at spreading news.'

'Gossiping, you mean,' I laughed, determined not to

wince at her ability to casually throw the 'C' word into the conversation.

'Got it in one,' she laughed back.

'In that case,' I said, peering through the window to see how much snow had fallen. 'I might wander into town. See if there are any last-minute presents to be had before I pack away the wrapping paper and ribbons.'

'You should treat yourself to one of the iced and spiced buns in the Cherry Tree Café,' she said with a wink. 'And while you're there, bring a couple home for me.'

The snow was only a light dusting, but as I was travelling on foot, I decided to wear the wellies Anna had lent me again. The idyllic icing sugar scene would soon turn to slush and the wellingtons would safeguard my jeans from any freezing splashes. Wrapped in one of Dolly's knitted scarves and hats, I set off, smiling to myself as I thought what Jonathan's reaction would be if he could see me going out in homemade gear. Not that his opinion could touch me anymore.

The town was busy for a Monday, but with the next day being Christmas eve that wasn't too much of a surprise.

'Hattie,' beamed Jemma as I crossed the café threshold and set the bell above the door tinkling, 'just the person. Grab a seat and I'll be with you in a minute.'

It felt nice to receive such a warm welcome. I almost felt like one of the locals.

'Now,' she said, popping a brown paper bag stamped with the café logo down on to the table, 'what can I get you?'

'Well,' I laughed, nodding at the bag, 'I'm guessing Dolly phoned her iced bun order in, did she?'

'She did,' Jemma confirmed. 'Not that she thought you'd forget.'

'Of course not,' I laughed. 'I think I'll have a bun myself please,' I told her, 'and a latte, to go with it.'

'Coming right up,' she said, keying my request in to her digital pad, 'and would you mind if I joined you?' she added. 'I have a proposition for you.'

It turned out to be more of an answer to a prayer than a proposition.

'Dolly happened to let slip that you've decided to stay here in our little town, for the time being at least,' she said as she served my order and sat in the chair opposite. 'She also told me why.'

I cut my bun into four pieces and nodded grimly.

'I still can't believe it,' I said sadly. 'I'm going to stay to look after her and of course, I'm every bit as determined as she is that she won't have to leave the cottage.'

'She said that too,' Jemma smiled. 'It's a great weight off her mind, Hattie.'

I was pleased to hear it.

'She also mentioned that you were going to need some sort of job to keep you occupied when you weren't pandering to her every whim. I think she's concerned that it will all become a little maudlin if you never leave the house.'

'How can it be anything but?'

'But you will need some balance,' Jemma went wisely on,

'and I was wondering if you'd like to take on a couple of weekend shifts waiting on tables in here. Goodness knows I could do with an extra pair of hands at peak times.'

It was a wonderful offer but I couldn't accept it.

'It's a very kind offer, Jemma,' I told her, 'and under any other circumstances I'd say yes straightway, but I don't know what's going to happen with Dolly. I might not be able to commit and what would you do if I had to cry off at the last minute? I'd hate to let you down . . .'

My words trailed off as Jemma shook her head.

'That doesn't matter,' she said. 'I'm more than happy to fit round whatever you can do. I have a couple of youngsters on standby to fill any gaps.'

'But wouldn't it be more trouble than it's worth, with me not always being able to turn up? It could get messy for you.'

'Life is messy,' she laughed. 'And I can handle a little more uncertainty in mine. I've always coped before and the locals are a good bunch. They're generally happy to hang on if there's a queue and I've got Lizzie and her team next door if I get desperate for an hour or so.'

I imagined myself sporting one of the café's trademark aprons and chatting with the locals as I took their orders. It wasn't a job I had done before, but it would be busy and Jemma and Dolly were right, it probably would be a relief to get out for a while, assuming my friend was well enough to be left.

'Don't decide now,' said Jemma, standing up.

'No,' I said, smiling, 'it's all right. I have decided. I would love to come and work here.'

'That's fantastic!' she grinned, placing a hand lightly on my shoulder. 'Come back and see me on the first Saturday of the new year and we'll talk about shift patterns and perks.'

'All right,' I nodded, 'but you have to promise not to ply me with too much confectionery.'

'Nope,' she laughed. 'I can't do that I'm afraid.'

I sat and contentedly ate my cinnamon and ginger laced bun. Working as a Saturday waitress in a small-town cafe might not have been a whole new career, but it was a start and the café was the best for miles around. I would be proud to be a part of the Cherry Tree team, even if it was only a small part.

When I arrived back at the cottage there were a couple of cars parked outside. One I recognised as belonging to the doctor.

'Doctor Harris,' I said as he came out of the door and closed it quietly behind him. 'How's the patient?'

'In excellent humour, as always,' he smiled. 'She's been holding court this morning, so she's in her element.'

'And what about her health?' I stole myself to ask. 'Not quite as excellent, I would imagine.'

You would never know by just looking at and talking to Dolly what was going on inside her. I think that's what made it all the more difficult to comprehend. She looked and sounded so well it was hard to marry that with the idea that she wouldn't be around to celebrate another Christmas.

'She's holding her own,' he said, 'and to be honest, Hattie, at this stage, that's as much as we can hope for. The fact that you're staying has been a huge psychological boost. She seems far more settled in her mind now that she knows she won't have to leave here.'

I was pleased I was able to do something to make Dolly's remaining time as stress free as possible.

'Anyway,' said the doctor, 'I'd better press on, and you've got a visitor so I won't keep you.'

'I've got a visitor?' I questioned, looking again at the second car parked along the pavement. 'Oh, that's Mr Matthew's car, isn't it?'

'It is,' said the doctor, unlocking his own. 'I'll see you next week, but if you need me in the meantime, just ring.'

I looked back to the cottage and could see Dolly peeping around the front curtains. When she spotted me, she beckoned me inside.

'Here she is,' she announced as I pulled off my wellies and unravelled my scarf. 'Did you get everything you needed from town, my dear?'

'I did,' I confirmed, handing her the bag of buns, 'and a little more besides. How lovely to see you, Mr Matthews.'

He was looking rather serious and I guessed that Dolly had told him her news.

'And you, Hattie.'

'What was the little more?' Dolly quizzed, her bright eyes narrowed as she studied my face for clues. 'Was it something from the Cherry Tree?'

'You know it was,' I laughed. 'I'm going to be working there for a few hours on a Saturday from the new year.'

'That's wonderful,' Dolly beamed, clapping her hands together. 'And Mr Matthews here has a proposition to keep you busy during the week.'

I had no idea why she thought that looking after her wasn't going to keep me busy.

'Oh?' I questioned, turning my attention to the headmaster.

'That's right,' he said, clearing his throat. 'I know it won't be easy to begin with,' he began, then faltered.

'He means while I'm still clinging on,' Dolly elaborated. 'Go on, ask her,' she urged.

Mr Matthews swallowed and started again. I really would have to have words with Dolly about giving folk a few minutes to come to terms with her prognosis before goading them into accepting it.

'I've been looking at the school finances,' he told me, 'and I have funds to take on another teaching assistant. Not full time, unfortunately, but for three days a week and with the possibility of extending to five from next September. Given that you've fitted into the school team so well Hattie and that the children clearly adore you, I wondered if you would like to be considered for the position.'

I didn't know what to say.

'But I'm not qualified,' I stammered.

'You can study for the appropriate qualification at the local college one evening a week,' said Dolly, shoving a pile of papers under my nose. 'The majority of the coursework is done at home or in school.'

I looked to Mr Matthews, who nodded in agreement.

'We'd love to have you on board,' he smiled.

'And I would love to say yes,' I began, 'but—'

'No but,' said Dolly sharply. 'There are no buts.'

'But,' I carried on nonetheless. 'I'll have to think about it.'

'What's there to think about?' she tutted.

'Well, for a start, I don't have anywhere to live.'

'You live here,' said Dolly, looking about her.

'For now, yes,' I said, 'but I have to think about the future . . .'

'The cottage is your future,' said Dolly, sounding impatient. 'I'm leaving it to you, Hattie. When I'm gone, the cottage and everything in it, including Tiddles, will be yours.'

Chapter 29

I really didn't think my mind had the capacity to cope with any more Christmas surprises, but Dolly had other ideas. I sat with her and Beamish that evening and relayed to him everything that the day had held – the two job offers which I had accepted and the extraordinarily generous gift of the cottage from Dolly – and told the pair of them that I felt quite giddy with it all, as if I was celebrating at least a dozen Christmases all at once.

'Thank goodness my imminent demise will balance things out a bit,' chuckled Dolly. 'Otherwise you'd be in danger of completely losing your head.'

'Dolly,' Beamish hissed.

'What?' she said, blinking and shrugging her shoulders.

'That makes me feel awful,' I told her.

'It wasn't meant to,' she said lightly.

'You shouldn't say things like that, Dolly,' Beamish scolded.

'Why not?' she carried on. 'It's my funeral. I can say what I like.'

I looked at her, wondering how to get the point across without eliciting even more gallows humour.

'I just wish you'd give folk a chance to take on board what you're telling them before you go bowling headlong into making such blasé remarks and spouting off ghastly gags.'

Dolly looked thoughtful.

'Point taken,' she nodded. 'I suppose it is a bit of a shock when you first hear it.'

'It's still a bit of a shock,' said Beamish leaning back in his chair and resting his head against me as I stood behind him.

'It's not just the diagnosis that's shocking,' I carried on, picking up the thread, 'but your whole attitude towards it, Dolly. You seem too accepting,' I added, in wonder, 'almost as if you're ready for it to happen.'

'I wouldn't go that far,' she sighed, settling Tiddles on to her lap. 'However, I do have the benefit of a life well lived behind me. My little life here in Wynbridge, and occasion-ally beyond,' she smiled, no doubt remembering her trips to the hotel, 'may have been simple but it's been full. I've filled my days doing the things I enjoy, working at a job I think I was good at and surrounding myself with people I love. Had I not ticked everything off my own personal Wish List,' she smiled, 'I might be feeling very differently.'

I could see the sense in what she was saying. As Beamish had pointed out to me before, it was all too easy to waste time, especially when you were young. It always felt like there'd be a next day, another year, a subsequent decade. Dolly's legacy was going to be a testament to the importance of living in the moment and squeezing the most into and out of every single day.

'I think I might write another Wish List,' I told her, looking over at ours hanging next to the fireplace. 'I think it will help keep me on track. Give me the focus to keep trying new things.'

'Are you going to add getting better at ice skating to it?' Beamish laughed.

I cuffed him lightly around the head and went to sit next to Dolly resting my head on her shoulder.

'I might,' I told him.

'I did enjoy that last trip to the rink,' she sighed wistfully. 'It felt good to be gliding across the ice on my blades again.'

'You were amazing, Dolly,' I yawned.

'I know,' she said. 'There's life in the old dog yet, but now I'm off to bed. It's Christmas Eve tomorrow and there'll be plenty to do.'

As she walked over to the stairs, I saw her look down at Beamish and he looked up and winked. Clearly the pair of them were up to something but I didn't have the energy to try and work out what. It was almost Christmas and I was sure all would be revealed soon enough.

All was indeed revealed straight after lunch the next day. Dolly, Beamish and I had spent the morning making sure we had enough of everything to see us through the twenty-four hours when the shops would be shut. Every present was finally wrapped and the larder and fridge were groaning under the weight of cheese, meat, puddings and of course the inevitable mountain of brussels sprouts.

It probably wouldn't have taken quite so long to check through it all had Beamish not insisted on kissing me every time I passed under the mistletoe which Dolly had made him hang above every doorway, including those upstairs. She chuckled every time she saw us and said on more than one occasion that our partnership was the most perfect last Christmas present she could have wished for.

'And talking of presents,' she added the next time she commented, 'yours will be arriving in a little while, Hattie so keep listening out for the doorbell, won't you?'

Beamish cut the volume of the radio and grinned.

'All right,' I said, feeling somewhat uncertain.

Given that Dolly had gifted me an entire house and also explained that there was a small financial legacy to accompany it which would mean I wouldn't be struggling to pay the bills while I established my new work routine, I didn't think I needed another present, but knew better than to say as much. Dolly in a determined mood wasn't a force anyone with an atom of sense argued with or contradicted.

A few minutes later the bell did ring and I was the one ushered to answer it.

'Will it need signing for?' I asked looking back over my shoulder as I pulled open the door.

Dolly and Beamish stood side by side, smiling idiotically.

'No,' Dolly laughed.

'Hello, sweetheart.'

My eyes swung back to the door.

'Mum!' I gasped, 'Dad!'

I couldn't believe it.

'Oh my god! What on earth are you doing here?'

I flung myself at my mother who wrapped me in her arms and held me tight.

'I've missed you so much,' she sobbed.

'I've missed you too.'

I wasn't quite crying, as I looked over her shoulder at my father's face, but I was close to it. For once Dolly didn't complain about the heat disappearing up the street and left us to our moment of joyful reunion.

'This is such a surprise,' I sniffed as the tears finally made a bid for freedom and I stepped back to let them in. 'I didn't think we were going to see each other until after the new year.'

'Well,' said Dad, hugging me hard as he followed Mum inside, 'we didn't like the thought of having to wait and when Dolly telephoned, inviting us to pay a surprise call, we thought we'd take her up on her kind offer and come straightaway.'

'When did you do that?' I asked Dolly.

She looked a little flushed, but not at all guilty.

'As soon as Beamish told me of your decision to delay your reunion because you didn't want to leave me,' she explained. 'He told me you were going to email and change your plans so I thought I'd interfere, just one last time.'

'But how did you get their number?'

She tapped the side of her nose.

I was too grateful to insist she told me. I couldn't believe my parents were actually standing in front of me, in Dolly's cottage. They both looked a little different, older and greyer around the temples and I cursed the time I had wasted not talking to them, as well as why.

'You must be Beamish,' said Dad, holding out his hand to my other half. 'Dolly's told us all about you.'

Beamish stepped forward and shook it firmly.

'Only the good I hope, sir,' he smiled.

'Apparently there was only good to tell,' Mum smiled back.

The atmosphere felt completely different to when Jonathan and my parents had been in the same room.

'Well,' said Dolly, as she bustled to the kitchen to put the kettle on. 'Isn't it wonderful that we're all finally together?'

'Absolutely,' we all happily chorused and then burst out laughing.

Later that afternoon Beamish and Dolly headed into town for the church Christingle service. I had been planning to go with them but in view of my very special visitors, I opted to stay behind and fill them in on what I was going to be doing with my life now I had eradicated Jonathan from it. I knew Mum especially would be thrilled that I was going to be working in a school.

'Don't worry,' said Beamish, planting a kiss on my cheek, 'I'll bring you back an orange.'

Once he and Dolly had gone, I settled on the sofa between my parents. I felt loved and cherished and safe. It was a feeling I hadn't enjoyed in their company for a very long time.

'If it's all right with you both,' I began, 'I'd rather not waste time telling you about how things finally ended with Jonathan.'

There was no way I would have been able to tell them everything. I dreaded to think how they would have reacted had they seen the bruises he had inflicted and it wasn't necessary to burden them with all that had happened that fateful Sunday when I had first heard from Mum again.

'Suffice to say he's gone for good,' I sighed, 'and I don't think any good would come from wasting time talking about him. We know now what sort of man he was and we're rid of him. That's all that matters.'

'I just can't believe we didn't see through him,' Mum sobbed. 'We went along with everything he said because we thought it was what you wanted, Hattie. We were so worried about losing you . . .'

'And he knew that, Mum,' I told her. 'He used everything I told him about David and losing the baby to manipulate my relationship with you until it broke.'

'But now it's mended,' said Dad, looking at Mum and smiling. 'So, let's do what Hattie is suggesting and move on love, yes?'

Mum nodded and blew her nose.

'And now you're with Beamish,' she sniffed.

She and Dad had both seemed quite taken with him and I could hardly blame them. I was pretty smitten myself.

'Yes,' I sighed happily, 'now I'm with Beamish and I know it looks like I've leapt from one relationship and straight into another.'

Dad shook his head and I stopped.

'What?'

'You don't have to justify anything to us,' he said, putting an arm around me. 'We're just relieved to have you back in our lives and see you so happy.'

'You are happy, aren't you?' Mum asked.

'Extremely happy!' I laughed. 'I can't believe I'm staying here in Wynbridge and I've got two jobs lined up.'

I explained that Dolly was also leaving me the cottage and it was every bit as much of a shock to my parents as it had been to me.

'She's also leaving me a little money,' I told them. 'Obviously I'll need to establish a regular income but I'll manage and I'm delighted to be working in the school.'

'And being able to study as you work is a real blessing,' added Dad. 'You've obviously made quite an impression here, love, and of course, we've got a little tucked away for you should you need it.'

'Have you?'

'Yes,' said Mum, leaning across and kissing my cheek. 'There's a little nest egg should you want to dip into it. We set it up when you left home and moved into the hotel.'

I didn't know what to say.

'Well I don't think I'll need it,' I told them both, 'but it's good to know it's there. Thank you so much. I can't tell you how happy I am to have you both back in my life.'

'And we're happy to have you back too,' smiled Mum. 'You probably don't realise it, but our lives just didn't work without you, Hattie. There was a very big chunk missing from both of our hearts.'

'But not anymore,' said Dad.

'Never again,' I said firmly.

They were getting ready to leave when Beamish and Dolly came back from church, with the promised candle and sweet studded orange.

'Won't you stay for tea?' asked Dolly.

Her face was pinched from the cold and Beamish insisted she sat next to the fire to warm up.

'Best not,' said Dad. 'It's a bit of a trek and what with it being Christmas day tomorrow, we need to get back to get the sprouts on.'

'You cheeky thing,' flushed Mum. 'They won't be going on until first light.'

We all laughed and I walked with them back to their car, hugging each tightly in turn before they climbed in. The car was one I hadn't seen before and I wondered how many other things had changed at home that I didn't know about. Not that it really mattered. I would be visiting them soon enough and besides, all I really cared about was that I had them back. The smiles on their faces told me they felt exactly the same.

'Look after yourself, my darling,' said Dad, once he had turned the engine over.

'I'll ring you tomorrow,' said Mum, leaning over the seats. 'And come when you can,' she added, 'but only if you can leave Dolly. I know things aren't going to be easy for you, but we're here, love. If you need anything you only have to ask.'

'And we can always come to you,' said Dad. 'Just pick up the phone if you need us. Merry Christmas, Hattie.'

'Yes,' nodded Mum. 'Merry Christmas.'

'Having you here has been the best present ever,' I choked as Dad put the car into gear.

I swallowed hard, willing myself not to cry until they had gone.

'Dolly said that she thought it might be,' said Mum, her eyes now glistening with tears of her own. 'She said it would be a wish come true.'

'Now get inside,' said Dad as he released the handbrake, 'before you freeze.'

I waved until they were out of sight and then found that I didn't want to cry. I bounded back up the path and into the cottage.

The Wynbridge midnight church service wasn't quite the reverent step into Christmas day that I had been expecting. Dolly was tired but insisted that she wanted to go, if only to make up the numbers, but there was no need to have worried about empty pews. Every reveller in town it seemed had spilled out of The Mermaid at closing time and headed for the church to celebrate the dawning of the day we had all been waiting for. The carols were sung with gusto, the vicar was on fine form, happy to indulge the more inebriated members of the congregation, and the service sped by.

Stepping out of the church porch, my hand clasped in Dolly's, was like stepping into a fairy tale. The snow was falling again, thicker now, and it was a safe bet that we were going to wake to a white Christmas. As far as I was concerned, it was the icing on the cake.

'Things have turned out pretty well, haven't they?' said Dolly, her thoughts obviously travelling along the same tracks as mine.

Aside from her sad news they had, but I knew she wouldn't want me to mention that now.

'Yes,' I answered, drawing her close. 'Yes, they have and I want you to know that I'll always be grateful that you invited me here again, Dolly.'

'I know you will,' she nodded.

'My future would have been very different had you not shown me another path. I'll always be thankful for your friendship and for leading me to Beamish.'

We looked over to where he was laughing with some of the congregation and pumping the vicar's hand.

'He's a wonderful man,' she smiled.

'He is,' I agreed.

He spotted us and waved and we waved back.

'You've got an amazing future ahead of you here in Wynbridge, Hattie,' said Dolly, looking up at me. 'If that's what you want. It is, isn't it?'

'Oh yes,' I smiled, enveloping her in a hug, 'most definitely. You've made my future here everything I could ever wish for.'

Acknowledgements

What an absolute pleasure it has been to spend another festive season in much loved Wynbridge with old and new friends. I hope you have enjoyed the visit as much as I have? As always, there is an ever-increasing list of people to thank for making the trip possible and this time I have a few very specific folk to hug for their support, encouragement and incredibly hard work.

No author could be happier with their merry band of readers than I am! My lovely #swainettes have been cheering long and loud this year and I wholeheartedly thank you all. Whether you are a blogger or a reader, you have championed both Wynbridge and Nightingale Square and that's hugely appreciated. Special thanks to @head_in_a_book_18 over on Insta for all the fabulous pics and to @GrumpyGirlie (Laura) who has really put in some miles to support me this year.

The entire Books and The City Team have also pulled

out all the stops again. Thank you, Jo Dickinson for your insight into editing *The Christmas Wish List*. I know our time together was exceptionally brief but I think we achieved great things in a short space of time. Thanks also to Rebecca Farrell for your equally insightful editing support and to Harriet Collins (publicist extraordinaire) who has been one step ahead of me this year and lined up some cracking events!

Thanks to Amanda Preston, my agent, who has been on hand to get me through what hasn't been the easiest few months and keep me on track. (Please, no one mention the words 'wisdom' and 'molar' in the same sentence as I may go into a rapid decline.) And huge and heartfelt thanks to my fellow authors, but more specifically my firm friends, Jenni Keer (you've been a trooper my darling), Clare Marchant and Rosie Hendry, for always being there when I need you.

I also have to thank my former colleagues from the school where I had the very great pleasure of working as a TA for a decade. I know that a couple of you will recognise yourselves within the pages of this book and I can confirm that Mrs Andrea Drake really did identify a long-lost tooth I found in a tambourine in the music room! Patsy, Louisa, Mike and Simon, you are all an inspiration and the children (and parents) are truly blessed to have you.

And finally, thanks to my family and Storm (the cat), for putting up with my piles of notes, incessant rambling and general neglect when I'm head down at the keyboard. I love you all.

Thank you, dear readers, for joining me once again on

another festive trip to Wynbridge. I wish you all a very merry Christmas and a happy and healthy New Year and, as ever, may your bookshelves – be they virtual or real – always be filled with fabulous fiction.

H x

Dolly and Hattie's Christmas Wish List...

If you enjoyed reading about the wish list that Hattie and Dolly put together, then why not create one of your own? Personally, I love a good list, and there's little in life as satisfying as ticking things off with a flourish.

Here are some simple and inexpensive ideas to kick things off, and all are guaranteed to keep your spirit soaring throughout the festive season. Some of the things are so much fun, you might even be able to tick them off twice!

Heidi x

1. Wear a festive jumper
2. Watch a pantomime
3. Watch a Christmas movie
4. Craft festive decorations
5. Bake mince pies
6. Take part in Secret Santa
7. Take a winter stroll
8. Visit the Christmas market
9. Go ice skating
10. Play Christmas music
11. See a reindeer
12. Drink mulled wine or hot chocolate

Don't miss the brand new novel from
Sunday Times *bestselling author Heidi Swain . . .*

COMING 2020
AVAILABLE NOW TO PRE-ORDER

If you loved *The Christmas Wish List,* then be sure to read Heidi Swain's previous novel . . .

Poppy's Recipe for Life

Treat yourself to a glorious novel full of food, sunshine, friendship and love!

Things haven't always been straightforward in Poppy's life but her dreams are finally within her reach.

She's moving into a cottage in beautiful Nightingale Square, close to the local community garden, where she can indulge her passion for making preserves and pickles. She may not have the best relationship with her family, but she is surrounded by loving friends, and feels sure that even her grumpy new neighbour, Jacob, has more to him than his steely exterior suggests.

But the unexpected arrival of Poppy's troubled younger brother soon threatens her new-found happiness, and as the garden team works together to win community space of the year, Poppy must decide where her priorities lie and what she is prepared to fight for . . .

AVAILABLE IN PAPERBACK AND EBOOK NOW

If you're looking for more festive fiction, then be
sure to read Heidi Swain's previous novel . . .

Snowflakes and Cinnamon Swirls at The Winter Wonderland

Moving into Wynthorpe Hall to escape the town's
gossip, Hayley finds herself immersed in the eccentric Connelly family's festive activities as they plan to
host their first ever Winter Wonderland. But Hayley
isn't the only new resident at the hall. Gabe, a friend of
the Connelly's son Jamie, has also taken up residence,
moving into Gatekeeper's Cottage, and he quickly makes
an impression on Wynbridge's reformed good-girl.

As preparations commence for the biggest event of the
season, the pair find themselves drawn ever closer to
one another, but unbeknownst to Hayley, Gabe, too,
has a reason for turning his back on love, one that
seems intent on keeping them apart.

Under the starry winter skies, will Gabe convince
Hayley to open her heart again once more? And in
doing so, will he convince himself?

AVAILABLE IN PAPERBACK AND EBOOK NOW